My Uncle Owes Me a Favor

Satiama

PUB

By Morrigan Milligan

To Hojin, Thank you for all you do!

First Printing, 2021
ISBN 978-17373757-1-5 (print); ISBN 978-1-7373757-0-8 (ebook)
Library of Congress Control Number: 2021940408

Subject Matter:
1. FICTION / Romance / General
2. FICTION / Family Life / General
3. FICTION / Friendship

Written by Maureen Ann Milligan under her pen name,
Morrigan Milligan.

PRINTED IN CHINA
10 9 8 7 6   5 4 3 2 1

*In Memory of
Honey*

*In Memory of
Uncle Sam*

Table of Contents

Part One
Buffalo

It was the 60s. We were in our late teens and early 20s. Vietnam, feminism, and civil rights were a steady diet on the nightly news. It was exciting. Hair was getting longer and longer, jeans grungier, and pot was available from a male cousin or two. It was the era of Easy Rider, Lawrence Ferlinghetti, and The Who. But when my cousins Cary and Carlo announced they were headed for Woodstock, our Sicilian-American parents had no idea what they were talking about. That news spread among us like wildfire. Sicilian mothers believed the men were designated protectors of the women. When Rosalie found out her brother Carlo was headed to Woodstock, she assured our moms that we'd be all right and, yes, we would stay with Cary and Carlo.

It was a fantastic experience on many levels. Along with half a million peace-and-love hippies squatting on muddy farmland, the four of us, beer bottles in our hands and passing a reefer, spotted our eldest cousin Rocco. We froze.

"Maggie, tell me that's not Rocco," Cary said.

"I can't," I replied.

We were sure he hadn't seen us, and we were trying our best to make out what exactly we were seeing. Rocco was entwined with another guy. But that was happening all around us; everyone getting physical with everyone. We looked at each other while never dropping the reefer that continued to pass among us. Then it became apparent with the full tongue kiss. Rocco was gay.

"Who knew?" Cary said, shrugged, and deeply inhaled the reefer. "Let's go someplace where I can pee without spraying someone."

We never discussed seeing Rocco because we were engaged in sexual, alcoholic, pot-smoking acting out of our own, kicking ass, and no names, please.

After Woodstock, it was easier for me to leave home. Rebellion was expected of my generation, except no one informed our parents. We had a voice. We took risks our parents never dreamed of. We thought of ourselves as more intelligent, as agents of change. I'm sure Rocco was caught up in all this when he decided to come out to his parents. He forgot who they were, the poor immigrants that shuffled into the Great Hall of Ellis Island. Rocco's dad, our Uncle Carmine, Aunt Zorah, and my mom,

Isabella, were born in Sicily. Aunt Bertha and Uncle Renato were born stateside. Family loyalty, tradition, and church were their core values. And the rules.

I escaped a considerable dose of this. My Irish American dad was a second-generation American on his mom's side and a third-generation American on his dad's side. From Northern Ireland to boot, read non-Catholic. We were pale-skinned redheads. Our looks quickly assimilated us. And my dad believed in girls being educated. I always knew that Dad's goal for me was college and a promising career. Mom would look at him in a huff when he'd talk with me about it. For her sake, he would add, "You never know, Maggie. If, God forbid, your husband dies young, you'll have something to fall back on." I knew that was code between us for college first, then marriage. I loved him for this.

When my female cousins were getting married right out of high school, in the spirit of feminism and free love that I never verbalized, I moved 1200 miles away for college. The summer between graduation and the beginning of graduate school, I went home. I'd be changing universities. A new city meant a unique living situation, so it seemed like the right time to go home. Mom and Dad threw a massive party for me, the first member of the Blake and Madonie families to graduate from college. All my cousins pitched in, making sure old high school friends got invited along with every member of the family. Dad made sure that his brothers, Mic and his wife May, and their kids and Uncle Jacob and his life partner Roy got invitations as well. Secretly I knew this gave Dad the excuse for buying half a keg of beer. The Sicilian side of the family drank the homemade wine my uncles made each year in Uncle Carmine's basement. Their other choice was straight-up whiskey.

There was a surprise in store for me. Cary had invited Jimmy Toscano and his band, Nickel Calamari, to play the event. Jimmy and I were an item in high school. He was a fantastic musician. There wasn't an instrument Jimmy couldn't play. He played trumpet in the marching band, piano for the choir, and guitar in his own rock and roll band. I felt so entitled. He was taller than most Italian guys, had hair like Elvis, and could swivel his hips better than The King. He wasn't hurting for attention from every girl in our senior class, but he and I had been going steady since junior year. Many of our classmates assumed we would marry right out of high school. But while I was liberating myself at Woodstock and reading Betty Friedan's The Feminine Mystique, Jimmy was also imprinted by Woodstock. He and I knew marriage was not for us. Not right out of high school. Jimmy was accepted at Berklee School of Music in Boston. We parted ways on Labor

Day weekend, 1969.

The Madoni Family owned three connecting lots on a street whose trees created a canopy over the road on the West Side of Buffalo. Three lots deep made the property more of an estate. The house facing the street was a Buffalo flat over flat West Side double. In the vast backyard space, there were two tiny homes we called "the rear cottages, first and second." It was the custom that when my aunts or uncles married, they moved into one of the cottages after the wedding. That was exactly what my parents did after they married. We moved from the property when I was six. My earliest memories are playing in the vast backyard with my older cousins Rocco, Sal, Cary, Carlo, and Rosalie, supervised by my grandparents plus Uncle Carmine, Aunts Zorah, Lena, Bertha, and, of course, my mom and dad. Family.

I could hear the music from the street as Mom, Dad, and I walked up the alley (a wide walkway just narrow enough that it can't be a driveway space between houses). I immediately knew it was Jimmy's Nickle Calamari band. Cary approached me, a massive grin on my face.

"Surprise!" he greeted.

"Is that Jimmy?" I asked, even though I knew it was.

"Go say 'hello.' He's excited to see you," Cary directed.
I approached the bandstand. Jimmy saw me coming. He never missed a beat playing the guitar or singing All You Need is Love by the Beatles. He was more handsome than I remembered.

It was a fabulous party. The gifts were amazing, status quo for our family. A lot of cash and designer purses, accessories, and promises for luncheons with my cousins Angela and Cary's wife, Ginger. At about ten o'clock, Nickle Calamari band members were breaking down. Jimmy startled me when he tapped my shoulder as I was talking with Aunt Zorah.

"Sorry! Didn't mean to scare you!" he said.

I spontaneously hugged him.

"Wow!" He hugged me back, then picked me up and twirled me around as I giggled with delight, just like we did when we were in high school.

"Boy!" I said, "That brought back memories! Cary said your band is really making it big. How are you? Why aren't you out on the road?"

"Just so happened that we came home because there was a break in our tour schedule, and it's my mom's birthday. Are you free tomorrow? How about we get together and take a ride, get some Ted's Hot Dogs, and talk. Catch up. How about it?"

"What time?" I replied.

We took a leisurely ride out to Niagara Falls, talking the whole way.

Moving to Berklee School of Music in Boston was the best thing Jimmy did for his career and band. He also loved the culture. Boston, or more accurately Cambridge, was the hotbed of countercultural expression. Timothy Leary was a household name. It hadn't been lost on Jimmy with his shoulder-length hair, full beard, and the faint aroma of pot. He could hardly believe that I wasn't involved in demonstrating for civil rights and feminine equality. But as I explained, south of the Mason-Dixon line, those agendas weren't as celebrated. I was still as much of a bookworm during my undergraduate days as I was in high school. I had a goal: I wanted a doctorate. I had to have the grades.

We spent most of our days together after that. Then he got a gig in Philadelphia and invited me along. The gig was a couple of nights, and the band had a bus. I immediately agreed.

Jimmy's bus was swank inside. There were bedrooms, so to speak, and in the common area upfront, someone was always playing music, or the band was rehearsing. It was so much fun. I had never been immersed in Jimmy's life like I was during that week.

Once in Philly, there were more rehearsals. When Jimmy's band wasn't at the venue, there was time for touring the city, sampling the food, and just hanging out at a charming hotel. I hadn't realized that Jimmy was doing so well financially. I must have thought it was like high school, a few bucks here or there for parties or school dances. I knew nothing of big-time professional music, and that was where Jimmy now lived. I was in awe.

The first concert blew me away. I had absolutely no idea just how excellent Nickel Calamari was. Jimmy played two of his own compositions. The crowd went bonkers. I was screaming along with everyone else and just as star struck. I had a good idea now just how all my high school female classmates felt about Jimmy and his band. But I got to go back to the hotel with the lead guitarist and singer.

This is the only explanation I have for allowing Jimmy to sweep me off my feet and down to City Hall to marry him before a Pennsylvania Justice of the Peace. When we got back to Buffalo, my mom was horrified, and Dad just grinned. We moved into one of Uncle Carmine's cottages. My aunts and cousins helped me set up housekeeping with the bare necessities. It was evident to them that we hadn't thought things through. By the end of my summer in the cottage, we both had realized that I wasn't going to be a groupie and follow him everywhere I was due in Houston for graduate school. Jimmy's life was in a bus on the road building a career he dearly deserved. He tried to swing the band by me in Houston whenever they were reasonably close, but that was maybe once a month during my first semester in graduate school. It was fun while it lasted. When I joined him at a recording studio in Detroit during Christmas break, we agreed to divorce and pursue our vastly different careers. I flew home from Detroit. Dad met me at the airport, and I told him Jimmy and I had agreed to divorce. I wasn't sad, more disappointed in myself.

"I'll talk with my attorney," Dad said.

I never questioned Dad. I knew I'd get my divorce once he took control.

Soon after the spring semester started, Rocco telephoned me from his new apartment in Houston.

It didn't take long before Rocco and I were partying together. One drunken night I spilled the beans about Woodstock. The joke was on us because Rocco had seen each one of us over the course of the weekend. His only comment to me was, "Nice tits, cuz."

As the work in graduate school took up more and more of my time, Rocco and I saw less and less of each other. I was aware that humanity had entered a new era of a deadly disease no one understood. While this disease was ravishing people in Africa, it was showing up in gay men in America. Classified as a virus that unraveled a person's immune system, it went undetected until Kaposi's sarcoma, a rare cancer, was first diagnosed. Researchers and physicians worked double-time attempting to identify the vehicle of entry. The 'zero' patient was an international flight attendant, a gay man. The critical puzzle piece explained why the virus was a gay man's disease in the US. A stigma soon attached, and the fight for lives afflicted with the HIV virus and AIDS began.

One afternoon while preparing for my class teaching undergraduates, my telephone rang. I was surprised. It was Aunt Lena. Did I know that Rocco was hospitalized? Did I hear he wasn't coming home once discharged? He had argued with his parents, announced that he could take care of himself. Aunt Lena wanted her son home so she could care for him, nurture him back to health.

I could hear the fear in her voice. The nightly news talked about gay men dying at staggering rates. Yet, medical researchers were making absolutely no progress in treating or stopping the disease's progression.

Suddenly Uncle Carmine got on the phone. "We really want Rocco home," he began. "His mother is sick with fear for her son."

Then it came. Something we cousins joked about; something movies stereotyped Sicilians with, something never spoken out loud unless one genuinely understood what was being asked.

Uncle Carmine slowly said, "Maggie, I would consider it a favor if you'd talk Rocco into coming home."

I froze. All at once, my Sicilian denial cracked wide open. There it was: validation of who we are.

"Here's your aunt again," he said.

"So, we'll be hearing from you, Hon?" said Aunt Lena.

"Yes. Yes, Aunt Lena, you'll be hearing from me."

"God bless, Maggie," she ended with and hung up.

The next day I headed to the hospital. Rocco looked sickly but acted himself. He insisted he'd be okay, that the medicine made him feel a lot better.

"And you'll go home after you're discharged," I punctuated.

He studied me a minute. "They called you," he said.

"Not only did they call, but your father would consider it a favor," I added.

Rocco flopped back into his pillows. "Oh, Jesus!"

"No shit!" I said. "So, you'll go?"

He looked at me long and hard. Then he softened and said, "Yeah. Yeah, I'll go."

We sat in silence a moment. Then, "Hey," he perked up. "Look at it this way: now you have an uncle who owes you a favor!"

I sat up a little straighter. "Hah! That's right!" In our family, this was a huge deal.

Divorced from Jimmy and back in Houston, I wanted to move and save money. No more checks from a husband making music on the road. I stopped at the graduate lounge and read the posting board for rentals. I was hoping that maybe I could share a place with someone in the Psychology department. Once the reality of the divorce sunk in, I realized just how much energy I was giving the marriage, but not in a good way. I was pretty much obsessed with when will Jimmy call? When will he swing by Houston and spend time, as in how many overnights would he stay with me this time? Sex was always good with Jimmy, and to say I didn't miss it while he traveled would be a lie. I didn't have Rocco in town anymore for distraction. His move back to Buffalo thrilled his mom and dad. His health improved remarkably. He also fell in love with a guy named Drew.

I was genuinely happy for Rocco. This was hard. My inclination was to feel droopy that my gay cousin found love and I just got divorced, which I knew didn't speak well of me on many levels. Too much psychology! Analyzing me was a favorite pastime, which I learned was indigenous to all graduate psychology majors.

I was reading the graduate lounge posting board when a woman walked up and, while juggling her books and purse, pinned a notice to the corkboard seeking another woman to share a house. Before she could turn to leave, I pulled down the flyer, with the bottom cut into many tabs with her phone number on each, and asked, "Is it your house, or are you posting this for someone else?"

"It's my house. Not far from here either. I live on South MacGregor Way, about two miles from campus. Why? Are you looking for a place to live?"

"Yes! Right now, I rent an apartment in Montrose, but I am looking to save some money. How about we get coffee or something? By the way, I'm Margaret Blake, Maggie for short," I extended my hand for a shake.

She took my hand and replied, "Hi Maggie. I'm Alice McLeod. Sure, how about the café in the student center?"

We exchanged information while we walked to the café and discovered we were starting the graduate psychology program. Alice was a native Texan that had lived in Houston since the age of four. She had never met a true Yankee before me. When I said I came from Buffalo, it made her laugh.

"There's a Buffalo, Texas, you know," she said, "big cattle auction place."

"Really? I guess I never thought about whether there were more cities named Buffalo. I always thought my Buffalo was the Buffalo! Pretty arrogant, right?"

During the coffee break, it was clear how comfortable we felt with one another. Neither of us was seeing anyone. Alice was empathetic about my divorce from Jimmy while at the same time thrilled to hear about how well he was doing in the music business. She had heard of Nickel Calamari and thought the name particularly unique. "One degree of separation from a rock star," she quipped. We laughed. It made me laugh as I thought about my week in Philly with Jimmy and the band; yeah, a true rock star. I liked Alice.

I gave notice to the apartment manager that I'd be moving out by the end of the month. Still, I started moving into Alice's house right away. The first time I saw her home I was surprised. Well, shocked was more like it.

South MacGregor Way curved around the park area of Buffalo Bayou with mansion-sized houses. The neighborhood was once most luxurious, just minutes from downtown Houston and the University of Houston campus. With the changing times, Houston money moved into the suburbs. The area was taken over by fraternity houses and well-paid professors.

Alice's parents bought the house during the era when oil ruled Houston and Texas, for that matter. Her dad, Mathis McLeod, was an original roughneck in the oil fields. He ended up being hired by Red Adair, the most famous oil field firefighter the industry had ever known.

For me to be appropriately impressed, Alice told me a joke about Red Adair:

A Texan died and went to heaven. Saint Peter showed him around paradise, but with every encounter of heavenly landscape, the Texan replied, "It's bigger and better in Texas!" Finally, frustrated, Saint Peter took the guy to the edge of heaven and asked him to look over the brim into the fires of hell! "Do you have anything like that in Texas?" he asked. "No, the Texan replied, "but I know a good ole boy in Houston who can put it out for you!"

That was Alice's dad's boss. Red Adair. Alice's parents met in West Texas when Red Adair was called in on a massive fire in a field where Alice's mom, Wilhelmina, worked for the oil company as the cook. The story goes that the fire was so intense it took five days for Adair's crew to put it out. During that time, Wilhelmina worked sixteen hours a day, keeping the men fed both in the mess hall and at the site. Volunteers from the town drove the food into the field and served it off the beds of pickup trucks. Wilhelmina never noticed Mathis during the emergency. While the men were working the fire, they were covered in soot, dirt, oil, and chemicals. They all looked like entertainers in blackface. After the fire was out, all hands cleaned up, the town threw a dance to celebrate the fire extinguishing, and they officially met.

Alice's mom said Red Adair was dancing with her, congratulating her on the excellent food, the hard work she put in keeping up with the needs of his crew when Mathis cut in. He was Adair's driller. This meant he was the lead crewman and answered only to Red himself. Red gallantly relinquished Wilhelmina to Mathis, who then touched the brim of his black cowboy hat as he greeted her with, "Ma'am." Once the music stopped, he did the same with another, "Ma'am." Wilhelmina was immediately smitten. Adair hired Wilhelmina. Firefighting oil well blowouts was intense, physically demanding, and dangerous oil fieldwork. Good food and lots of it was mandatory. It didn't take too much time before Mathis and Wilhelmina were an item, and Alice was on the way. They married in the Harris County courthouse, Red Adair as best man.

Now, Mathis and Wilhelmina were retired and living on a cruise ship! Mathis's rationalization was he had been landlocked most of his life, so now he wanted to see the world. They had left several years prior, their address the next port of call for the ship that traveled around the world. Alice had no idea when or where they'd land once the cruising got old. Meanwhile, Alice was thrilled to live in the two-story "mini-mansion," as she called it, rent-free.

My rent would help pay utilities and property taxes. I had two upstairs rooms for myself: one a bedroom, one a study. We were both in the throes of researching dissertation topics which meant every available minute was spent reading.

By the end of my first year of grad school, I was exhausted. An inventory of events made me feel even more so: a new city; a new university; a long-distance marriage that ended in divorce after five months; an encounter with my uncle asking for a favor; moving in with Alice; starting as a teaching assistant with undergraduate courses; all the time thinking about a dissertation topic. By the second semester's end, I was finally comfortable with the flow of my own course work and my teaching schedule; I was relaxed living with Alice. My grades were A's, thankfully, after earning only B's first semester. There was no such grade as a C in graduate school. When school was out for the summer, I was surprised that I had absolutely no desire to spend any time in Buffalo. I just wanted to be lazy at the house. Sleep in late, graze food all day instead of eating on the run, take long baths, go to movies and sip iced tea while lounging on the back screened-in porch of the house in that huge wicker settee with a thick cushion. I couldn't care less about reports of Houston's summer heat and humidity. Bring it on! My pores needed cleansing anyway!

Mid May, I was sprawled out on that wicker settee with an opened book on my chest, an iced tea on the table next to me. I had just dozed off when Alice flew onto the porch allowing the screen door to slam me awake.

"Well, that's very white of you," Alice quipped.

I wasn't exactly sure what that meant. "What?"

"Let's skip town for the summer."

"What?"

She handed me a flyer:

Summer Excursion Course
"The Diversity of Humanity"

Lead by
Dr. Honey Tibbett
Course Description:
Social Psychology 7052: The curriculum involves traveling by train, with overnights in New Orleans, Birmingham, Atlanta, Charlotte, NC, and July 4th in Washington DC. The focus is on US regions with cultural and ethnic diversity, documented through daily journaling and returning to Houston, a thesis paper.
Five Credit Hours

"Wow! This actually sounds wonderful," I said with the flyer in hand.

"Then you'll go?"

I hesitated a moment only to realize I had no good reason for saying no. "I'm in."

"Great! I've already signed us up. But, first, you'll have to meet with Dr. Tibbett and fill out some forms, registration, and release of responsibility, things like that. She is on campus until five this afternoon. Want to meet her?"

"Sure."

"Come on, the deadline is soon."

Honey Tibbett was so unlike any female professor I've ever met. Stunning at five-eleven, long brunette wavy hair and tortoiseshell framed glasses, rosy cheeks, and a huge smile, she stretched her hand across the desk to greet me.

"You must be Maggie. Hi, great that you came right in. We've got to get your forms into the registrar's office to assure you get the credits!"

Alice and I sat down; I proceeded to fill in the forms.

"How many have signed up so far?" Alice asked.

"You two."

Surprised, we looked at each other. "Just two?" Alice repeated.

"So far, oh, and my good friend Patty, Patty Odin."

"How many do you expect?"

Honey shrugged. "Just those who are intended to make this trip," she said smiling.

I looked up from the forms and met Alice's eyes.

"Is there a deadline for signing up? I didn't notice one on the flyer," Alice asked.

"Today at five," Honey answered.

We exchanged looks again, with silent giggles. There was something about how this was unfolding that appealed to me.

"With any luck," Honey commented as I handed her my completed forms, "it will be just us, the four of us."

It was ten days before we left for New Orleans. Honey insisted we meet her life-long friend Patty Odin. Patty lived in the Heights, one of the oldest communities of Houston. Heights Boulevard was lined with tall "painted lady" houses. Patty's house was painted purple, with green trim and yellow gingerbread accents.

"I love your house," I gushed when Patty opened the front door.

"Mardi gras colors: purple, green and gold; Chakra colors as well: purple and gold, crown Chakra, green heart Chakra.

"You must be Maggie and Alice. Come in, come in. Welcome!" She hugged us both. My hug was tight and seemed a little longer than I was accustomed to, but there was warmth and sincerity. I wiggled loose when I felt a furry thing brushing my leg.

"Ah! Who is this?" I asked, as I picked up the beautiful black cat with its obviously engorged.

"That's Natasha. She gave me a litter of seven little ones a week ago. Follow me, I'll show you."

We dutifully followed Patty to a hallway closet whose door was ajar. Inside was a low- slung wicker backet with these little mouse-size kittens moving around. Four of the kittens were pure gray, and long haired, two were all black, and one had a perfect circle of white fur at the base of her neck. I picked her up, inspecting for her sex.

"Oh, Patty! She's darling!" I gushed.

"If you want her, you can have her once it's time to separate them. I have a good friend, Janice, who will take all of them in while we're on vacation. Once back, she'll be ready for a new home," Patty explained

I held the small kitten up to my face and listened to her quiet squeal. I kissed her face and said, "Moonbeam! I'm so pleased to meet you; I'm so looking forward to taking you home with me, Moon!"

Honey turned to Patty, "One down, six to go!"

Patty was holding Natasha, "Guess who's getting neutered when I get back?"

At four-foot eleven inches, Patty standing next to Honey was a Mutt-and-Jeff image. Both ladies wore billowing cotton caftans, sandals and their long hair flowed. In contrast, Alice and I were in cut-off jeans, tees, and flip-flops. My hair was pulled up into a not-so-tidy bun on the back of my head. I felt so underdressed, no longer hip. I wanted to look like Honey and Patty!

The month of May was already humid and hot. Patty's dining room was comfortably air-conditioned. It was a display of porcelain tchotchkes, books, a round wooden table, and unmatched wooden chairs. The table settings didn't match either; a visually delightful jumble of patterns. Lunch was fresh prosciutto-wrapped melon, spinach-and-hardboiled-egg salad with bacon dressing, homemade bread, pea-and-candied-walnut salad, and iced tea by the pitcher.

"Peas and walnuts! I thought my mom was the only cook who made peas and walnut salad!" Alice said. Wilhelmina's cooking, my Sicilian family's cooking, Honey's lack of cooking became the topic while we ate. Over tea and cookies, Patty introduced herself to us.

"I've lived in Houston all my life. Right out of high school, I married my sweetheart, had three children then divorced him when the drinking got so bad, I knew I was at risk.

"Several years later, I married a guy from North Carolina, moved there with him, pulling my youngest, Lorraine, Raine for short, along. Little did I realize he was a binge drinker. That's when I realized I was to blame for where I found myself."

"You blame yourself for his drinking?" Alice asked.

"No, I blame myself for picking the same guy, another drinker. But I was young. I didn't know what I didn't know.

"The drinking progressed from binge to daily. I knew I had to get out of the marriage. But this guy was different from the kids' daddy. When my second husband drank, he became mean. I started praying fervently, asking God for a way out and back to Houston without causing Raine or me any harm. That's when I learned I had The Gift."

Alice and I exchanged looks. We looked at Honey. She smiled.

"The Gift?" Alice repeated.

Patty and Honey exchanged smiles, more expressive of the cat who killed the canary.

"As I said, I prayed every day to God for a way out," Patty continued.

"And what did God say?" Alice asked.

"God never answered. My mother did. My deceased mother instructed me to plan my husband's funeral. And in a small town, news travels fast that you are planning a funeral for a husband that is at work daily, isn't sick, but is a mean drunk."

Now Alice and I were laughing! "No kidding!" I said. "What happened?"

"Well, he got wind of it all, got spooked, and I was home before my birthday and in time to enroll Raine back into her Houston school before classes started in August."

"I'm sure there's more to this story," Alice said.

"Yes, there is. But let's leave it for the train ride," Honey suggested.

When I graduated with my Ph.D., I told the family they had to come to me. It was a ceremony I didn't want my parents to miss. To my surprise, Uncle Carmine and Aunt Lena, Uncle Mic and Aunt May, Uncle Jacob and Roy, my cousins Cary, Rocco, and his partner Drew attended my graduation as well. Alice's home had plenty of room. My mom and Aunt Lena took over the kitchen. The men walked the property and immediately started fixing what, in their opinion, needed fixing. Alice sat on the back porch sipping tea, smiling all the while with Aunt May. Aunt May, the only non-Sicilian aunt who confessed to Alice she had absolutely no idea what "they" were cooking in there.

"I think they're a hoot!" Alice confessed, laughing.

The heat did pose a challenge for a few in my family. "What's the matter for you?" Uncle Carmine asked. "Back in Sicily, it's-a like this every summer."

The family stayed another week beyond graduation. Patty invited them all to rest and relax at her bay house on Bolivar Peninsula, just 60 miles south from Houston, to Galveston, and across the ship channel by ferry to Bolivar. My family was fascinated with the bay houses up on stilts. Patty did an excellent job of explaining hurricanes and flooding. Her home was spacious, with three bedrooms and ample sleeping arrangements with fold-out sofas and futons in the living area and the deck. I hadn't seen my mom in a swimsuit for 10 years. Even Uncle Carmine wore Bermuda shorts with black socks and shoes. The cooking resumed as my aunts invaded the kitchen. This time Aunt May joined in because potato salad and coleslaw were her specialties, and cold food was the fare.

This allowed Alice and me to present our plan to my family about joining a psychology practice at the Houston Medical Center. Mom was deflated, but Dad and the uncles and cousins were all supportive. No one really had any experience opening a doctor's practice, so they deferred to our better judgment.

Alice and I took some additional time off after the family left and before we met with Frank Dorr and Honey, Frank's partner, the psychologists we were joining. Then there were many legal talks, paperwork, and we leased a new and more extensive office suite. But it flowed smoothly. Honey, Frank, and Patty guided Alice and me through the business process of a psychology practice. In about 6 weeks, we were up and running.

I hadn't been home in about ten years when I received the invitation to Aunt Zorah's 80th birthday party. I knew I wanted to attend. I felt I could handle the Sicilian pressure of "Are you seeing someone?" and "Why aren't you married?" and "Girls these days! No respect for family!" That last quip was about not being married, no kids, and not living around the corner from your mom or mother-in-law.

I was a Ph.D. psychologist with a thriving practice in Houston. But even as my chest puffed with self-worth, I knew that in my mom's world, there was nothing I did that resonated with her peers when they got together and talked about their children and grandchildren. Yet, I knew that my dad was proud of me. I was proud of myself.

Dad and Mom met me at the airport. I was immediately zipped away home where Mom had a traditional Sicilian meal prepared. My favorite homemade meatballs and sausage were served with thin spaghetti, then salad. In Sicilian households, salad arrived after the entrée, followed by espresso and sweets. Tonight, cucidati, homemade Christmas cookies. Mom constantly freezes a dozen or more for special occasions, like tonight. She also served ice cream.

I sat with my parents as they watched a TV movie and talked about the characters during the commercial breaks as if they knew them in real life! And they managed a question or two for me about life in Houston and how the business was going. It was fun, and it felt good to be with them again.

As I settled into my bedroom, I was exhausted. Sleeping was no problem. The party was scheduled for Saturday. The next couple of days, I wanted with Mom and Dad, hanging around the house.

"When you finish your breakfast, get ready, Aunt Bertha is expecting us for lunch," Mom informed me.

"I'm just finishing breakfast!" I pleaded. "And I was hoping the three of us would hang out, maybe later get a hot dog at Ted's. Unfortunately, you can't get a charcoal-grilled hot dog in Houston."

"Bertha is expecting us, and to make it easier for you, Lady Jane, Aunt Eve, and my brother Renato are going to be there too. Kill two birds with one stone."

"Hmm," I thought. Mom used that title when she thought I was being too pretentious (which meant Irish). But, after being called Lady Jane, I knew I had no recourse.

As I dressed, I mused to myself, "I bet you a dime to a dollar that my cousins will be there too. Let me count. Cary, Ginger, their four kids, Carlo, maybe even Uncle Joe's sister Jane and her husband. That's about fourteen people. Yup, sounds about right." When my dad turned onto the street where Aunt Bertha lived, the cars parked along the curb would make anyone think a party was going on in someone's house.

"Ciao Bella!" Aunt Bertha greeted me with a huge hug and kisses on each cheek, followed by Uncle Joe, Uncle Renato, and Aunt Eve. My cousins were far more modern in their greetings.

It was a wonderful afternoon. My cousin Cary's kids were all young adults. I just loved their names. Cary's wife Ginger was a movie buff. The kids' names reflected this: Maureen (the firstborn), O'Hara (the first boy), Irene (in the middle), and Dunn (the "baby" boy). We all had asked what if the last child had been a girl? "No chance," Ginger answered. I sat with each kid and had a thoughtful conversation. No one pumped me about whether I would ever get married, and my cousins were interested in my practice, living in Houston, and my friends there.

Uncle Renato approached me and teased, "A doctor! Must be making money hand over fist."

"I wish," I said. "Don't get me wrong. I'm doing okay. But my student loans take a huge chunk out of my monthly income. Huge."

"What is it you do, exactly," he changed the subject. I gave him a crash course in psychotherapy, testing, behavior modification, and other various treatments our practice offered. An art therapist was working with us, which I pointed out as very current in my field. He seemed impressed. I was thrilled. He was the only uncle who asked me anything about my practice of the aunts and uncles present. I gave him a lot of credit for asking, taking an interest in me like that.

When I was a kid, Uncle Renato was always a little scary to us, the cousins. His moniker "the Mechanic" was rumored to mean he "fixed" situations. That was scary and an eerie evil connotation for kids entering middle school.

While I watched my mom for the first time, I could see her pride in having her daughter the doctor at home. It made me pause for a moment. I wondered if I had missed other moments like this in the past because I just wanted to get away from the family, be on my own, live my life the way I wanted. It was a moot question.

Around six, Rocco crashed the party. "Hey! Our turn! Aunt Bert? Are you done with this lovely lady?" he called out.

"Yeah, take her!"

Drew and Rocco took me by the arms as in escorting me out the door. My parents were laughing. Mom called out, "Have fun!"

"Where we goin'?" I asked.

"Just get in the car, lady," Drew said, impersonating Jimmy Cagney.

Soon we were on the Youngman highway headed for the suburbs. Then we weaved our way through a Clarence subdivision. After about half an hour later, we were pulling up in front of Rosalie's house. My cousin Rosalie was Uncle Renato's daughter and my Woodstock companion. Rosalie had a brother, Giancarlo (we called him Carlo). The cars parked in the driveway on the street gave away that a party was happening. As I walked into the backyard, a chorus of "There she is!" greeted me. Danny, Rosalie's husband, was grilling steaks. Gaggles of kids were in the in-ground pool. My cousins hugged me, handed me a margarita, and guided me to a lawn chair. I got comfortable. This was wonderful.

"So, a doctor, huh?" Angela said.

"Yes, a psychologist, Ph.D. type doctor," I added, not that I thought Angela needed the Cliff notes. She was my oldest female cousin. Uncle Carmine's daughter and the mother of his only grandchildren: Maria, Isabella (after my mom, we called her Izzy), and Carmine (after his grandfather, we called him Car). Angela did it "right:" married her high school sweetheart a year after graduation; complete cosmetology school first so Jimmy could complete junior college. Marrying into Uncle Carmine's family almost assured the guy would become a part of The Family Business. So why did he finish junior college, the cousins wondered among themselves.

Angela sat down next to me. "You got more education than you know what to do with, don't you?"

My first reaction was some sarcastic remark that it beats shampooing old ladies' heads all day. Still, I just tipped my huge margarita glass in her direction and said, "Yes!"

I was the only university graduate among my cousins. I had turned away from the family formula of marriage and grandchildren for your parents, plus living around the corner. Yet, I had no regrets, even though I knew I had sacrificed marriage and children for my career.

Soon after my divorce from Jimmy Toscano, I would fantasize about what it might have been like if I left school and followed Jimmy? How might it have worked if I got pregnant, moved back home, and reclaimed the cottage my aunts had set up for me that summer of my marriage. I stopped that train of thought when nausea hit.

Angela was long gone after my "Yes!" She was looking for a soft spot but found none. I watched the kids in the pool, trying to figure who belonged to who when Rocco sat down next to me. If anyone understood the sacrifice of the family "formula," Rocco did when he came out with his parents.

"A penny for your thoughts?"

"Hah! Angela, kids, the marriages around me," I confessed.

"That? Why would you let that bother you?" he joked. "I get it. I think it would make a difference in my family if Sal would have kids. Give my dad a Madonie grandson, just so Renato's grandsons aren't the only Madonie grandsons, you know?"

"Carlo has children?!" I gasped in my best interpretation of shock. "I never got a wedding invitation!"

"Stop! Rosalie's kids don't have the Madonie name. I was just saying when or if her brother Carlo gets married, his sons will be Madonie, that's all," Rocco explained.

"Oh! You scared me for a moment. Carlo all married and with kids! Like Sal, it's going to take extraordinary women to marry those two. But Sal's bride would have to be willing to be upstaged by the groom in a wedding dress more spectacular than hers!" We both fell out laughing.

"Perfect, Cuz," Rocco said, relaxed some then, "A doctor. That's great! You must be making money hand over fist."

"You are the second person today that has said that to me, but my student loans are killing me."

"Let me guess, Uncle Renato, he asked how much money you make, right?"

"Yes. Let me ask you a question: where else can you go to borrow money, and the balance grows while you're making payments? Where? Sound familiar?"

"Yeah," Rocco replied, "Easy. Stevie D. You sure these student loan people aren't in a family business?"

"Who is Stevie D?"

Surprised, Rocco said, "You don't know who Stevie D is?"

"No. Remember I lived out of town for the past ten years!"

"Right. Uncle Augustine and Aunt Lucy?" Rocco started.

"Uncle Carmine's, I mean, your dad's first cousin. They head The Family Business," I said.

"Very good! You have been paying attention. Aunt Lucy's brother is Leo. Leo Bataglia. Leo married Jane Rizzo. Aunt Bertha married Joe Rizzo, Jane's brother." Rocco continued.

"Oh, the in-laws of Uncle Augustine and Aunt Bertha, who would be at every Madonie event in life, would invite their brother and sister! I get it." Maggie felt pleased with herself.

"Now you got it. Leo and Jane had two kids, Stevie D and Lucy, who married this cool dude Rich Jones. Did you know that they have two kids, and one is named Elvis? But not Elvis Presley, Elvis Costello! You know who that is, right?" Rocco asked.

"Yes. I've heard of him. What is their daughter's name?" I was getting tired of Sixty Questions.

"Diana." It was apparent that the pause was intentional.

"Okay. Diana. What? What?" It was obvious I was missing something.

"You don't get it?" Rocco was incredulous.

"What?!" I could feel the alcohol.

"Princess Diana!"

I didn't get it. "Back to Stevie D. What does the 'D' stand for?" I asked.

"All he ever says is 'You don't want to know,' so I don't know."

Now I laughed out loud. "Come on! What, he's trying to act like a hood? Floating loans on street corners?"

"I remember Stevie D from high school," Rocco continued. "He's a cool character. Always standing off to the side, never said much, but scored big on the football field and with the girls. And his wife, God rest her soul, Donna Del Marco, hung onto him like fleas on a dog. If Stevie D ever tried to shake her off, it didn't work. They married right out of school."

"His wife is dead? How did that happen? Did he 'whack' her?" I asked, joking.

Rocco didn't flinch. "No, car accident. Seems one night they got into a fight, and she drove off . . . ended up dead," Rocco said flatly.

"Wow. Sorry to hear it. I'm assuming he works for your dad," I continued.

"Not directly. Uncle Renato. Leo and Stevie D work for Renato."

"What does he do?" I was trying for a bit of insight into The Family Business.

"Let's keep it simple and say he's in transportation."

"I thought you said loan sharking! I could use someone in finances!" I reminded him.

"When I said Stevie D's name connected to loan sharking, all I was thinking about is it takes a ball-buster like Stevie D," Rocco explained.

"Oh. Wait a minute! I was just thinking, your father owes me a favor! I could have used it!"

We looked at each other and broke out laughing again. I chalked it up to the margaritas.

Aunt Zorah's party was more like a big Sicilian wedding: the music, the lasagna, the antipasti, homemade wine, homemade bread, and cannoli. The cake was giant. We all hoped Aunt Zorah wouldn't spit on the cake while blowing out the 80 candles. It took five cousins almost ten minutes working together to get all those candles lit simultaneously.

Mom, Dad, and I were gathering our to-go bags of cannoli and cake, ready to leave the party, when Uncle Renato approached me.

"Hon, come here," he beckoned.

I left Mom's side and walked with Uncle Renato.

"You got anything planned Sunday after Mass?" he asked.

I didn't dare tell him I hadn't been at Mass in twenty years. I just said, "No."

"Good. Come over to Uncle Carmine's house. Be there at three. He kissed each cheek and walked away. I was surprised. In a Sicilian family, when someone kisses you unexpectedly, you ask yourself, "Was that a kiss of love and respect or the kiss of death?"

Mom and Dad calling my name snapped me out of it. I told Mom, "Uncle Carmine wants to see me tomorrow. Do you know why?"

"No," she said. "Don't' worry about it."

Sunday afternoon at Uncle Carmine and Aunt Lena's home was warm and fragrant from all the cooking. We greeted with hugs and kisses.

"Carmine is waiting for you in the dining room. Are you hungry? Could you eat a little something?" Aunt Lena asked.

"I smell the bread. How about a slice or two of your bread with butter," I replied. It was easier to just ask for something instead of getting into a tug-of-war of "no thanks" and "just a little something." I went into the dining room.

Aunt Lena served coffee, warm-from-the-oven bread, and butter. Then, before any conversation started, Aunt Lena and Aunt Zorah (who lived with them) left the room, leaving me with Uncle Carmine, Rocco, and Uncle Renato.

"How you doin'?" Uncle Carmine asked.

"I'm good, Uncle Carmine, really good."

"So now you're a doctor? What kind of doctoring is it anyway? You cut people open?" he asked.

"No! I'm a psychologist. I dissect the brain with words to learn what makes people tick." The small talk was nerve-racking.

"This is interesting. I could use someone like you in my business." We all laughed. My laugh was a little nervous. What is he getting at?

"I bet you want to know why I asked you here," he said. He was obviously good at reading people.

"Rocco came to me," Uncle Carmine reached out affectionately and patted Rocco's face. "He said things would be better for you, but you got this . . . this . . ." he turned to Rocco again, "What did you call it?"

"Student loan debt," Rocco answered.

"That's it. Student loan debt," Uncle Carmine repeated.

"Oh, that! "I tried sounding nonchalant. Now I'm legitimately nervous.

"So, how much we talkin' about?" He took a slab of butter, spread it onto a chunk of warm homemade bread, then folded the slice to dunk it into his coffee.

"Ah, well, I'm really not sure. I just make the payments and try not to think about it too much."

"Come on, Cuz, how much?" Rocco coaxed.

"Two hundred thirty-five thousand dollars," I said quickly, flatly.

"Mamma Mia!" Uncle Carmine declared.

He was sitting at the head of the table directly across from Uncle Renato at the opposite end. After Uncle Carmine sipped his coffee, all the while shaking his head no, he looked at Renato.

"Renato, we can do something about this, no?"

"We can," Uncle Renato replied without even looking up from dunking his bread into the coffee.

"Then, Renato, fix it, okay?"

"Okay," he replied and stuffed the wet bread into his mouth, brushed his hand together, shaking off crumbs, and smiled at me, with puffy cheeks like a squirrel.

My head was turning left and right as if I were at a tennis match.

"Good!" Rocco injected.

"What just happened?" I asked in disbelief.

"The loan, the student loan," Rocco answered.

I panicked. "I'm not asking for any money!"

Uncle Carmine said, "Who said anything about money. Forget about it." He focused on his next dunk.

I looked at Rocco with a "help me understand" look, but he only smiled in reply.

"Besides," Uncle Carmine said as he reached across to me and pinched my cheek the same way he did when I was a kid while calling me his Irish angel. "I owe you a favor."

Rocco walked with me the blocks between the complex and my parents' house.

"Is he serious? He's going to pay off my student loans?" I asked Rocco.

Rocco confessed, "All I know is what I heard: 'Renato, fix it.'" Rocco imitated his dad's gravel voice. "Let me know what that looks like, okay?"

We hugged.

A day later, I was back in my own home, 1200 miles away, unpacking. I couldn't "forget about it!" though. It didn't keep me awake nights, but I wondered how this would manifest, this, "Renato, fix it."

My first clue came at the end of the month when no money had been automatically debited from my checking account. I wanted to call the loan people but didn't. Having extra money felt good, yet I wondered if it was the "fix" or a mistake. My answer came a week later. I got a letter from the loan company informing me that my loan was 100% forgiven, my balance zero, and best wishes for a bright career. If they could be of service in the future, just call.

I re-read that letter several times. I wanted to telephone someone but didn't know who right off the bat. Then I decided I'd wait and see if next month my account is or is not debited the loan payment.

It wasn't. I called Rocco. "Why are you surprised?"

"Really? Two hundred thirty-five thousand dollars?"

"Just call him and say thanks," Rocco suggested.

"That simple?"

"He owed you a favor, remember?" Rocco paused, "I owe you my life as a result," Rocco reminded me.

I had forgotten. If Rocco hadn't returned home, reconciled with his parents, and with medical advances, Rocco was alive today.

"Are you there?" he asked.

"Yeah. Yeah, I'm here," I said softly.

"So, forget about it," Rocco said. "Enjoy your life! You worked hard for the Ph.D. And come home more often, okay?'

"Okay. I love you."

"Love you, too. Bye."

And that was that.

My receptionist interrupted my session with a client, which, the rule was, only in case of an emergency.

"It's your Aunt Zorah. She said it's an emergency,"

I made my apology to my client for leaving the office.

I picked up the phone and immediately asked, "Aunt Zorah, who died?"

My Sicilian genes kicked right in.

"Come-a home right now," she commanded.

Now I'm no longer the level-headed psychologist. "What's going on?"

"You just come-a home right now," she said with a firm tone.

I was silent. I thought maybe if I didn't answer, she would cave.

She did, a little. "Your mother, she needs you."

"Then something happened to my dad? Is he all right?" I could feel my voice softening.

"You come-a home?"

"I need to know what kind of emergency. I have clients with appointments to see me. What is going on?" I hoped she would accept my reasoning.

Now it was her time to pause, and finally, she said, "Your father, he's a-dead."

I froze.

"How soon you get home?" she asked.

"I'm leaving my office right now. I'll call from the airport and let you know what time I'm getting into Buffalo. Tell my mom I'm on my way." I turned to Alice and exclaimed, "My dad died. I will end my session with my client, head home, pack, and get a cab to the airport. I know I'm dumping my appointment schedule on you . . ." I started to apologize.

Frank, the senior psychologist, joined us, listening. He offered, "I'll go in with you and sit with your client, process the therapist running out on her? Him?"

"Her. Thanks. I'll introduce you; tell her my dad died as I get my purse, okay?"

Honey had joined us. "What's up?"

"My dad died. I don't know when, I just got the call, I have to fly home!"

Honey offered, "Of course! We've got it here. Do you need anything else?"

"Honey, do you still have a key to my apartment?"

"Yes."

"Will you take Moon to Patty, like I did when I went for the party? This time I don't know just how long I'll be, and Patty won't mind caring for Moon," I said.

Frank asked, "Got everything covered here? Then, let's go in and tell your client that you're leaving now."

Once I had my flight information, I called Mom and Aunt Zorah answered.

"How's Mom?"

"Who knows? Bella, always cry over everything, so now she cry all the time."

"Can I talk to her?"

"No. She just went upstairs after lunch. She need-a rest. What time I send Rocco to get you?"

I told her my arrival time in Buffalo. At first, on the plane, I had no thoughts; I felt numb. When I was home for Aunt Zorah's party, I could see that my parents had aged in the ten years I hadn't seen them. Somehow a kid gets into denial and thinks that parents will be around forever. I was so glad that Dad and I had danced at the party. That was the memory I replayed in my mind.

By the time the flight attendant offered me the meal, I had flipped into all the unknown answers for the questions running like ticker tape in my head: does my mom know how to write a check? Is there a will? Insurance? Funeral arrangements! If Mom is crying non-stop, I doubt she'll be coherent enough to make funeral arrangements.

The same attendant who placed the meal before me paused at my row, "Miss, are you all right?"

I was surprised by the question but realized that tears were running down my cheeks. Embarrassed, I said, "My dad died. I'm heading home."

"I'm sorry for your loss," she said and moved on. Minutes later, she appeared again with a hot towel from first class. Handing it to me, she said, "This will soothe you. I'd like to bring you a complimentary drink," she posed.

"That's a good idea, bourbon and water on the rocks."

After a second drink, I dozed off into a no-dream sleep.

I was awakened by the same attendant, and I heard the announcement that we were preparing to land. She had another hot towel for me. I gratefully accepted it and pressed the towel to my face. It felt terrific and even picked up my spirit some. What a wonderful gesture. I'd never forget it.

I disembarked, headed for the exit at a quick pace. Once past security, I spotted Drew immediately. He rushed to me, grabbed, and hugged me hard. I hugged back. This lasted until Rocco arrived, who interrupted Drew and resumed hugging me. I was relaxing.

"Home; I'm home. I'm here. I can handle this now," I thought. "What happened? All that Aunt Zorah said was my dad is dead. No details; what the hell happened? He was fine when I was home."

We were walking rapidly towards baggage claim. I had my tickets out, and Drew took them from my hand. All the while, Rocco was explaining.

"All I know is that he went upstairs for a nap after breakfast and when your mom went to wake him for The Price is Right, he was dead; didn't wake up." Rocco kept it simple.

"Poor Mom."

Drew appeared with my luggage, and each had me by the arms and guided me outside to a waiting car, more like a mini limo.

"What is this?" I asked.

"I know a guy. He offered to drive us so I wouldn't have to park," Rocco said as I was offered the back seat of the black Lincoln Continental.

We headed down Genesee Street and onto the 33. I sat between Drew and Rocco.

"We're going directly to your house. Aunt Zorah and Ethel are waiting for you. They've been cooking since they got there. Your mom is a mess; she can't seem to stop crying. Uncle Renato tried to ask her about funeral arrangements, a will, and all that, and she just bawls louder," Rocco explained.

"Do you know how she handled finding my dad dead?"

"Yeah, she dialed 911. That's how the family was notified. The ambulance wouldn't take him because he was . . . dead a while, the corner had to be called; gave us time to get to your mom. All our aunts and uncles showed up. And, of course, Aunt Zorah and Ethel took over."

When the Lincoln turned the corner onto the street where Mom lived, cars were parked in all directions.

"People are still here? It's almost two a.m.!" I was more disappointed than grateful because I was exhausted and selfishly wanted to be with Mom alone. But that's not how this works in a Sicilian family.

A couple of cousins-in-law were sitting on the back porch. They moved their cars from the driveway so the driver could pull in all the way to the back. I entered the house through the back porch and heard the murmurs, "Maggie." "Maggie's home. Do we wake Bella?"

Uncle Renato was the first person out the back door; he opened his arms, and I fell right into them. I just sobbed.

"It's going to be alright," he whispered, hugging me tightly.

I could smell the sauce and bread and coffee. I walked into the kitchen. Aunt Zorah gave me tissues. She hugged me, released me to Ethel.

Ethel Murray. She and Aunt Zorah had been friends since the 1930s when they worked downtown as secretaries. Well, I know for sure that Ethel was a secretary. Aunt Zorah worked for The Family Business, so no one knows what Zorah did. These ladies were always together; took vacations together; movies; Ethel was Zorah's plus one. No one ever questioned their relationship. Even when I was a kid, if my cousins in one house came down with chickenpox or the flu or something, Aunt Zorah and Ethel practically moved in and helped nurse everyone back to health. Once our grandparents got old, Aunt Zorah cared for them. Uncle Carmine and Aunt Lena moved into our grandparents' house when they became empty nesters. After our grandparents died, Zorah continued living with Carmine and Lena. Ethel lived in her family home; her brother married and moved to Cleveland. I met him maybe twice.

Ethel escorted me over to the kitchen table, had me sit down, and got me a glass of wine. Aunt Zorah followed up with a plate of spaghetti with meatballs. The bread was already on the table. For some odd reason, as the two ladies walked back to the stove and sink, Ethel put her arm around Zorah, leaned in with a side hug. It made me stop short. Was it possible? Why would I consider this now? Most likely because over six years as a psychologist had opened my eyes to humanity!

Without my noticing, my cousins had joined me at the table. Cary and Ginger, Rocco and Drew, Carlo, Rosalie, and Danny; Sal slid in next to me on my chair, put his arm around my shoulder, and said, "No worry, I won't let you fall off!"

The questions started: how was I doing? Did I need anything? Just speak up, just call, whatever you do, don't do this by yourself!

The commotion woke Mom. When she entered the kitchen, everyone stopped and looked her way.

Mom wailed something incoherent and rushed to me. I jumped up so fast Sal landed on his ass. It was the comic relief we needed.

"Get up, stupid! What? You can't let your cousin sit by herself?" Mom quipped. Then she turned to me, and in my embrace, Mom began crying again.

I hugged her, whispering through my tears, "We'll get through this; we'll get through this together."

Her answer was, "When you're finished eating, go to the dining room and pay your respects."

I knew exactly what she meant. My aunts and uncles were in the other rooms. Sitting at the head of the dining room table was Uncle Carmine. Next to him on either side were Uncle Augustine and Uncle Renato; Aunts Lean and Eve sat nearest their husbands, while Aunt Bertha and Uncle Joe filled out the table. I walked around the table, hugging, and kissing them all.

Uncle Carmine motioned, "Come here, sit, sit." He put a small juice glass in front of me and filled it halfway with wine.

I sipped; it was homemade, room temperature, and stout.

"Doll, Renato is-a going to help you through this whole thing. You-a no alone in this, we are all here to stand by you. Renato, tell Maggie what will happen," he nodded at Renato.

"Tomorrow, I'm sending a car around; you and Bella have to go to the funeral home. Take with you the clothing you want your dad to be buried in. Then," Uncle Renato leaned in as if a secret would be shared, "the undertaker will take you to pick out the coffin."

I was startled. I hadn't expected that. Then, of course, the family picks out the coffin.

"I can see that you're tired," he said, "Lena, let's-a go home."

Uncle Carmine stood up. "Let's all go home and let Maggie and Bella get some sleep. They have busy, sad day tomorrow."

With that, people did start milling about, paying respects to Mom and me as they filed out of our home. The only two left were Aunt Zorah and Ethel.

Ethel came to me and whispered, "Dear, I drew a bath for you."

I felt cared for. Those two ladies had been taking care of the Madonie family for years without a peep.

I slept like a log: it must have been the wine. Then, finally, Ethel gently woke me, telling me it was time to get up as there was a long day ahead of me. How well I knew.

I was surprised to see Uncle Renato at the breakfast table with the man I had never seen before. I kissed Aunt Zorah and Uncle Renato good morning, then got myself a cup of coffee.

"Hi, do I know you?" I asked as I sat across from him.

Before the guy could answer, my breakfast was presented, my favorite, a slice of bread with the center torn out, buttered. The slice was then placed in the skillet and an egg broken into the middle, fried, just looking at it brought on tears.

"Are you okay?" the guy asked.

I wiped my eyes. "Yes. Silly, isn't it? Just looking at breakfast feels like love."

"Nice. And you're right. By the way, I'm Stevie D."

Just then, Rocco arrived, kisses all around, coffee in hand, slapped Stevie D on the back, and said, "Well, here he is! Stevie D!"

"We've met," I said, not looking up from the food.

"Oh," he sat down. "How you doin'?"

"To tell you the truth, I don't know yet. Where's Mom?" I directed the question to the ladies standing at the stove.

"I go get her now," Aunt Zorah said and headed up the stairs.

The room was silent. I could hear the birds chirping. I was dreading Mom joining us, more out of fear about how she would act today. When we heard feet on the stairs, all eyes fixed in that direction. Mom entered the kitchen, made a beeline for me, grabbed me from behind in a hug, and began sobbing into my hair, "I'm all alone! Oh God, I'm all alone!"

I didn't know what to do. I tried twisting around, but she had a good grip on me. Aunt Zorah unlatched her and made her sit down. Mom just sobbed, and the day was just starting.

I knew the drill. Sicilian families flocked to funerals. First, there is the wake that lasts for three whole days. Then, between the viewings from two to four and seven to nine, we flock to someone's house for supper. After nine we go home. On the day of the burial, it starts with prayers at the funeral home; people get to say goodbye and pay respects to Mom and me. Next, there will be a procession of cars, driving at a slow speed, to the church where the Mass for Christian Burial is offered for his soul. That is followed by the next leg of the drive to the cemetery and graveside prayers. Uncle Renato (most likely) will invite the attendees to a meal at a pre-arranged restaurant. It was exhausting just thinking about it. How will I ever get through it with any sanity? How will I handle my mom?

In the house, Aunt Zorah was handling Mom quite well. But once Mom and I got into the car for the funeral home, it was on me. She could be histrionic, and if any event gave her permission to behave this way, it was Dad dying.

Aunt Zorah was preparing Mom's breakfast; Mom was holding a handkerchief in her hands over her face while she quietly cried. Where did she dig up the handkerchief? Who uses handkerchiefs anymore? I rolled my eyes, then realized I had an audience. Stevie D. had a big smile on his face as he raised the newspaper high enough to block him.

I excused myself and lit up the stairs like a scared cat. I closed myself off in the bathroom, literally shaking. "Get a grip, Maggie," I was telling myself. "Be the strong professional." I had to get ready for the day.

Ethel was sitting on the top step in the hall. She startled me, but her smile said, "I know, hon, I know. Time to get ready for the funeral home. I just thought I'd give you a hand."

"Thanks." We entered my bedroom. "Ethel, I have no idea how one plans a funeral. Who gets the church? Where should we have the luncheon? Who do we get for pallbearers?"

"Well, there's your Uncle Mic's oldest boy and your cousins, to start with," she answered.

I froze. "Uncle Mic and Uncle Jacob! I forgot, completely forgot! Do they know? I've got to call them; how could I forget to call them?"

Ethel had her hand on my back, rubbing while saying, "Breathe, breathe, breathe. Renato already talked to them right after it happened. Your Uncle Mic said if at any time you need to get away, he'll be here in a heartbeat." She leaned in a little, nudging my shoulder, "If I were you, I'd escape to them after this funeral coffin business is over and eat some ham and cabbage!"

We both laughed. I was as ready as I could be, not caring how I looked. Ethel and I returned to the kitchen. I got another cup of coffee. Uncle Renato was reading the newspaper, and Stevie D was gone. I went right to the phone and began dialing Uncle Mic's number.

After my call, I felt much better. I apologized for not calling him when I arrived in town. He invited me for supper tonight; I said I'd get back to him.

Zorah was chopping something for the next meal. Ethel was cleaning up the breakfast dishes. We heard Mom's footsteps coming down the stairs. All stopped. She entered the room like Gloria Swanson in Sunset Boulevard. Wearing a black dress, black hose, and black shoes, her head was covered with a black tulle netting, long enough to touch her shoulders. She also was wearing a pair of black cotton gloves.

"What the . . ." I thought. "Uh, Mom, what are you wearing?" I asked.

"My funeral dress!" she snapped.

"And that veil on your head?"

"Jackie O," she replied.

"Jackie O?"

"Yes. You remember, when President Kennedy died, Jackie wore a veil covering her face! Like a widow should! I always thought that was smart."

"Are you planning on wearing it all the time?" I asked.

"No, of course not! How are people going to kiss me at the wake if I have this over my face? But, when I go out, I'm wearing it." She sat next to me at the table.

Aunt Zorah placed half a meatball sandwich in front of me. "Mangia. You be out all afternoon," she looked at Mom, "Bella, you wanna a meatball?"

I smiled to myself. Aunt Zorah, with the crazy people, just keep moving forward.

Stevie D walked in, "car is ready," he announced. He did a double take at Mom, then looked at me as if asking, "What the . . .?"

At the curb in front of our house, a black Lincoln limo was parked.

Stevie D opened the rear door for Mom, me, and Uncle Renato. Before the door was closed, Rocco climbed in as well. "Sorry, I'm late."

"How can you be late when you weren't expected?" I asked.

Before Rocco could answer, Uncle Renato said, "Be on time from now on."

I thought, "Keep your mouth shut."

"Aunt Bella, what's that thing . . ." He didn't get to complete his question. It was the way Uncle Renato looked at him that shut him up.

Once downtown Stevie D weaved around some back streets of a seedy neighborhood of warehouses. He pulled the limo into an alley and parked. A steel side door next to us opened, and I recognized Mr. Edward, the funeral director. A younger man stood next to him, and I assumed it was his son. Stevie D, the perfect chauffeur, jogged around the car and opened the door.

Mr. Edward greeted us with condolences, ushered us into the building. Once inside the foyer of the warehouse building, on the wall in three-foot gold letters, it read, "AMERICAN CASKET COMPANY."

Mom moaned loudly and feigned a slump into Stevie D. He righted her. "Here we go," I thought.

Mr. Edward led the way down a hallway to a freight elevator, the kind that opened from top and bottom, not side to side. We all stepped into it for the ride up several floors. The old elevator creaked and stopped with a jolt. The son opened the doors to a warehouse-size room full of opened caskets popped into full view.

Mom inhaled a scream and fainted. Rocco and Stevie D caught her and carried her to a chair.

"Sam, smelling salts!" Mr. Edward gasped. The young man pulled the ampules from his coat pocket, cracked it, peeled back Mom's veil, and waved it under her nose. She came around quickly.

Uncle Renato took over. "Rocco, Stevie D, take Bella downstairs and outside for some fresh air. Wait in the limo. Maggie and I will pick out a coffin for Georgie; we'll be out of here in thirty minutes. Go!"

Mom was sobbing again into a cotton handkerchief. Rocco helped her off the chair and back into the elevator.

"Wow," was all I thought and hadn't realized I'd said it out loud.

"Yeah," Uncle Renato answered. "Bella, always the crier. Come on, Doll, let's get this over," he said as he gently took my arm and motioned to Mr. Edward to move forward.

I had no idea that people had to walk through a warehouse floor of opened coffins, listening to the undertaker droll on about cherry wood, mahogany, eggshell color silk lining, or "against Mr. Blake's fair complexion, doeskin tan might suit him best." With every pause over a coffin, after hearing the particulars, Mr. Edward and Uncle Renato would stand closer together as Mr. Edward wrote what I assumed were prices on a small notepad and showed it to Uncle Renato.

After about six coffins into this ordeal, I asked, "Do we have to look at more?"

"No, doll; which one do you prefer?"

"I have no clue," I said and slumped a little. Then, I felt a strong hand in the middle of my back, pushing a little, supporting me. I turned. Stevie D. I didn't realize he had joined us.

Uncle Renato approached me and took my hands in his. "Doll, I know all these decisions are yours to make now, but I'm here to help. Let me be your front man on this:
I bring you the information, we talk, you decide, and I take that decision back to whomever. How's that?"

I sighed audibly. "Fine. May I go now?"

He gestured to Stevie D, who stepped next to me. Uncle Renato said, "I'll meet you both at the car in a few minutes."

Stevie D gently put his hand on my back, guiding me back through the labyrinth of coffins to the elevator. I was never so happy to get out of a place in all my life.

Once in the limo, I just leaned back and took in some cleansing breaths to get the musty smell out of my nose.

After about fifteen minutes, the limo door opened. Uncle Renato climbed in over Mom and me. Mr. Edward leaned in, saying, "Mr. Blake will be ready by seven, family only, tonight. Are you all right, Mrs. Blake?"

Mom leaned forward and said, "Thank you so much, Mr. Edward. I'm sorry for fainting; I feel much better now."

"Make sure you eat. You'd be surprised how many times a family member faints, and it has more to do with not eating. We'll see you tonight, thank you." And he backed out and closed the door.

"Stevie D, back to Bella's house," Uncle Renato directed.

We rode in silence. All I could do was look out the window. It was a sunny day in June. I watched the scenery pass, lost in reading retail signage. It was a game I played with myself: a game of no thoughts. I wanted an escape from this surrealistic event. Yet, I was right in the middle of it all with a mom who had already surrendered her position.

Back at the house, Aunt Zorah had the dining room table set for supper. As we stepped in, Mom headed directly for her bedroom. We heard that door slam shut.

"I'll just go change my clothes and be back in a minute," I said.

While I climbed the stairs, I could hear Aunt Zorah ask how it went and the men relating the details. I was sure we were all wondering how she would handle tonight.

Supper was a combination of leftovers from the two a.m. dinner plus a fresh green salad. We passed platters and bowls of food in silence. Mom was absent.

After a glass of red wine, I asked, "What next, Uncle Renato? "

"Viewing starts at seven," he said without looking up.

"No. I mean, how does all this get paid for? Who will be pallbearers? Where will we hold the luncheon after the cemetery? Did anyone call the priest from their parish?"

Ethel reported, "I called the church the morning George died. Father Antonio came right over and sat with Bella through it all. Father Antonio said he'd clear the day, four days out, for the funeral Mass. So that's all set."

Uncle Renato was scooping meatballs and more spaghetti onto his plate, "Doll, Mr. Edward, and I wrote the obituary for the newspaper. It will be in the Courier Express tomorrow. As for the pallbearers, my Carlo and Rosalie's husband Danny, Bertha's Cary, Carmine's Sal, and Rocco, plus Angela's husband, Jimmy. That's six, all we need."

"Wait, there are no Blakes. There has to be one of my Irish cousins, I insist!" I said, surprised that they were left out.

Uncle Renato stopped and looked at me, "Maggie, I'm sorry. I wasn't thinking. Of course, I'll call Mic and ask his three oldest boys to be pallbearers."

"Sal and I will sit out," Rocco said.

"No. You, okay. But Jimmy and Danny will step out. It's more important that Georgie's nephews are pallbearers than nephews-in-law." He leaned back in his chair and announced, "This is better, three pallbearers from each side of the family. Good. Okay, Maggie?"

"Perfect, thanks," I answered.

Stevie D sat next to me at the dining table. He was very attentive, holding platters and bowls while I moved the food onto my plate. He refilled my wine glass without my requesting and made sure the grated cheese bowl was within reach. After pie and coffee, Uncle Renato rose from the table, nodded to Stevie D.

"Hon, I'm headed for a nap. Stevie D will drive me home and return. He will drive you, your mom, Zorah, and Ethel to the funeral parlor. You don't have to walk in right at seven. It will be a slow night tonight," he said, then added, "And, make sure your mom eats something before you leave here."

Ethel insisted that she and Zorah would wash up the dishes, but I just kept clearing the table and started washing them. I needed something to do. If I stopped, I'd start crying, and I just had no more strength for that. When Stevie D returned, he picked up a towel and began drying the dishes.

"You don't have to do that. They can just sit there and dry," I said.

"Isn't about the dishes," he replied.

I didn't look up.

The funeral home was the usual over-the-top faux antique décor. It made me think of my grandparents' living room back when I was a kid. Mr. Edward, his son and another somber undertaker man, and a middle-aged woman with a warm smile greeted us. Mr. Edward shook with two hands then escorted us into the viewing room.

Mom wasn't more than three steps into the viewing room when, seeing the opened casket at the far end, she let out a groan and fainted dead away. Rocco and Sam caught her.

"Lower her to the floor!" I directed. She was a rag doll. Out cold. The smiling woman ran for water and a wet cloth for Mom's head. I kneeled next to Mom and held her hand; my tears flowed. The somber man had cracked an ammonia inhalant capsule, and Mom started to revive. The woman returned, carefully lifted Mom's veil, and placed the cold cloth on her forehead. Seeing that bunched-up veil on her forehead made me smile.

We helped her to a chair that she insisted be right next to the casket. Before she sat, she reached into the coffin and touched Dad's hands, kissed his forehead. I was right next to her. When she sat, I moved in and kissed Dad's forehead. My lips met a stone. This surprised me. I was accustomed to kissing the sagging soft cheeks of my elderly dad and the aroma of "Old Spice." It was true: my dad was dead.

Mom pulled the veil down over her face and positioned herself next to the head of the coffin. People were arriving. One by one, my aunts, uncles, cousins, cousins-in-law, their children (no age restriction for funerals in a Sicilian family) approached the casket. Some kneeled for a moment; others paused and bowed their head. Then each approached Mom, leaned over, and air-kissed her from cheek to cheek. Me? I was kissed lips to skin. After about an hour of being kissed, I excused myself for the ladies' room and washed my face.

The family milled about quietly. The younger kids made a game of running around weaving in and out of the rows of chairs. No-one stopped them.

Mr. Edward announced that he was turning out the streetlight. The family took the cue, began saying good night. Mom allowed Uncle Renato to take her arm, escorting her towards the car. I was two steps behind her when Stevie D caught up with me. I automatically took his arm, he smiled at me.

"Someone for me," I thought. This had never happened to me before.

We were in the corridor headed for the car at the rear of the building when we heard voices coming from the front street entrance.

"They sound drunk," Stevie D commented.

I stopped abruptly. "They are!" I turned and high-tailed it down the corridor and came to a stop just in time to see Sam, the young undertaker, holding the two men at the door with an arm across the threshold.

"The viewing for tonight is over; it will resume tomorrow at two," Sam said, but these blokes weren't having it. Each carried a six-pack of beer with a few missing bottles. I strolled forward now in their sight. They pushed poor Sam aside and made a beeline into my opened arms.

"You're late!" I declared.

"Never heard of such a thing, closing awake! Why, my mother, bless her soul, is rolling over in her grave!" Uncle Mic said.

"How are you doing, doll?" Uncle Jacob asked as he hugged me and kissed me.

I squeezed them both. "Much better now; is my name on one of those bottles?"

"You don't have to ask," Uncle Mic said as he twisted the cap off and handed me the beer.

Stevie D was at my side. "Uncle Mic, Uncle Jacob, meet Stevie D, my bodyguard!"

They all shook hands. No one questioned or even laughed at what I thought was a joke: my bodyguard.

"Are you Leo Bataglia's boy?" Uncle Mic asked.

"Yes." Stevie D sounded humble.

"Hmm, seems no introductions were necessary," I commented.

Uncle Jacob handed Stevie D a beer, "Well, it is a family business, Margaret Ann."

"Lead us to him," Uncle Mic requested.

Standing at the casket, both men made the sign of the cross and kissed their thumbnail. I never understood the thumbnail kissing but knew this wasn't the time to ask.

"Ay, they did a good job," Uncle Mic noted. "He looks just like himself. Stevie, get us four glasses, would you please?"

Stevie D obeyed; the uncles pulled up chairs in a semicircle in front of the casket and sat. With their glasses in hand, a bottle of whiskey appeared, a two-fingers measure was poured for everyone.

"Here's to a dear, loving brother!" Uncle Mic toasted.

"The most unconditionally loving brother," Uncle Jacob added and lifted his glass again. "Now, Margaret Ann, tell us what's planned."

I ran through the agenda of the next three days as best I knew.

Another two fingers measure of whiskey poured as Uncle Mic spoke of what the Irish had planned. "We have the Abbot Road club reserved for the party after the funeral. And the day after tomorrow, we'll all be here in force," he turned to Stevie D. "Tell Carmine the Blake family will be occupying the place day after tomorrow, with all due respect."

"Yes, I will," Stevie D acknowledged, then added, "and it's Renato that's coordinating this for Maggie and Mrs. Blake."

"Renato's good man, yes, tell him too," Uncle Mic said.

The whiskey had loosened my tongue. "And how, exactly, do you know who, exactly, is Renato, Uncle Carmine, or for that matter that Stevie D is Leo Bataglia's son? Hmm?" I could hear my own slurring speech.

"Now, darlin', we've been family since before you were born. So don't worry about it," was Uncle Mic's reply. "You are expected on Abbott Road after we bury your father."

"Oh, I don't know. Mom has been acting flakey. And how am I going to get there?"

"I'll get you there," Stevie D answered.

I looked at the faces of the three smug men sitting before me. "Okay," I said, "Salute," and downed the whiskey.

Around midnight Mr. Edward appeared. I had no idea all that time had passed. He insisted we leave. Uncle Jacob pocketed the empty beer bottles and poured the last of the whiskey into our glasses. We stood, swaying, holding up our glasses high next to the coffin; my uncles sang Danny Boy. When we got to the front door, Mr. Edward made himself scarce so we could have our good-byes. I hugged my uncles tight and didn't want to let go. I was imagining how much better my days would go if they were with me each day. But Uncle Mic did say that day after tomorrow the Irish would be present. After hugs, there was a pause, and Uncle Mic and Uncle Jacob turned to face Stevie D.

"Leo Bataglia's boy, right?" Uncle Mic started. What was going on? I was so tipsy.

"Yes, sir."

"And you'll be at Margaret Ann's side the entire time: wake, luncheons, suppers, evening visitation, the Mass, the cemetery," Uncle Jacob drilled.

"Yes, sir."

Uncle Mic put a hand on Stevie D's shoulder. "Good, good. Now, if anyone of those goombahs disrespect Margaret Ann, you let me know, got that?"

I thought, oh my God, it's the booze talking, but Stevie was cool; he answered, "Yes, sir."

Now Jacob moved in, with his hand on Stevie D's other shoulder, "And, if Margaret Ann comes to us in tears, or angry or any way that says you disrespected her, well, there will be hell to pay."

"Hey! What are you two talking about? Stevie D is family! He works for Uncle Renato!" I injected, making them unhand Stevie D and turn to acknowledge that I was in the foyer with them.

"Now, Margaret Ann, don't get your Irish up . . ." Uncle Mic started.

"I could say the same to you," I countered.

"Give us a hug, we'll go peacefully," Uncle Jacob said.

We hugged, but on the way out, Uncle Mic turned and said to Stevie D, "Don't think I didn't notice how you look at her!" The door slammed behind them.

Mr. Edward stepped into the foyer so fast I was startled. Stevie took my arm and we started walking down the hallway to the back door and parking lot.

"What the hell was that all about?" I could hear my own slurring of words.

Stevie D smiled broadly, "Just your uncles letting me know they know what I know."

"Huh?" And we were at the car, I fell into the seat, and didn't remember the ride to mom's house.

The following day, I was awakened with that unmistakable churning in my stomach. I bolted into the bathroom, and out it came, projectile fashion. There was a slight knocking at the door.

"Hon, are you alright?" It was Ethel.

I opened the door with a towel covering my mouth, "No."

"Come on now, brush your teeth and here," she handed me a tall glass of green something.

"What? No, no, my stomach . . ."

"Clean your mouth and drink this down. Its hangover cocktail from my family, guaranteed to work wonders. Come on, get started," Ethel directed. "You're forgetting, I'm Irish. By the way, Stevie D told me Mic and Jacob officially started the Irish wake."

I drank the concoction down. "Did we ever!"

"Stevie D should have known better," she said more to herself.

"I'm sorry," I said immediately. It was the Sicilian guilt, even if you're not guilty.

"We have to pull you together for today. It's going to be a full day, all about business. All the families will be around today," she said as she pulled large towels from the cupboard and ran warm water for the shower.

"Business? What do you mean?" I asked.

She stopped dead. "Hon, all the families in The Business will be there today to pay respects to Bella and Carmine and you, of course. It's expected," she explained.

"I hadn't thought about that." I sank onto the edge of the tub.

"Hon, you're shivering," Ethel draped a bath towel over my shoulders.

Once in the shower, I could think about what was going to happen today. All my life, the Family Business was somehow just out there. No one talked in front of the kids. We had whiffs of information here or there, an overheard conversation. Most of the few details we had come from Rocco and Sal. Angela would prance around like the princess because her dad, Uncle Carmine, was head of the family. Yet, none of us really had any idea of what the Family Business was. Uncles would disappear months at a time. Police would drive by the Madonie complex from time to time. But for the most part, much of the conversations were spoken in Sicilian, and none of us spoke Sicilian, let alone understand it to glean anything.

When I entered the kitchen, Mom, Ethel, and Aunt Zorah were present. Then I saw Stevie D. What?

"Good morning," I said. I poured myself a cup of coffee and sat at the table.

"What are you doing here? How's your hangover?" Forcing a smile, I asked Stevie D.

"No hangover at all," he smiled. "You never noticed how much I didn't drink. I still had to drive you home. And I'm here because today I will drive your family back to the funeral home. So that's what I'm doing here."

"Oh." I felt stupid

"Are they always like that?" Stevie D asked.

Aunt Zorah placed a plate of poached eggs on dry toast in front of me and a glass of orange juice. "Mangia! And drink all the juice; hangovers need orange juice."

"You mean with Uncle Mic and Jacob? Yes, well no, but at celebrations and wakes, funerals, picnics, you know, they're Irish, I'm Irish too," I explained.

"So you are," he added with a smug smile as he lifted the morning "Courier Express" in front of his face.

I lowered my head and smiled as well. I ate in silence. Every now and then, Mom would sigh audibly, but no one paid any attention. She eventually left the table, announcing she was going to get dressed. Once I heard the door to her bedroom close, I turned to Stevie D and asked him about the day in front of me.

"The families will show up today," he started.

"Do I have to be there? I will know absolutely no one," I pleaded.

"True. But if you weren't there, it would be disrespectful, in bad taste. The families are not only paying their respects to you but also your mom, George Blake's widow and Carmine Madonie's sister." He was folding the newspaper and placed it on the table. "Your dad worked with these families. As Carmine's brother-in-law, some of the families had known your dad since before you were born, as your Uncle Mic said.

"This is bigger than just you and your mom, Maggie," he said.

I was looking directly into his eyes. They were a hazel green, not the expected brown of a Sicilian man.

I exhaled. "I still won't know anyone."

"Well, how about if I stand behind you, as close as I can get to your right ear, and as the families approach the casket and before they get to your mom and you, I'll tell you their names and if possible, a little about their background, how they're connected to your dad. Okay?"

I was leery, "Be discreet. It would be embarrassing to get caught."

Aunt Zorah slammed a plate of fresh sliced bread onto the table. It stunned us both. I had forgotten we weren't alone in the kitchen.

"Something you want to say, Aunt Zorah?" I asked the obvious.

She pulled out a chair and sat down. "You been gone a long time; I be there all the time. Today," she was shaking her index finger at me, "You make me proud! The families, they are family! I go check on Bella now."

When I was sure she was on the second floor, I said, "Wow! Who knew?"

Stevie D and I locked eyes then burst out laughing.

We rode in the back of the limo in silence. I concentrated on watching the buildings quickly pass by as Stevie D weaved through the narrow streets of the West Side. Mom wore a new veil today: black lace and shoulder length. I wondered how much of her sight was obstructed by the lace pattern.

Once we stepped into the viewing room, a murmur went up, "The widow is here." Stevie D escorted Mom up to the coffin where Uncle

Carmine stood. Mom dropped to her knees onto the cushion of the kneeler. She bowed her head, the sobs started. I surprised myself when I thought, "On cue! Really?" Then countered it with, "Come on, Maggie; why can't you accept this is your mom grieving?"

Stevie D brought my attention back. Mom was off the kneeler and hugged Uncle Carmine, then Uncle Auggie, and it seemed that they were telling her something. The room had started humming again.

Without realizing it, Stevie D had me standing at the kneeler. I turned and looked directly into his eyes, "No." I reached into the coffin and stroked my dad's hair. His hair was still soft. I stood behind Mom. Mom turned and included me. Uncle Carmine and Uncle Auggie embraced me. Uncle Carmine had Mom turn to look at a viewing room just next to this room and pointed that he'd be just over there. When I turned around, I caught sight of the long line of people ready to approach the coffin, Mom, and me. I felt light-headed.

"What the hell is that rotten egg smell?" I thought as I swiped my hand under my nose and shook my head side to side. Opening my eyes, I muttered, "What . . ." I looked up at a circle of faces directly over me: Stevie D, Carlo, Uncle Carmine, Mom, and Sam, the undertaker's son.

"She's awake now," Sam said.

"Let her rest a minute," Mom directed.

"Are you okay?" Stevie D asked; he was holding my hand.

I came into awareness that I was prone on the floor; chairs around me were askew.

Embarrassed, I looked at Stevie D, "I fainted, right?"

He smiled, "More like a head dive into the chairs. You have a goose egg on your forehead."

I reached up and felt the cold cloth. "Nice."

"Feel like getting up?" Stevie D asked.

I looked around; no one had moved from over me. "Yes."

Uncle Carmine and Carlo reached out their hands; I took hold and was on my feet. I swooned; Stevie D had his arm around my waist. "Wow! Sit down here."

Mom sat next to me, the veil now lifted, folded back onto her head; she handed me a small paper cup. "Drink this."

I obeyed and couldn't stop myself as the aroma of the liquor hit my nose, the drink was in my mouth, and I swallowed. I winced. "What was that?"

Mom said, "It will help. Stevie D get a chair for Maggie next to the coffin. I'll stand," she turned to me, "you sit."

"I'm okay; I can stand!" I protested.

Stevie D set the chair then asked, "Mrs. Blake, how about I take Maggie outside for some air. Five minutes."

Mom allowed this. Stevie D led me out through the adjoining viewing room. I spotted a table with bottles of whiskey, small paper cups, and a box of cigars.

I walked the parameter of the building in the parking lot, at first in silence. I kept taking big cleansing breaths. Passing the front of the building for the second time, I spotted a diner down the street. I headed in that direction. Stevie D followed.

I found a back booth and slid into it. Stevie D did the same. A waitress set down two glasses of water with ice, "Nice lump you got there, Hon," she quipped, "What will you two have?" She was poised with pad and pencil.

"Coffee; are your donuts fresh?" Stevie D asked.

"Yes, sir, brought in fresh each morning."

"Peanut stick?" Stevie D asked.

She nodded and turned to me. "Chocolate shake."

"Chocolate shake," she looked at Stevie D, "you take cream, Hon?"

I had half the shakedown before I could breathe easier. Stevie D never interrupted the silence. But my eyes began swelling with tears.

"What to talk about it?" he asked.

"Oh, just the absurd nature of it all; plus knowing my family sees me one way but knowing that isn't me anymore, hasn't been for years and years. They have no idea who I am today. They just fast-forward what they believed about me from the past and proceeded.

"But not my dad; he never did that. We talked by phone every Sunday. He was always interested in the latest goal I achieved. And he always asked about my good friends, Honey, Patty, and Alice ."

"Honey, Patty, and Alice," Stevie D repeated.

"My best friends in Houston. Alice and I lived together in her house during graduate school. She and I were invited to join a psychologist practice that Honey and Dr. Frank Dorr had, and we did. Honey was one of our grad school professors. Patty is Honey's dearest friend. Patty is the eccentric among us. She is so fun!

"What?"

"You're smiling as you talk about your friends," Stevie D said.

Now I was aware of my smile, made it more expansive, and said, "Don't take this wrong, but they are my family now."

"I think I understand," he offered. "How are you feeling?"

I was slurping the bottom of the glass through the straw, "Okay. Ready."

As we walked back, I realized Stevie D was a little taller than most five foot two or four, Sicilian guys. He must have stood at least five feet eight, tall for a Sicilian. That kind of went with the fact that his eyes were hazel green.

"May I ask you a personal question? How did you get so tall, and hazel green eyes to boot? You are Sicilian, aren't you?"

"On the Rizzo side of the family, I'm told that my great-grandfather married a Swedish woman he met during World War 1 at a Red Cross station. Every now and then, those genes surface, like with hazel green eyes and being taller than the average Sicilian." He paused and added, "Grandma Herta; it means 'of the earth.'"

"Herta," I repeated, "I like it, Herta."

As we walked into the funeral home Stevie asked, "Are you going to stand or sit?"

"Stand; I feel okay now. And I don't want people bending over me, creepy."

"Okay, good; I'll stand just behind you and give you the lowdown on the families, the who's who."

"What is that other room for? Uncle Carmine holding court?" I asked.

"Exactly."

I was startled and turned my head to look directly at him. "He's serious," I thought. When I entered the viewing room, a murmur went up, "Here she is."

The showing of respect hadn't started yet. I was scanning the room for Mom. Then I saw her; she was in the adjoining room, sitting in an overstuffed chair with a small paper cup in her hand. I headed toward her. Uncle Carmine saw me first and started towards me.

"Better?" he asked. Mom was right behind him.

"Mom, what are you doing here? Why aren't you receiving people?"

"Hon, I was waiting for you. These people came to pay respects to us."

I took a deep breath that raised and lowered my shoulders. "Okay, let's do it."

Mom pulled her veil down over her face. We got into position, and the men in the suits also took their places. The parade began.

Like a sports commentator, Stevie behind me and at my right ear began, "Approaching the coffin now is Ralph Zito and his family. They control the professionals and institutions for the family," Stevie D whispered.

I turned my head slightly, and I talked out of the corner of my mouth, asking about the first people approaching the coffin. "They're so tall and fair; they don't look Sicilian."

"Northern Italy," was all Stevie D said just as Ralph Zito was shaking my hand, as did the five men that followed him. They didn't return to their chairs in the viewing room; they walked straight to the adjoining room where Uncle Carmine was holding court.

"The next family is the Cellentani family. Russell Cellentani and his sons take care of transportation."

"Of what?" I whispered out of the corner of my mouth.

"Goods," was all I got out of Stevie D with no time for more.

I saw the next group of people were members of Mom's church. I turned to Stevie D and asked, "Goods?"

"And any problems, if they occur, they have a way of turning a screw and getting results."

"Now you're playing with me," I accused. He nodded his head for me to turn and be greeted by Mom's Altar and Rosary Society chairwoman.

I was eyeing the next gaggle of suits. The difference between these men was the age gap. There was an older gentleman, maybe my dad's age, and three guys, late teens, or early twenties. Stevie D didn't say anything to me. Instead, he left his position behind me, came around, and hugged the older man.

"Dad, this is Maggie. Maggie Blake," he introduced.

"You're Georgie's daughter. So awfully glad to meet you, and I'm so sorry for your loss. Your dad was a great guy. One thing I can say about Georgie is he never met a stranger!" He hugged me and kissed one cheek instead of a handshake. He made me smile.

"That's right, Mr. Bataglia, Dad had the Irish gift for gab!"

"Maggie, these three sorry excuses for gentlemen – don't let the suits fool you – are my sons."

"Your sons?!"

Each stepped forward one by one.

"Sorry for your loss. I'm Capra," he said, shaking my hand.

"I'm Stevens, sorry for your loss," the next young man said.

And finally, "Sorry for your loss, Ms. Blake, I'm Wilder."

"It's nice to meet all of you. Thank you for coming," I said.

"Keep moving," Stevie D said gently.

"Why do your names sound familiar?" I asked just to hold onto the boys a little longer. They were a surprise, and I wanted them to linger a bit longer.

Mr. Bataglia headed for the adjoining room, "I've heard this story."

"Your names are not as typical family names," I asked the young men.

They exchanged looks and grinned. "Our dad named us after movie directors," Capra answered.

"Really?" I coaxed.

"I'm Capra as in Frank Capra Bataglia," he turned to his brothers, "he's George Stevens Bataglia, and he's Billy Wilder Bataglia!" They were grinning.

"You obviously enjoy your names," I mused.

They all nodded yes, and their dad moved them on.

"They are a handsome bunch," I said to Stevie D, but it was all I could get in before the priest from Mom's church was shaking my hand. While others moved around the Battaglia boys and me, the priest had waited. I was embarrassed. We shook hands, and he assured me all was ready for the Mass of Christian burial.

Stevie D was positioned again. "Here comes the Ditalini family."

The sight of the Ditalini family took me back a bit. None were taller than five feet, at the most; just a short family but all wearing exquisite suits.

"Who are the Ditalini's, and where do they buy their suits?"

"In Rome. Believe it or not, they are geniuses at what they do. They get the big picture."

No time for more questions as Anthony Ditalini was standing before me, and I could not take my eyes off the fabric of his suit. He noticed. I'm only about five feet two inches, but Anthony Ditalini was looking up at me.

"Nice fabric, isn't it? But I'm here to express my condolences for your loss. Georgie, well, what can I say about Georgie? What a guy! Such a good storyteller! Love the guy, so sorry for your loss. I know it's a long day for you."

I was now surrounded by short men as he continued, "Allow me to introduce my family," and one by one, the men and one young woman stepped forward, each shaking my hand.

"Anthony junior; Carmelo; Pasquale; and Dominic; and the Princess, Clare," a beautiful Sicilian woman stepped forward, but I was looking down at her. She was looking up with a compassionate smile. The group exited into the adjoining room.

Anthony Ditalini hadn't left; he approached me and pulled in Stevie D just by looking at him, "Now, if there is anything we can do for you, anything at all," he looked up at Stevie D, "All you have to do is call." He pointed a finger at Stevie D, "Capiche?"

"Yes. Capiche." was all Stevie D said as the two men shook hands.

At four-thirty p.m. Uncle Renato was encouraging people to leave. Stevie D took the initiative with Mom and me. Once back at the house, I didn't get past the sofa before I had kicked my shoes off and flopped down in exhaustion that was more emotional than physical. I threw my arm up onto my forehead, and the pain of the lump reminded me it was there. My yelp summoned Ethel.

"What?" Ethel asked.

"Oh nothing; I just hit my head when I fainted this morning."

Stevie D handed me an ice bag. "Here, I thought this might help the swelling go down."

Tears were rolling again, yet I was laughing. "I'm a mess!"

He was sitting on the edge of the sofa next to me, "Yes, you are." He took my hand and kissed the back of it.

Aunt Zorah served cold cuts, fresh bread, a green salad, and thin spaghetti with oil, garlic, and Romano cheese. Uncle Renato and Aunt Eve joined us, as did my cousin Rosalie and her husband, Danny. Uncle Carmine herded the suits to his home for supper. Yes, they would all return for the evening as well.

I dug right into the pasta. "Where are the kids?" I asked Rosalie.

"With my in-laws; they'll be there tonight."

While sipping wine, the conversation was about who was at the wake. It was a kind conversation, saying how good people looked who hadn't been seen since the last funeral or wedding. It was about how respectful people are to come out on an afternoon and sit with us. It was about appreciation.

Once we returned and were in place, Stevie D realized I didn't need a narrator. So many people I did know from the neighborhood, from the church, Mom's Altar and Rosary Society members, and the priest once again. A beautiful woman approached me, smiling, extending her hand.

"Maggie, this is my little sister Lucy."

The man behind them now pushed between them in a joking way, "I'm the in-law, Rich Jones." It made us chuckle.

"Nice to meet you both, and thank you for coming out tonight," I couldn't take my eyes off Lucy. She made me think how statuesque she was, like Sophia Loren. Maybe those Swedish genes?

Stevie D broke the spell, "You think I named my kids strangely? Ask Lu what she named her kids."

"Okay, I'll bite; what are your kids' names?"

She smiled, "Elvis and Diana!"

"Aren't you too young to be an Elvis fan?" I asked.

"Not Presley, Costello! Elvis Costello! And Princess Diana, that one is obvious," she laughed.

Rich leaned in, "I had nothing to do with it, well, nothing to do with their names! It was all Lu!"

"I love it, and I have heard of Elvis Costello." Then I remembered that Rocco had told me about Stevie D's sister's kids' names when I was home last. Wow, I must be stressed, I thought, that it didn't even ring a bell while Lucy was telling me.

"Let's move it along, Maggie. The line is backing up," Stevie D said.

"Please, come by the house tonight, please, say you will," I encouraged.

All three exchanged looks, Stevie D shrugged, and Lucy said, "We will; we'd be honored. Thank you. See you tonight."

The evening dragged on. I'd look at my watch only to realize just minutes had passed and not the hours it felt. There was no conversation, really. It was "sorry for your loss," and "he was a wonderful man." I was beginning to regret having lived so away for so long. But in the scheme of things, if anyone understood why I moved out of Buffalo, it was Dad.

By the time Mr. Edward announced the lights out front were being turned off, I was more than ready to leave. I search out Stevie D.

"Come on, let's go," I told him.

"I'll see if your mom's ready," he answered.

"Can't we just get out of here?"

He stopped, "Are you alright?"

"No."

"Wait right here, sit, I'll be right back."

"Don't say anything to my mother!" I called to him as an afterthought.

"Not my plan," he said half over his shoulder.

After a few minutes, Stevie D and Rich Jones approached.

"Ride with us," Rich said.

I jumped up and followed him. Over my shoulder, I said, "Thanks, Stevie."

Rich headed away from the west side, where my house was. I just kept quiet. I didn't care. He pulled into the parking lot of the Anchor Bar. We all got out and went inside.

Rich ordered a pitcher of beer and a platter of wings. Lucy broke the silence. "We thought you might need some good ole Buffalo comfort food about now."

"I'm sorry; I'm really not good company."

"No need to be sorry. I'd be a mess if my dad died. So just relax, no one here to pester you."

"You're reading me like a book," I quipped and drank half a glass of beer before coming up for air. Rich was refilling my glass without my protest.

"What is it you do in Houston, Maggie?" Lucy asked.

"I'm a psychologist and psychotherapist," I smiled and shook my head,

"I could use a little help now."

Rich answered, "That's understandable. You're too close, the grieving daughter. It's like a surgeon can't operate on family."

"You know Rich, I never thought of it that way! I was beating myself up because I believed I had slipped into 'little Margaret Blake,' half Irish, half Sicilian from the west side, and somehow Dr. Blake had disappeared. It felt disorienting. Thank you. You gave me some clarity."

Stevie D walked in as I was talking. He took a glass and poured himself a beer. "You okay?"

"I'm better."

"Your mom said to tell you, 'Take your time,'" he reported.

"Hmm. I feel as if I'm failing her; I feel so useless."

"You're not failing her," Lucy said, reaching out and putting her hand on my arm. "You're home. You're here with her, at her side. That's what counts, your being home."

The platter of wings arrived. Good ole wings, celery sticks, and blue cheese dressing. No one did it better than the Anchor Bar. Our conversation turned to the foods I missed because I lived in Houston and the foods I've come to love, like grits. After all, I lived in Houston. After a while, we were comparing notes on the kids we knew in high school. Before I realized it, several hours had passed.

It felt like minutes.

When I woke the following day, I lay quietly staring at the ceiling. I felt my forehead; flat. I couldn't accept there was yet another day of awake. I wished I were back in Houston with my friends and my cat. I knew I sounded so self-centered. Get a grip, Maggie. I threw back the thin blanket and sheet, swung my legs, and planted my feet on the floor. But I sat there. The tears started. I couldn't do another day hearing, "I'm sorry for your loss."

There was a soft knock at the door. "Come on in, Aunt Ethel!"

Slowly the door opened, "Are you decent? It's Stevie D."

I scrambled, pulling the light blanket off the bed, and wrapping it around me. "Okay."

A glass of green liquid entered through the crack in the door first. I started to laugh.

"I'm not hungover!" I protested.

Stevie D pushed the door open, "Ethel seems to think you might be and gave me directions that I had to make sure you drank it all. Then tell you to hurry up!" He handed me the glass and left. His smile was huge.

I shifted myself to sit with my back against the headboard and drank. I knew it would make me feel better.

We rode in silence to the funeral home. It was a different silence this morning. We were exhausted. We had stood for two days next to a coffin. Neighbors came by with casseroles and baked goods, sat a few minutes over coffee, or insisted they just wanted to drop by during the off hours. The parking lot of the funeral home looked like a mall lot the day before Christmas. I was confused a minute until I saw a truck with signage: KEG BEER/home delivery.

"Oh . . . my . . . God," Mom lamented.

I was smiling from ear to ear.

"I mean, Mic and Jacob already visited, right?" Mom added.

I caught Stevie D's reflection in the rear-view mirror; his smile was reassuring. My inclination was to bolt out of the limo and run into the building, but Mom took twice as long adjusting the tulle veil over her face. Once inside, the sound of bagpipes filled the air. Mom stopped just inside the door to speak with Mr. Edwards. I continued towards the viewing room, and when I stepped in, a rush of women encircled me: "Oh, hon, you look so pale, how you feel?" "Let me hug you, Maggie. It's been too long." "Let me look at you, Margaret Ann, just the image of your father!" "And he looks just like himself, doll." Add the hugs, kisses, stroking my hair, holding my face in their hands, I loved it; all of it. I caught a glimpse of the women who already had greeted me rushing to Mom, taking her by both arms as one lifted the veil off her face so they could kiss her cheeks. Then, they walked her to the casket and fell onto their knees to pray with her. I had to chuckle.

I was escorted to the casket as well. Aunt May had one arm, and my cousin's wife Cate had the other. I felt so different. In all honesty, and with some Sicilian guilt, I felt alive. I eyed the room behind me where Uncle Carmine, just the day before, was holding court. The men were gathering there, but each had a beer. I could see Uncle Mic and Uncle Jacob, and Roy, Uncle Jacob's partner, ever since I could remember. I left the women and walked into the room. Uncle Renato, to my surprise, met me with a hug.

"The Irish know how to throw awake," he said as he hugged me.

I laughed, forgetting myself. Then I saw the keg. Uncle Mic was walking to me, holding out a glass of beer.

"Didn't Mr. Edward protest?" I asked.

"I don't remember. The Ladies' Auxiliary of St. Bridgit's Church was hauling in the corned beef at the same time," he said with an Irish lilt in his voice and smile. "They've set up in the viewing room on the other side of Georgie," he directed.

"Maggie, your mom is asking for you," Stevie D said as he approached. Uncle Renato took my beer, and I returned to daughter duty. Once I was in position, I could, indeed, smell the food. It made me smile. The room wasn't a quiet din, like the day before with the Sicilians. It was downright ordinary.

At the end of the afternoon visitation, I told Mom I was staying. Uncle Renato offered to take her back to the house with Zorah and Ethel. Stevie D stayed with me in case I changed my mind. But I knew I wouldn't. There was food, drink, and more conversations I wanted to have. This was the first time since my high school graduation that I'd seen my Irish cousins. Many were there with wives I had never met and kids as well.

Uncle Mic insisted Mr. Edward lock the door to the outside. I think he complied so no health inspector could just walk in and see the keg, smell the food. The food was so good: mashed potatoes, cabbage, corned beef, and beets with onion. Irish soda bread and bread pudding rounded out the menu. Where the coffin was, chairs were moved to the wall, the bagpipers started again, and the girls started dancing in the traditional Celtic style: straight body, all the action in the legs. This began when the British occupied Ireland. Women in protest stood at their kitchen windows, their upper body still and legs dancing in defiance. It was quite a moving tribute to Dad. We were clapping to the music, encircling the dancers. From where I stood across the room, I eyed Uncle Carmine in the other room watching. We locked eyes. He blew me a kiss.

The women were mindful of the time. The place was cleaned up and ready for the seven o'clock viewing. Mom arrived on time. I could see her nose sniffing under that veil; the aroma of corned beef hung in the air.

I made a quick run to the restroom, washed my face. I did that several times a day now. While Mom deferred people's kisses with the veil hanging over her face, many compensated by kissing me cheek to cheek. I slipped a tube of lotion into my pocket for these face washings. The soap in the restroom was harsh. I stood looking at myself in the mirror: my hair was flat, I hadn't rolled it since I arrived; I had grey circles under my eyes which highlighted the redness from the on and off crying; my cheeks were reddened too now that I scrubbed my face, and my clothes just hung on me. Ethel bought the dress for me a size larger than I told her, just in case.

Walking out of the restroom, the aroma of perfume caught my attention.

I turned a corner and caught sight first of the suits, next to the wives with arms looped through their suit's arm. I watched for a minute; it seemed each wife had the same sway to her butt.

The wives of the suits didn't socialize with the Madonie women. It just didn't happen. The Madonie women were, well, the first ladies. The wives hoped for an invite to the big house that never arrived. I figured they compensated by becoming socialites, if only in their minds.

The wives wore pastel linen suits. No color was repeated. They also wore tiny hats with veils (veils!) and a handbag placed in the crux of the arm for each. The accessories were complementary to the color of the suit, for example, a pale pink suit accented with a deep rose handbag and matching pumps. The jewelry varied from obviously expensive jewelry to just expensive jewelry in bad taste.

The only Madonie events I ever saw the wives attend were weddings and funerals. Quickly, I headed into the viewing room for my position next to Mom. I used the entrance through the viewing room where the drinking took place. I wanted to watch the wives enter the main viewing room where the Irish gathered. Dad's brothers, nieces, cousins, sisters-in-law, and nephews were also greeting people. There was no light din, people were speaking with their natural volume, to be heard over the bagpipes. Bless the Irish; they had their own set of manners for a wake.

The Irish greeted with hearty handshakes. I could see the surprise of the wives. My Irish aunts gave hugs without warning, which made the wives step back, and upon release, straighten their suits and tulle hat veils. A few wives were tweaking their noses. The aroma of corned beef was prominent. And there was one wife, Connie, the only woman I had a name for, who was as wide-eyed as a deer in the headlights.

I tried to stifle my giggles. Mom jabbed me in my ribs. I straightened up just in time for greeting Ralph Zito and his wife . . .

"Stephanie," Stevie D whispered into my right ear. That made me smile, which the Zito family took as pleasure at meeting them.

Before the next couple approached, they stopped to kneel and pray. I was aware that Stevie D was gone, then quickly returned. I said, "Where did you disappear to?"

"I took a break, ma'am," He faked a southern accent.

Again, my smile was mistaken as a warm greeting to Tony Ditalini and his wife, Connie. I had met Connie during my summer married to Jimmy Toscano. I never saw Connie next to her husband before. While Connie was a little shorter than me, she was taller than Tony. It made me smile just a little wider.

"Stop enjoying yourself so much," Stevie D teased.

"Too much beer; besides, it's an Irish wake. I'm Irish!"

About an hour into the evening viewing, the noise among the three viewing rooms was like a wedding reception. People flowed back and forth, all with a glass of beer in hand or a corned beef sandwich. I knew Uncle Jacob pushed boilermakers, insisting it would ease the grief. Therefore, if you had a beer in your hand, you chased the whisky with it. Mom and I had abandoned our posts for overstuffed chairs in the beer room. After I kicked my shoes off. That seemed to give Mom permission to kick her shoes off as well. I looked around. I hadn't realized that Uncles Carmine and Renato were still here, as well as Aunt Bertha and her husband, Joe. Zorah and Ethel shared a love seat, taking a well-deserved rest. I gazed at them for a while, watching their expressions and gestures. I made a mental note to inquire more about how long they had been friends. Would anyone tell me that there was more to it?

Many of us at the same time realized that the bagpipes had stopped. I sat forward some and looked around. Mr. Edward stood in the main viewing room next to the bagpiper while he folded up his pipes. Oh, it must be nine or after! Mr. Edward had a few words with Stevie D.

"Mrs. Blake, Mr. Edward wants you to hang back so he can talk about tomorrow and how the morning will unfold," Stevie D told Mom.

My warm feeling was draining.

When we arrived home, Mom went straight up to her bedroom. I sank onto a kitchen chair. Aunt Zorah immediately put on a pot of coffee while Ethel pulled cold cuts from the fridge. Stevie D sat next to me. We were joined by Uncle Renato. No one spoke until Aunt Zorah placed a wine bottle on the table, along with small juice glasses.

"Ah! Grazie," Uncle Renato said, pouring wine for each of us into the small glasses.

I sipped the wine, hoping it would help me sleep.

"Hon, the pallbearers, I talked to all the men tonight. They know to be at the funeral parlor early," Uncle Renato reported.

"I'm worried about Mom," I said.

"You're stating the obvious," Ethel said.

I grabbed a slice of homemade bread and piled bologna onto it with mayo. I scooped Kalamata olives and hunks of provolone onto my place as well. I sunk my teeth into the sandwich. Couldn't remember the last time I ate a bologna sandwich. The wine was a good match. I thought a minute about whether I'd get sick mixing it with all the beer I drank, but I didn't care.

I paid attention to the conversation around the table. I knew tomorrow was the day. Once my plate was empty, I drained the last of the wine in my glass and said, "Good night." Aunt Zorah grabbed my arm and made me lean in for a kiss from her.

I woke at five a.m., sat straight up, pulled my knees to my chest. Mr. Edward's outline ran through my head: prayers at the funeral home; a parade of people saying last goodbyes, paying final respects; closing the coffin; into the limo; to the church; Mass; then onto the cemetery, prayers, and that's it. Mom. What will it be today? Stoicism? Tears? Drama? When I got out of bed and headed for the shower, a freshly laundered black dress was hanging from the curtain rod in the bathroom. I sat on the toilet seat, looking at it.

No. No, not today. No black today! I went back into my bedroom and searched my closet where Mom stored old clothing, even some of my old things. I pushed things from side to side, not sure what I was looking for, but I'd know it when I saw it. And there it was: a grey flared cotton jersey skirt and a pink chiffon blouse with a deep rose camisole. Perfect! I knew I'd be comfortable, and, today, the color will help me get through the day. The grey was for the funeral, and the pink was for my love for Dad. It didn't matter if no one else got it.

When I walked into the kitchen, I expected the "evil eye" from Aunt Zorah. Instead, she turned around and greeted me, paused, then said, "Sit, I bring coffee."

That was it.

Mom entered the room. I could hardly believe her. The veil today was almost opaque. How the hell would she see where she was going?

"Bella, you see through that?" Aunt Zorah asked.

Mom folded back the lace. "No," she sighed deeply, pulled the lace off her head, and tossed it on the table. "Ethel, will you see if you can find my small black hat and veil?"

Ethel nodded yes.

Mom looked at me, reached across the table, and took my hand, squeezing it, "It's over today, hon."

"I gotta frittata," Aunt Zorah announced and set the pan on the table. "Mangia! It's a long day today. A long day."

And we did. We ate hardily.

Stevie D arrived on time, as usual. But Aunt Zorah insisted he eat before we left.

"You look beautiful," he said.

"Thanks," I said, "I needed something different, soft, more me."

"It works."

When we arrived at the funeral home, the directors lined up the cars for the funeral procession from here to the church to the cemetery. There were about a dozen cars already. Mom and I walked into the main viewing room arm in arm. The kneeler was removed. We stood at the coffin; Mom stroked Dad's cheek. There was no way I was going to touch the body again.

"Mom, Dad's wearing his wedding ring," I whispered. I wondered whether we should take it off him.

She also whispered, "Where it belongs."

My Irish relatives were seated in a row of chairs just behind the front row. Mom sat down, and I walked into the next row to kissed and hugged the Blake's.

I walked through the funeral home closure and the Mass without tears. Mom was being held up by Uncle Renato and Zorah. But when we got to the cemetery, it was different. Mom started to sob uncontrollably. After the prayers, Uncle Renato, and Aunt Zorah guided her to the coffin. She touched it with one hand and slumped into Uncle Renato. They walked her away.

I stood still, staring at the casket and the bouquets of flowers draped over it. My arms were crossed tightly over my chest. No one moved. Mr. Edward came to my side and whispered, "Maggie?" I didn't move, didn't acknowledge him. I saw the priest fold his arms over his prayer book and bow his head in my peripheral vision, looking at the ground. No one moved because I hadn't moved. I couldn't. I couldn't walk away. Walking away was the final separation, no going back. Walking away meant I would leave behind the only person in the world that I knew loved me unconditionally. Walking away and I'm no one, empty. Just leave me here. Go! All of you in your best funeral attire and words of condolences that rolled off your tongues as if rehearsed, go! Leave me right here. My face was wet with tears. I started shivering. I didn't care. Go! Leave me! My head was pounding.

A soft familiar voice in my ear, "Maggie?"

I couldn't move.

"Maggie, I'm going to take your arm, and we're going to walk up to the coffin so you can say goodbye," the voice said.

I allowed it.

At the coffin, the person leaned forward and placed a hand on the coffin. I did the same. For the first time, I turned my head. It was Stevie D who held my arm.

Our eyes met. He nodded, and with a slight pull on my arm, I slumped into him and allowed his arm around my waist, holding me up and leading me to the limo.

As I climbed in, Mom reached out with her hand. I grabbed it and sat next to her.

"You okay, Hon?" she asked.

I nodded yes.

Uncle Renato got into the back with us, Stevie D rode shotgun.

"The Madonie complex," he called over his shoulder to the driver.

I quickly reacted. "NO! Driver, Abbott Road Irish-American Hall!"

"What?" Uncle Renato and Mom said simultaneously.

"Maggie, we're expected at the compound; the catering is all set up outside there. Uncle Carmine planned the luncheon; everyone will be there. We can't go to South Buffalo!" Mom countered.

The limo took a turn.

"Where you goin'?" Uncle Renato asked the driver. He had now moved down the long seat behind the driver and stuck his head through the opening in the window, "Madonie complex," he said with a stern tone.

Now Stevie D was facing Uncle Renato. There was a quiet conversation. The drive continued the trek to South Buffalo.

There was a heavy silence in the limo all the way to the front of the Abbott Road Irish American Hall. Stevie D popped out of the front seat and walked back to open the back door to the limo. He reached in with a stretched-out hand to me.

I took his hand and climbed out.

"Show your face, pay respect to Uncle Carmine!" Mom said.

Stevie D closed the door, and the limo pulled away.

I hurried into the hall. I wasn't a foot in the door when all my cousins and the Ladies' Auxiliary of St. Bridgit's Church rushed me and passed me around like a doll, hugging and kissing me. The music was festive, and people were dancing. It was wonderful. Aunt May made her way to me, took my hand, and guided me to the table where Uncles Mic, Jacob, and Roy sat.

"Praise be to God! Here she is! Herself!! Uncle Mic said as he stood and hugged me. Then Uncle Jacob hugged me, Roy pulled a chair out for me, and someone poured me a glass of beer.

"We didn't think you'd make it," Uncle Mic continued.

I took a long draft. "I think it was Stevie D's doing," I looked around, "Where did he go?"

We all looked around. Then I spotted him, and I had to laugh. The widow Edna McCullough, a neighbor of Uncle Jacob's and the Blake family before my grandparents died, put a platter of food into Stevie D's hands. He was being polite; Mrs. Edna McCullough was at least twenty years older than Stevie D. She'd been widowed about five years, and it was apparent the fire in the furnace hadn't died. Stevie D would back up with each advance!

"Excuse me, I have a rescue to attend to," Uncle Mic said as he left the table.

I turned around just as Aunt May placed a platter of roast beef dinner in front of me. It smelled wonderful. I dug right in, realizing how hungry I was. It was almost three in the afternoon. We had left the house at eight am. By the time the bread pudding was placed before me, I had leaned back on the wooden folding chair, stretched my neck back as far as I could, looking at the ceiling when Stevie D's face was looking down at me. It made me laugh!

I sat up straight. He sat next to me.

"And how is the Widow McCullough?" I teased.

He shrugged. "The food is good! Are you feeling better?"

"Yes. I just couldn't stand one more minute of the Sicilian funeral. I . . ."

"Maggie, I'm here for you; no explanation or apology necessary. Just let me know when you want to leave . . . if you ever want to leave tonight."

I had permission to be with my uncles, and Aunt May. I felt refreshed, didn't want to just sit anymore; I poured myself more beer and got up. I headed into the crowd. When my great extended family realized I joined the celebration of Dad's life, they all came around me, introduced new babies and girlfriends. The neighborhood men asked me to dance. The ladies wanted to know if I'd thought about moving home now that Mom was widowed. My cousins wanted to congratulate me on my doctorate. The first doctor in the family, even if it was "only" a Ph.D., they teased! I lost track of time.

While dancing with Roy, a guy tapped his shoulder to cut in. Rocco!

"What are you doing here? Mom sent you to fetch me?"

"No. Not exactly; my dad said if you weren't coming around tonight, 'it's-a alright,'" he said, mimicking his dad accent. "But he invites you and your mom to his house Sunday, 'after Mass' (using Uncle Carmine's accent) for supper around five. I'd go if I were you. I think its business," Rocco warned.

"Should I leave now? Go there?"

"No, not necessary. You've been the perfect Sicilian daughter. I really think my dad gets it that now you had to be the perfect Irish daughter. He's okay with it. He really likes you, you know."

I smiled. "Nice to hear."

"And I brought a car because Stevie D doesn't have a car here to take you home. You may say 'Thank you, Rocco,' now."

"How are you getting back?"

"Drew, the second car; we're here until you leave. I needed a break too. Boy, can we get intense! The Irish, however, now they know how to work off grief."

The pace of the music picked up, and people began moving back, allowing for the dance floor to clear. At the same time, the classical dancers from around took to dancing, this time in full costume. It was such a tribute to Dad's memory. He financially supported the group for years. The crowd was clapping, keeping time with the dance. While standing watching, I became aware of just how tired I was. It was as if the energy just drained out of me. I walked away towards the table where my uncles and aunt, Stevie D, and Drew sat.

"Darling, let the boys take you home. You look exhausted and so pale," Aunt May kindly said. "It's late; no one expects you to stay up all night with us. But be sure, we'll be here when the sun rises!"

"I agree, doll," Uncle Jacob said. "It's okay to leave. But, like May said, this party is just getting started; after all, it's only ten p.m.."

"All of a sudden, I'm drained," I said.

"Any time you're ready," Stevie D added.

"But I couldn't go through the crowd again. Suddenly, I just don't have the strength," I attempted to explain.

"I know the back way out; just follow me," Uncle Mic offered.

We all stood hugs all around with reminders to call them and make sure we all got together one more time before I left for Houston. I agreed. Uncle Mic took us around the back of the bandstand, far away from the crowd, through the kitchen, and out the back door. The cars were out front.

One more round of hugs and into the car. I was in the back seat and fell asleep.

Once home, Stevie D gently woke me and walked with me inside. Aunt Zorah and Ethel were sitting at the kitchen table.

"Hi," I sheepishly said.

"You want a sandwich?" Aunt Zorah asked.

I stood behind her chair and hugged her neck, "No. I'm full of roast beef and bread pudding," I said.

"And beer!" Ethel added.

"Yes, so I'm headed for bed. Where's Mom? Upstairs?"

"She went straight up," Aunt Zorah answered.

Stevie D was standing in the door frame, leaning. I walked over to him, kissed his cheek, and said, "Thanks for everything. Really, I couldn't have gotten through it without you," and I kissed his cheek again. I had my hands flat on his chest when I reached up to kiss him. He didn't move, just smiled, but I could feel his heart as it picked up speed. "Good night," was all he said.

Once on the second floor, I approached the closed door to Mom's room. "Mom, are you still awake?"

"Come in, hon."

She was sitting on the bed in her nightgown, drying her eyes and blowing her nose. "I'm glad it's over, you know what I mean?"

"Yes. It's been a long week, even though it's only Thursday," I climbed onto the bed and sat Indian-style opposite her.

"Was there something you wanted?" she asked.

I sighed while looking down at the pattern on her thin summer blanket. "What is it, hon?"

I looked up. She had bags under her eyes and dark circles. Her eyelids were puffed and reddened from all the crying, and her latte completion looked sallow.

"Mom, we really hadn't had a chance to talk at all since I got home. I feel bad about that."

"What was there to talk about? I knew you and Renato were handling the funeral arrangements, and, to tell you the truth, I was glad. After the trip to the casket company, well, that was enough for me. Anyway, that's over now." She started crying again.

Tears were rolling down my cheeks as well. "Mom, I'm so sorry!"

"Sorry? Sorry for what?" She managed while blowing her nose.

"That Dad died."

"Oh, Maggie," she gave a little laugh. "What do you have to be sorry about? Your dad was so proud of you!"

"I know, Mom, you keep telling me that. But what about you? You lost your husband, have you thought about what's next for you?"

"Well, every time the thought crosses my mind, the only thing I'm sure of is I'm staying right here until I figure it out."

"Stay here in the house?"

"Yes. It's my home! I'm in no way leaving my home. Don't get any ideas about moving me someplace or other! I'm staying right here!"

"Mom, I have no such plan. Are you considering living alone? I'm asking because Uncle Carmine seems to have a different idea."

"Like moving Zorah in with me?"

Surprised, I said, "You figured that out too?"

"Oh, please! How long have I lived with this family? Every time something happens to any one of us, Carmine farms out Zorah. After Ma and Pa died, illnesses, babysitting, and not only for us, but for his goombahs! It doesn't surprise me that he thinks Zorah needs to take care of me now!

"Don't get me wrong, I was really relieved she was here during the wake and funeral. Couldn't have gotten through this without her and Ethel, but it's time for her and Ethel to go home and leave me to myself! I just want to walk around my own house without walking into someone who isn't a part of this house, this family. That's you and me now. We are the family of this house!"

"Uncle Carmine expects us for supper this Sunday."

"He does? When did that happen?"

"The message was delivered by Rocco at the Irish Center. But he didn't say why. He said it was business."

"Never ceases to amaze me how my brother takes charge of everything! Georgie dies, and Carmine feels it's his responsibility now, taking care of me." She held up her fists and shook them towards heaven. Then she allowed her arms to slump. Shaking her head, smiling, sniffing her running nose as she reached for a tissue, wiping her nose, then crawled to me and pulled me into a hug; that hug turned into her cuddling me in her arms.

"Do you want to live alone?" I asked.

"No."

"No? Then what? . . . Oh, wait. . . . No, I want to hear you say it."

She was rocking me. "Okay. I'm not ashamed that I want you to move home and live with me. There!" She kissed my head.

"I thought so."

"You will?" This sounded like a plea.

"I didn't say that. I said I was right that that's what you'd say. And why won't Zorah live with you? You said, 'That will never happen,'"

"I know that Zorah has a life that Carmine and the rest know nothing about."

"You know this because . . .?" Mom piqued my interest.

"Because she told me, an awfully long time ago, and I'm not saying. It's in no way my story to tell; it's Zorah's."

"What? . . . No, wait. . . .. It's about the relationship between Aunt Zorah and Ethel. They're much more than unmarried lady friends," I sat up and looked Mom straight in the eyes.

She crawled back so she could lean against the headboard. "Listen to you, Dr. Blake, psychologist. You're rather good. Yes, there was a saying when I was a kid, 'Still waters run deep.' If that doesn't explain Zorah, nothing does!"

"How about a couple of Tylenol for those swollen eyes?" I offered.

"If you insist," Mom said as she sunk under the sheet and thin summer blanket.

I brought her the pills, water and tucked her in as Dad had always done for me.

"Good night, sleep tight . . ."

She said with me, ". . . and don't let the bedbugs bite!"

As I prepared for bed, I was thinking about Zorah and Ethel. But when my head hit my pillow, I was out like a light.

I woke naturally. No Ethel, no alarm, nothing. It was eleven a.m.. I stretched and listened for a minute. Quiet. No 'Italian' voices heard from downstairs. Today was curiously silent.

As I descended the steps, the kitchen was empty, but there was fresh coffee. I poured myself a cup.

"Mom?" I walked through to the living room. I found her watering the plants.

"Good morning, sleepyhead," she said without turning to look at me.

"Good morning. Where is everyone?"

"Gone. I sent them home."

"Aunt Zorah and Ethel?"

"Yes." She walked past me, kissed my cheek, and asked, "What would you like for breakfast?"

I followed her, "Eggs, scrambled, and toast."

"Coming up!"

I sat at the table, watching her get to work. Sipping coffee, I wondered about this energy. It was the psychologist in me. I had a week of seeing my mother in a decompensating state over my dad's sudden death, and yet today, she was . . . normal.

"You alright?" I finally asked.

Placing a dish of scrambled eggs and toast before me, she answered, "Yes," and sat next to me.

After a few bites, I added, "Forgive my psychologist mind, but this energy today is a one-eighty turn."

"I'm entitled, don't you think? Enough of the crying and deep grief for now."

I wasn't satisfied with her answer.

She could read me like a book. She slumped a bit. "Honey, I'm tired of crying. I'm tired of the attention. I'm tired of the grieving widow's role. Today I'm just me! Me, Isabella," she moved off the chair and refilled our coffee cups.

Sitting again, she reached across the table and grabbed my hand, and squeezed it tight. "Today, no tears; I want to breathe, and I'm getting that chance. I called Renato and asked him to take us for a ride on his boat."

"This afternoon? Just Uncle Renato?"

She paused. "I never asked. I suppose he could bring Eva. Maybe someone to drive his boat; of all the years I've taken a ride on his boat, I have never seen him drive that boat. Maybe he'll have someone to drive the boat."

"Well, it's a beautiful day for a boat ride," I said, wondering who else might be tagging along.

It was about forty-five minutes before we were out on Lake Erie moving along with a comfortable speed, my cousin Carlo, Uncle Renato's unmarried son, at the wheel. Uncle Renato played host, getting us into life jackets and comfortable deck chairs, visors all around to protect our eyes, and then, finally, an ice-cold drink in our hands. Mom and Aunt Eva were chatting away.

I was leaning back, eyes closed, and enjoying the wind on my face. What a fantastic idea! Mom and I needed this kind of a break, especially today, something completely different from what we had been doing all week long. Brilliant idea!

About an hour into our ride, we were invited below for an early supper. It was all cold foods: boiled shrimps; a calamari salad with greens, chopped onions, bell peppers, and tomatoes, served with lemon wedges and fresh Italian bread and iced lemonade or tea. Once we were munching cookies for dessert, Uncle Renato nodded towards his wife. She invited Mom back up on deck. That left Uncle Renato and me alone.

"Oh, no," I thought. "It's a set-up!"

"Anisette?"

"Sounds great," I feigned.

As soon as he placed the petti glass in front of me, I took a swig. I was bracing myself.

"I know how smart you are, Maggie, so I'll cut to the chase," he said laughing.

"Thanks. Is this about moving in with my mom because if it is I . . ."

He interrupted me, "No."

My face gave me away.

"You're surprised," he laughed. "No, Carmine can handle his own agenda. I'm here on behalf of a heart-sick guy. And to tell you the truth, I'm as surprised as you are that we're here, now, and I'm about to talk with you about love." He was shaking his head as if it were an unbelievable topic for conversation.

I stared at him, squinting. I'd been told I automatically do this when I hear something I don't believe.

There he sat, just shaking his head.

Finally, I repeated, "Love? Did I hear you right?"

He straightened up in his chair, turned sideways a bit, and propped one arm on the back of the chair. "Yeah. I'm surprised too. Me, an emissary for love." He was shaking his head again. We cousins knew Uncle Renato was called 'The Mechanic' because he fixed things, but love? I understood where he was coming from!

"Okay, the suspense is killing me. Who are you an emissary for?" I pressed.

He got up and walked the minimal space in the lower deck mess, oblivious to me, uncomfortable.

"Come on, Uncle Renato, sit, sit, talk to me," I coaxed with a soft voice.

He did. "Bella, I accepted the request to talk on . . . on his behalf because you both need love in your lives. I'm as close to him as I am to you. I've seen the same, sort of, events in both your lives. You tried marriage with that musician, whatshisname, Jimmy Calamari? . . ."

"Jimmy Toscano is his name, Uncle Renato; Nickle Calamari is Jimmy Toscano's band."

"Whatever; I watched you follow him around, then . . ." Uncle Renato exaggerated a shrugging of his shoulders.

"I was a lot younger then, and I had stars in my eyes. He's made it big you know."

"Forget about him! You had a heartbreak that keeps you from marrying again, bottom line, am I right?"

"Well, there was school and my career . . ."

"Am I right?"

"I just haven't been looking . . . at all."

"Exactly! That's what I see in both of you! So now you can imagine my surprise when he approached me last night like some love-sick dog asking me if I'd talk to you, feel you out, so to speak, and talk with you!"

I was stunned. "I'm speechless," I managed.

"Ain't that right!" He leaned in, elbows on the table now. "This is serious. I've never seen this guy like this . . ." He sat up and gestured with his arms in front of him as if he had no words for what he experienced. ". . . a lovesick puppy! For God's sake!"

I sat back a little, stifling a smile; the gesture was comical and so Sicilian! "Uncle Renato, who are you talking about?"

"Stevie D!"

It was a pie to my face.

"Doll, are you alright?"

"Stevie D?"

"Yes!" Again, arms waving, "Stevie D wants me to ask you if he can date you! He wants to know if he can go to Houston and hang out with you! He wants to know if you will really consider moving back home." He took a big sigh of relief. It was out, all of it, like a cleansing exhale after a close call.

I just stared at him.

"Doll?" He poured another anisette for me.

We sat in silence for another minute. "Uncle Renato, what do I say?"

"Do you love him?"

That startled me. "I've never thought about it!" I downed the anisette. My Italian voice kicked in unconsciously, "Who falls in love attending your father's funeral? Answer me that?" I heard the defensiveness in my voice. "I'm sorry. I'm blown away. I didn't come home looking for love."

"And that's the best part," he offered as he pointed a finger at me, "you weren't looking for it; it came to you. That's the best way."

I sat gently shaking my head; I come home for my father's funeral, and suddenly, whew.

"Doll, this is all you need to know today. Sunday you and your mother will be at Carmine's for supper. I'll be there too. Hear your Uncle Carmine out. Go into it telling yourself that you don't have to make any decisions now, not Sunday, not today. I know that it's a lot thrown at you, like a chain reaction wreck."

"So, if I get the hell out of town on Monday, no one will be surprised or stop me?"

"Well, that's not exactly what I was going for, but if that's what you have to do, do it," he said with a shrug.

"Hey! You two! What are you doing? Don't want our company?" It was Aunt Eva yelling down at us.

"Aspetta!" he answered. "Doll, Stevie D is a good man."

"I know, Uncle Renato, I've felt that."

It was around ten when Carlo dropped Mom and me off at home. The summer days were long, with sunset around nine in the evening. I loved that about summer. Mom started a fresh pot of coffee once in the kitchen. I just slumped into a chair.

"How about some cheese and bread and fruit? Not so heavy that we won't sleep," Mom asked, her head in the fridge.

"Sounds perfect," I answered. "Mom? What do you know about Steve D and his wife?"

She set the table with food and sat. We started helping ourselves. The grapes were refreshing.

"Donna. Her name was Donna. The story was that they had a fight, she took off in her car and got into an accident that killed her. Left the guy with three sons: one in high school, one in middle school, and a toddler.

"What mother does that? Just goes crazy without taking her kids into account. Any good woman knows when you fight with your husband, it is him that gets thrown out!"

I knew the implication of the sentence was "any good Sicilian woman."

"Nothing else, Ma?"

"Stevie D is a member of Renato's crew, along with Leo, his dad. The Rizzo's -- you know Jane Bataglia is Bertha's sister-in-law -- so not so much said. Bertha is protective of her in-laws. I don't blame her; they're good people, like the Blakes.

"This has to do with the long after supper conversation Renato had with you, right?" she asked.

I smiled. "Bingo."

"So?"

"Well," I sat up and did my best to sound sarcastic, "seems Steve D loves me and wants to date me and wants me to move back."

Mom just smiled while cutting her next chunk of cheese. "No kidding," she said.

"Mom! He can't be serious! Who falls in love at a funeral? Who?"

She was sitting back and still smiling and taking her time with grapes, smiling.

"Mom, get serious! I live in Houston; I have a career I worked hard to get! What the hell is everyone thinking?"

"Me thinks she protests too much," Mom said with a smirk.

"You're joking, right?" I said with a mouth full of bread and cheese.

"Hey, got anyone waiting in the wings I don't know about?" she asked.

"No. Anyway, he saw me at my worse, crying and fainting and emotional; probably just a knee-jerk reaction to rescue the damsel in distress. You know I'm no damsel in distress. I can take care of me; been doing just that for over ten years and quite well, I might add."

"No one said anything about you not able to take care of yourself; didn't you say he loves you? That doesn't automatically mean 'rescue.'"

She started clearing the table and said, ". . . protests too much."

I attempted to get out of my chair as if in protest. But I didn't know what that would look like, so I just got up and started helping her. "Well, the pressure is building," I said with a sigh.

"What pressure?"

"What pressure? You're kidding! Right? Uncle Carmine's invitation for Sunday is all about him wanting me to move back; you want me to move back and now, love!"

"Don't be so dramatic! What would you tell a client?"

"That's not fair!" She didn't just go there.

"Something like, 'you have choices.'" She mimicked me.

"And what about a client who comes from a strong Sicilian family who still believes in the asking and honoring of favors?"

"Oh, that; that just makes life interesting!"

Ah! Sicilian denial! "I'm going to bed!" I announced, kissed her cheek, and took off before another word could be said.

Sunday, I woke early with the aroma of fresh coffee waffling up the stairs. Popping out of bed, I thought I'd ask Mom about another day of just us, maybe going to a TED's hot dog stand and enjoying my favorite Buffalo fast food, a light lunch before we went to Uncle Carmine's. By the time I walked down the stairs, I heard voices, Aunt Zorah and Mom; their voices didn't have a friendly, sisterly loving ring.

Here we go again.

"Morning," I said as I made my way right to the coffee pot.

No one responded. Oh, come on now!

Sitting at the table, joining Ethel, Zorah, and Mom, I said facetiously, "What's up? Silence; then Mom said, looking at Zorah, "May I?"

Zorah nodded yes.

"Your aunt has run away from home. Seems our brother Carmine announced to her that he has every intention of seeing her move in here with me now that my husband has died, without asking her. He told her that after dinner tomorrow, she'll be moving in here."

"Wait a minute! I think tomorrow is all about Uncle Carmine asking me to move home and move in with you, not Aunt Zorah!" I countered.

"Si! But-a Carmine, he no-a thinks you do this, move back. So, when you say 'NO,' then he says I move in, but I say 'NO.' I say, 'no more,' I say, she got a daughter, she move in!' But-a me, no, no more," she nodded her head one downward solid jerk.

I thought, "Oh shit."

Zorah continued, her arms crossed over her large, soft breasts, her head now tilted up and back, her face set. She looked sternly at Mom. "Nobody think you can live alone. Nobody. Georgie, he do everything; everybody know this. You think living alone is easy?"

Mom sat a moment, looking at Zorah as if she were formulating something in her head. Then slowly, Mom started carefully, "Zorah, you aren't the only one who has never had a chance to live the life you were meant to live."

Zorah and Mom locked eyes.

Like watching a tennis match, I looked at Mom, then Zorah, then Mom, then Zorah. It was Ethel that broke the spell. "Ladies," she said softly and then spoke directly to Mom, "I think no one can know how much a dominating man can hold a woman back. I know, Bella, that your Italian culture also holds women back. But this is the first time we've heard you say you could be someone else. God, Bella, you could have said something about this years ago! Especially to us!"

Mom was drying her eyes, "I didn't mind," she finally said, "it wasn't until Maggie left for college that I wished I were working or volunteering. Georgie never would stand for it. I think he saw me as one of the 'wives.'" She looked directly at Zorah. "God, Zorah, you know how we -- you, me, Bertha . . . Mama even -- were happy that we weren't like the wives! We didn't have to be because we are The Madonie's! I think, though, that I just went with the flow in this house. I was older, and Zorah, you've been working all your life! Then Georgie died.

"Zorah, I'd like very much to learn how to live my life on my own," then she turned to me, "and this in no way changes anything about my wanting you home in the same city with me, with family."

Whew. "Mom, I had no idea." Mom and I decided walked the three blocks to Uncle Carmine's house. Aunt Zorah and Ethel followed.

Mom broke the silence. "You nervous?"

"What do you think?"

"I am! Zorah and I may, for the first time, stand up to our brother! You may be witness to a Madonie Family First if we live through it!" She nudged me playfully.

"Mom, Zorah, and Ethel, there's more there, right?"

"Shh! That's Zorah's secret to tell when she wants to if she wants to."

"I can keep a secret; just ask my clients!"

"As I said, doll, it's not my secret to tell."

As expected, the house had the aroma of baking bread, sauce, and the heat of an oven that has been on all morning. Aunt Zorah and Ethel immediately began helping in the kitchen with Aunts Lena and Eva. Uncle Carmine, Rocco, Drew, Sal, and Uncle Renato were already sitting at the dining table, sampling the antipasto, and drinking wine. The conversation was in Sicilian with Drew, the odd man out. He immediately rose, smiling at Mom and me, pulling out our chairs.

"They still talk Sicilian in front of you!" I commiserated, whispering.

"Hey, I consider it as being inclusive because they are comfortable knowing I'm in no way offended. Were you ever offended when they switched into Sicilian?" he whispered.

"No. I see what you mean," I approvingly nudged him, "except when I knew it was about me!"

Without missing a beat in his conversation, Uncle Carmine gestured to Sal to fill our wine glasses and every wine glass on the table.

Uncle Carmine picked up his glass, "Salute!"

"Salute!" the rest of us around the table said.

"Maggie, how you feel?" Uncle Carmine asked.

Surprised to be singled out already, I hesitated, almost choking mid-sip.

"Take your time. I know about Stevie D," he said, peeling a pomegranate. In my peripheral vision I could see Rocco, Drew, and Sal smirking in delight on the topic of Stevie D being introduced.

Ay yai yai yai! My face must have registered the horror I felt about this situation being announced over the Sunday dinner table in front of all these guys! It was one of those moments when I'd see my mom throw her hand to her mouth and bite her index finger. Instead, I shot a glare at Uncle Renato.

He shrugged. The aunts arrived with bowls of food, platters of meat, a large bowl of green tossed salad, and warm homemade bread. Aunt Lena was arranging the table while instructing the other ladies, "Sit, sit."

Once everyone was sitting, her very presence in silence caught their attention. She began with crossing herself, "In the name of the Father, Son, and Holy Ghost, Bless oh Lord, for these Thy gifts . . ." In the end, we joined her in an "Amen."

During the prayer, all I could think was that the Holy Ghost was never upgraded to the Holy Spirit as Rome decreed! This made me smile.

"Mangia!" Uncle Carmine announced, and immediately everyone reached for the item before them, shoveled food onto their plate, and passed the bowl or platter. Rocco was busy slicing a warm loaf of bread. All the comments were about just how wonderfully luscious the food looked and how good it smelled. It was the comfort of the moment, the family familiarity of the table, all the anxiety that brought me to this event vanished.

If a cannoli is homemade and fresh, you can hear the shell crunch when you bite into it. As Uncle Carmine slurped his coffee then bit into a fresh cannoli, that sound was music to my ears, and I also bit into the cannoli I held in my hand. The taste amazing; my entire life's experience in this family wrapped up in a shell stuffed with ricotta, chocolate chips, walnuts, and candied cherries, topped with sprinkled powdered sugar and moist ends dipped into coconut shreds. A tiny gem.

"Okay," Uncle Carmine announced, "we're here to discuss what we do with Bella now that Georgie, God-rest-his-soul, is gone."

In a heartbeat, Mom retorted, "Excuse me! 'What to do with Bella?'"

People moved in their chairs. The women looked at each other.

Mom continued, "I'd like trying to live on my own, Carmine."

He shrugged, nodded his head in understanding, "Then Maggie is staying."

"No," Mom continued. "No, Maggie has no plans for moving back. She got on a plane to bury her father, not move back to Buffalo. Her home and career are in Houston."

My head spun to look at her as I thought, "Way to go, Mom!"

Now Uncle Carmine was in his "hump" gesture: a smile, a semi-shrug, and nodding his head with shoulders rounded forward as if saying can't believe what he's hearing. Then he sat up straight, "Bella, Maggie isn't that selfish. She understands family, and she knows that her mother needs her."

Nothing to say here except 'awkward pause.'

"No!" All heads snap in the direction of that voice; then another, "No!" from Aunt Zorah. Her face was turning red. I think she had never had this much attention at one time in her life. She straightened in her chair, held her head up and looked straight at Carmine, and repeated herself, "No!" At the same time, Ethel lowered her head to hide a broad smile.

"No," Uncle Carmine echoed, "no what?"

"No, I will not move in and live with Bella," Aunt Zorah stated.

"You would leave your sister all alone in that big house at her time of need following the death of her husband?" he asked.

She softened some, "Yes. She no need me. She wants-a to live alone anyway. She say so! Just now, she says she try living alone. And if no work out, it's Maggie's responsibility. It's her mama."

I was impressed with Aunt Zorah's declaration, but I became aware that all eyes were now on me. As I looked around, I felt my face flush.

Mom turned to me, "There is nothing that I'd like more than you move back here with your family, near me," she said, reaching out and taking my hand.

I stammered, "I still have a lot to think about, Mom, especially with my practice, my clients."

I glared at Uncle Renato. I thought, "Don't start merging agendas now," hoping he got my message with the 'evil eye' glare I was giving him. He turned away. I grabbed a cannoli and stuffed it into my face. Uncle Carmine caught the 'evil eye' shot between Renato and me.
I looked at Rocco for support, and he just smiled, very passive-aggressive of him, I thought.

Before I could say more, Uncle Carmine said, "Make me an offer."

"Excuse me. Are you talking to me?" I asked, genuinely surprised. I'm in a scene from The Godfather.

He nodded yes.

"Uncle Carmine, housing and office space is the easy stuff. Its licensure and building up a clientele that's the hard stuff. I'm not licensed in this state.

"I didn't come home looking to move back. Look, Mom said she wants to be on her own. What's wrong with that?" There was no movement in his camp. "How about a year? How about Mom gives it a go on her own over the next year? I'm sure she'll be able to say what's working for her in that amount of time. Now that all of us know the subject of my moving back is on the table, it will give all of us time to think about it as a possibility."

There was a pensive silence.

"Scusi," Uncle Renato addressed Uncle Carmine.

"Oh my god, here it comes," I thought in a mild panic.

Uncle Carmine gestured a "Yes," with a wave of his hand and a nod of his head.

I braced myself, looking at Mom. "Damn, stop smiling," I tried to tell her telepathically.

"Maggie, with all my heart, I know it's right to add that Stevie D wants time with you as well. This year you talk about, maybe not only for your mother, my dear sister Isabella but also for Stevie D to court you, so to speak."

In my life, I had never heard any of my uncles be so Sicilian formal, and no one sounded more like a matchmaker than Renato did at this moment. In my peripheral vision, I could see Rocco, Drew, and Sal just dying with amusement. I dare not look in their direction.

Before I could reply, Uncle Carmine said, "Renato, your advice on this matter."

I thought, "What?"

Uncle Renato sipped his espresso, placed the small cup on the saucer, and answered, "With all due respect, I think Bella should live on her own as she wants, and Maggie returns to Houston knowing the wishes of her family, and we talk more at a later date if Maggie accepts all that is proposed here."

I was doing okay until that last provision. I sat stunned a moment and, at that moment, before I could speak, Uncle Carmine was on his feet holding his wine glass and saying, "Salute!"

Everyone got up and did the same. I lagged but did, in the end, join them.

Once seated, I asked myself, "What just happened?"

Aunt Ethel, Sal, and Drew began clearing the table. Mom moved to kiss my cheek and then joined them. I felt stunned. Somehow, I had agreed to be courted by Stevie D! Oh my God, how do I get out of this? Whack him? This thought made me smile.

Once dishes were cleaned, and Ethel was sweeping the kitchen floor, Mom and I started making our parting kisses all around. When I approached Uncle Carmine, he took me into a bear hug and said, "Doll, I would consider it a favor if you moved back within the year. Regardless of what my sister says, she needs you, and you know this is true." He kissed each cheek of my face. Now I'm genuinely freaked.

Mom and I started walking the blocks back to our house. I was still thinking about this favor in Uncle Carmine's eyes. I was watching the sidewalk just in front of me. The neighborhood was old, the curb was lined with tall trees, and the pavement was an obstacle course of broken cement, small, pointed mountains from roots pushing up. Suddenly Mom nudged me. I looked at her; she nodded her head to look forward.

There he stood, leaning against his car, arms crossed over his chest, a smile on his face. Stevie D approached Mom and me. "May I escort you beautiful ladies' home and protect you from falling on this broken path?" he asked with such chivalry. He stood between us, arms bent and extended, and she and I looped our arms into his. Mom laughed, somewhat like a schoolgirl, in my opinion. He did, though, make me smile.

"Who called you? Rocco?" I inquired.

"Yeah," he fessed up easily.

Once at our house, Mom excused herself and left Stevie D and me on the porch, awkwardly at best. I spoke first as I sat in a yard chair, "Now what?"

"Well, I know Renato talked with you," he began, "and I guess, well . . . how you doin'?"

I started to laugh. The more I tried to curb the laughter, the harder I laughed, and now I was rocking my body in the chair, convulsing in laughter. Tears running down my face along with snot running out of my nose, I motioned to him that I needed a Kleenex. Thankfully, he got what I was gesturing for and handed me the crumpled one he had in his pocket. I didn't care; I just wanted to mop my face. The laughter was contagious. He was laughing and asked, "What did I say that was so funny?"

Catching my breath now, I managed to say, "God, that felt good!" I turned to him and said, "Just what I needed: a really good laugh. Man, nothing let up after we buried my dad like I thought it would. I thought once Dad was buried, I'd have a few peaceful days with Mom, then I'd quietly get on a plane back to Houston, meet my girlfriends, tell them all about the funeral, then go back to my life. Boy!" I was shaking my head "no."

"I had no idea it would get crazier than it already was!" I declared.

Still smiling, a little stiff now, he asked, "How crazy?"

Incredulously, I said, "Stevie, really? Do you think that Dad's funeral was a normal American funeral? Huh? And do you really believe people fall in love at a funeral, especially the funeral of one's father?" It was out of my mouth before I realized what I was saying. I startled myself and tried back paddling, "I'm sorry! I didn't mean it like that!"

But Stevie D, smiling, settled back into the chair, and asked, "How about we drive to Niagara Falls? Get a few beers and sit by the Rapids?"

"What?"

"You heard me. We drive up to the Falls and hang out. Talk. Don't talk. Drink a few beers, and if we stay late enough, I know a guy who makes the best pizza in the Falls."

That seemed a logical offer. "Okay; just give me a minute to grab my purse and tell my mother."

I hadn't realized that Stevie D's car was a Mustang convertible, top-down. Red. It looked so very inviting. I was more convinced that this was an excellent idea, but I needed a guarantee, "Hey, you won't mind if we don't talk on the way up there, will you?"

"Suits me just fine; anyway, with the top down, we would hardly be able to hear each other."

He was right. The day was perfect. Still sunny, and with the top down there was a good breeze. I didn't care about how messed up my hair got. I just slid in my seat until my head rested on the seatback; I put on sunglasses, closed my eyes, and just felt the warmth and the breeze.

On Grand Island, Stevie D took the exit for a side street and a convenience store. He came out with a six-pack of beer and a bag of ice, placed it all in the trunk, and we were on the road again. It was only another twenty minutes before we were driving along the Rapids and parked. There were a few benches to choose from for sitting.

Cooler in one hand, Stevie D took my hand and guided me to the edge of the turf and a park bench. Once we each had a beer half gone did the conversation begin.

"To answer your question, I'm better, now," I tipped the beer bottle towards him.

"How was dinner?"

"You tell me. I know Rocco must have reported to you!" I threw my head back in a laugh. "You seemed to know when dinner was done and showed up on the street!"

He raised his hands, "Guilty! . . . Yeah, Rocco called me. I would have called Renato later tonight if Rocco hadn't called," he looked sheepish, "Sorry."

"Thanks."

"I never realized that anyone could walk right into the Rapids from the Park, that there is no barrier! No wonder people wade out and commit suicide. It's easy to access." I had no idea what brought that on.

One thing, silence with Stevie D was always comfortable. We allowed it now. He passed a new beer to me after a while. I just felt good to relax and stop my brain. The sunset was in progress with fading light and just a tad cooler. The only sound was the roar of the water over the American Falls not so far away. So familiar and comforting that I knew I was home. There is nothing like this in Houston, no rushing water sound, no cooling off with a sunset; which do I prefer? I had no answer.

"You haven't met the real me, you know," I finally said.

"You don't think so? Why?"

"Well, for one, I had no idea that my dad was going to die. When I was here for Aunt Zorah's party, he was fine. Then, the call came and sent me into shock," I explained.

"Okay. But what about how you handled the arrangements?"

"You mean how Uncle Renato handled the arrangements. You know that; you were there."

"And you handled your mom."

"Fainting dead away isn't my idea of handling it," I confessed.

"What is okay with you then? You were in extreme grief, you fainted, you are a daughter, what's wrong with that?"

I shrugged

"Look, I know you came home to bury your dad. I know you weren't looking for anything more than that and some time with your mom. It's all an adjustment. Believe me, I know. You know my wife died, so I know something about all this.

"I just want permission to get to know you without the pressure," he offered.

I looked at him knowing my eyes were squinting, "You really believe that? No pressure?"

"We won't know if we don't give it a try. Let me go back to Houston with you."

"No! Oh, no, no, no! You can visit me, at some later date," I countered.

"How about Labor Day weekend?" he suggested.

I paused for an awfully long time as to in no way impulsively give an answer I'd regret once back in Houston. "September?"

He nodded yes.

I thought, "The remaining days of June, all of July, and August. Okay."

I said, "September; that's better. Okay, visit me Labor Day weekend."

"You were right; this pizza is amazing," I said with a mouth full.

"Joey says it's the pans. The pans were his great-grandmother's, and no one ever scrubbed them with an SOS pad, ever," Stevie D explained. "Must be something to that."

"How long have you known about this place? Do you come to Niagara Falls often?"

He gave me a Sicilian shrug. "Come on, you know how it is with us! Niagara Falls is where we went to play, blow off steam. You haven't been away for so long that you don't remember that from high school?"

I smiled. "No, I do remember, and you are right. I just thought that as adults, y'all might not 'blow off steam' in the Falls anymore."

"Say, what's with this 'y'all' stuff? I've been meaning to ask you."

"Let's see: four years of undergraduate work, six years of graduate work, and all the years in my career, that makes, four plus six plus ten is – BINGO -- twenty years living south of the Mason-Dixon line. Now, don't you think that after twenty years among Southerners, I'd pick up some of the jargon?" I was being sarcastic.

"All right, but it sounds weird coming from you! I mean, I grew up in your family! No one says 'y'all' except you!"

"Speaking of growing up in my . . . our family, exactly what is the Family Business about these days?" I jumped at the opportunity to ask.

He looked up, surprised as I had hoped. I intended to catch him off guard in hopes of getting a straight answer.

"What do you know about the Family Business?" he countered.

"Nice," I thought. "Well," I began, "I know that no one talked about it; that we, as a family, had a lot of respect. In high school, the undercurrent among the other kids was that we were Madonie's and don't mess with us. And, judging from the Suits, The Business is still alive and well. My question to you is precisely what kind of business is The Family Business?

"I remember the police coming to our house to talk with my dad. I remember my uncles talking about men in jail, even one guy who was sent to Sicily. I remember Mom being incredibly nervous when Dad was working with her brothers. I remember my Irish uncles wanting to work with my Sicilian uncles as well, in their neighborhoods. I understood that best because the conversation was in English, no flipping into Sicilian among the Blakes."

Stevie D was eating a slice of pizza, sipping his beer, but paying close attention to what I was saying. "I have a professional license. I am in no way allowed to become involved in criminal activity or with criminals! This is where I get totally freak out." It felt like a considerable risk saying that to him, and inside, I was a total wreck.

"Hmm, I see," was all he said as he patted his mouth with a linen napkin.

My stomach churned, but I picked my pizza slice, intending to show my calm, then blurted out, "How in the world can I move back home into my family? My family, the Madonie family, and their Business? When I was a kid, it didn't matter . . . much. We joked about Uncle Renato being 'The Mechanic' and that goon Pasquale something-or-other being 'Crusher.' We were kids! But now, there is no more plausible denial."

He was leaning back on the back two legs of his chair, the way men like to lean back, making every woman who sits across from them wish they would fall on their heads so they would no longer lean back on the back two legs of the chair. He just looked at me, seemingly amused.

"We've changed," he finally said, sitting up on all four legs of this chair.

"Changed? How?" I let the pizza slice plop down onto the dish.

"You have to trust me; we've changed. It's a good business now. We help people."

"Help people how?" I pushed a bit.

"I'm not the one who can tell you."

"Then who can?" I pushed.

"Your Uncle Carmine; he's the only one who gets to tell all about The Business and, usually, only to people he decides to bring into The Business."

There was an eye-staring stand-off.

"What if I go and ask him to tell me what The Business is?" I wondered aloud.

"Go ahead. My money is on that he won't say."

Smugly I countered, "You think he won't tell me?"

"Nope. He won't tell you."

"What makes you so sure?" Was he being arrogant?

"You aren't in; you aren't any part of The Family Business. Maybe he likes it that way."

"You seem sure of yourself." I poked.

"Maggie, I've been working in The Business all my life. I understand the rules."

I didn't want to give up. Yet, I, too, understood some of the rules; I understood that all Stevie D was saying was absolutely the truth. Unless I was 'in,' as an employee in The Business, I would never know the exact workings of The Business. Also, I'm a woman. I was aware growing up that the women had no idea about the comings and goings of any of the men. And, again, it was deliberate. An unspoken rule in their families: no questions, no answers, no knowledge, the safer for all was the bottom line of family life.

"Stevie, Uncle Carmine asked me to move back as a favor, again," I said.

He leaned in on his elbows, "Really?" He was smiling.

"You think that's great, don't you?"

He was shaking his head, "That's a trick question," he said.

"Damn right it is!"

"Yup, damned if I do, damned if I don't; what do you mean 'again'?" he asked.

"Rocco never told you about why he came home all those years ago?"

"No. And we weren't that close then. I was just getting started . . . ah . . . full time and had a young marriage and kids. I knew he was back, but that's it."

I quickly recounted the story about Uncle Carmine asking a favor and getting Rocco to return home when he was first sick. And I told him about how Uncle Carmine repaid the favor by somehow having my student debt erased. Now he was asking again for a favor; all I could think about was the thousands upon thousands of dollars of debt I don't have because of Uncle Carmine! All that debt was just erased. In good conscience, I just can't skip the fact that I'm being asked for a favor again, now.

He had a smug look on his face. "You have to move home."

"You're enjoying this, aren't you?" I elbowed him gently.

"Maggie, I want to get to know you better. I want to hang out with you, I want . . . never mind that, what's the problem?"

"You wouldn't understand." How much do I trust him? Is he trying to endear himself?

"Try me."

I slumped and took a breath, "You wouldn't understand because you're not a woman. All I've accomplished is so against the grain of how I was raised. It was hard-fought, in my eyes anyway.

"This isn't just a movie, this is about who I am now, and they, my family, don't know me as I am today. They don't realize that I don't fit here anymore. So, if you want to be helpful, then help me get out of this favor."

We stared at each other again. This time it was longer, and I wouldn't speak first if this took all night.

"Joey! Check! Let's go, Maggie. It's late."

There was no conversation all the way back to Buffalo. The drive was calming for me. The night air was so fresh because there was no humidity here. In Houston, at night, the humidity can be eighty or ninety percent, just as high as it is during the day. But here, while driving along the Niagara River, there was a breeze, and I was chilled.

"There's a blanket in the back," Stevie D said. "You look cold."

I turned around and retrieved the blanket. Now I was comfortable and still able to breathe in the clean, cool air.

I got out of the car at the house without an escort. I told him it wasn't necessary, and he said he'd call me before I left. I said I didn't know exactly when that would be, but certainly before the week was out.

Once he drove away, I sat on the porch. It was then I realized I still had the blanket wrapped around me. Oh lord. The tears just quietly flowed from the throbbing in my head.

I finally gave up sitting and went inside. Locking the door behind me, the house was quiet, which means all are asleep, even the furniture. I made my way to the stairs in the dark. Everything was neat, in its place; even the kitchen appeared spotless in the muted darkness. I loved growing up in this old house. Most of the homes on the west side of Buffalo had been built during the 1930s. It was easy to date the house: no closets in the bedrooms! And if there was a closet, maybe it was five feet long and two feet wide.

I'd seen our house go through all the decorating crazes of the times: from hardwood floors to covering them up with wall-to-wall carpet; wallpapered walls to flat paint; window shades to vertical blinds to drapery; kitchen linoleum to faux tile to ceramic tile; claw foot bathtubs to built-in tubs with showers; narrow windows pulled out for picture windows instead. And that was just the inside of the house! The basement, while growing up, felt like a dungeon. Then during the late 1950s, it became vogue to finish off the basement and make a game room or a canning room or just a finished area for parties. No one had driveways or garages. The streets were narrow because, at the time the city was mapped out, only the wealthy drove cars. Everyone else took a bus. No one had the imagination for a car in every household that needed a garage. Yet, even with changes to the house and the bumper-to-bumper parking on the narrow street, there was charming on the west side of Buffalo. A charm that people had tended to over the years. The neighborhood was still a neighborhood people knew each other by name.

I doubted that anyone in my apartment complex in Houston would know me if they ran into me at the grocery store, let alone know my name.

When I woke, I realized I had slept very well. It must have been all the fresh air and just the right amount of alcohol. In the hallway between my room and the bathroom, I could hear voices coming from downstairs in the kitchen. Hmm. Company already. Entering the kitchen, I saw Ethel first, then Aunt Zorah, and Mom busy at the stove. The aroma of coffee drew me straight to that pot, and I poured myself a giant mug of the hot brew. When I turned to face the table is when I saw Sal. My cousin Sal was sitting there eating eggs fried in the hole of slices of homemade bread. There was something about that egg-and-bread fry that tasted so good.

"Mom, may I have what Sal's having?" I asked.

"Coming right up, doll!"

Sal (short for Salvatore) was the middle child of Uncle Carmine and Aunt Lena. Rocco was the eldest child, and Angela was the youngest. Sal, so far, hadn't married, and, as far as I knew, worked in The Family Business. He had a peculiarity that was one of the family secrets that everyone knew: crossdressing.

"What brings you here so early in the morning?" I asked.

He smiled and shrugged. "I never really got to talk to you during the wake and funeral, what with Stevie D monopolizing your time!"

Ethel leaned over the table, placing a platter of fresh cinnamon buns. Looking at Sal, she offered, "That was his job, his assignment, remember?"

My head snapped to look at her. "What do you mean by 'his

assignment'?"

Sal, very matter-of-fact, said, "His job, Renato assigned Stevie D to look after you, never to leave your side in case you needed something, for the entire wake and funeral, just like Rocco was assigned to watch over Aunt Bella. It's procedure," he waved a hand smiling,

Ethel quipped, "Oh! You've forgotten how things work in The Family!"

I looked at Ethel, "Is that true?"

Sal and Ethel said at the same time, "Yeah, pretty much."

Aunt Zorah was placing a plate of fried egg in bread in front of me, "Who you think was gonna take care of you? Your Mama? No, your Family, we-a know how to take care of you."

I was torn between launching into the egg and being indigent about being 'assigned' to Stevie D. I chose the egg. After a few marvelous mouthfuls, I asked, "So all along, Stevie D was just doing his job?" I said it that way deliberately to see how they responded.

Mom spoke up first as she joined Sal and me at the table with her own plate of egg and bread fry. "Well, at first. But anyone with eyes could see that he was falling for you."

That I didn't expect!

Sal laughed and shook his head, "Ain't that the truth!"

As Aunt Zorah and Ethel joined us, I looked around at their faces, and they all seemed too smug.

"Wait one damned minute! Nothing is going on between Stevie D and me!"

They smiled, shook their heads, and just kept eating.

Mom looked and me and lipped, "Protests too much."

"Hey, anyway, the cousins are gathering out at Angela and Jimmy's house around lunch, and I've come to take you there. But first, maybe you'd like to drive around, shop, do something different before we head out?" Sal said.

What a relief! "That sounds great!" I turned to Mom, "You didn't have anything planned for today, did you?"

"Just gathering up your father's clothing to donate to Catholic Charities. That's why Zorah and Ethel are here, to help me."

Surprised that she was venturing into this chore so soon, "Oh! Do you want me to stay and help?"

"No," she breathed deeply and sighed, "no, I decided that the sooner I cleared out his clothing, the better. The other things around the house that were his, well, they're okay, they're just things he liked, and that's easier to take. But his clothes, I don't want to look at his clothes and know he'll never be here to wear them again."

I reached for her hand, "That makes sense. Are you sure you don't want me to help?"

"Yes. Go and be with your cousins. After all, you really haven't had time to visit them," she held my hand and placed her other hand on top of mine, "Go and enjoy the day."

It was settled. I turned to Sal, "Should I bring anything? Food? Drinks? Anything?"

"I was thinking about stopping at Camillo's Bakery and picking up some cannoli. No one had time to make cannoli, and no one ever refused Camillo's cannoli. And we can drive around and just talk some before we head out, okay?"

"Sounds great," I was thankful for the rescue.

Once in Sal's car, he immediately began with, "This is no spontaneous invite."

"No? Really?" I said sarcastically.

"No. Rocco called me after Sunday's dinner with my folks. He called Angela, too. The two of them put their heads together and said we, the cousins, needed to get hold of you and see how you felt about all this, give you some support, and maybe, even give you some advice, if you want it."

"Really? Hmm. And just what 'about all this' is all this about?" I asked. I wanted to know what my cousins knew.

He was headed into Black Rock, where Camillo's Bakery was. "My dad can be . . . persuasive. I know he wants you to move back home, live with your mother."

I laughed. "Now that's what you call an understatement! Your dad asked for a favor."

"Whew, he's serious," Sal said, shaking his head.

Pulling into the parking lot, Sal added, "The bakery is a coffee shop too, now. How about espresso and some fresh biscotti?"

"You've got room for biscotti after those wonderful cinnamon buns at my mom's?"

He smiled broadly as he opened the car door, "Yes!"

He was right; the espresso was excellent. I had forgotten just how good espresso is when presented with a bit of lemon twist and a lump of sugar. He wasn't wrong about the biscotti, either.

"Is there anything else?" I poked.

"Anything else, what?"

"Anything else that the cousins know?"

"Oh! Stevie D; yes, they know about Stevie D asking Uncle Renato if it was all right for him to hang out with you when he wasn't assigned to anymore." He was so matter of fact.

"Everyone knows!" It was my Italian voice.

"What do you think?" Sal replied.

"What do you think about it? You were there, you heard at all firsthand," I said.

"Who, me? Nobody asks me my opinion, you know that?" he said with a twinkle.

"You trying to tell me you have middle child syndrome? No attention, so you find a way to get attention," I said, nudging him.

He laughed! "Not fair. And I don't do that for attention, I do it because it feels good, natural - hey! Stop being the psychologist! I'm just a humble employee in my father's business. I'm not the golden child; that would be the first-born son, Rocco, and I'm not the child that produced the grandchildren, although my children would carry on the family name, a minor glitch. Thus, no one asks the child with no distinction, but the distinction he does have is an embarrassment. But they don't talk about it and ignore it, that way they can believe it doesn't exist!"

"Stop! I feel like I'm at the opening narrative for a soap opera!" I said, laughing.

He smiled beautifully with a twinkle in his eye. Sal, my unassuming cousin who you could count on for anything you needed.

"I'm the sheep headed for slaughter?" I mused.

"NO! You're the damsel being rescued, and your champions are willing to whisk you away to whatever country you choose where you'll feel safe from the encroaching villain."

He made me laugh! It felt good, laughing. "You're a trip!" I leaned into him and kissed his cheek.

It took about half an hour before arriving in Clarence at Angela and Jimmy's house. The house sprawled on five acres had a in ground pool and three-car garages plus a golf cart garage. The number of cars in the driveway and on the street validated that the cousins were gathering for my benefit. Wow! But instead of feeling their concern, I felt nervous that this moving to Buffalo was far more serious than I had believed.

The gathering started behind the house at the pool. There was a wonderful space around the elaborate grill (more like an outdoor kitchen) with cushioned chairs and an awning for comfort. Unfortunately, the sun was hot, and there wasn't any breeze. Clarence was too far inland from Lake Erie to benefit from the breeze off the lake, the way it was on the west side.

I made my way through the greetings, hugs, and kisses: Angela by my side, there was Rocco and Drew; Angela's daughters Izzy (Isabella after my mom), Maria, and son Car (Carmine after his grandfather/Uncle Carmine); then Cary with wife Ginger, their kids Maureen, O'Hara, Irene, and Dunn (yes, the movie stars); Rosalie and Danny and their kids Paul, John, and George (Ringo the dog was home) and finally, my bachelor cousin Carlo (Giancarlo.) By all accounts, Carlo was a healthy, straight, all Sicilian-American guy. Why he was still a bachelor, no one knew. By the time I was handed a tall Long Island iced tea and found a seat under the awning, it became apparent to me that my cousins were serious about an intervention.

There was small talk before the luncheon spread was ready. My cousins took turns telling me about their lives and their kids' accomplishments, much to the embarrassments of the kid. But it was fun to hear about how full and normal my cousins' lives were. I had to remind myself that Rocco, Cary, Carlo, Jimmy, and Danny all worked in The Family Business as far as I knew. And it occurred to me that Stevie D was a cousin-in-law to Cary. Cary's dad, Joe Rizzo, was brother to Stevie D's mom, Jane Rizzo Bataglia; his dad, Leo, was in The Family Business.

The good news was Stevie D, and I weren't blood related. Wait! Why did that even matter?

When the food was ready, Angela placed a colossal roasting pan of baked macaroni on the table. I burst out laughing!

"What?" she asked, looking puzzled.

"Baked macaroni?" I asked.

"Yes. What's so funny about that?"

"This is a picnic lunch, right? Because, if memory serves, all Madonie family picnics always had baked macaroni as the main noon course," I started to explain. "Do you know that most American families, when you say, 'picnic food,' think of fried chicken or hamburgers and hot dogs, steaks, even ribs, and sausage? But, no, you can tell the Sicilian families because the aunts set out the huge pans of baked macaroni!" I narrated.

Now she was laughing. "Okay! Okay! I know! The first time, oh, this was years ago when we first moved out here. The kids were small; we were invited to a potluck picnic for the junior soccer league Car belonged to. I brought a pan of baked macaroni. Well, you would have thought no one had ever seen a pasta dish before in their entire lives. I guess it was because it was a hot baked dish that got them. I explained how our family always brought a pan of baked macaroni to family picnics. Now, those same soccer moms, they ask me specifically to bring baked macaroni to the potlucks!"

She enjoyed telling me her soccer mom story.

The baked macaroni was excellent. It had been years, most likely all the years I had lived south since I last ate baked macaroni. Once the dishes were cleared and the desserts came out, my cousins gathered around the table with me. The kids sensed the cue to clear away from the adults. I became aware that the discussion time was at hand.

Rocco opened the topic. "Maggie, this is what we know: Now that your dad is buried, God Rest His Soul, my dad wants Aunt Zorah to move in with your mom. His opinion is that Aunt Bella, your mom, won't take care of her affairs as a husband does. On the other hand, Aunt Zorah and I might add since her birthday -- turning 80 has done something to her -- declared that she, Zorah, had no intention of moving in with your mom.

"Let me tell you, my dad was not happy about this, not at all," he was shaking his head. I didn't even want to know what that looked like: when Uncle Carmine is unhappy with someone's rebellion.

My cousin Cary spoke up. "The fact that you made a statement about how it might be a good thing if your mom tried living on her own didn't sit well with Uncle Carmine, either."

"I had no idea!" I was astonished.

"Yeah," Rocco continued, "My dad has a way of never letting you know exactly what he thinks. He sees Aunt Bella differently than we do. We all think it's a great idea for her to try living on her own. I mean, it's not like she's abandoned or anything; there's family all around her. So, what's the big deal? My dad, he has his old-fashioned ideas about taking care of the women in the family."

Rosalie added, "Aunt Zorah is making the men think differently about that! My dad is on the fence about it all." She looked directly at me, "Maggie, my dad is so impressed with your accomplishments! He brags all the time that he has a nice doctor! And then there's the issue about Stevie D. My dad was really freaked out that Stevie D approached him about you!" She laughed with the other cousins, imagining our Uncle Renato, The Mechanic, being approached with an issue concerning love.

I replied, "Yes, I know. He demonstrated just how weird it was for him when he first told me about Stevie D coming to him."

Carlo asked, "Maggie, what do you think? Any decisions yet?"

There was a hush. I took a deep breath. "I'm returning to Houston on Friday. Mom will be living on her own this first year without Dad. She'll assess whether living alone works for her. I have no intention of moving back . . ." -- it didn't take a Ph.D. psychologist to see and sense that this statement didn't land well on this audience – ". . . at this time." They relaxed.

Angela got up and filled wine glasses, encouraging people to pass around the dessert trays and asking anyone if they needed anything more.

When that all settled, it was Rosalie who asked the tricky question. "Maggie, I'm surprised I'm going to say this; I feel as if I'm in a movie, but, with all due respect, as you are my older cousin, how do you feel about Stevie D?"

Again, the communal table held its breath.

Yikes! If there were ever an event where I could be candid with the people around me and honest with myself, it was here and now. Yet . . .

All eyes were on me. I slumped back into my chair cushion. "Whew!" I took an audible sigh. "That's a hard question for me to answer," I started. I leaned back into the table, "Who goes to a funeral, the funeral of her father, and falls in love? Who does that??" I thought I was making a point for absurdity.

There was silence. Remarkable silence; I looked around, and there was some shifting, but no one was giving up anything in the moment.

Finally, Rocco said quietly, "You do?"

The pregnant pause; my mind darted around, looking for a cryptic answer. Finally, "In your opinion."

"Maybe so, but I was closest to you and Stevie D during the entire wake and funeral. And I say there was chemistry between the two of you. Are you willing to admit to that? Chemistry?"

The mood lightened, heads were nodding in agreement, and I conceded, "Okay, yes, there is chemistry between Stevie D and me."

I finally said what was stuck in my craw. "I was his assignment, for God's sake!"

That stopped everyone cold. Now they knew that I knew what they always knew during my dad's funeral. Explain away that, I thought.

Cary spoke up, "That aside, my cousin is crazy about you," he offered.

"I get that. Just let me go home to Houston and get grounded. Do all y'all realize that in ten days, I've lost my father, had to bury him, then faced the unexpected expectation of my mom and Uncle Carmine that I should move back here and live with my mother, dropping all I've built in Houston over all these years, just like that?" I snapped my fingers.

"Sounds disrespectful to you," Carlo said.

"Thank you!" I said directly to Carlo.

"Maggie, we want to help," Rosalie said. "I'm sorry if that isn't coming across. We know better than you what it's like living in this family and trying to have your own life. That's why we gathered here today, to offer you suggestions about how to get around anything you know isn't for you. We've all done that and were able to keep the peace between this generation and theirs."

"That is the first good news I've heard today," I said. This made everyone relax.

She continued, "For example, just tell my dad and Uncle Carmine you are open to all possibilities. This way, they'll feel no doors were shut."

"Okay, I can do that," I relaxed as I answered.

"And no sneaking out of town!" Rocco added, "Pay your respects all around like a good Sicilian girl!" Everyone laughed.

I bowed from my waist while still sitting, "Yes, sir! I can do that as well!"

The following day, Aunt Bertha called Mom and me to join them for supper tomorrow night. I can't remember when Aunt Bertha ever called me in my life. She was the shy, wallflower sister. Never had anything much to say when the sisters (Zorah, Isabella, and Bertha) at family gatherings. Bertha wasn't outgoing like Aunt Zorah, or should I say, intrusive? As I thought about Aunt Bertha, I realized that she was most ordinary, and what I mean is Aunt Zorah never married, lived at home, and worked in The Family Business; Mom had the distinction of marrying outside the ethnic group to an Irishman, thus bringing about a halt to Sicilian being spoken all the time at family events. I remember my grandfather (Carmine, also, Papa to the grandchildren) saying he respected my dad and made the effort to learn more English than ever before to communicate with Dad. Dad being brought into The Family Business was a big deal and had its advantages.

Aunt Bertha married another Sicilian, Joseph Rizzo. As I mentioned, Uncle Joe had a sister, Jane, who married Leo Bataglia. Their eldest child is Stevie D. As I was thinking about the strangeness of the invite to Aunt Bertha's for dinner tomorrow, I began piecing together who just might be at that dinner. Cary was the only child of Aunt Bertha and Uncle Joe. But he wasn't the only 'only' child in the family; I was the other one. I imagined Cary and his wife Ginger would be present.

I called Cary later in the afternoon.

"Hey, your mom invited my mom and me to supper tomorrow. Are you planning on being there?"

"Yeah, as a matter of fact, we are. Not the kids, just Ginger and me."

"Anyone else I should know about?" There was too long of a pause. "Oh no! Don't tell me that Stevie D is going to be there too! What in the world . . ."

He interrupted," In my mother's defense, I think it's cute," he said, laughing.

"Cute? Cute! What's cute about it? Isn't it more like pushy?" I protested.

"Lighten up. It's our family. Uncle Leo and Aunt Jane, my cousins Stevie D and his sister Lucy, their kids, which, knowing kids today, may or may not show up at a supper with their parents and grandparents and some old lady from Texas that they just met at a funeral they were dragged to," he said, trying to be funny.

"Stevie D has three boys, right?" I knew I was right but wanted validation.

"Yes. They're not really 'boys' anymore; Stevens is, what, eighteen or nineteen, I think, and that makes Wilder sixteen, and Capra is nine. I tease Stevie D that Capra was an afterthought! Lucy has two kids, a boy, and a girl, Diana, and Elvis," he reported. Diana is fourteen, and Elvis is twelve. So, as I said, no telling if the grandkids will turn out for this family supper," Cary sighed.

"Okay. . . ."

"What are you worried about?" Cary asked.

". . . The last time I saw Stevie D, I said what I had to say, and I told him no visiting me in Houston until Labor Day, meaning September," I replied.

"Doesn't answer my question," he remarked. "What are you afraid of?"

". . . I guess . . . that the family will get the wrong idea. Between you and me, and I do mean what I'm about to say is not for anyone else's ears but yours, can you do that for me, say you won't make it part of a guy conversation?"

"Relax. Okay. I know exactly what you mean. Promise. Now tell me, what's up?"

"There is no way I'm thinking about moving back here. I've got a life in Houston, twenty years in the south. It feels like home. Mom really does need to be on her own and find out just how capable she is of taking care of herself. She can't do that if I move back. And I'm a licensed psychotherapist who took an internship and an exam, not in New York State. I have no idea what it would take to be licensed in a different state. Big issue!"

There was a pause.

"Well, I suspect once you return home to Houston, things may just clear up for you in ways you never imagined. I find that's usually true for me; I get all wound up about something, and once I kind of let it go, watch and wait, allow all the forces of . . . of . . . of the Universe, for lack of a better word, I'm usually amazed how it works out."

I was smiling now. "You know something, cuz?"

"No, what?'

"You are a very wise man," I said. I could hear him softly laugh.

"Thanks. See you tomorrow at supper?"

"Yes. Thanks," and we hung up the telephone.

Mom and I walked to Aunt Bertha's house. She lived within a dozen blocks of Mom's house and her brother's, Uncle Carmine. When I walked into the house, memories flooded about how each house resembled the other among the sisters and sisters-in-law. When one woman got something new or trendy, the others followed suit. I'm not sure if it was jealousy, or one-upmanship, or just a keeping up with the Jones kind of behavior. When I was a teenager, it hit me that this was their habit. I realized it over a coffee pot. Tall white plastic thermos-lined coffee pots were all the rage. I my mom was the first to buy one. With an Irishman in the house, coffee was a necessity at each meal. But the other families drank wine with meals and espresso after. But, within the month, each aunt and aunts-in-law had a tall white thermos-lined coffee pot! Ours was used daily. Theirs were used at family functions. After that, I would take notice: peeling off wallpaper and painting; toaster ovens replacing toasters; crockpots; wall decorations of felt cut-outs of family profiles glued to dinner plates. Crazy.

I was greeted with hugs and kisses on each cheek after Aunt Bertha wiped her hands on her apron. Uncle Joe entered the kitchen with arms extended, welcoming me into his embrace. I tried to look over his shoulder into the other rooms to see who else was present. Cary came into the kitchen; Ginger was helping Aunt Bertha cook.

"Come onto the patio," Uncle Joe said and guided me through the dining area to a set of French doors that were new to me. "We added a patio a couple of years ago; it's so nice in the summer."

The patio was extensive with a red and white striped awning like the ones I remember over the store windows on Grant Street.

And there they were. Sitting at a large patio table, Leo and Jane Bataglia, their grandsons Wilder, Stevens, and Capra, and their dad, Stevie D. The boys stood and kissed Mom and me on the cheek like good Sicilian kids are taught how to respect their elders. Then Stevie D approached me. First, he hugged and kissed me on each cheek, then he kissed Mom.

Mom sat across from Leo and Jane, and a conversation immediately started. I was still standing next to Stevie D. I could hear bits and pieces of Mom's discussion about how I was returning to Houston on Friday. No, Zorah wasn't moving in, Mom wanted time to settle in for a while on her own, and yes, she'd like it if Jane came by for a visit.

Stevie D said, "I hope you don't mind."

"Mind? Mind what?" I feigned.

"Remember, Bertha and Joe are my aunt and uncle, too," he stressed.

I nudged him, saying, "Convenient for you, right?"

With that, we joined the table. The conversation was now about the weird and funny happenings at the wake and funeral that Mom and I most likely missed. The most significant event for the boys was the night of the Irish wake, with booze and corned beef and cabbage! They had never seen that before. It was topped off for them with the Irish dancing during the supper break when the doors were locked to the public. They now loved Irish wakes! It really tickled me.

I was comfortable, to my surprise. No one focused on me like my cousins did the day before at Angela's house. Ginger and Cary were a lot like Cary's parents, unobtrusive and mild-mannered. It occurred to me that I hadn't ever really experienced them separate from the large family gatherings before. Compared to the over-the-top personalities, the loud Italian voices, and the general cacophony of kids, they were a quiet, shy couple who always worked with the others, never needing a spotlight. That was Aunt Bertha and Uncle Joe.

On our walk home -- I had declined Stevie D's offer to join us -- I commented to Mom, "That was amazingly different."

She looked at me in surprise. "What was so different? It was Bertha and Joe; how was it different?" She stopped walking. "What are you talking about?"

I searched for words, "Well . . . they're quiet, they don't ask a lot of questions, they are a part of the conversation, not the moderator, you know. It felt like when I'm with my friends in Houston. I was so comfortable! They are lovely! I never realized it before."

Mom just shook her head and smiled, "You are so weird," was all she said.

We walked in silence for another block. The air was light, and the moon was full.

"Mom," I started, "before I leave on Friday, I want to make time to stop in at Uncle Carmine's and Uncle Renato's and thank them for all they've done for me, us, this past ten days." This was me, following Rosalie's direction.

Again, she paused, "What brings this on?"

"Yesterday, my cousins offered some advice for navigating the family," I said.

She tossed her head back in a laugh, "Anything I can use?" She teased.

"I think you and Aunt Zorah held your own with Uncle Carmine the other day. You should be proud of how you handled your big brother!"

"Thanks, but I know how it works in this family: one flub and in moves Zorah! God, I just wish she would have it out with him and move out of his house. She should have done that after Ma and Pa died."

"And why is that?" I was careful how I asked, hoping Mom would slip up and tell me Aunt Zorah's secret.

"Here we are! Home again, home again, jiggety-jig!" And up the front porch steps she went.

"Wait! Mom! You're ignoring me!" I ran after her in fun.

The day before I left, Mom and I spent time with the attorney and bank manager. I wanted to co-sign everything necessary in case something happened to Mom. She was happy to have my interest, support, and back-up. Then in the late afternoon, we found time to stop by at my uncles' homes and enjoy an espresso and biscotti with each of them. I took the opportunity to let Uncle Carmine and Uncle Renato know that I was open to the suggestion of moving back to Buffalo, and as icing on the cake, said I would research how a psychologist gets licensed in New York State. They both welcomed this.

Whew. It made me feel better, too, to my surprise. My cousins were right.

Rocco and Drew drove Mom and me to the airport Friday morning. I told her she didn't have to see me off. I said that more for me than her. I knew when I hugged her goodbye, I would break down and cry. At this point, I had no idea when I'd see her again, and the thought crossed my mind that sometimes a spouse dies soon after their life partner has died. I shook my head to clear that thought.

I had a window seat on the flight. I like looking out the window and ignoring the guy next to me. I hate talking to people on planes. There was a five-hour flight before me, and I wanted the time to just mellow out, chill, no thoughts. I called Alice and Patty; Alice would be at the office, and Patty said she'd meet me when my flight arrived. I tried to talk her out of it, but she insisted and won me over, saying that we would head out to her place on Bolivar for a shot of sea air once I arrived. For Patty, the fresh air off the Gulf of Mexico cured all. I also knew that the unspoken agenda would include margaritas!

As it turned out, I slept most of the flight. Houston's Hobby Airport was easy to navigate. I headed right to baggage claim because I knew Patty would be waiting at the curb. It was the rule among us: no one need park the car and enter the airport for returning friends. It was a good rule.

I had to wait about five minutes for Patty. Finally, she pulled up and got out of her Jeep, and hugged me. It felt so good.

"I'll throw that suit in the back; get in. There's a bottle of cold soda with your name on it."

The diet Dr. Pepper hit the spot. No one drank Dr. Pepper in Buffalo. That was strictly either Coke or Pepsi. The story goes that the original formula for Coca-Cola had cocaine in it, small amounts but cocaine. The Southern Baptists were strictly against that, and Dr. Pepper took hold.

"Whew! I'm back. God, what a trip!"

"How is your mom doing?" Patty asked.

"She was a mess during the wake and funeral. But interestingly, once we buried Dad, she kind of snapped out of the daily crying. I'm sure she's not out of the grief, but it shifted.

"Then we met with Uncle Carmine, who, by the way, would 'consider it a favor' if I moved home and lived with my now widowed mother!"

"Oh, no! You're kidding!" Patty took her eyes off the road, and the car swerved. "Oh!"

"Sicilians don't kid about favors. No, not kidding. And, if I wasn't willing to say yes that very day, then he would have Aunt Zorah move in with Mom. Aunt Zorah put her foot down and refused to move in with Mom. Mom said she wanted to live on her own, and, somehow, for now anyway, Uncle Carmine is 'allowing' this.

"Mom really stood up for herself. That was a first for me to watch! And I think she's right. She went from her father's house to her husband's house. She wants to be her own person, and I want to give her the space to do that," I explained.

"And, if she needs you, you can revisit the possibility of moving back," Patty said.

This surprised me. "You think I should move back?"

"I didn't say that. I said you can revisit the idea."

"But why would I do that? I've made a home here. Two decades, right here! Oh, wait, have you been talking to Alice?"

She smiled and shot me a look, "Who me?"

"Oh, I get it now. You know about Stevie D."

"Alice may have mentioned him by name."

"Please, let's leave that conversation for the deck at your house, okay? I'm pooped. A swim sounds really good right now, along with a margarita."

We were on the Causeway Bridge between the mainland and the west side of Galveston Island. It was a busy waterway. The hurricane of 1900 had destroyed the docking of ocean-going fright, tankers, and the like in Galveston. While the Island was rebuilt, Houston deepened the channel and created a port for Houston. To this day, ships move up the channel, into the Bay, and onto Houston's port, while Galveston hosted cruise liners.

Once on the Island, Patty drove directly to the Texas Department of Transportation's free ferry between Galveston Island and Bolivar Peninsula. The ferry takes cars across the channel where Galveston Bay met the Gulf of Mexico. Once on the ferry, we exited the vehicle and climbed a ladder to a lip of a balcony with a bench. It was very private on that bench, and the breeze was great as well as the view. The ferry was way too noisy for a conversation, so we sat in silence and enjoyed the view and the ride. It's a thirty-minute ride. There were times when all of us -- me, Patty, Honey, and Alice -- would walk aboard the ferry, leaving the car behind, and just ride back and forth. Usually, times when words wouldn't make any difference, but the sea air might.

Back on a road, we headed into Crystal Beach; I asked Patty if we could stop at Coastal Groceries and Tackle. The market had a sandwich sign by the road that read, "LIVE BAIT." Inside I headed straight for the telephone and called Alice. I asked her to join Patty and me at the bay house and see if Honey could make it out also. With that done, I did some shopping for foods I had missed while in Buffalo: a box of grits, klatches for breakfast, and two quarts of their homemade gumbo. Patty insisted that she had a fridge full of food and drinks, there was no need to shop. I just looked forlornly at her, and she laughed.

At the check-out, I spotted a small ceramic creature that made me smile. It was an angel in a bikini and flip-flops and a sheer fabric cover-up that had slits on the back of the fabric so the wings could poke through. I bought it for Patty.

Patty's home was on the water's edge, down a sand-packed gravel road. She inherited the four-bedroom Bay house from her grandfather. Like all Bay houses, it stood on stilts, sixteen-foot-tall stilts. A deck encircled the house, and every room had a sliding door onto the deck. The house was weatherproofed for the hot summers and the cold winters. Under the house was a parking space for two cars, the laundry with lavatory and shower, plus storage. As much as we liked coming to the house in summer, we also loved being on the beach during autumn and winter. Something about being on the beach during the winter months was invigorating.

We hauled my luggage up the steps to the front entrance. I announced, "First thing, I'm going in for a swim."

"Knock yourself out. I'll make the Margaritas," Patty offered.

It wasn't long before I was out far enough in the Gulf that the house and the few people on the beach looked a foot tall, and there was no one around me. This was all on purpose, of course. I slipped off my swimsuit. I hooked it over my shoulder like a purse, and I swan horizontal to the shore. I just loved the feel of the water on my bare skin. The first time I swam naked, I was surprised how different it felt to be butt naked. And ever since when I swam on my own, like today, I made sure I spent half of the time nude.

I floated on my back awhile, looking at the clouds overhead. I breathed deeply, exchanging the airplane air in my lungs for good ole Gulf air. Then it hit. I straightened up, started treading water while I sobbed. The burst of tears, and gut-retching sobs shocked me. Was I still in grief? Okay, I told myself, of course. The crying stopped as spontaneously as it had started. I began swimming horizontal to the shore again.

I lose track of time while swimming in the Gulf. I've learned that if I get out far enough, there is no other sound but the waves, making and unmaking white caps as the water undulates toward the shoreline. The Gulf is transparent green. I'd think how I'd love to visit Hawaii and see blue water, but the Gulf was all I had, and it was good enough. When I first swam in the Gulf and got a mouth-full of water, I was surprised that it was salty! I guess I forgot that the Gulf was saltwater. The Great Lakes are freshwater, and until I attended college and made my first trip out to Galveston Island, I hadn't much thought about saltwater or freshwater swimming. The saltwater made my skin feel as if it was shrinking when I came out of the water. The outdoor shower under Patty's house got a lot of use.

When I saw Patty on her deck, looking out through binoculars, I knew I'd been in the Gulf long enough. Better put on my suit and swim in for that margarita.

I ambled back to the house, towel drying my hair. I took a shower before climbing the stairs. The house faced east. The deck would be comfortable. And as promised, sitting on a short side table next to the lounge chair was a salted rim Margarita and a platter of tamales.

"AH!!" I shouted in glee! "Tamales! Where did you get tamales? Oh, thank you, thank you, thank you!" I sat and dug right in. Each modest cornhusk package of cornmeal nested subtly spiced pork and steamed to perfection, so they won't fall apart when the husk is pulled off. Tamales are a winter seasonal festive food. No one makes tamales during the summertime.

"When I heard you were coming home, I ordered a batch from my housekeeper Maricela. She is willing to make them for special occasions, like you, coming home after burying your father. Maricela agreed that qualified for a batch of tamales," Patty explained.

With my mouth half full, I managed, "They are wonderful! Thank you."

"You want to start talking about home now?" When Patty slid into the Adirondack's chair, her feet stuck out like a kid in an adult chair. It was cute.

I sipped my drink, "Do you mind if we wait until Honey and Alice arrive? Then I only tell the story once. Then I can get all y'all's opinions at once. It's Friday night! We can stay up late, right?"

I ended up dozing off. I had no idea how long I slept, but Alice and Honey woke me clamoring up the stairs for their weekend stay.

"Hey, Buffalo Gal! Won't you come out tonight, come out tonight, come out tonight! Buffalo Gal, won't you come out tonight And dance by the light of the moon!" Honey leaned over and kissed my forehead.

"Don't quit your day job!" I teased.

"How are you doing, darlin'?" she asked, towering over me.

"A swim, margaritas, and tamales; I'm doing SOOO much better!" I reported.

Honey and Alice settled into chairs or on full-body lounges; they kicked off their shoes and whipped off their bras from under their blouses. Patty pushed a small cart onto the deck with fresh margaritas, the shaker for refills, and bowls with handles filled with hot gumbo and rice. There was a place of hot cornbread, and butter on the side. It was a perfect deck meal.

"Okay, shoot," Honey opened, after sipping her drink and a mouth full of gumbo.

"Is that my cue to start talking?" I asked, while devouring a cornbread square.

"Skip the jokes, just start talking," Patty directed, "I'm dying here waiting!"

"Where do I start?"

"How about with Stevie D?" Alice offered.

"No," Honey said, "Tell us how your mom got through the funeral; I know you always worried about that day coming."

That seemed as good a place as any. I started with getting into Buffalo after midnight the day Dad died.

"All during all this time, Stevie D was always right by your side. And, if I understand you correctly, the only time he wasn't with you was while you slept," Patty summarized.

"Yup. Pretty much," I answered.

The gumbo was as good as the tamales. I asked Alice about our practice, my clients. Honey and Alice said all went well. They also mentioned that Frank, our senior partner, was acting more depressed than before, and Alice was concerned. Honey reported that her daughter Dawn arrived home with a new beau in tow. Honey thought this guy might be "the one" for Dawn.

I left the deck for a cover-up, headed for my luggage in one of the bedrooms. While I rifled through the clothing, I felt a warm fury creature rubbing my leg. Moon! I scooped her up, sat on the bed and we gave each other a proper lovey-dovey hello! Then, I remembered the little ceramic angle I bought for Patty. Holding Moon under one arm, and the ceramic angel in a bag in the other hand, I returned to the deck. I gave Patty the gift and settled into my chair with Moon on my lap.

"AH! I love her! I'm naming her Myrna Loy," she said spontaneously, "I'm going to place her on the kitchen shelf next to the window and sink. I love Myrna Loy, and this gal's lips are puckered like I remember Myrna Loy doing. Thank you, Darlin'!" She set the tchotchkes on the cart.

The breeze off the Gulf felt cool. We headed inside where Patty started a low fire in the living area fireplace, just enough to take the chill off the house. I mused to myself: how Texan of her! The house cools from the air conditioning running all day, now needing a fire to warm it up again!

Honey initiated resuming the conversation, "When did you know that Stevie D had feelings for you?"

"It was a day after we buried Dad. Uncle Renato invited Mom and me out on his boat. It was wonderful to be doing something so hugely different than heading to a funeral home every day and shaking hands with people you don't know.

"I've got to laugh when I think about Uncle Renato trying to get around to telling me that Stevie D wanted to see more of me, romantically. Uncle Renato was so uncomfortable. He even confessed that! Talking about love! The Mechanic in the Family," It was amusing to me remembering this.

"The 'Mechanic?' What do you mean?" Alice asked.

- 90 -

"The Family Business. See, some of the men have nicknames related to the jobs they hold, and...," I stopped, knowing I probably didn't have any more of an explanation.

"You mean that's for real? I thought that was only in the movies!" Alice said.

"Where do you think the movies got it from?" Honey poked.

"What does 'The Mechanic' do?" Alice asked.

I shrugged, "Fixes things."

My friends exchanged looks. Then they broke out laughing!

Patty explained, "Now we feel like we're in a mobster movie!"

"Believe me, it's not funny. For instance, have any of you thought about my license to work as a psychologist? No criminal activity, anyone think about that?"

They sobered up all at once.

"No," Honey was the first to admit. "No, I hadn't thought about that. Whew! You're right; this isn't an easy question."

"As a kid, living at home, I never knew exactly what my dad did other than he worked for Uncle Carmine in the Family Business. Mom and Dad didn't talk about it in front of me, ever. And now, Stevie D, still very much in the Family Business; are you getting the picture now?"

There was a pause while Patty refilled the margarita glasses and asked, "What does the 'D' stand for?"

"The 'D,'" I was confused a moment.

She stood and looked at me incredulously, "Yes, the 'D,' Stevie D."

Now I burst out laughing! I remembered back a few years at Aunt Zorah's birthday party when Rocco brought up Stevie D for the first time, and I asked him about the 'D' in Stevie D's name. All Rocco said, I remembered, was that he didn't want to know.

"I don't know!" I confessed.

Now we were all laughing, and if not for the arms of the chairs, we would have been on the floor.

"'Devil,'" offered Alice.

"No, no, has to be something he does for the family; how about 'Destroy?'" Patty offered.

"No, it must be something like Uncle Renato being 'The Mechanic' who 'fixes' things; something like that," Honey directed. "I got it! 'Damage!'"

Patty said, "I like that! It isn't destroying anything but inflicting damage, yeah, that fits!"

"It's the margarita talking now!" I protested, plus I was exhausted. "I'm going to bed!"

"Just relax a minute. Let's drink up, and we'll all go to bed," Patty said.

It was quiet. We all watched the gas flame of the fire for a minute. It was Alice who broke the silence, "I love it here; at night, you can hear the Gulf."

"Yes. No need for a sleeping pill," Patty added.

"I had a rough week," Honey offered. "I'm happy to get away from the city. It is so damned hot in Houston. I don't know how they live in New York City among all those tall skyscrapers. Houston doesn't have as many, yet you can literally feel the heat rising off the pavement when you walk on the street! I hate it."

"Well, one nice thing about Buffalo, after the sun sets, the night cools down, and there is a breeze off Lake Erie, a cool breeze, like here, the breeze off the Gulf is always cooling."

"That would be something you'd gain, Maggie; summertime that was bearable," Patty said.

"Patty, you're forgetting winter can be a bitch!"

One last belly-laugh among us as we all got up and headed to the bedrooms. My room was on the northeast side of the house. The opened sliding door allowed for the Gulf breeze to waft through the bedroom. Everyone kept their bedroom doors open when it was just the four of us: allowed for a nice cross breeze.

I woke early, Moon curled at my side. I took advantage and crept out of the house wearing my swimsuit, carrying a towel and flip-flops. Didn't even stop for a bottle of soda from the fridge, didn't want to wake anyone. It was eight a.m..

Once at the base of the steps, I put on my flip-flops and headed for the beach. I was looking forward to a swim before breakfast. I knew that later that morning, we would all most likely swim. On the beach, people swam before eleven a.m.. By high noon, all bets were off. The sand was so hot you could feel the heat through your shoes. Even under a beach umbrella, it was sweltering. It didn't take long to learn that the beach was off limit from around eleven until three.

When I got to the water's edge, there was another towel thrown down. I tossed mine next to it. I looked out to sea and just barely saw someone bobbing on an inflated raft. It must be Patty, I thought.

I swam out, and sure enough, Patty was laid back on the raft with a sun visor on her head.

"Good morning! You're up early. Did you sleep okay?"

I swam around her, "I slept beautifully. Getting in an early swim, couldn't pass that up."

"And don't be shy; I'll hold your suit for you if you want to skinny dip!"

I nudged her float, making her think I would dump her into the Gulf, "How do you know about that?"

"Binoculars! It's amazing what one can see on zoom with binoculars!"

Laughing, I stripped and hung the suit over my shoulder as usual.

"You don't trust me," Patty whined.

"That's right!" I laughed and began my horizontal swim.

By nine a.m., we were all around the kitchen table drinking freshly brewed coffee and enjoying the klatches. Then, as I predicted, we all headed for the sea and a late morning swim. There would be no more swimming until after the undeniable heat of the noon sun.

Lounging in the living room with cold drinks in our hands, Alice opened the conversation, asking, "Patty said your Uncle Carmine wants you to move back home. Are you...?"

"Right now, I say no. . . ."

"But you're thinking about it," Alice said.

I was defensive, "Come on, Alice, all we've built up, our practice, hell, and our lives together! I'm not going to pack up and go. Besides, I really want to give my mom the opportunity to live independently and have her own life and voice! Living on her own is something really new for her."

"What about Stevie D?" Honey asked.

I threw my head back and moaned. "I don't know! Besides, he saw me at my worst. I'm sure all this 'may I keep you company' crap is the damsel in distress knee jerk reaction. He doesn't know me in my own setting, here, with all y'all. I'm a different person here than when I'm home. in Buffalo."

"I wish I didn't understand that" Alice said. We all laughed.

"Yup, home is where no one sees you past the age of whenever you left," Patty offered, "so in my case, I left home at eighteen. When I'm among my siblings and cousins, I'm Patty-the-eighteen-year-old-hippie."

"And what's the difference now?" Honey cracked.

Patty threw a pillow at Honey.

"Thank you," I said. "And the last time I talked with Stevie D, I told him he wasn't allowed to visit me until after Labor Day. By then, Stevie D will be a fast-fading memory for me, and hopefully, he too will see that he was just reacting to his male ego need to rescue."

My friends exchanged looks.

"Okay, I saw that! What gives? Come on, tell me," I pressured.

Honey spoke up, "Maggie, let me theorize for a moment: What if your mom just wants you to be in the same city with her after all these years?"

"You trying to get rid of me?" I joked.

"Just wanted you to keep an open mind; to tell you the truth, I'd love for

Dawn to live closer to me. I know all the reasons why young people must move away. Believe me, half my counseling at the university is about just that. Yet once kids are older and the rebellion has died out, adult kids and parents can have a whole new relationship and genuinely enjoy each other. But, well, as a mom . . . let me just say I can see your mom's side," Honey said.

There was silence.

"My cousins gave me the same advice, too; they said that I just needed to let Uncle Carmine and Uncle Renato know that I'd keep an open mind about moving back. So that's what I plan to do; Mom's success on her own or not will be a factor that influences me."

"Okay. I have one burning question," Alice said.

"Go ahead," I encouraged.

"Well, is Stevie D . . . what did Sonny's wife call him? An Italian stallion?"

It took me, Honey, and Patty a minute to pick up on the reference to The Godfather movie. When it clicked, I threw a pillow at Alice, "I haven't slept with him yet!" I yelled through the laughter.

"AGGH! She said 'yet'!" Patty was pointing her finger at me.

Honey chimed in, "Freudian slip!! And you know what that means!"

"Oh, come on!" I pleaded.

"Just what I thought," Alice accused.

"Y'all! Stop this! I have absolutely no interest in Stevie D on any level!"

My friends exchanged looks and burst out in another round of laughter, and then Patty said, "She protests too much!"

Echo of my mom's comment.

Our fun was interrupted by a resounding knocking on the front sliding door. Patty hurried to see who was calling on us.

Once Patty saw the person on the deck, she smiled and slid the door open, "Drake! What brings you here? I've not ordered anything?"

It was the teen who worked at Coastal Groceries. Patty had him step into the house, into the cool climate. "Ms. Patty, there was an urgent phone call for," he looked down at the note, "Dr. Blake and the answering service said she was staying here, and she needs to call this number because the man insisted it was important."

"Let me see that, Drake. Have a seat. Want a Dr. Pepper?"

"Yes, Ma'am."

Patty took the note, handed the boy the soda, and then read the message. She walked over to me and gave me the piece of paper. I started reading and almost fell off my chair. Instead, I stood up in disbelief, "Oh no! What the hell?"

Honey and Alice gestured and asked, "What?"

"I can't believe this! The nerve of him! No, wait, not just him, the family! It's the family!"

Honey and Alice's facial expression begged Patty to enlighten them.

Patty got a couple of dollar bills out of her purse and handed them to Drake, "Thanks, darlin'," and showed him out the door. Returning, she flopped in a chair and said, "Cousin Rocco is in Houston and looking for her."

"What?" Alice and Honey sat straight up in delight.

"You heard me," Patty said, looking like the Cheshire cat herself.

I was pacing; I was so angry.

"Oh! This is the gay cousin of the first favor," Alice said.

"Yes. The nerve!"

"Well, take my car, drive up to Coastal and invite him down. The more, the merrier!" Patty goaded.

I stopped cold. I looked at her as if she had just sprouted a second head. "Are you crazy? He followed me! I'm livid!"

Honey said, "You don't know that. Maybe something happened."

That made me turn on my heels; grabbed my purse, "Keys! Keys!" I demanded from Patty. I flew out the door and down the steps, and up gravel road kicking up sand behind the car.

I got to Coastal Groceries in record time. The answering service gave me the number of the Marriott Hotel.

"Hello?"

"Rocco? What the hell are you doing in Houston?"

"Hi, Cuz! How you doin'? Where are you?" he casually asked.

"Again, what the hell are you doing in Houston?"

"Okay, looking for Aunt Zorah, she ran away from home, if you can believe that."

"What?" I was sure I didn't hear him right.

"Aunt Zorah. After you left, Dad and Zorah had a showdown over her moving in with your mom. I wish you could have been there watching the two of them go at it! That Zorah, she can hold her own, and ever since her birthday, she has her own ideas, like moving in with Ethel.

"You know, I always heard stories about Zorah, from when she worked for The Family when she was younger. What a looker she was, could wrap any guy around her little finger, then kick him to the curb. It never seemed to faze her I was told. No wonder she never married; guys feared her," he drooled on.

"As much as I love family history, I'm in no way convinced this is really why you're in Houston," I challenged.

"Mags, I flew down, and Aunt Zorah and Ethel are driving. If they make good time, they will be here on Monday. My dad told me I must bring her home. Now, tell me, how am I supposed to do that? Hey, where are you? Can I come over?"

"I'm on Bolivar; at Patty's."

"Galveston?"

"Across the Bay from Galveston, Bolivar Peninsula; have you rented a car?"

"Yes, give me the directions. How long will it take me to get there?"

When I hung up the phone, I was relieved yet pissed off. My idea of being home was getting away from my family and getting a perspective on all that happened. I thought I would be free of them when I told Stevie D he couldn't visit until Labor Day. Little did I figure anything else like this would crop up.

"Well?" was the question asked of me when I re-entered Patty's house.

I quickly explained. "Stop laughing!"

"Come on; your eighty-year-old aunt ran away from home with her friend because her brother wanted her to move in with your mother?" Honey recounted.

"You've got to admit, Maggie, this is the fodder for a good sitcom!" Alice said.

"To tell you the truth, I think my Aunt Zorah and Ethel are a lot more than 'friends,'" I said.

"Lovers, you mean lovers, right?" Alice said.

"Alright!" from Patty. "So, what do we make for supper now that we have company coming?"

"I need a swim," I said as I left the room, grabbing a towel from the deck and down the steps towards the sea.

I tipped toed through the hot sand to the Gulf's edge. Once out far enough in the water, I started to cry. The real emotions of the previous weeks came rushing back. The psychologist in me knew that meant I hadn't processed any grief or anything else. It was as if I was still in shock, but now, with the tears, that veneer was washing off. I thought about what Rocco said: Aunt Zorah and Ethel running away from home. I started to laugh. Oh god, the drama of a Sicilian family! That's what I had missed since moving away. I surmised that all the talk about my mom being on her own and exploring a life for herself had spurred this for Zorah. My understanding of Zorah's life was she had always lived at home. She worked in the Family Business; when her parents became elderly and fragile, she cared for them. After both died, her older brother, Carmine, and his wife, Lena, moved into the family home. Meanwhile, when the grandbabies started, Aunt Zorah went where needed; cared for mother and baby until a routine was established, and the mom felt okay to take it from there. That was for all the cousins!

As far back as I could remember, Ethel was a part of my memories. I heard that Zorah and Ethel met while both were working downtown during the nineteen forties. When I was a teenager, Zorah and Ethel took vacation together. I now wondered what Zorah told Mom about the nature of their relationship. As I rehashed what I did know, it now seemed to me that Mom had known about Aunt Zorah and Ethel for a long, long time.

Oh, what the hell! Dad is dead, and the Universe has shifted.

I became aware that my skin was hot in the water; time to swim back.

No one spoke to me once back in the house. Patty was in the kitchen, dicing something. Alice was curled on the sofa with a book, and Honey was nowhere to be seen. I took a Dr. Pepper from the fridge.

"I'm sorry," I said to Patty.

"For what, Darlin'?" She walked to me and gave me a hug. "Darlin', has it occurred to you that the dynamic in your family has changed? And now you are part of that dynamic, no matter what you might have thought when you returned home?"

I sat at the kitchen table, "You took the words right out of my mouth." And the tears started again.

"Good. Cry. That means you are finally feeling something," she said as she grabbed a whole watermelon and began slicing it.

I headed for my bedroom, grabbing a Vanity Fair Magazine on the way. Moon joined me. I'd just hide out until Rocco arrived. Patty woke me about an hour later because Rocco was in the kitchen dicing onions for the sauce.

"You're kidding, right?"

"No. When he arrived, the first thing Rocco asked was to allow him to make a kettle of sauce for the weekend because there were so many ways to have sauce. Who knew? Why argue!"

Sure enough, with a kitchen towel tucked in the waistband of his Bermuda shorts, there he was at the sink slicing and dicing.

"Hey! Cuz!" He hugged me. "Thanks for having me here. I wasn't looking forward to the weekend in the hotel."

"Where's Drew?"

"He had to work, and Dad insisted I leave immediately. Crazy, huh?"

"Rocco, I'll be honest with you, the last thing I expected when I arrived home was the family following me. I need time on my own, Rocco! I need distance from all the . . . drama. Can you understand that?" Tears were rolling down my cheeks without the heaving or catch in my throat; I felt terrible immediately for having said all that.

He just looked at me for a long minute. The guilt was building in me.

"Mags, I get it; I just didn't want to be alone this weekend. I promise, no family conversation, none, nil. But, to tell you the truth, I can use the break too."

I rushed into his arms, hugging him. "Agreed! No family talks at all!"

Just then, Alice walked into the kitchen, "What smells so good?"

"Meatballs frying; hi, I'm Rocco," he extended his hand.

"Alice, Maggie's partner at work, are you really making spaghetti sauce?"

"Yes. I hope that's okay?"

"You bet! I love Italian food!"

"Great! Oh, by the way, Mags, Carlo, Cary, and Sal will be here Monday. Well, not here, they'll be checking into the hotel where I'm at . . . Mags, don't look at me like that! It wasn't my idea! Honest! They have business at the Port of Houston, and it just happened to coincide with Aunt Zorah running away! No one planned it! Really! Mags, you've got to believe me!"

I burst into tears, took off to my room, slamming the door like a teenager who just broke up with her boyfriend. While I buried my head in a pillow, Patty entered the room with Moon. They sat quietly on the foot of the bed.

"Darlin', what's the worst thing that could happen with your cousins here, in Houston?" she gently asked.

I rolled over to face her. "I lose my privacy! My seclusion! My time for me! I didn't have a minute to myself for the last ten days. A lot happened during that time! What about me?"

Patty moved next to me. "Darlin', they have to leave at some point. Just hang in there for another week."

I recognized it as an attempt to comfort me. Little did she understand how Sicilian families operate. Drying my eyes and blowing my nose, I nodded in agreement. Maybe having my cousins here was just what the doctor ordered: allow my three best friends to step out of their WASP frame of reference!

After a fantastic meal of spaghetti and meatballs, Rocco had charmed his entire audience of women, me included. I never realized just how funny he was. He and Alice made plans to hit the roadside markets early Sunday morning. Alice said she knew a few shrimp boats near Kemah where you could buy fish and shrimp right at the dock. Rocco was chomping at the bit for the experience. He held to his promise: no Family conversation.

Alice gave up her room and bunked with me.

"He's really nice," she noted.

"He's had a hard life, being gay in a Sicilian family and HIV positive," I said.

"What about his partner, Drew?"

I paused, "To tell you the truth, I have no idea about whether or not Drew is positive. It never comes up in a conversation, that's for sure. But Rocco has really taken care of himself all these years. When HIV was first diagnosed, no one knew that people could live positive for years; so many people died right off the bat. Remember the quilts?"

"Yes! Now that you bring it up. Never hear about them anymore," Alice reflected.

"Amazing, isn't it? Wait until Cary, Carlo, and Sal get here. When my cousins get together, that's another story!" I warned.

"You ready for the lights out?" she asked.

"Yes." I climbed into the bed next to her. "Here Moon, 'kiss kiss kiss,'" my mommy noise for Moon was an audible kiss. In a heartbeat, Moon was on the bed, circling the space between Alice and me.

With the lights out, "Now, tell me who, exactly, are Cary, Carlo, and Sal. First and foremost, are they married?"

I gave her a hard nudge, "Cary is married. Carlo and Sal are still single, and if I say so myself, they are handsome men."

"Ah, Sicilian and not married; are they gay also?"

I shoved her again, "NO! It isn't unusual for Sicilian guys to marry right out of high school or later, in their late thirties. No one seems to mind about the guys. Now with the girls, the expectation is she needs to marry right out of high school. I was lucky my Irish dad wanted to see me go to college. Mom couldn't fight him about that."

She shoved me back, "Enough about you! Tell me about Carlo and Sal. Would I like either of them?"

"AH! I see what you're after! An Italian stallion!"

And with that, a pillow fight broke out, screaming and all!

We abruptly stopped when the overhead light flipped on. Patty. "Ladies!"

We froze, just as if we were twelve years old.

"Why wasn't I invited to this party?" She climbed on the foot of the bed. Out of her pocket she pulled a bottle of bourbon. Before Alice or I could say anything, in waltzed Honey with four short, stubby glasses, each with an ice cube. She closed the door, but not before Moon made an unapproving sound and walked out of the room.

Once we each had a sip of the sweet nectar, Honey said, "Maggie, Monday, I'll free up my schedule. Then I'm back here for the week with you."

"With me? What are you talking about? I'm going back with you. I'll be back to work, the latest Wednesday," I countered.

Patty started, "Maggie darlin', Honey and I been talkin', and we think it best for you to stay here . . ."

Alice interrupted, "Maggie, you take off until after the July 4th holiday. You've been saying you need the time for yourself."

I slugged back the bourbon and grabbed the bottle from Patty, pouring myself another. "Yes, without my cousins, time for myself!"

"Darlin', how often have you started to cry just today and stopped yourself?" Patty asked.

I sipped, long. "But my cousins will be in town. At least at the office, they can't get to me," I reasoned.

"Exactly why I want you here, darlin'. When they visit here, well, it's neutral territory, not your place, not their hotel rooms, but a house belonging to a woman who is old enough to be their auntie. It's an advantage for you, darlin', don't you see that?" Patty was persuasive.

"I wish I could take the week off," Alice lamented.

"You've got to hold down the fort with Frank," Honey directed.

"I know, but I looked at the appointment book before I left Friday, and it's light next week. . . . Maybe I can move some Friday appointments to Thursday and be back here Thursday evening. Is that okay? I hate to miss something," Alice said.

"Maggie, what's wrong?" Honey was the first to notice.

I slid my glass onto the bedside table then rolled over and started sobbing.

"Maggie, you're entitled to your grief. Holding off causes more trouble than it's worth. We're all worried about you, Mag. Your cousins showing up gave us, at least gave Patty and me, a heads up. Things are serious; your Uncle Carmine is a man to be reckoned with. We're beginning to understand," Honey concluded.

Sunday night was a mass exodus: Rocco, Alice, and Honey packed up and headed into the city. I was finally alone with Patty. The sunset around nine in the evening. Patty and I watched from blow-up rafts on the Gulf as the sunset behind the house, to the west. I was grateful that Patty didn't need any conversation.

Honey was back as promised. We three settled around the kitchen table for supper. Patty made salads and tuna sandwiches. Cold beer hit the spot. Moon, smelling tuna was ever present. Patty put the empty cans on the floor for Moon to lick.

"You didn't leave Frank and Alice swamped, did you?" was my first question.

"No; surprisingly, the appointment schedule was light. I think people are beginning to travel for summer vacation. Get out of Houston, amazing how the city holds heat. I'm almost inclined to move out of Houston myself during the summers," and under her breath, but loud enough for us to hear, "if Dawn would only ask."

"Where is Dawn now?" I asked.

"Asheville, North Carolina. She has a teaching position at a small, private high school. She teaches drama. And, somehow, she became a member of the Director's Guild of America! Amazing, isn't it?" Honey boasted. "She created her own theater group, Dawn of Thespians. It's an entire theater group, and she produces, directs, and engages high school kids as well. They've won awards.

"Remember, when you were in grad school, Maggie, when we'd all get into the car and drive out to Austin for Dawn's productions? I swear I don't know where she gets her talent; all I know is that I'm immensely proud of her!"

"You need to let us know when we all can drive up to Asheville and see something. What a great trip that would be," Patty offered.

"How's Raine," I asked Patty.

"On baby number three, bless her heart." Patty swigged her beer.

What regular people didn't know about the South is when someone says, "bless (her/his) heart," it is closer to a northerner saying, "Poor kid," or "What a doofus."

"Wow. When did she get married?" I asked. It seemed like the logical next question.

Patty was up getting cold beers from the fridge, "Who said anything about being married?"

I had to smile. It was hard to tell if that made any difference to Patty, considering her hippie roots.

"Where is Gideon now? And Kingsley?" I moved on.

She looked at her watch as a joke, "Gideon right now is packing up his apartment in San Antonio for his move to Ann Arbor, Michigan. I can't imagine a boy born and reared in Texas moving to Michigan for the next three years of his life! But that's the match for internship; starts July 1: University of Michigan Ann Arbor."

I started to laugh, "It's not so bad, Patty! Look at me! I was raised in Buffalo and now live in Texas; he's doing the opposite."

"Darlin', it's easier to move from a cold climate to a warm climate. Well, time will tell," Patty concluded.

"Aren't you thrilled to have a son that's a doctor?" I asked.

She exchanged looks with Honey.

"What?" I pressed.

"Darlin', do you think I'd be thrilled if I were a vegetarian all my life and one of my children became a butcher?"

I choked on my beer, "What?"

"Maggie, I understand how Patty feels. She raised her kids with spiritualism, mindfulness meditation, herbal medicine, mind/body wholeness, and healing before it became vogue. A shaman would have been welcomed, but a western medicine doctor?" Honey explained.

"You do see my reservations now, don't you?" Patty asked.

"Well, Honey and I are psychotherapists, and you don't seem to mind that," I said.

"And you both studied Dr. Carl Jung, dreams, spiritual roots to physical problems, and you guide people's minds! That's different!"

"I guess so," I wasn't sure.

"Now, Kingsley! He's in Oaxaca, Mexico learning how to fire clay in the Aztec tradition of above-the-ground firing! That's more like it, as far as I'm concerned," Patty declared.

"Really? I mean how amazingly interesting! . . . Firing above the ground and all," I commented.

"I should have realized the difference in the boys; Kingsley and Raine always at my side, attempting any of the arts and crafts I did, while Gideon had his nose in books, not comic books, the classics. At the time I thought, 'great!' he's an intellectual. Now I wish I had thrown in a lot of Dr. Seuss!"

Honey reached across the table and touched Patty's hand, "Sweetie, there is absolutely no shame in having a medical doctor in the family . . . not even your family!"

"I did my best at his graduation. I'm so happy that Raine and Kingsley were there, too, so they could shout and applaud. I cried. But Gideon will never know that my tears were about my disappointment!" She got up and started clearing the table, "Ice cream, anyone?"

Honey was laughing, "Patty Odin! If I didn't know you so well, I'd believe that last statement you made, but I know how proud of Gideon you truly are!" She grabbed some dishes as well.

"Have you got chocolate ice cream?" It was time to change the subject.

Later, when we settled on the deck, the topic did come up about how I was doing.

"Haven't cried all day. I do feel better without Rocco around, that's for sure," I said.

"But you do know it's okay to cry, and crying is a relief," Patty offered.

"I'm ready to wash the day off. Who's up for a swim?" Honey announced.

Less than twenty minutes later, we were all in the Gulf. It was the best part of the day for me, just as good as my early morning swim. It felt cooling on my naked body, and I relished the silence. No thoughts, no questions, no chatter. I hoped that Honey and Patty knew the next couple of days I wished for silence before all hell broke loose.

Patty arrived back from Coastal Groceries early afternoon Wednesday. She was quiet.

"What's up?" Honey asked.

"Nothing."

Honey and I helped unpack the groceries, and I came across a scrap of paper that a message was scrawled on saying something like, "the guys and the aunts, if that's okay, Alice." I stood still reading it when Honey read over my shoulder. Finally, she took the piece of paper out of my hand and approached Patty.

""The guys and the aunts, if that's okay, Alice,' Let me guess, you called Alice back," Honey said, reminding me of cross-examination by an attorney.

Patty was cleaning lettuce. "As a matter of fact, yes, I did call Alice back."

Now I was standing on the other side of the sink, Patty between Honey, and me, "And you said . . . what?"

"That it was fine and bring their swimsuits and . . ."

I reached across Patty turning off the water. My eye caught the ceramic angel in the bikini, "Myrna, did you hear Patty say, 'that was fine,' or are my ears playing tricks?"

"Myrna has nothing to do with it!" Patty joked.

"Patty, what were you thinking? The girl needs rest and support, not more stress!" Honey said.

Patty turned around, drying her hands on a towel, "In my defense, who wants a beer," she grabbed three from the fridge, "It's better to keep your enemies closer, right?"

I started to laugh.

"She's hysterical," Patty was alarmed, "Honey, you're a doctor, do something!"

"Cut it out!" Honey took a swipe at Patty's arm with a towel, "Let's sit and re-group, make a plan. Plan our defense!"

"Look, it's better having them all here, get a big picture. From what you said, there are differing points of view among them about you moving back, your mom on her own, and who knows what. Until we ask or at least are open to hearing what they have to say, we'll never know!" Patty explained.

Honey and I exchanged looks. We nodded in agreement.

"Surprisingly, that's not a bad plan," Honey admitted.

"But we also have to plan the sleeping arrangements. Maggie, how about the aunts in your room? Honey will share with Alice. Maggie, you with me. The guys can fight over the fourth bedroom, and then there are the pull-out beds of the living area sofas. That covers it. Sound okay?" Patty asked.

"Make sure you let the guys know that there is a lavatory and shower downstairs under the house. They can use that," I directed.

"Perfect," Honey agreed.

"What about food?" Patty asked.

"You really don't know about Sicilian people, do you?" I stated. "You won't have to worry about food. I'll bet you this house that my Aunt Zorah, and Ethel and the guys will arrive 'bearing gifts' of the magnitude you have never experienced."

"Sounds scary," Patty commented.

"If they were Greek, but they're not, they're Sicilian," Honey said.

"To my Family!" I said, sarcastically raising my beer bottle towards the middle of the table.

Honey and Patty did likewise, "To Family!"

I just had to laugh! The quiet of the three days alone with Honey and Patty had worked its healing magic. Today the fact that half a dozen of my closest relatives would crash my best friend's Bay house was no longer a horror, just a headache. This should be interesting.

Thursday morning, we skipped our swim before breakfast. We used the time to change sheets, put out towels, and unfold the sofa beds to see whether the previous guests left the sheets on. They had. We made those beds as well. In the lavatory under the house, we stocked towels, soap, shampoo, and toilet paper. Patty made room in the fridge for the promise of food. Honey took three large Igloo coolers to Coastal Groceries for ice. One cooler would be for "clean ice" to put in drinks; the other two for packing drinks.

By lunchtime, we grabbed our suits for a quick swim before it was heat prohibited. It was that or a shower, and why shower when the Gulf is at your doorstep? Settling into lunch of leftovers from the previous days, we agreed that we felt the house was as ready as possible.

"Maggie, I want to set down some strategies for us, the three of us, so you know we're here for you," Honey offered. "All you have to do is come to one of us. If you're feeling overwhelmed by the conversation, say something, like 'meet me in the loo.'"

"In the 'loo?' How crazy is that!" Patty complained. "Just touch my shoulder and say, 'Elvis just went home.'"

I started to laugh, "That's from Men in Black! Tommy Lee Jones tells Will Smith that Elvis didn't die, he . . ."

Together Patty and I said, "'He just went home.'"

"I'll use that!" I declared.

"Oh God, how did I get mixed up with these two?" Honey asked the Universe.

Patty replied, "We know you love us. But seriously, Maggie, I'm concerned this might be too stressful with your aunts and all. Be open; the Universe knows what She's doing. Walk into this next phase with the intention of willingness to go the distance, and sometimes, you don't have to."

"And sometimes you do," Honey added.

Patty threw a kitchen towel at her.

My heart ached with love for my friends.

After lunch, I was resting in Patty's bedroom with a magazine. Moon sitting straight up with ears piqued, was the first hint that the guests were arriving. Then I heard the cars, then Sicilian voices under the house. They had arrived. I sat on the side of the bed, took a deep breath, and told myself that it would be okay; this was my territory.

When I got on the deck, Cary and Rocco were admiring the enormous outdoor grill Patty had stashed under the house. Sal and Carlo were unloading suitcases while Aunt Zorah and Ethel were surveying the view of the Gulf. Patty was already among them, giving directions.

"Are you ready for this," Honey asked. She had joined me on the deck.

"As long as all y'all stick to me like white on rice," I replied.

"Spoken like a true southern lady!"

I bounced down the steps. Hugged and kissed my aunts (Ethel was as much my aunt as Zorah, after all these years.) One by one, Sal, Cary, Carlo, and Rocco kissed me as they passed headed for the steps with bags of groceries and lugging suitcases.

"Whose suitcases?" I asked.

"The aunts," Sal answered, "looks like they're moving in, right?"

Boy, that was the truth.

About an hour later, all rooms were assigned, and Sal got the last of the bedrooms. The guys were planning on grilling Italian sausages, working out the details with Patty.

I asked Aunt Zorah and Ethel if they wanted to swim before supper? They said yes! I was a little surprised. I can't remember ever seeing them in a swimsuit, ever, even with family outings at Crystal Beach in Canada. We all changed, except Patty. She seemed to be drawn in by the testosterone of the cousins. So far, all was relaxed.

When we returned to the Bay house, I spotted Alice's car. Once inside, Patty was setting the table for supper and Alice was helping all the while talking with Carlo, and Sal.

"There you are!" I hugged her from behind.

"I hope you didn't mind," she offered. I faked strangling her; we laughed; I knew that she knew exactly what I meant.

"Of course not!" Patty answered.

By the time the sun was setting (and the aunts were surprised it wasn't setting over the water like every movie they had ever seen), we were all quiet. The air on the deck was wonderful, with just enough breeze. Patty made perfect sangria. I got the sense that my family was only tired. No one wanted or needed a conversation, and, best of all, no one pretended they did.

Around midnight, I woke from the sound of a knock at the bedroom door. Up on one elbow I called out to come on in.

Alice and Honey, dragging blankets with them, entered. This woke Patty.

"What' going on?" Patty asked,

Honey answered, "We just wanted to talk, now that everybody is here!"

"You mean now that my family is here, right?" I corrected Honey.

"Yes, it's exciting, don't you think?" Honey asked

"Depends on whose shoes you're standing in," I answered.

"How are you doing, Maggie? I'm sorry for springing them on you, but Rocco called the office and asked me for direction to Bolivar! I didn't think, I just gave them to him. That's why I telephoned Coastal Groceries, to give all y'all a heads up," Alice explained.

We three talked and talked, in the dark, like schoolgirls at a sleepover.

Alice said she was happy I wasn't angry with her about sending the cousins and aunts out to Patty's house. That event felt like so long ago.

Rain pelting the house woke me Friday morning. Oh no! When it rained, it usually rained all day. The entire day inside this Bay house with my relatives. I flopped over on my side, then realized I was alone in the bed. No Patty. I lay quietly for a few minutes. I did hear muted voices. As I walked through the living area, the three guys were still sleeping. It looked like a dorm room. In the kitchen, Aunt Zorah was making French toast, and the coffee aroma beckoned. I grabbed a cup and joined the ladies at the table.

"Did you sleep okay?" I asked Ethel.

"Oh, my dear! The air is exceptional! Must be the sea salt," she replied.

Patty placed the first plate of French toast before us. Mangia! Zorah said as she joined us.

After a few mouthfuls, Honey poked the elephant in the room, "So, tell me, ladies, what brought you to Houston? I mean, driving all that way! "

Ethel and Zorah exchanged looks. It was Ethel who spoke, "We ran away."

It was as if someone punched the "pause" button. Patty and Honey exchanged looks, then tried to get me to say something, but I filled my mouth with fried bread and maple syrup, shrugging my shoulder. This forced Honey to follow up.

"Ran away? You're joking, right?"

Aunt Zorah extended her pointed index finger in Honey's direction, "No-a joking! I run away! You know my brother Carmine!" Ethel was patting Zorah's forearm.

"There was a . . ."

"Fight, a-bigga fight . . ."

"Confrontation . . . between Zorah and her brother; Maggie, tell your friends what Carmine's expectations are of us . . . I mean of Zorah," Ethel said.

Oh no, I was being dragged into it. I stated very matter-of-factly, "Uncle Carmine thinks Aunt Zorah should move in with my mom since I'm not moving home. Aunt Zorah told him that she has had enough of caring for everyone else and said no, she wouldn't move in with Mom. I can only guess that after I left, just this past Friday, Uncle Carmine pushed too much."

"Dear, that's an understatement," Ethel replied. "Maggie, you most likely weren't even off the ground in the plane when Carmine insisted Zorah move in with Bella! We tried to reason with him; we reminded him that the agreement was Bella would live on her own, see how she does. We didn't expect his total disregard for all of us," she paused and pointed to me, Zorah and herself, "that Sicilian thing that women don't know what they want or have a brain in their heads!"

I sat spellbound! This was the most I had ever heard from Ethel.

"Zorah came to my house so upset. I said to her, 'Zorah, enough is enough! It has been over fifty years that you have kowtowed to Carmine.' Then I said, let's leave! Let's just get into my car and drive away, far away, and that's your 'NO!' There is nothing he can do if you aren't in the city any longer, is there?" She turned to me, "Dear, Houston was as far away as we could imagine where we knew someone!

"Little did I know he would send a posse after us!" Ethel concluded.

That lightened the mood some; we all smiled. Patty got up and served more coffee. Just then, we heard a gruff "Good morning" from a male voice who obviously just woke. But by the saucer-sized eyes Alice and Honey cast over my shoulder to whoever was behind me, all I could think was, "Oh, no, he didn't;" I turned, knowing just who I would see. Oh, yes, he did.

It was Sal, in mules with faux fur uppers and wearing two-piece pink baby doll pajamas with white eyelet ruffles.

"Good morning Sal," I said.

"'Morning; I didn't expect it to rain in paradise," he poured himself a cup of coffee and leaned against the counter sipped the brew. "What do you do when it rains at the beach?"

"How about joining us? The French toast is to die for," Patty invited.

"Zorah's French toast?"

"Yes," Ethel said.

"I'll get changed and be back," he said, taking the coffee mug with him.

I called out, "Please do!" Then I said to my friends, "Now you've met the real cousin Sal!"

"I no-a notice no more," Zorah said as she got up, started making more French toast.

Alice leaned across the table as if to whisper, "Has he always been like that, I mean, a cross-dresser?"

"Yes," is all I said.

"I think it's cute," Patty offered

The Ph.D. psychologists at the table looked at her as if she had two heads.

"It's a shame, I know," Ethel said. Again, Ethel has an opinion? I wasn't accustomed to Ethel in a conversation. "I think it's because his parents were too focused on Rocco being gay when Sal was a young child."

"Did I hear my name" Another waking male voice?

"Morning," was the chorus from the kitchen table.

Rocco was scratching his ass and pouring himself coffee at the same time. "May I join you?"

Before anyone could answer, I jumped in, "NO! Get dressed!"

"But you're still in PJs!"

"That's different," I was firm.

He left without further protest. Carlo and Cary entered the kitchen soon after, waved, got coffee, and left. Good.

"We have them trained," Honey mused.

All I could think of was how we keep Ethel talking; I had never heard about our family's history from someone who was not a blood member before. Ethel speaking up today reminded me that she and Zorah were always together; Ethel said fifty years. The impact of what all those years meant was sinking in now; I was curious for more information.

Soon the kitchen table was crowded with all of us except Zorah and Patty, who kept the French toast, coffee, and orange juice flowing. The guys talked about how huge Houston's airport was (they had arrived at Intercontinental and not Hobby, which would have been closer). Then they had to wait for the aunts. It usually took me three days to drive from Houston to Buffalo. It took the aunts five days to drive from Buffalo to Houston.

"I must admit, I'm pleased you invited us to come out here, Patty," Carlo said. "It is stifling in Houston. Even at the dock, the humidity is extreme."

"The docks?" Alice picked up, "What were you doing at the docks?"

The men eyed each other. Rocco spoke for them, "Business. The Family has business with shipping some exports out of the Houston docks."

Now the women surveyed each other. I thought, "No, please leave it alone!"

"Does Tommy Jimenez still work for us?" Ethel asked, "Out of Houston?"

Before one of the men could answer, Aunt Zorah said, "No. He be our age, Tesoro mio. He's a kid take over, Pedro. Sal! Put-a the cat down! No animals at the table!"

I was thinking hard; I'd heard that before: Tesoro Mio. But what? A term of endearment for sure.

Rocco turned in his chair to face Zorah in the kitchen. "And, how do you know that?" At least he was smiling.

Zorah shrugged. "You-a boys, you think me stupid! But I-a work in the Family before you was born! And when you was born, I slap your ass and clean your minchia!"

The family at the table burst out laughing! The slang we all were exposed to and learned never left us. The guys started teasing Zorah with other Sicilian phrases and slang; Carlo got out of his chair, holding the waistband of his Bermuda shorts, and asking Zorah if she wanted to see that he wasn't small anymore!

Honey, Alice, and Patty got the gist of the comment. We all had a good belly laugh.

The conversation came back to what do you do when it rains at the beach? I brought up touring NASA or taking in a movie. There was a mall just south of the city with an IMAX theater. Or we could just sit around, talk, nap, read, eat, and drink?

The guys opted for a movie at the mall. They were out the door by noon, warning us that they might be out late, don't hold supper, and don't wait up. I was impressed that they did straighten up the living area making it decent enough to occupy.

"Hey!" Honey got our attention, "We have movies here as well!" Patty had a nice DVD collection.

"Nah," Zorah said. "The quiet, si, just the quiet."

Each of us went separate ways. I retreated to Patty's bedroom. I needed to regroup after the morning, Sal's baby dolls and Zorah calling out the guys about small penises! Yet, Zorah did know all about The Family Business. How interesting. I realized that when someone is elderly, like Aunt Zorah, we seem to forget these "old people" most likely had very full and exciting lives filled with events, just like anyone experiences in their twenties, thirties, and forties. I had forgotten that myself. If we (meaning Honey, Patty and Alice, and me) could get Zorah to tell that story. Wow! What I'd learn about my own family.

I woke from a nap and jumped out of bed. Moon was not amused. My anxiety was my friends were entertaining my aunts! But when I entered the living area, the women were sitting around, all looking comfortable, a pitcher of Sangria on the coffee table, along with a platter of cheeses, bread, olives, and veggies to munch. Zorah and Ethel sat on the love seat.

"There you are!" Patty said.

"You-a okay?" Zorah asked.

"Yes. A little overwhelmed by the guys this morning! How about all y'all?"

"Dear, we're fine! Remember, it's you that hasn't been around family like this in an awfully long time," Ethel said.

How true. I grabbed a glass of Sangria and sat on the sofa next to Alice, folding myself like a pretzel. "What are we talking about?"

"Zorah's early days in this country. Did you know that your grandparents had three young children when they immigrated to the US? Carmine, Zorah, and Isabella," Honey informed.

"I think I knew that; yet, put that way, it sounds different. Bertha was the first child born state side, right?"

Ethel said, "Yes! Amazing, isn't it? Her dad, Carmine, wanted to have a successful business before they had any more children, thus the gap between Zorah and Bertha."

"That is crazy! And they were Catholic!" I said, implying the rule of no birth control.

Zorah said, "Mama was sixteen when Carmine was born, then me, right away, six years later Isabella. Papa," Zorah tapped the side of her head, "He was-a smart. When Bertha born, Mama, she only," she shrugged, "just thirty-five, still can have babies. I got-ta help, a lot!" She laughed. "People in our neighborhood, they think the babies be mine! Papa, he get angry! He start-a pushing the buggy up and down the street, saying, 'my bambina?'"

Honey asked, "How old were you, Zorah?"

"Eighteen. Just-a eighteen, helping Mama with babies, and start-a working in-a The Business with Papa.

"Papa, his business a-good; we always have money. Other families with lots of kids, I can see how hard for them, no money, bad jobs, but Papa, he was smart.

"When Mama stop-a nursing Renato, I start-a working downtown, in an office, with Papa, instead of running errands for him from the house."

"That's when we met," Ethel added. They looked affectionately at each other.

Alice continued, "What was that like? What year was it?"

Zorah and Ethel looked at each other, and Ethel said, "Around nineteen thirty-three or four. It was an interesting time. The country was in the Great Depression, and Prohibition was in full force. It was wild!"

"Is that how Grandpa made his money? Smuggling booze?" I edged.

"Hmm, small stuff. Papa, he had bigger ideas," she offered.

"Gambling!" Honey injected.

Zorah laughed out loud. "Now you gotta something!"

Ethel quietly added, "And numbers; running numbers."

"What does that mean?" I asked.

"It's-a gambling, too," Zorah answered.

"Did you ever shoot anyone? Kill anyone?" Alice asked.

For a moment, we all just stared at Alice. "What?" she asked defensively.

"No, dear, not the women," Ethel answered.

Oh my God! Not the women?

I gulped then asked, "So, people in our family did kill other people?"

And, without skipping a beat, Aunt Zorah shrugged and said, "Who knows?"

Ah, Sicilian denial -- alive and well!

"I think we need supper! Something in our bellies to soak up all the wine; who's with me?" Patty stood and announced.

"I'll help," Alice was up off the sofa, and I followed.

"Are sandwiches and leftovers, okay? I have grilled sausage, fruit; Maggie, will you make a green salad? Honey, how about cutting up this watermelon?

"Zorah, Ethel, what will it be?" Patty asked.

Zorah sat at the table, "I did breakfast! I sit this out!"

We all laughed. Ethel was setting the table. At the sink, while I was washing lettuce and tomatoes, Honey stood next to me with the watermelon and quietly said, "The plan is just keeping the ole girls talking. You in?"

"Hell, yes!" I smiled.

We were all wiped out after supper. Long about seven p.m., a clap of thunder startled us.

"That was loud," Ethel declared.

"Not unusual for the beach," Patty offered. "I think because it's such an open space. Who's up for coffee?"

One more time, we gathered around the kitchen table. Patty put out fruit, pastries, and fresh coffee plus a bottle of Kahlua.

"May I ask you both a question?" Honey addressed Ethel and Zorah.

The ladies exchanged looks, smiled, and nodded yes.

"Given that I'm a psychologist and all, I'm curious, on many levels . . ."

"Yes, we're lesbians and have been together since 1940!" Ethel offered.

Someone hit that pause button again!

"Ah, you hit the nail on the head!" Honey said.

"Aunt Zorah! Why haven't you told me?"

"No business of yours . . . until now. Now that I run away from Carmine, best you know why I am tired of being pushed around by him. If Isabella can get a new life on her own, me too!"

"I guess I see that now," I said.

"What's the plan?" Patty asked.

Again, Ethel and Zorah looked at each other. "To tell you the truth,"

Ethel started, "we have no idea. Just getting out of Buffalo was such an incredibly heady, wild, and wonderful fete that the plan hadn't progressed past getting here with Maggie."

"So," I started, "you don't know where you want to wind up?"

They shook their heads no.

"Well, you are welcomed to stay here as long as you need to while you figure it out," Patty said so quickly that my head spun around to look at her.

"I do know that we want to live as who we are, back in Buffalo," Ethel offered.

"That much makes sense," I managed to say.

"You have no money issues, I assume," Honey broached.

Aunt Zorah laughed. "I-a saved real good! The Family Business pays good. I work for Carmine a long time, and I take care of all the family babies!"

"My home was willed to me by my parents," Ethel said. "I worked until retirement and saved. And I get Social Security." She turned to Zorah, "I'd love for us to live in my house, back home, eventually."

"Aunt Zorah, do you get Social Security?" I asked.

She laughed while saying, "You think Carmine, he report-a to the government so we get Social Security?"

We all laughed.

"Hadn't thought about it like that," I said with a red face.

"The problem will be the boys," Ethel said.

"The boys?" Honey asked.

"My nephews," Zorah clarified.

"How so?" I asked.

"They here to take me home. Carmine's orders! And they no go home and say 'oh, Carmine, she no wanna come home!' No. They no can say that."

"Well then, we'll just have to give them a story that Carmine will accept," Patty announced.

Ethel and Zorah looked at each other, shaking their head in disbelief. "Dear," Ethel started, "That will be some story! I have yet to witness Carmine accepting a 'no' from anyone."

My friends and I exchanged looks. I knew Ethel was utterly correct.

Finally, Patty said, "Well, we'll just have to win them over."

A puzzled look ran among the faces.

"The boys! The guys! We will have to show them such a good time that when they return, they will be praising the lifestyle here and reassuring Carmine that Zorah and Ethel are doing great!" Patty fantasized.

I burst out laughing! I was the only one who was laughing.

"What?" Patty asked. "Why can't that work?"

Ethel reached for the Kahlua, poured some into her mug and into Zorah's, then said, "Every time, in the past, when we tried to move in with each other, the roof came down around us. Carmine is big on how the family looks. And having two ladies living together, well, in those days, anyway, let's just say, we've been down this road before.

"All we could think of was getting out of Buffalo and avoiding that whole 'how things looks' stuff that always comes up," Ethel concluded.

"But Ethel? Rocco and Drew live together! Uncle Carmine doesn't seem to have that problem with them."

"They no women, and they young, and for them, it's-a different. No one gonna say anything to Carmine about his-a son being queer," Zorah explained. "But his-a sister, all these years? They no stop talking about us."

"I still think that if we win the boys over, it will work out, and you can return to Buffalo and move right in together," Patty said.

There was a collective silence.

"But wait," I started. "Do we really know what the guys think? No, we don't. And I propose we use the time to get them talking about what they think about the situation . . . not only Aunt Zorah's but mine as well." I turned to my friends, "Y'all said to me that I really have no idea how my cousins think about me and Stevie D, and I needed to allow them to tell me. Y'all said I might be surprised or at least get an angle on how my cousins thought about it all. Why can't that be true for you too, Aunt Zorah? Get the guys as allies, not just extended arms of Uncle Carmine."

The ladies exchanged looks.

"That's what I've been saying!" Patty announced. "When do your cousins plan to leave Houston?"

"I have no idea," I answered.

"Well, as soon as they arrive back here, we'll start creating conversations around Zorah and Ethel staying at least through July 4th weekend. That's two weeks from now," Honey said.

"I like it," Ethel said.

Zorah took Ethel's hand and said, "Me-a too," and reached for the Kahlua bottle and headed into the living area.

A cool breeze wafted through the Bay house; it was around midnight. The rain stopped. We opened all the doors and turned off the air conditioner. I felt as loose-limbed as a rag doll. I carefully rolled over to face the opened sliding glass door, and not disturb Patty or Moon. The aunts told us stories that made me laugh so much that I thought I'd pee my pants.

"Again, who did you dub 'The Mayor'?" Patty asked.

"Toni Ditalini," Ethel said. "Maggie, you met him at the wake. He is the guy that is about four foot something, as is his wife Connie and most of their kids! Calling him The Mayor came to us after we saw The Wizard of Oz, remember, the Munchkin mayor?"

"Oh no!" I was laughing with a picture in my mind of Tony Ditalini no longer in that gorgeous suit but in the mayor's costume from the movie! "You don't mean it?"

"He-a went to dances for people like him, even back then," Aunt Zorah added. "He meet Connie there. They are perfect together!"

"And, what about Anita and Stephanie?" I asked my aunts.

"Ah, Anita and Steffi," Aunt Zorah began, "They be gold diggers."

Ethel patted Zorah's forearm, "Now, be kind!"

"No need to be-a kind, the truth is the truth! Anita, she had her eye on Renato, The Business, it's-a no secret the Madonie Family is wealthy," she shrugged, a gesture of matter-of-fact. "Carmine, he meet Lena riding trucks with our cousin Augustine. Lena, her family," another shrug, "on the north side, but we help each other out.

"Papa, he-a talk with Lena's papa, and they think Carmine and Lena a good match. Lena, she-a knows about The Family Business," one more shrug.

"Well, what about Anita and Steffi? Neither got Uncle Renato, obviously; how did Aunt Eve score?" I asked, even though I thought I was pushing it a little, even with all the Kahlua on board.

"Let me tell!" Ethel said. Zorah nodded yes. "It was beautiful to watch!" Ethel began. "Basically, Genève Adriano ignored, and I do mean completely ignored, Renato. It was the best catch a woman ever made using this technique. Not once did she falter!"

We were all rolling in laughter! Ethel's words were spoken with such precision that we got it just how extraordinary the fete had been!

"Details! Details!" Alice demanded humorously.

Zorah was smiling and laughing as well, "She no answer the phone when he call her! And he-a always slam down the phone and Papa say if he break-a the phone, he pay for it out of his wages! And one day, he-a break-a the phone! Papa right there, so Renato, he-a finished the job by pulling it out of the wall! Then he say to Papa, 'There! I get you a new one!'"

"What did Grandpa do?" I asked.

"He just a shake his head, then look at the rest of us and say, 'ah amore'!"

"How did they finally get married; I mean, if she was ignoring him so completely?" Alice asked.

Ethel answered, "She acted . . . contemptible."

"Contemptible?" Alice echoed with a questionable tone.

Ethel poured Kahlua into her mug; no more pretense of needing coffee. "Mm, yes; think Sophia Loren!"

"Oh!" We all said at once and then rolled in laughter!

"And that worked?" Alice continued.

"Yes. And they have Carlo and Rosalie to prove it!"

"Hey! I've got an idea!" I announced.

"No, you are not thinking about treating Stevie D that way! Are you?" Alice said.

"That's a difficult game to pull off," Patty said.

"I agree; plus, the relationship like that must start from the get-go; switching now won't work," Honey added.

I thought about it a moment. I'm no Sophia Loren.

I fell back into a deep sleep, that when I woke, the sunlight was coming through the sliding glass door that was still opened. Patty was already gone from her side of the bed and Moon had abandoned me also. The guys were sleeping in the living area, and a pile of luggage was at the front door. I started coffee, and Ethel joined me.

"Oh my God! I've heard never get drunk on sweet drinks! Got any aspirin?" Ethel asked, holding her head.

I opened the cupboard where Patty stored all that stuff.

Ethel looked around, "Where's Patty? In her room?"

"No. And obviously not sleeping with the guys in the living area."

"On the deck?" Ethel offered.

I headed out to the deck and peered out at the Gulf; no one in the sea as far as I could tell. The guys were stirring as I entered the house. Zorah was now in the kitchen and started to cook breakfast. Carlo, Cary, and Rocco moaned a morning hello as they each grabbed for the aspirin bottle and a mug of coffee; still no Patty.

"What time did you get here?" I asked.

"Around six a.m.. We waited until the sun was coming up because we knew we'd never find Patty's place in the dark. We checked out of the hotel, and here we are.

"By the way," Rocco continued, "we," he made a circular gesture with his arm to include everyone in the room, "need to talk!"

"Humph!" was all Aunt Zorah said.

"Have any of y'all seen Patty?" I asked my cousins.

They looked at each other like little boys keeping a secret.

"Right here!" Patty and Sal entered the kitchen. Both were dressed for the day.

"Where were you?" I inquired like an irate mother.

"Well, I heard the boys on the deck, so I let them in." She was a little too sheepish.

"But you didn't come back to bed," I said.

"I invited her to sleep, and I do mean 'snore sleep,' with me instead of waking you!" Sal said.

The guys were amused.

Zorah dished up scrambled eggs and threatened to dump them in the guys' laps if they didn't stop snickering at Patty and Sal.

"Oh, okay." I felt stupid. I clumsily ended the conversation.

Over coffee and donuts, the cousins brought with them, Rocco started the conversation.

"Aunt Zorah, my dad expects one of us," he motioned to the cousins," to assist you and Ethel back to Buffalo."

She ignored him.

"Aunt Zorah, what do you plan to do? Stay here?" He said it like that was such an impossibility.

"Yes, we-a plan to stay here; Patty, she invite us to stay as long as we want, and we-a want!"

That took the guys by surprise.

"It's true. I offered Ethel and Zorah my home for as long as they needed," Patty confirmed.

"Aunt Zorah, what do we tell Uncle Carmine?" Carlo asked.

"My dad isn't going to like it," Rocco said, "and to tell you the truth, I really don't want to be the one to have to tell him."

"Then, I-a tell him. Where's the phone?" Zorah said.

"Darlin', there is no phone here. But the next time we head up to Coastal Groceries, we can use the phone there," Patty said as she poured everyone another cup of coffee.

"Come on you guys! What can Uncle Carmine do if Aunt Zorah doesn't go home? I mean, really?" I asked.

"Make us very uncomfortable," Cary said.

"It would go better if you did call Uncle Carmine, Aunt Zorah. It would take the pressure off us for sure," Carlo offered.

"Okay. Patty, next trip to the grocery store, I call," Aunt Zorah said.

The guys physically collectively sighed.

"Who's up for a swim?" Sal asked as he left the table for his room. The others followed. I started clearing the table with Patty and Alice. Honey began washing the dishes. Ethel and Zorah were in an embrace that none of us wanted to interrupt.

Patty and I took rafts out. We held hands to keep us close enough to talk while floating.

"What? No naked swimming?" she asked.

"Not with my cousins in the same pond! . . . By the way, why didn't you come back to bed in your own room?"

"Sal offered to share his bed, and I just said yes without a thought."

"I see a return to your old hippie days!" I teased.

"I'll admit he's cute . . ."

"Cute with a problem."

"You mean the crossdressing?"

"Yes."

"Why does it have to be a problem? It's who he is, right?"

"Yes. It's . . . a psychological condition," the psychologist in me said.

"I'm going to disagree with you, Doctor. I believe it is also just a fetish. Have you ever talked with your cousin about his crossdressing?"

She had me there. "No. Okay. Maybe one day I'll have that conversation but not this weekend."

"Anyway, I think he's cute and kind. Great mix," she said, smiling.

Once on the deck, Cary sat with me. We were alone. I knew something was up.

"Maggie, I'll be leaving Sunday night, back to Buffalo. I got to get back to work. This little trip pulled me away from stuff that can't wait any longer. But I wanted to say something, okay?"

"You will anyway, right?"

"I guess so. Okay, here goes. If you love Stevie D, don't push it away. And, Maggie, I think the reason Uncle Carmine and your mom want you home is because they're getting older, and now that we're adults, we can have quality time with them. It's not like it was when we were teens, always arguing and bickering. God! Since I've had kids, my relationship with my folks has improved one hundred percent. It's amazing. I never thought of my dad as an ally. It's nice for my kids too. Remember how we were always plotting our grandparents against our parents? That doesn't happen with my mom and dad and my kids. Mom and Dad are so supportive, but I think they're a little different, being that we're Rizzo's. Anyway, Maggie, I just wanted you to know what I think. If you stay in Houston, so be it. But . . . well . . . all I'm saying is think twice before kicking love to the curb, your mom's, and Stevie D's."

I just sat there. I was stunned for a moment.

"Thanks, Cary. I'll remember this for a long time," was all I could muster.

At lunch, Carlo and Sal surprised us. They asked Patty if it was all right if they stayed on until after the July Fourth holiday! That was two weeks away. Of course, before I could open my mouth, Patty said yes!

"I'm leaving with Cary Sunday," Rocco said. "But before I go, Maggie, we need to talk."

"You too?"

"What? Can't we talk?" he assumed an innocent posture.

I just rolled my eyes.

Patty and Aunt Zorah left for Coastal Groceries after lunch. Everyone was camped inside the air-conditioned house. Zorah said she'd talk with Uncle Carmine. When Cary and Rocco got into Buffalo early Monday morning, Uncle Carmine would know she wasn't coming home for now.

I retreated to the bedroom I was sharing with Patty. Lying on the bed, I just stared at the ceiling with my arms folded behind my head. Cary had surprised me, talking about love, and talking about how a relationship changes once kids are adults. I intellectually knew this. I counseled people about just that. How easy it was not to apply the best advice I give out to myself. I was an adult now. The wake and funeral were no measure of what my relationship with my mother could be. I was disconcerted. I left the bedroom through the sliding glass door onto the back deck. Afternoon siesta had set in throughout the house. I sat in one of the Adirondack chairs. I loved how the chair reclined; Patty's chairs had footrests as well. Wearing sunglasses and a large, brimmed hat, I rested better.

"May I join you?"

"Sure," I said without moving. It was Rocco's voice. I looked at him without lifting my sunglasses. I really didn't want to talk.

He perched himself on the edge of the other Adirondack chair. His knees seemed level with his chest. "Maggie, remember the favor my dad asked from you way back when?"

I lowered my sunglasses on my nose. "When you were in the hospital? I was in college?"

"Yes. Dad wanted me home, and I wouldn't go. I was so full of anxiety: I was gay, tested positive for HIV, hadn't done anything to create a career for myself, and had run away from my mom and dad because I believed they were embarrassed, even ashamed of me. Then you popped into my hospital room and said my dad wanted a favor from you: to get me home.

"Well, we all know how there's no refusing or ignoring a favor, especially in our family. Maggie, going back home was the best thing I did. My assumptions about how my parents felt about their gay son were wrong. My mom was happy I was home because she wanted to nurse me into health," he sat up straight and threw out his chest, "Look at me! It worked!"

"And the cocktail of medications that came into being along the way," I added.

"Yes, and the cocktail of medications I take daily. But my point is I underestimated my parents. I think you might be underestimating your mom and, more importantly, and please don't get angry with me, Stevie D's love for you. And Maggie, I'm your oldest cousin, and we've traveled many the same roads, and I can see it in you that you love him too."

I took my sunglasses off and looked into his eyes for a full minute. "What are you suggesting?"

"Before you sign off on never coming home, will you spend time with Stevie D? Time like as boyfriend, girlfriend?"

"And how do you propose I do that?"

"Call him; invite him here, now, for an extended stay, just like Aunt Zorah and Ethel are staying," and he laughed, "And Carlo and Sal. Say, what do you think is up with that? I didn't see that coming. I mean, once I get home, not only do I have to say, 'Gee, Pop, no Zorah, and no Carlo and Sal either!' Guess how great that's going to go over. Believe me, it will make more work for the rest of us, for sure!"

"I don't know about Carlo and Sal. Do they need a vacation?" I asked.

"You haven't answered me about Stevie D."

I threw my head back and hit the chair a little harder than I had anticipated. "Ouch!"

"Well?"

"Rocco, before I showed up in your hospital room, how did you feel? Before you knew that your folks wanted you home so desperately that your dad was asking for favors?"

"Terrified. I thought I was on my deathbed."

"I don't feel that I'm on my deathbed, but I do feel terrified."

"And what would you tell a patient you were seeing?"

"Not fair!"

"Oh yes, it is fair! You're a great psychologist . . ."

"How would you know?"

"I know. So, what would you tell your patient?"

"Client . . . I'd tell my client that she should face her fears while holding the hands of the people she can identify as supporting her," I said, reluctantly.

He slapped his knees. "There! You have your answer! Do you need me to stay?"

"No. No, go home with Cary."

"You'll call Stevie D?"

I squinched up my face.

"Maggie," he prompted.

"Can it wait until Monday? I want to talk it over with Honey, Alice, and Patty, seeing theirs are the hands that will be supporting me," I asked.

"And Zorah and Ethel and me and Carlo and Cary and Sal and Ginger and Rosalie and . . ."

"Okay! Okay! Okay! I get the picture!" I started to laugh.

"It's about time!" he said as he stood, towering over me.

Rocco left the deck. I leaned back, replacing my sunglasses. Uncle Carmine did ask for another favor. "Ah yai yai, yai!" I said to myself, borrowing an old Sicilian expression.

Aunt Zorah marched up the stairs onto the deck, waking me. I walked around to the front of the house and sat in another Adirondack chair. She joined me, pulling over a regular folding chair to sit on, most likely knowing it would take two people to get her out of the Adirondack chair.

"He-a no happy," she offered, "and I call him collect!" She amused herself, saying that.

"You told him you weren't returning to Buffalo now," I repeated clearly for validation.

"No going home now," she said,

"Okay! Then, what's the plan?"

"No know yet," she confessed.

Honey came through the sliding glass door with cold beer cans in a bucket of ice.

"Heads up! Time to cool off," she announced.

"Ah," Zorah said

"Gimme gimme!" I stretched out my arm, wiggling my fingers for a can of beer.

The sun was off the Gulf, heading behind the house. The guys joined us on the deck. Ethel emerged and hugged Zorah hard. No words. No one spoke. It was the most supportive atmosphere I ever felt folded around us.

Rocco and Cary will be hassled once home. Zorah and Ethel are embarking on a new life together. I have a lot to consider and resolve, what with Carlo and Sal staying on. But I also have my dear, dear girlfriends Honey, Alice, and Patty, open and unconditionally loving. I told myself, "Just drink in these moments."

By mid-afternoon Sunday, the guys were helping Cary and Rocco pack. They would ride to the airport with them and come back in the rented car. Zorah and Ethel retreated to their room. Patty was straightening up the living area after the guys left when I asked her, Honey, and Alice to sit down because, Elvis just went home.

I started talking quietly, not wanting to disturb Zorah and Ethel in their room.

"Would you be more comfortable talking to us someplace private?" Honey asked.

"Yes, I would," I answered.

We all looked at each other a moment, then Patty spoke up, "Let's go to the Sea Wall. The ride on the ferry will do us good, and the Sea Wall is as private as you can get this time of day."

I gently knocked on the door to the aunts' room, and, before they could open it, I told them that the four of us were going out, don't wait up! They called back a choral "Okay!"

We rode in silence to the ferry; once on the boat, we left the car and headed for the bench on the lip of a balcony for the ride, and when the boat pulled into Galveston, we were back in the car, off the ferry and headed down Sea Wall Boulevard for a less tourist spot on the Sea Wall.

The Sea Wall was built after the hurricane of 1900, that devastated the Island. It stretched ten miles parallel to the Gulf of Mexico and stood seventeen feet high, hopefully, high enough to contain any swell the Gulf attempted to rush the Island with. The further south, along the Sea Wall, small parking areas popped up, with benches and picnic tables. We found a deserted area and pulled in.

We disturbed a flock of pelicans, that with our presence, took off simultaneously and gave us a terrific show of grace, and wingspan, in flight!

Pelicans departed, we gathered around a picnic table. Patty plopped the Igloo cooler at the end of the table, opened it, and passed our wine coolers.

"Okay, spill!" Alice said.

I filled them in about the conversations Cary and Rocco had with me. I had to admit to them that I did have feelings for Stevie D, but I couldn't be sure what kind of feelings they were, with the wake and funeral going on at the same time. He was there, always, catering to my every need. Hell, he was assigned to me by Uncle Renato! Yet, he suffered through the evening at the Irish Center and Dad's Irish wake! And this was the most important question I had for myself: were my feelings hinged on Stevie D's attention during that week? If so, then that's not really love, and he may just be kidding himself that he's in love. What would it look like if he was just another goombah attending the funeral of George Blake, Carmine Madonie's brother-in-law?

"She's got a good point," Alice said. "What do y'all think of Carlo?"

"Who are we talking about here? Maggie and Stevie D or you and Carlo?" Honey asked.

Alice shrugged, "Why not both? Why do you think Carlo and Sal wanted to stay on until the holiday?"

"Now that's an excellent question," I replied. "Any inkling why, Alice?" I deliberately asked.

"Well, I think they're nice, and Carlo is so funny," Alice offered.

"Hmm," Patty commented.

"Don't 'hmm' me!" Alice said, laughing. "What did you do in bed with Sal Saturday morning? Hmm?"

"Sleeping," Patty said unconvincingly.

"Oh boy! Is this going to be a mess!" Honey said.

"No kidding. I wanted to ask whether or not y'all think I should call Stevie D tomorrow?" They shot looks at me. "I know, it's turned into an episode of a soap opera!"

"Maggie, take time off until after July 4th weekend. You've got plenty of PTO," Alice offered.

"I like that idea," Honey agreed. She leaned in, elbows on the table and looked directly at me, "Maggie, don't run from this. You've lived away from home for so long that you need to get a bead on how your family thinks, as well as sorting out your feelings about Stevie D. I like the idea of him coming here, at some point, and seeing him outside his element, as Patty said. That's good advice."

"Wow, not exactly what I expected," I said. Yet, my cousins' advice had been right on before, and probably was now. We were quiet. "Okay. I'm going to drive into Houston tomorrow, pay my rent, and get some clothes, unload my suitcase. I'll call him while I'm there. Patty, I'll need your car."

"So soon? I didn't think we were done discussing the pros and cons of his coming here earlier that Labor Day weekend!" I could tell Honey was annoyed.

"Sounds like a plan, and yes, take my car," Patty said.

Alice announced, "Now, what do y'all think about Carlo?"

"I think a better question is 'what do you think about Carlo?'" Honey said.

"Well, now that you asked, I think he's delightful, and . . . I'd like to get to know him better," Alice confessed.

"Now tell us something we don't know," Patty said.

"Well, you don't know that his staying over until after the holiday was because I asked him. Monday when I get back to work, well, I've asked him to my place for supper," Alice continued.

"Too many people at the Bay house, right?" Honey was more facetious about the question.

"Yes! There really isn't any space here for a face-to-face conversation," Alice said

"Hmm," I muttered.

"What? He's your cousin! Is there something you're not telling me, like Sal's crossdressing? If there is, please, speak now!"

"Or forever hold my peace?" I joked.

Alice laughed, "Yeah, something like that. You know, no man has ever impressed me the way Carlo did when I met him. He said the same thing that he was taken by me. We want to explore that, and fortunately, we don't have the complications like Maggie has with favors and family. Carlo is a free agent . . . so to speak," Alice concluded.

"Ah, 'so to speak,' is just that! You do realize that his dad, Renato, my Uncle Renato, is second in command, so to speak, of The Family Business!" I declared.

"Yeah . . ." she hesitated, "Carlo did mention that."

"Oh, so you have had a few conversations about the family?" I was being haughty and knew it.

"Yes, but just bits and pieces. We want to sit down with each other, alone, uninterrupted and just talk."

"I think that's a great idea," Honey pronounced. then added, "Exactly what you need to do with Stevie D, Maggie.

"I said I would call him tomorrow and ask him to visit sooner rather than later. But it sounded like you didn't agree with that." I pointed out to Honey.

"It's about me, remember!" Alice joked.

Honey turned to Patty.

"Oh no, you don't!" Patty said playfully.

"Oh yes, I do! Tell us about Sal, Patty." Honey was smug.

"He's cute!" Patty quickly stated.

"And...," Alice said.

"When he gets back from the airport, we're going out to check out the night life," Patty explained.

"Where are you sleeping tonight?" Alice asked.

There was silence. Then we burst out laughing.

"I know you know that you're way older than he is, right?" Honey commented.

"What does that have to do with anything?" Patty asked.

"Are you serious?" I asked.

Patty shrugged. "I like him, a lot. He's good company. He holds his own in a conversation, unlike men my age, these days. He's never been married, so there are no complications with wives, ex-wives or children… that I know of!"

"No wives, no children," I reassured her.

"And the crossdressing thing, well, that's him. I'm comfortable with it, to my surprise, if you must know, I'm really comfortable with all of him."

"The sage has spoken," Honey said feigning a prostration with arms outstretched in Patty's direction.

"Or just, she told us!" Alice quipped.

After about two hours, we headed back to Bolivar and Crystal Beach with the same routine as when we left the peninsula: drive onto the boat, climb the narrow ladder to the narrow deck with the bench, enjoy the ride in silence, drive off the boat, home, rather, to Patty's Bay house.

We arrived in time to see Zorah and Ethel heading for the sand path to the beach.

Ethel shouted a big wave with swinging arm, "Come join us!"

"Sounds great!" All of us rushed to get changed. It was the perfect time, around seven o'clock, for a swim. The sun was off the Gulf, and the breezes were gentle. We'd work up an appetite and we'd sleep well because of the air and exercise, and knowing the solutions to our problems.

"Hello?"

"Aunt Eve? This is Maggie."

"Hello, doll! How are you? Say, is Zorah with you, I hope?"

"Yes, she and Ethel are here, well, not here, on Bolivar at my girlfriend's Bay house."

"Oh, good! I don't know Bolivar, but as long as they're with you! They made it, driving all that way. What were they thinking? But I heard from Lena that it was a knock-down-drag-out fight. I wish I were a fly on the wall; I would have loved to watch someone stand up to Carmine! But, doll, why did you call? Nobody died, right?"

Ah, the Sicilian knee-jerk reaction to a surprise phone call. "Nobody died. In fact, Aunt Zorah and Ethel plan on staying until after the Fourth."

"That's good, but it's going to make Carmine crazy. Happy I don't live in that house. What's wrong, doll? Are you okay?"

"Is Uncle Renato there? I was hoping to talk with him."

"Yeah, he's right here; it's about Stevie D, right? Just say yes, and I'll get the details from Renato when you hang up."

"Yes."

"Oh, doll! I was praying that you'd come to your senses! Okay, Renato is right here. I'll give him the phone," and I could hear her calling him to the phone, "Hon! It's Maggie!"

"Maggie?" He answered.

"Yes. Hello Uncle Renato. How are you?"

"Good. Good. What's up?"

"Ah, well, I've been thinking and talking with my girlfriends, not to mention that Rocco and Cary were here and added their two cents . . ."

"My Carlo made it there too, right?"

"Yes, and Sal. It's been a packed Bay house! But we're all getting along. Rocco and Cary should be back in Buffalo today."

"Good, good. Now, what is it you want?" I froze. "Maggie? Maggie? Are you there?"

"Yes, yes, I'm here. Uncle Renato . . . I'll spit it right out. Will you ask Stevie D to call me today? I'm here at my apartment, but I'll be driving back to the Bay house this evening. I've decided to take a short leave from work until after the Fourth, and there's no phone at Patty's house, just the phone at Coastal Groceries. If Stevie D wants to talk to me, I'd like to invite him here, he really must call me soon, at my apartment." I finally inhaled.

"Wow. Okay. Don't you have his number?"

Surprised by his question, I answered, "No. He always called me or just showed up."

"Oh yeah, that's right. Okay, doll, you got it. I'll call him right away. Anything else? Is Zorah okay? When are they headed back?"

"After the Fourth, as far as I know. They still need to make some plans.

Uncle Renato, they really just want to live together in Ethel's house as who they really are with each other."

"I know, doll. I agree that it's time. I'm on Zorah's side. I'm thinking about how she stood up to Carmine. I think I'll let my big brother know that I'm on her side; she should live as she wants. Are you okay? I mean, with all of this, you cousins and Aunt Zorah crashing at your house?"

"Yes, Uncle Renato, I'm okay. And you must know I have wonderful girlfriends. Patty has a Bay house that faces the Gulf of Mexico, and she immediately opened it up to everyone: Aunt Zorah and Ethel, and even all my cousins. We've all been there, on Bolivar peninsula; that's the opposite end of Galveston," I quickly added. I knew that he knew about Galveston.

"That's a good friend, doll, really good friend. But you, how are you?"

"The tears are just at night but not every night. How's my mom? I haven't talked with her since I got back because I went right out to Bolivar where Patty has her Bay house."

"Bella? She's okay. Don't worry about Bella. We're watching out for her."

"Thanks, Uncle Renato."

"Okay, doll, I'll get in touch with Stevie D."

"Thank you."

"Ciao Bella."

"Ciao."

I hadn't realized that I brought home so many dirty clothes. Doing the laundry was an excellent chore as I waited for the phone to ring. Still, it didn't stop the monologue in my head, trying out different conversation openers. Finally, I just plopped down onto the sofa and cried! What am I doing? How did it get this far? What the hell?

The phone rang.

I sat straight up as if an intruder had just entered my apartment with a gun drawn. I jumped up and grabbed the phone off the charger.

"Hello?"

"Maggie, Stevie D . . . How ya doin'?"

I plopped back onto the sofa. "I'm okay. How about you? Busy with work?"

"No. I got some time off . . . I was pretty busy there for a while, what with your dad dying and all."

Yeah, with the bodyguard or assignment or whatever they call it, I thought, but asked, "Any plans?"

"No. Just home with the boys; school is out end of this week. It's a mess around here! I keep saying I need to hire a housekeeper, but every time I do, they don't last!"

"Three boys, that's a handful," I tried to make light.

"Renato told me to call you; more accurately, he said you asked him to ask me to call you. Is that right?"

"Yes. Stevie, do you know that Aunt Zorah and Ethel kind of ran away from home, and Uncle Carmine sent Rocco, Sal, Cary, and Carlo here to bring her back home? As if they're in their twenties back in Sicily?" It was pressured speech, and I recognized it.

Stevie D was laughing. "Yeah, Renato told me because Carlo and Cary . . . ah . . . work with me. I had to rearrange a few guys so I could still be off this week. They're okay, Zorah and Ethel, right?"

"Yes. They just want to live together as who they are."

"Who are they?" It was a genuine question.

"You haven't picked up on that?" I asked.

"On what?" He was sincere.

"Zorah and Ethel are a lesbian couple!" I blurted out.

"Hah! Now things make sense. Talk about a double standard. Carmine is okay with Rocco and Drew, but not Zorah and Ethel. I guess it's the age. I mean, with Zorah and Ethel, guess they had to keep their secret, right?" He peddled back some.

"Yeah. It was a different time when they met," I added.

"Are you ever going to get around to telling me why you wanted me to call you?"

This startled me. I took a deep breath and sighed audibly. "Okay. How about visiting me soon, here in Houston?"

"Seriously? You want me to visit, soon? I don't have to wait until after Labor Day?"

"Yes. If you want to . . . come whenever is convenient for you and your work." I breathed deeply again. "I'm taking off from work until after the July 4th holiday. Originally, it was to give me time to think, then boom! Family fell from the sky into my lap."

"Maggie! That's wonderful! Thank you! What changed your mind, dare I ask?"

"Let's just say I realize I need to explore my feelings, away from a wake and funeral. And this weekend, being surrounded by cousins: Rocco, Cary, Carlo, and Sal, I heard a lot of opinions I never got to hear back home, what with the funeral and all." I was beginning to feel relaxed with him; his voice was even, with no hint of emotion. I could picture his face in my mind. "Let me know what you decide."

"The boys will be out of school end of this week; I'll have a talk with them. Sometimes they have summer plans I know nothing about!"

"I'm at the Bay house until after the Fourth . . ."

"The Bay house?"

"Oh! Sorry. My girlfriend Patty owns a huge . . . well back home, we'd call it a cottage by the lake, but here the cottages are up on sixteen-foot stilts to avoid getting flooded during hurricanes. When I arrived Friday, Patty picked me up and took me straight to Bolivar to her Bay house. It's not on Galveston Island. Bolivar is a peninsula across the Bay from Galveston, where the locals go for R & R." I realized I was babbling again.

Politely he said, "I'm sure it will all become clearer when I get there. Is there another phone number where I can reach you?"

"There's no phone at the Bay house. Call my office and talk with Alice, and she'll make sure I get your messages. Oh, by the way, Carlo is staying on until after the Fourth. I think it has something to do with Alice!"

"What about Sal? He's one of my crew, too."

"Patty."

"So that's why. I'm anxious to get to Texas. It seems all the answers to why my life is turned around are in Texas!" He mused.

I laughed. "So, that's it, Stevie."

"I'm so glad you asked me to call you, Maggie. I'll let you know the plan as soon as I talk with the boys."

"Okay. Bye Stevie, bye."

"Bye."

I stayed overnight at my apartment. By the time I completed all the chores, it was rush hour, and getting stuck in traffic on I-45 south was in no way my idea of a good time driving. When I got to the Bay house the next day, I learned that Carlo had moved out of the house and into The Galvez Hotel. No one said why but I remembered Alice saying they had no privacy. Well, him in a hotel, I'm sure that will be private enough.

The remaining house party (Aunt Zorah, Ethel, Patty, Sal, and me) settled into a routine. Seemed we naturally fell into the balance of chores. Aunt Zorah made breakfast, I threw together a lunch, and supper was up for grabs. Some nights we all went out together for seafood, and some nights Sal grilled, and some nights it was leftovers on your own. Surprisingly, it worked out well.

I enjoyed the morning swims alone. I think everyone in the house knew it was therapeutic for me. I was happy no one joined me so I could swim nude. Zorah and Ethel made late afternoon their time for swimming. Sal and Patty could be seen headed out for a swim just as the sun was setting.

I was very aware that Sal and Patty were becoming an item. The confirmation came the second Friday we were together. Around eight in the evening, Patty showed up all decked out in a lovely summer dress and wedges.

"Going someplace?" I asked.

"As a matter of fact, yes."

"Where may I ask," I continued.

"I'm not sure; someplace on Galveston Sal found."

I noticed the raised eyebrow look Aunt Zorah and Ethel exchanged. Ethel muted the TV. I took a chance, "Something you two want to share?" I asked.

"Well, Sal . . ." Ethel looked at Patty, "Dear, are you ready for anything?"

Patty laughed, "I think I know what you're getting at . . ." and before she could say anymore, Sal entered the room.

Okay. Let me give a fashion editor's description. The gentleman wore a stylish brunette wig that unfortunately enhanced his Roman nose. His choice of lipstick was exactly right, considering. The white sleeveless halter top tied in a knot mid-chest showed just enough chest hair. The capris slacks in a lavender flower print were tasteful for a sixteen-year-old girl. The gentleman selected a leather shoulder strap, natural straw bag, and ballet flats in lavender that complemented his slacks. Accessories included several bangle bracelets and dainty hoop earrings.

I didn't know Sal had pierced ears!

We all just stared. I smiled broadly to keep from laughing nervously. I realized that all my life, while I knew that Sal was a crossdresser, I had never seen him in women's clothing other than the baby doll pajamas when he first arrived. This was . . . amazing.

Patty walked to him, hooked her arm in his, and said, "Are you ready, Babe?"

"Yes. Bye, all! Don't wait up!" Sal offered. And out the door they went.

There was silence for a few minutes. Ethel unmuted the TV. It was only Aunt Zorah, Ethel, and me. Alice was commuting on days when she had a few appointments, but she stopped at The Galvez first. We never knew when she'd pop in here.

Ethel muted the TV and got my attention, "Are you alright, dear?"

"To tell you the truth, that was the first time I ever saw my cousin all decked out in women's clothing! I'm speechless!" I confessed.

Aunt Zorah got off the sofa and headed for the kitchen, "You get-a used to it." When she returned, she handed me a cold beer and another for Ethel and herself.

"Thanks. I need this!" I said as I reached to accept the long neck.

"Pay no attention. Been too long now for him to-a change," Zorah added.

I moved into the bedroom that Alice and Honey vacated. I was happy to be by myself again;   Moon joined me. I liked retreating there, during the high noon hours, and, like now, with the house so quiet. I amused myself with magazines Patty picked up at Coastal Groceries, and I napped. This routine was becoming wonderfully comfortable to the point that the thought of returning to work, seeing clients, seemed less and less appealing. Oh God, I was going soft! What am I thinking? I must make a living; I have a career! But . . . not today.

On the Friday of the July 4th weekend, Alice and Carlo showed up around eleven a.m.. She bounced up the stairs. Patty and I were on the deck. I lowered my sunglasses to watch Alice. Patty looked at me. I looked at her knowing we both were thinking the same thing. She got laid.

"Hi! We're here!" Alice announced.

"So, I see," Patty said. "Looks like you'll have to move back into my bedroom," she said, looking at me.

"Oh no, that won't be necessary! I'm staying with Carlo at The Galvez this weekend," she answered, realizing Patty had tricked her into telling all.

"Hi Maggie, Patty," Carlo said after he unloaded grocery bags inside the house. "Have you heard from Stevie D, Maggie?"

"No. Alice, any messages for me?"

"Ah, no . . ."

"Ah, I've heard from Stevie D," Carlo interrupted. He looked sheepish.

"Sit down. You look like you're going to faint," Patty directed.

Just then, Aunt Zorah and Ethel joined us, carrying a tray with a pitcher of iced tea and glasses. "Soon, no-a good out here!" Aunt Zorah remarked. "What's-a wrong with you?" she asked Carlo as she handed him a tall glass of iced tea.

"Maggie, I'm not supposed to say, seeing that he hasn't told you yet," Carlo started.

"He...Stevie?" I asked.

"Yeah," Carlo replied reluctantly.

"What?" Patty pushed.

"He's here; well not here, he's on Galveston, at The Galvez . . ."

"Really?" I thought this incredible.

"Yes, with his boys. They arrived Wednesday, but he didn't want you to know until next week, so he and the boys are hanging out, they visited NASA yesterday, and I guess just waiting. But the boys are having a blast! I can't remember any time that Stevie D took the boys on vacation," Carlo offered.

"Why doesn't he want me to know he's here? I called him a week ago and told him it was okay to visit. All he said was he'd check with the kids. He wanted to wait until school was out. How strange," I was thinking out loud.

"Drive over to the Island, check out The Galvez," Patty offered.

"Yeah," Carlo agreed. "He'd probably be relieved if you did that."

I looked at Aunt Zorah, "What-a you looking at me for? Go, go, you gonna go anyway no matter what we say."

I noticed Carlo had recovered. Didn't realize that he was that afraid of telling me Stevie D was in the same state, hell, the same county for that matter! This is so weird! What is it about Stevie D? I keep forgetting that these men work with each other, and there is a strict chain of command among Sicilian Families. Stevie D is older than Carlo, Sal, and Cary. Rocco and Stevie D are about the same age. But Stevie D has his own crew, if the current Family Business still runs with crews, then that makes Stevie a boss. No one ever hints at what the existing Business is about. Not even a drunk Aunt Zorah. I always thought that I knew what The Business was but had my doubts those activities continue.

That night I couldn't sleep. The air was on, the room nice and cool, and the moon was full. I sat up, arms wrapped around my knees tucked under my chin, staring at the moon. I needed to talk to someone. Patty!

I softly knocked on her bedroom door, whispering, "Patty? Can I come in?"

No answer. I knocked again, "Patty?"

From behind me, I heard, "Over here!"

Patty was standing in the doorway of Sal's room. I stood up straight. Hesitated.

She waved me in. I walked to that room, a little scared.

Patty was crawling back into bed with Sal. She was wearing a knee-length slumber tee. Sal sat up, re-adjusted pillows for them both to sit up facing me as I sat, legs folded, on the foot of the bed. Sal was wearing a cotton baby doll pajama top, pink.

"What's up, Cuz?" he asked.

"Stevie D is already here, on Galveston, with his three sons, already."

"Okay," Sal said, then gestured for me to continue.

"What do I do? Go there? Wait until he contacts me? But over the holiday weekend, he won't get ahold of me because the office is closed, and he doesn't know about how we call through Coastal Groceries, and what if he thinks I changed my mind about wanting him here, and what do I do with his kids? He never indicated that he might bring his boys with him and how is it that . . ."

"Whoa! One item at a time!" Sal interrupted.

"Darlin', take a deep breath and relax!" Patty said.

Feeling foolish but following directions, I did relax and waited for more input.

"Good," Patty said, "Now, what do you want to do?"

"I'm not sure. Like I told you before, Patty, I can't be sure that my feelings for him are real or just because he was so gallant during my dad's wake and funeral, catering to my every need, because I was his assignment, by the way. But I'm not that woman. I know how to take care of myself and am in no way a damsel in distress that needs rescuing, and so what are my feelings about anyway?"

"Take a breath, girl, before you pass out from CO2 retention!" She wasn't as gentle with her direction this time.

Sal leaned forward, "Maggie, I've known Stevie D a long time. In fact, I think since Donna died. I had just been assigned to his crew. To tell you the truth, since his wife died, I've never seen Stevie D date or bring a girl to gatherings the family had. Not once. Watching him around you at the wake and funeral (which, by the way, was way more attention than any of us guys would have put into it) was a huge topic of conversation for his guys! If you ever tell him I told you this, not only will I deny it, but I know a guy, ya know what I mean?" He laughed.

"Oh, I'm so scared!" I mocked.

Sal reached out a hand across the bed towards me; I reached also and took his hand. "Cuz, it's about time you both had happiness. Look at me!" He leaned back, and his arms swallowed up Patty as they rocked back and forth laughing!

"Now I feel as if I'm intruding!"

They stopped. "No, no," Sal said, releasing Patty. "Cuz," he put one arm around Patty, but all I could see was the hairy armpit exposed with his reach and the pink baby doll pajamas. "I've found someone who loves me for exactly who I am!"

Patty had a massive grin on her face.

I looked from her to him and back to her.

"That was fast" was the only thing I could think to say that wasn't negative or a jab about the sex obviously going on here.

"So, you'll take my car and head for The Galvez tomorrow morning?" Patty asked.

"How about after lunch, when they're most likely be in the hotel avoiding the heat and sun," I offered.

"Sounds great! Take your swimsuit. Stevie D loves to swim. He's been known to even swim during the winter at the Y," Sal said.

"Really?" I have no imagination about Stevie D's leisure life. Boy, have I got a lot to learn.

"After lunch sounds perfect," Patty added.

I got off the bed, walked around to Patty, kissed her cheek, and hugged her. Then I walked around the bed to Sal and did the same. I hooked my little finger in the strap of his baby doll pajamas, "Pink's your color!"

The lobby of The Galvez is fantastic. Built in 1911, its original grandeur was unmistakable. I sat in the spacious lobby that occupied the entire seaside of the hotel with windows that stretched to the ceiling and from wall to wall. The Gulf breeze wafted through the area. I leaned back, allowing my head to rest on the back of the high-back chair, taking deep breaths of what felt like clean air.

"Maggie?" The voice was his!

I snapped forward. "Ah, hi!" was all I managed.

Three young men joined him. I didn't remember their names.

"Hey, it's Maggie, from the funeral!" the shortest boy said.

His brother elbowed him hard. "What I say?"

"Boys, this is Doctor Maggie Blake, and yes, you met Dr. Blake at her dad's funeral. Her dad worked with your Uncle Joe and your grandfather," Stevie D explained.

"Hi boys! I must admit, I don't remember . . ." pointing to the youngest who spoke up, "You are, don't tell me, Capra?"

"Yeah!"

"And you," the next boy was as tall as his dad yet lacked the filled-out physique a young adult, ". . . are Stevens?"

He looked disappointed. "No, I'm Wilder," he elbowed the brother, "he's Stevens."

"Well, I'm delighted to meet you under very different circumstances!" I got up, "Welcome to Texas! What have y'all been doing?"

"You really say 'y'all'? Aren't you from Buffalo, like us?" Capra asked.

"Yes, I'm really from Buffalo, but I've lived in Texas for many years now. I've picked up the lingo."

"Sounds funny," he added.

"What brings you here?" Stevie D asked.

"To meet you," I said straightforwardly, then just smiled and stared into his eyes as a challenge to ask me more about how I knew he was in town.

"Okay!" was all he could manage. "Well, we were headed to the pool. It's way too hot to walk out on the sand, so we thought we'd cool off at the pool."

"It just so happens that I'm wearing my swimsuit under this caftan!"

He looked a little surprised. "Then let's go!"

We continued walking through the lobby. The boys took point, knowing exactly where they were going.

Stevie D was silent for a while and then said, "Carlo."

"Carlo?" I echoed.

Stevie D just looked at me like one does when they are being bull-shitted.

I smiled. "Okay, Carlo. Seems there is a mutual interest between him and my girlfriend, Alice. How long are you staying here, in Galveston?" I ended up asking.

"How much time do you need? The boys are out of school, and, to tell you the truth, this is the first vacation I think we ever took as a family. It's a big deal for them," Stevie D said.

"Then, if you'd like, bring the boys over to Bolivar, Patty's Bay house, where I'm staying for now, along with Aunt Zorah and Ethel."

"They're still here?" he looked surprised.

"Zorah and Ethel? Yes," I answered.

"Bet you money that Carmine is really pissed," Stevie D said, shaking his head and smiling.

"What can he do? They want to live together! What's Uncle Carmine's problem?"

"Let's see, how can I put this? Zorah is a retiree from The Business, everyone knows her, and it wouldn't look good. Best I can do," he answered.

"And what exactly is the business?" His opening was perfect.

Stevie D moved close and draped his arm over my shoulder, "No one can tell you that, except Carmine himself."

An answer! I was stunned.

We were at the pool. The boys were already in the water, splashing each other. No one else was around. Way too hot for most.

"This heat isn't bothering you?"

He shrugged and then cannonballed into the pool! I was drenched. The water war, boys versus Dad, was on, and for the first time in quite a while, I realized I was laughing, laughing in fun, no nervous laugh, just laughing, then stripped off my caftan and jumped in joining them.

I was invited to join Stevie D and the boys for supper at the new Moody Gardens. I hadn't been there, so it really was a treat. It was the most relaxed I'd been in a month.

Once we placed our food orders, drinks were served. Cold beer for Stevie D, a gin and tonic for me, and soda for the boys (who became embarrassed when ordering "pop," the Buffalo slang for soda pop.) I asked the boys, "Tell me, how is it that the three of you ended up with names of movie directors?"

"Our dad is crazy?" Stevens answered. The eldest at eighteen, Stevens was the image of his dad. I learned that after nine months in Europe (while some kids take their senior year of high school trips to New York City, Stevie D arranged for Stevens to visit Sicily) home base being in Sicily with a cousin of his Grandpa Leo, he traveled to all the usual places. He came home speaking Sicilian surprisingly well and made amazing Sicilian pizza, or so he said.

"Dad loves movies, the kind you go to the show to see. Not so much when they come to TV," Capra offered. The youngest at nine, he was beginning to sprout.

"Yeah," Wilder said. He was seventeen, and would enter his senior year of high school in the fall. "We have the movie directors' first names as well, but Pop here called us by their last names since the day we were born."

I turned to Stevie D, "And, what was the reason for this?" I mused.

"I guess because I was tired of repeating names, you know, Sicilian families," he shrugged. "Do you know exactly how many Carmines there are in your family alone?"

I had to think a minute: Uncle Carmine, one, Angela's son, two, Cary, three, oh and if you count our dead grandfather, four. "Four."

"Exactly; I have a goombah, and they have seven Sams in their family. I think that's crazy."

"Did your wife approve?" I spoke before I thought, and now I was aware of that moment of awkwardness that followed. "I'm sorry," I said, all within seconds.

Stevie D answered, "She wanted to use the first names, Billy, Frank, and George, but that was too ordinary for me. Their names are B (period) Wilder Bataglia, F (period) Capra Bataglia, and G (period) Stevens Bataglia. I think it worked out really well," he turned to his sons, "What do you think, guys?"

They all joined a chorus of "it's great" and "fine" and how much they liked their names.

After walking around Moody Gardens, I was invited up to their suite. They had a sprawling three-room suite: two bedrooms and a living area with a small kitchenette. Stevie D called down for a bottle of wine for him and me and a pizza for the kids with soda.

"They just ate!" I declared.

"Obviously, you know nothing about raising young boys!" Stevie D teased.

The boys departed into their bedroom with the pizza. Stevie D and I got comfortable in the living area. We caught up on what was going on between Uncle Carmine and Aunt Zorah. We had a good laugh about it, yet we felt for Aunt Zorah and agreed by now she should be allowed to live her own life.

"Thank you for this," Stevie D offered.

"For what?"

"For showing up today, spending time with us; you're invited to stay over if you like. I can bunk with the boys. Say you'll stay over. I like having you here with us," he gently pressed.

It took no thought, "Okay. Then I'd like all of you to come out to Patty's place and join the herd there for the fireworks and grilling and swimming in the Gulf."

"It's a deal."

Like an old married couple, Stevie D found a pay-for movie we agreed upon and settled into each other for the duration of the show. Once it was over, there was absolutely no pressure for anything else: he got a few items out of his room, kissed my cheek, and headed for the boys' room. I sat on the side of the bed for a few minutes reviewing the day. "Wow," I thought, "I've got to watch out; that was all too comfortable."

A gentle knock on the bedroom door woke me. I reached for the clock first. Two-thirty. "He's got to be kidding me!" I thought. "This is his plan? Try to get into my bed in the middle of the night?" I opened the door just enough to speak through.

"Doctor Blake," Stevens said, "I'm sorry to wake you . . ."

"Stevens! Is something wrong? Someone sick?"

"No . . . ah . . . I'd like to talk to you . . . if you don't mind . . . Do you like tea? I can make us a cup of tea?"

"I'll be right out," I said. I threw on my caftan and joined him in the living area. He had turned on just one lamp. The windows faced the Gulf, and the sound of the waves was soothing.

"Doctor Blake . . ."

I interrupted, "Call me Maggie, please. What's on your mind, Stevens?" I was in therapist mode.

"I . . . ah . . ." he laughed nervously, "I guess I hadn't thought it out!" The kettle whistled, and he ran to the kitchenette. "Whew, I don't want to wake anyone!" He handed me a cup.

I dipped the teabag a few times, giving him time to start over again.

"Doctor . . . ah, Maggie. Whew, I'll just spit it out: you make my dad happy. Do you know how long it's been since I've seen my dad happy? I can't even remember a time, even when Mom was alive," he was waving one hand/arm in the Sicilian manner, and I thought how well he had learned!

"Maggie, I wanted you to know it. Since Mom died, well, this is the first real family vacation we've had. And he's so happy! . . . And it's you, Maggie. Dad is in love with you.

"Whew, there, I've said it!" He leaned back in relief and sipped his tea.

I started to laugh. He was so ridiculously charming in his mission.

"Stevens! I'm so flattered!"

"Maggie, I'm not flattering you. I mean, that didn't come out right. Dad loves you. My brothers and I have talked it over, and we hope you might love Dad too or think about falling in love with Dad.

"I know you've spent time with each other, I mean your dad's wake and funeral, which I know that isn't the best of times, but you did see what a great guy my dad is. He is considerate, and we haven't seen him this happy. He's always good to us, never mean or anything," he finally took a breath.

"Stevens, relax! Okay," I put my cup of tea on the coffee table, "I'll let you in on how I feel, but you must promise that you won't discuss anything we say here with your dad. Okay?"

"I'd like to tell my brothers. I mean if you let me tell them. Then he leaned in the direction of where their bedroom was located, "so they can go back to bed and stop listening at the door!"

I heard soft shuffling behind that door. I took a deep breath because I was fully aware that if I told Stevens how I felt, and he told his brothers, then I was raising the hopes of three innocents in this cat-and-mouse game between their dad and me. It was a point of no return, in a way.

"Maggie? Are you alright?" Stevens asked with genuine concern in his voice.

I had spaced out for a moment, wondering how I got in this situation.

"Yes, yes. I'm fine, Stevens. You guys are great! And you're right. Your dad and I did spend a lot of time together during my dad's wake and funeral. To tell you the truth, I wouldn't have gotten through it as well without him.

"Now I ask myself, are my feelings for your dad because of all the nice things he did for me in my deepest grief? Or are my feelings for him really for him minus the nice things during my dad's funeral when I was a mess? Do you understand that?"

"Yeah, yeah, I think I do. And I think that's smart of you. Is that part of why we're here taking our first-ever family vacation? You were on Galveston Island?" he asked, smirking.

"Technically, Bolivar Peninsula," I corrected amusingly. "I did invite your dad. But, in all honesty, I didn't expect you guys! That was the bonus."

"Maggie, I'm not so young that I don't know it takes time sometimes before someone knows for sure about whether or not they are in love, so take your time. But, if we had our way, you'd only get a week!"

I laughed, covering my mouth in case I was too loud and waking the guys. "Stevens, I'm so touched and impressed over how much you care for and think about your dad."

"When Mom died, boy," he shook his head, "Maggie, we were scared Dad would do something crazy, too, and then what would the three of us do? But, no, he sucked it up. My grandparents, Mom's parents, came to the house; I thought Grandpa would kill my dad. Wilder was so scared he called our other grandpa to hurry over to our house. What a scene!" He looked up at me, his eyes tearing up, "Maggie, I'll never forget that night as long as I live.

"In the end, once everyone calmed down, Dad said his living tribute to Donna, that's Mom's name, was to raise the three of us the best he knew how with all the advantages he could give us. Grandpa Leo told Grandpa Dominic that he stood behind Dad and would make sure that happened.

"The three of us heard it all. Capra was only four, but I held him the entire time that night, and his eyes looked like a deer in the headlights. He might not have understood what was being said, but he understood yelling. Yet Dad and our grandpas acted as if we didn't," he looked straight at me again, "how could we not hear them? But it was never acknowledged. And Dad has kept his word. Now he's happy. He's happy because he's in love. I know it, and I love him so much I want to see him keep it." He was blushing with his final remark.

I leaned across the sofa and hugged his neck. Forehead touching forehead, I said, "You have my word that I take all of this seriously. I do have strong feelings for your dad. I'll continue sorting them out come sunrise!"

"Thanks!" he hugged me, quick release, kissed my cheek, and jumped up off the sofa.

When the door closed behind Stevens, I flopped back on the sofa. The encounter was so incredible, just utterly amazing.

The noise that woke me was the room service setting up breakfast in the living area. I showered and shampooed, then joined the guys.

Stevie D approached me with a kiss on my cheek, "How did you sleep?"

I sensed an edgy look from the boys, "Great! I loved the sound of the waves during the night. Very much like a lullaby." The boys exhaled.

Over breakfast, we planned. They would pack a few things for a couple of nights at Patty's place. Then, we'd grocery shop at Walmart because we were springing four more people on Patty. Also, I suggested a few inflatable rafts the boys could use as mattresses because, most likely, the living area would turn into a dorm room for the men.

Patty was entirely welcoming. Honey had arrived with Frank Dorr, our colleague. Once I had Honey away from the crowd, I asked her, "What possessed you to drag along Frank? He's such a gloomy Gus?"

"Yes! Exactly. I had a --let's call it an informal session --with Frank this week. Believe me, if anyone needs to be surrounded by people as demonstrative as your family, it's Frank."

"Really? That bad?"

"Yes," she took my arm with one hand and led me to the kitchen, "Let's make sangria!"

The guys gravitated to the grill and the area under the house; the ladies claimed the deck. Everyone swam in the Gulf well before noon, and downtime hours were initiated with a huge meal and lots of laughter.

Alice and Carlo took my room. Patty was shacked up with Sal. The boys found a board game they set up in the kitchen, and to my surprise, Aunt Zorah and Ethel joined them. The men had the living area with the TV, and I retreated into Patty's bedroom, Honey in tow. She and I flopped on the bed. It didn't take long for her to fall asleep. I was glad; I needed a break.

It was crowded. On the verge of feeling overwhelmed, I reminded myself that my life had made a significant one-eighty. The jury was still out on whether it was for the better.

By four p.m., the guys had piled into two cars and hit the road for fireworks. Patty encouraged them to bring back fresh fruit if they saw a farmer's roadside stand or fresh fish from the back of roadside pick-up trucks vendors. She assured them that the produce and fish would be fresh. "That's how we do it in Texas," she told them. The sun was beginning to move behind the house, so the deck was comfortable. The ladies assembled, each with a drink of their choice in hand.

"I love weekends like this. When my kids were young, they'd each have a guest or two over, and it felt just like this! There's a lot of really nice, loving energy here now," Patty said.

"It's a like a holiday. . ." Zorah started, and Ethel interrupted, "It is a holiday!"

"You-a know what I mean, like a holiday when you and I," she smiled at Ethel, "we get into the kitchen early and cook all day! People, they a come in and out of the kitchen; grab a hunk of bread and dip it into the sauce; we slap-a their hands; we laugh a lot!"

That made everyone smile. I gave it a half-smile. I had forgotten all about what it was like on holiday with Sicilian family.

Honey added, "Thanks to Patty, Dawn and I were always part of the gang during the summer months. But I loved best the Thanksgiving and Christmas gatherings. For me, there is nothing better than this house during the winter."

"And" Patty spoke up, "because Honey loved it so much, she paid for the winterizing!"

"You didn't have to say that!" Honey protested.

"Yes, I did! I'm not the doctor here! I'm the hippy mom with the tarot cards and crystals!"

"Did someone say tarot cards?" Alice asked.

"Yes! Are you interested?" Patty answered.

"Yes! How about right now? I want to know what's in my future!"

"An Italian stallion," Zorah quipped. The group was stunned for a second, then we all broke into gut hurting laughter.

Patty jumped up, heading for the kitchen. Alice followed.

Zorah and Ethel excused themselves and headed towards the shore. That left Honey and me.

She moved to a chair next to me. "What's going on, girl?"

I sighed. "A lot." I filled her in: Stevie D on Galveston with his sons; all the outings we did together culminating with Stevens and my late-night heart to heart.

"How do you feel?" The quintessential therapist's question was hanging in the air for several minutes as I stared into the glass I was holding.

Then I looked up at her, "I don't know. Yet, I feel that I want to move, soften my attitude towards him . . ."

"You mean toward yourself."

"Toward me?" That was incredulous!

"That's what I said: toward you. Maggie, I don't know if you're scared or what, but you are the only one in the way! We all see it. Are you afraid that what you believed about yourself is no longer true? The self-sufficient doctor might, in the end, need love and family, like the rest of us?" Honey posed.

"Ouch! What do you mean, 'needs family?' All y'all have been my family since graduate school! I've had a family, thank you very much!" I said with a nod of my head.

"In a way, that's true. But, this family, the cousins, Aunt Zorah and Ethel, your blood family, God, they're great! How can you possibly be resisting them?"

"Because you don't know what it's like back in Buffalo. The Sicilian code of conduct for women and all things family! They're great here because that code doesn't stretch this far," I argued.

"Well, that might have been true while you were growing up, but from what I see and hear, the rules are being severely bent, even broken," Honey countered.

I calmed down. "I see that too, and I don't trust it; I'm waiting for a long arm to reach out and bite Aunt Zorah in the ass. Trust me, the other shoe hasn't fallen yet," I warned.

"God! Good thing you weren't an English major, mixing metaphors like that!" Honey joked.

"Very funny; but believe me, once I told Stevens I'd take it very seriously, I realized I agreed to this courtship, or whatever you want to call it. That's as far as I've gotten," and before Honey could quip, I went into the house.

When the guys returned about two hours later, they came bearing gifts: multiple fireworks, corn on the cob, watermelon and fresh shrimp, and half a dozen fish. The cousins fired up the grill. Stevie and the boys took to the shore with the fireworks, far enough away that it wasn't deafening. The men encouraged us, the women, to leave the house for the beach: supper was all theirs, and they'd let us know when it was ready. It was a gift to us.

We quickly changed into our swimsuits, grabbed rafts, and headed for the shore. We didn't have to be told twice.

After supper, Stevie D asked me to join him on a walk along the shore.

"Thanks for having us here. The boys are having a great time, and they really like you."

I smiled. The night was perfect: the breeze was just enough; the sun was setting behind all the beach houses, and the crashing of the waves on the shore the only music I needed.

"You're doing a great job raising them. They're very compassionate boys. If you don't mind my asking, how old were they when their mother died?"

"Stevens was fourteen, Wilder was twelve, and Capra was four." He was looking at his feet and occasionally picking up a seashell, which mostly were oyster shells.

"They were young. Did you have any help? I mean, you still had to work."

"The wonderful advantage of working in The Family Business," he said with a knowing smirk. "My dad and mom really kicked it up a notch with the boys. "Mom met them at my house after school, and Dad took them to all the sports they were involved in when I was out of town. I had Capra in daycare. Mom picked him up on the way to my house when she headed there for the other two after school. It worked very well."

The silence didn't bother me, and Stevie D didn't seem to need a constant babble.

"I've got something to say but let me say it all before you comment or even reject the idea. Okay?"

"Sure," was all he said.

"I'm calling this," I gestured the two of us, "a courtship. I know that might sound corny, but it fits because I'm attempting to get out of my way. My friends, my good, loving-me-like-a-sister friends tell me that's what I do, get in my way. I'm listening to them. I accept what they tell me as true even if I don't see it in me. You asked Uncle Renato if you could call me, visit me, hang around with me? My answer is yes. I'm open to all of that.

"Whatever you say, please don't make fun of me," was my closing plea, which, after I said it, felt foolish.

He stopped in his tracks and gently grabbed me by my arms, turning me to him. "Maggie, this is wonderful news. And the farthest thing on my mind is making fun of you! I love you, Maggie. Now, I'll be bold and say I feel that you love me, too, but it scares the hell out of you!"

With that pronouncement, I crushed him in a hard hug. I know tears were rolling down my cheeks. I didn't let go until I knew I wouldn't cry outright; it took a minute or two.

"Now what?" I asked as I wiped the stream off my face with my index finger.

"Well, I plan on staying the rest of the week, but at The Galvez. We haven't had a vacation ever. I like it here. And there's so much to do around here. I want to drive up to San Antonio and see the Alamo, and I hear there's an amusement park in that area."

"Yes, Six Flags Over Texas."

"Six flags? What does that mean?"

"Texas was under the rule of six different countries in her history: Spain, France, Mexico, the Republic of Texas, the Confederate States of America, and the United States. Six flags."

"Wow, that's confusing but interesting. When the boys ask, I'll sound brilliant. After that, it's back here for the remaining days until we fly home next weekend.

"When do you plan on returning to work?" he asked me.

Without telling Honey, Alice, or Patty, I answered, "Wednesday; this coming Wednesday. I'll help Patty clean up after this holiday party is over, and then I'll need a day at home to get things back into a routine, including Moon and me!"

"What about Zorah and Ethel? When are they leaving?" He asked.

"I have no idea! They seem to love it here, much to my surprise. I thought the heat would get them, but not so far. It surprises the hell out of me! Have you heard anything about them back home? From Aunt Bertha?" I asked, remembering my Aunt Bertha was also Stevie D's Aunt Bertha.

"Ya know, Aunt Bertha and Uncle Joe are pretty different from the others if you don't mind my saying. She did say that Zorah left because she was angry with Carmine. But nothing more; just isn't her nature."

"Well, I'm sure this isn't over between Uncle Carmine and Zorah. I'm kind of waiting for the other shoe to fall," I said.

"Maggie, changing the subject, once I'm back in Buffalo, what's best for you? Do you want telephone calls, letters, or, and don't reject this next suggestion offhandedly, but I can arrange to visit every couple of weeks."

"Letters?" I was laughing. "Every couple of weeks? Are you crazy?"

"What? You think I can't write?" he nudged me playfully, "And yes, I could arrange to be here every couple of weeks. We have business at the port."

He had no idea that wasn't why I was laughing, "I like the idea of letters! And" I took a deep breath, "visits. There I said it!"

He stopped in his tracks. "Really? You are serious about giving this a shot? I'm free to visit?"

"Yes. I'm giving it a shot, and I invite you to visit," I whispered more in fear than anything else.

He pulled me to him and kissed me soft, long, and with passion. How did I keep from melting right there? Okay, reasonable risk so far.

The fireworks shot off Galveston Island were usually spectacular! The sun was fast fading behind the beach houses. We all headed to the shoreline with chairs and tiki torches. The guys filled a cooler with beer, soda, and iced tea. There was leftover pizza from lunch and chips. I love the summer months. It was almost nine-forty-five p.m. before the fireworks started. The long days during the summer were so welcoming. I leaned back on a low-slung lounge chair. There was a lot of chatter going on around me. This was a new configuration of the family for me: Honey, Zorah, and Ethel were huddled under a beach umbrella (for what reason I have no idea.) Carlo and Alice were talking and laughing with Sal and Patty. Stevie D was throwing a Frisbee with the boys until it was so dark, they couldn't see the thing anymore. Then Stevie D pulled up a beach chair (a sawed-off lawn chair) next to me.

"I've got something to ask you, permission, so to speak," he said.

"Oh, pray tell, what?" I quipped.

"While I think 'Maggie' fits you very well, but I'd like to call you something no one else does. What do you think about that?"

"Hmm; depends on what it is," I held my breath; please, not Margaret.

"Innamorata," he whispered.

"Innamorata? It means?"

"Sweetheart, but a formal, special sweetheart," he explained. "There's a song Innamorata sung by Dean Martin that's a knock-out."

I gave him a full, warm smile, "I'd like nothing better," and leaned over and kissed him quickly. But not so quickly that it escaped the audience all around us! The hoots and hollers went up as if their favorite team just scored a touchdown. I blushed.

Stevie D just waved them off and called out, "Carlo, throw me a beer!"

The fireworks distracted the group. Oohs and awes accompanied each burst. Enjoying the explosive festival, I turned to see if Stevie D was enjoying them as much as I was. What I saw was his boys all hanging off him, obviously needing to be somehow touching him and checking his face for enjoyment.

Dragging all the beach equipment back up to the house was a challenge in the dark. The boys wanted to sleep out on the deck, but Patty said there would be nothing left of them in the morning once the mosquitos got hold of them. That killed that idea.

I was walking up the dunes with Frank. "How did you like the fireworks, Frank?" I asked for openers.

"Great! Can't remember my last July fourth; maybe when my kids lived home," he said with no expression.

"Thanks for holding down the fort for me while I buried my dad," I said, more in an offering to keep the conversation going.

"You're welcome. It was a pleasure; really, your clients are interesting."

"Anyone in crisis while I was gone?"

"You were missed, for sure, but everyone was gracious enough that I sensed they truly dug in and worked with me," he turned and looked at me, "it was gratifying," he reported.

"I'm glad it worked out. I've needed the time off."

"When are you returning? Not that I'm in a hurry or anything. Take all the time you need," he offered.

"Wednesday; I'll help Patty house clean Monday, and then head home; get my place opened up, so to speak, and be back to work Wednesday," I reported.

"Okay!" He flashed a smile.

Alice just took over the third bedroom with Carlo, no conversation about it. That left Honey and me in Patty's room.

"Are you sure?" Honey asked.

I started to laugh, "Honey, I know that Patty and Sal have been sleeping together since the second night they met, but that's not my style. And his boys are here, too."

"Oh, I wonder what he wears to bed."

"Stevie D?" I was confused.

"No! Sal!" she clarified.

"Pink cotton baby-doll pajamas, with lace," I answered matter-of-factly.

"You know?" She was surprised.

"Don't ask."

Honey and I settled in, waiting for the rotation in and out of the bathroom. It was necessary to dash at the right moment and beat the next guy out. I missed my chance to Zorah, so I strolled into the living area to see how the dorm was set up. There was hardly any walking room around the sofa cushions on the floor with the rafts, pillows, light blankets, and clothing scattered everywhere.

"A mess, right?" Stevie D asked.

"It looks like fun. Where's Frank?" I asked.

"He's showering downstairs. I wouldn't blame him if he stayed downstairs," Stevie D said. "Even with screens, mosquitos find a way inside. Anyway, I think he needs to be around the boys. Their energy is infectious," I commented.

"No kidding; I think I'm keeping up with them. Once I hit the pillow, I sleep like the dead."

Just then, Zorah motioned to me from the bathroom to hurry and get in there. I ran! Then, releasing the bathroom to Honey, Patty motioned me into the kitchen.

"What?" I asked; she seemed so secretive.

"What would you say if Sal stayed?" Patty asked.

I squinted my eyes at her.

"Stop that!" she demanded.

"What?" I said through squinted eyes.

"Stop squinting your eyes! You do that when you can't believe what you've just heard!"

"You're right! What did I just hear? That Sal is moving in with you?" I replied.

"No! No, he's just staying on," she explained.

"Because of Aunt Zorah; still trying to get Aunt Zorah to let him drive them back to Buffalo?"

"Not exactly . . ." Patty squirmed a little.

"Not exactly; then what exactly?" I pushed.

She gently punched my arm, "Stop being difficult."

"Okay," I opened the fridge and pulled out the wine. She pulled out two glasses from the cupboard. We stood by the sink, and I poured the wine.

"Now, start again," I asked once I had a good sip.

She continued to whisper, "Sal wants to stay. He says he can work from here for a while."

"I think you want that too," I assessed.

She swirled the wine in her stemware. "Yeah. Yeah, I want him to stay. For a while."

"You know you're about, hmm, twenty years older than he is, right?"

"Thirteen years, he's thirty-seven, and I'm fifty. It works out well. And stop making it more than what it is!" She pushed back.

"Didn't mean to; just forgot how old he is," I stared into the glass a minute, then sipped the wine. "Patty, what about Sal's . . . crossdressing?"

"Makes him all the more interesting," she didn't skip a beat.

"He's not a replacement for Gideon or Kingsley?" It felt very risky to ask. Her sons were so opposite of each other, Gideon the medical doctor and Kingsley the artist, yet the psychologist in me thought maybe . . .

"Don't be silly! Sal is older than my oldest son, and my sons are my sons! I love them, but I do know the difference between a mother's love and love with a lover!"

"My," I thought, "she didn't use the word fuck as I expected. This is different!"

"Thank you for saying that. The psychologist in me slipped out there a minute," I explained.

"So, you're okay if Sal stays?"

"Why do you need an okay from me? I'm leaving after cleaning up on Monday. I'm going back to work Wednesday. And, by the way, I'm taking Moon. If you can stand Sal, Aunt Zorah, and Ethel here like The Man Who Came to Dinner, go for it!" We toasted with our glasses, clinking ever so quietly.

"Hey, you can be a spy for me. See if Sal will tell you anything about the Family Business. And, maybe even Aunt Zorah will say more about what it is," I suggested.

"I'll keep that in mind," we clinked again, which this time brought Frank around the corner.

"I thought I heard whispering! Ah! Any of that wine left?"

We poured him a drink and sat at the table. Stevie D also joined us. The conversation centered around what to see in Texas within close driving distance. Stevie D also learned about how Alice and I joined Frank and Honey's psychology practice once we were graduated. Before anyone knew it, Honey and Sal joined the group, and we talked until two a.m..

Stevie D's first letter came about two weeks after he got back to Buffalo. It was cute. A lot of talk about what he and the boys did with their last week in Texas and the let-down of returning home, where it wasn't as exciting every day. Stevens took off for parts unknown, camping with friends. Wilder, it seemed, was holed up in his room with comic books and VHS movies. He, Stevie D, was catching up with work. He hoped I was back into the swing of things on my job. He signed off "with love, S."

I returned the superficial chatter.

# # #

As it turned out, July 4th came and went, but with no movement from the 'Zorah and Ethel camp,' at all.

Then, the day came when I was wonderfully comfortable at the office. Between clients, I even thought, "I'm back, I'm home, and I'm back in my element!" It felt good.

Alice knocked on the door as she opened it, allowing herself in. "Remember how you said that the other shoe hadn't fallen yet when it came to the situation with your Aunt Zorah and Ethel?"

I sat up straight, "Yes."

"You were right. There is a gentleman to see you."

"Who?"

"He said he's your uncle."

"NO!" I flew from around the back of my desk and into the waiting room. There he sat: Uncle Renato with a GQ magazine in front of his face and Marcello Mastroianni smiling back at me.

"Uncle Renato?"

The magazine came down. He stood with his arms up and out, inviting me, "Ciao Bella!"

We kissed each cheek simultaneously, and I enjoyed his embrace. "What are you doing here?" I asked as I straightened up.

"You got an office?"

"Follow me." As I passed Alice at the receptionist desk, I instructed, "No calls and hold the next client with apologies!"

She nodded yes, and I could see she was on the verge of laughing. I could have smacked her. Just wait until Uncle Renato learns you're sleeping with his beloved only son Carlo and you're not Sicilian, I mused to myself.

I closed the door behind us. "Have a seat, please."

He walked around, checking everything out, went behind my desk to read the framed degrees on the wall, then sat in my desk chair.

I slumped into the chair across from him.

"I hear Stevie D spent time with you over the holiday, with his boys. Good, good! How do you feel about him now?"

I fidgeted a little, realizing I was avoiding looking at him. "Stop that," I told myself, "You are not the patient here."

I took a physically exaggerated breath and said, "We're courting." Then I jumped to my defense, "I know that sounds corny, but it does describe the time we plan to take together to get to know each other . . . away from a funeral and family."

Uncle Renato threw up his hands in a hallelujah salute and said, "That's great!"

"But you didn't travel all this way just to ask me about how it's going between Stevie D and me." I challenged.

He sat silent for a moment, looking straight at me. I held his gaze. "You're right. Cut to the chase: where's your Aunt Zorah?"

"As far as I know, your older sister and her partner are staying with my girlfriend Patty on Bolivar, at Patty's Bay house."

"Take me there."

"After office hours if that's okay. I think I have maybe two clients more; then I'd be happy to drive you out to Bolivar."

He slapped the desk with both hands. The bang startled me, and I jumped. "Lunch?"

"I have a client waiting. But, in forty-five minutes, I'll be free for lunch."

He exaggerated the approving nod of his head. "I'll wait."

"Ah . . ." But it was too late to change his mind about where he was waiting; he was up, around the desk, and out the door just that fast.

After a few notes about the last session, I leaned back in my chair and told myself to calm down. It was only the second time in my life I'd seen Uncle Renato out of Buffalo, out of his comfort zone. The first was my

Ph.D. graduation. I thought a moment. I never had an opportunity to 'treat' Uncle Renato as a way of saying thank you for all he'd done for me, for Mom, and now, a sorta matchmaker between Stevie D and me. I decided it was time to say thanks.

I grabbed my purse. Uncle Renato was busy reading an old People magazine.

I interrupted, "Are you ready for lunch?"

He replaced the magazine, "Sure."

"My treat! I have something very Texan in mind. My way of saying thank you for all you've done for me: dad's funeral, always being there for Mom and me, and now with Stevie D."

He was standing, "Forget-about-it!"

"I will, over some delicious Texas barbeque!" I looped my arm through his and out the door we headed.

Part Three
Buffalo

Uncle Renato spent the weekend with Zorah and Ethel. Patty reported daily when she made excuses to leave the Bay house so the three could hash things out. Sal went with her. She called me from Coastal Groceries. She had no idea what kind of progress was made. Finally, on the Saturday night, Uncle Renato told Sal he needed a lift to the airport, he was flying home Sunday.

And that was that, for now.

About eight weeks later, Alice opened my office door as she knocked. "Hey, got a minute?" This was code for "I have a personal problem."

"Yes, just making some final notes before I pack it in and head home. You are coming out to Patty's for the weekend, right?"

"Yes. Four glorious days! No labor for Labor Day, I can hardly wait, but I wanted to tell you something else," she said with a plop onto the sofa. I moved away from my desk and joined her.

"What?"

"Carlo," she paused, looked coy, and then blurted out, "asked me to marry him!"

I was stunned. Sure, Carlo hadn't left Texas since he chased Aunt Zorah and Ethel here back in June. And yes, he and Alice had been an item almost from the get-go. But marriage?

"Wow, I don't know what to say," I was honest.

"Say you're happy for me! But here's the glitch," she broached carefully, waiting for me to say something.

"What?"

"He wants me to move to Buffalo."

I burst out laughing! I didn't know why. I just burst out laughing!

"That's not the reaction I was expecting, but okay, what's so funny?"

I composed myself. "To tell you the truth, I'm not sure. Maybe because my family wants me to return to Buffalo, and here you are, moving!"

"I didn't say I'd move," she was completely serious.

This sobered me up. "What? Why?"

"Because of our practice, we built something here, the both of us. Can you remember a time when we weren't joined at the hip when it came to graduate school and then into this practice? There was no way I was going to agree to a move like that without your input.

"Let's face it, it's our practice, and it's your family I'd be marrying into, so the way I see it, you've got a stake in this, almost as much as I do."

"This is incredibly generous of you," I replied.

"Why are you so surprised?" She reached over and took my hand. "You're like the sister I never had!"

I placed my hand over hers and said, "Yeah, I feel the same way."

"Do you want to wait until Stevie D arrives before we talk more?"

"Ah, what? What does he have to do with this?"

"Maggie, you know when he gets here, he'll most likely propose. Those letters he's sent you, the courtship as you keep calling it, well?" In the next moment, she was slapping my thigh, "And stop squinting your eyes at me! You always do that when you don't want to believe something! So, what time does Stevie D get in?"

"Late tonight; he wanted a full workday today, so he said he'll just take the limo to The Galvez. We'll meet tomorrow for lunch."

"Mafia guys put in long hours like other suits?" she joked.

"Careful," I said, pointing a finger at her, "you're about to marry into this family!"

"Yeah, yeah, yeah!" she teased. "I am so happy that Frank decided we all needed a four-day weekend for Labor Day! Oh, by the way, Honey invited him to join us again."

"I know, she told me, and I told Patty."

"So . . ." She implied a question that needed an answer.

"So, what?"

"Do you think Stevie D will propose to you this weekend?"

I got up and headed back to my desk, "I have no idea! Now get out of here so I can finish this work and get going! By the way, congratulations! OH! Is there a ring?"

"Not yet, but we're going shopping this weekend!" Alice said as she almost skipped out of my office.

As I drove out Interstate 45, with Moon rattling around in her carry case, I said, "Yeah, I know. It's a lot! Alice and Carlo; his expectation that she move to Buffalo, and then, that last letter from Stevie, about marriage. I don't think this is going to be the relaxing weekend I was hoping for. Now, settle down. I promise you a can of people tuna when we get to Patty's," and, she did. Moon settled down. I swear, she understands English.

I was feeling bad because I had sort of lied to Alice. Stevie D had already proposed in his last letter. He said he was asking in a letter because it would give me time to think, then he'd be there and, well, we'd be together. I wondered if he knew anything about Carlo proposing to Alice and asking her to relocate to Buffalo. I was too much a Sicilian to believe this was all a coincidence. There was no such thing as a coincidence in my family.

Traffic was heavy for a Thursday. Moon registered her displeasure with an audible sound. Exactly why I wanted to leave Thursday, I knew that tomorrow would be much worse. I'd stop at Coastal Groceries and browse. I loved their homemade baked goods and the fresh fish. I wanted to contribute something to the weekend, even though Patty never hinted that it was expected. She always seemed surprised when any of us brought bags of groceries for the house. And more than ever, I felt she had outdone herself on the generosity scale. I never imagined Zorah and Ethel, at their age withstanding a hot summer as they did. All had been decided when Uncle Renato visited after the Fourth of July. The ladies would return and live in Ethel's house after Labor Day weekend. Uncle Renato said he would send Cary and, since Carlo was already there, he could drive the ladies back, one in Ethel's car and the other in a rental. The ladies declined to fly back because they had had so much fun driving down to Texas. They wanted to imagine the change of seasons on the trip back. No one mentioned that it might be too soon for autumn leaves, but no one brought it up so that they could get the ladies on the road and back to Buffalo.

It was after seven in the evening when I pulled up to the Bay house. Aunt Zorah and Ethel waved from the deck. Patty greeted me as she came through the door.

"Here you are! Are you hungry? How are you doing? How long has it been? I think the last time I saw you was when your uncle was here, right?" She took Moon's case and left me holding the grocery bags. She set the case on a kitchen chair, opened it and Moon practically jumped into Patty's arms. "I made gumbo and rice and cornbread; this way, people can eat whenever they get here," she informed me, as she was noodling up to Moon.

"Please give Moon the can of people tuna I promised her, a reward for the car trip here. I've got my bag to get from the car, and then I'll eat."

I stopped on the deck. I leaned in and kissed each lady on each cheek. "How are you two? God! Look how tan you are! How are you holding up in this heat and humidity?" I sat on the edge of a chair.

Ethel spoke first, "We love it! It's like being in Sicily in the summer, Zorah says, so what's not to like?" They smiled at each other.

"I've never been to Sicily, but I understand. Are you ready to go home?" That was my real question.

Aunt Zorah spoke up, "We've-a been talking to Renato. He calls at the grocery store. They-a know us now and come get us quick. He's-a calmed down, Carmine. It's-a all over now. I go live with Ethel," she gave a pronounced nod of confirmation.

I got up, hugged each lady, and said, "I'm so very happy for you both."

When I entered the house with my bag, I asked, "How in the world did Coastal Groceries get involved?" I started to laugh.

"Well, to tell you the truth, I was surprised at first that young Drake would drop everything and drive here for Zorah until I learned about the twenty-dollar tips. Seems to make it all worth his while, and it's only been about three or four times since your uncle left."

"Thank you. That explains it. This looks good; got a beer?" I stirred the gumbo to get the veggies off the bottom of the pot.

"Coming up." As she placed the long neck on the table, she asked, "How are things going between you and Mr. Wonderful?" Patty asked.

"Stop that! I hate when you say that! What if a guy were Mr. Wonderful? You're mocking me!"

"Believe me, there are no 'Mr. Wonderfuls' in the world! Take the word of an old crone! Now, tell me what's been happening," Patty said.

I tried to think of a comeback, but with all the years I'd been counseling women after a break-up with 'Mr. Wonderful,' I had nothing.

"Okay. We've been writing letters. Some of his are long; some aren't so much, just a chat about the boys and the summer break. But in one letter, he talked about Donna, his wife that died in the car crash. That one was hard to read. I'm going to ask Aunt Zorah about it. She knows so much more than anyone believes she knows," was all I offered as I dished into the gumbo.

"You're right about that; I have no doubts that Zorah knows what you need to know."

"Ask-a Aunt Zorah what?" she said, entering the kitchen and sitting down with us at the table.

I jumped in before Patty could speak and before I swallowed my mouth full of cornbread. "Stevie D's dead wife."

"Eat-a your food before you-a choke!" she reprimanded me.

I washed it all down with a sip of beer. "He wrote a letter about it all. I don't know if I ever told you that the night I stayed at The Galvez over the July Fourth weekend with Stevie D and the boys, his oldest, Stevens, woke me in the middle of the night and talked to me about it. Stevens said they worried their dad might do something stupid as well; he said that Donna's father got into a fight with Stevie D that their grandfather, Leo Bataglia, had to stop.

"Do you know anything about that?" I looked Aunt Zorah directly in the eyes.

Ethel had joined us as well as Sal. It seems my voice carried and enticed them to the kitchen table. I didn't mind talking about it in front of everyone. There was a time when I'd be huffy about nosy family members, but all summer long, my family managed to invade my life here in Texas. I surprised myself that I had gotten comfortable with this.

"Yes." Aunt Zorah answered.

"And . . ." I coaxed.

"I-a know all about Donna. I babysit her. Her father was part of Carmine's crew, so, naturally, when the baby is born, Zorah is sent to help the mama," she said, shaking her head side to side.

Carmine had used her to express his generosity.

"She was a spoiled kid. The last kid for Angelina, ten years between the brother and sister; Angelina no-a happy with being pregnant at her age; and the father, Antonio, he-a spoiled Donna, perfect name, prima donna, like-a she was the woman of the house!

"Anyway, Donna, she-a hounded Stevie D when they both in high school. He, not so much; I think maybe she pregnant when they marry, but no. Maybe he just want her to stop chasing him. Who knows?

"But, that night, she a very selfish girl, three children! She never think of her babies. What mother do that? If-a the husband no home, comes in late, he's the one that you throw out! Very selfish, she left her babies," Aunt Zorah was shaking her head side to side. The silence in the room was pressing. I lost my appetite.

"He-a asked you to marry him, right?" Zorah questioned. That snapped everyone's head, looking at me.

I spontaneously sat up straight and exclaimed before thinking, "How did you know that?"

"Renato, he-a tell me, last phone call. Stevie D, he's-a talking to Renato," again she was shaking her head side to side but this time with a big mischievous smile on her face, "Renato, he-a says Stevie D got it bad for you," now she was wagging a finger at me. The table exhaled and laughing with her.

"Hey, Cuz! Is there going to be a double wedding? You and Stevie D, Carlo and Alice?" Sal asked.

I sarcastically answered, "And you and Patty?" This made Patty punch me in my arm.

"Stop that!" she demanded. "I'm in no way marrying again . . . when shacking up is so much fun!"

Waves of laughter changed the general tenor of the room. Patty and Ethel started serving more gumbo, cheeses, fruit, and a bottle of wine appeared on the table. The evening was set.

Moon got mushed cooked shrimp, Patty's treat for her.

"What's so funny?" Alice and Carlo were entering the kitchen, loaded down with grocery bags.

Sal spoke up first, "A double wedding: you and Carlo, Maggie and Stevie D!"

"He has proposed! You lied to me!!" Alice said as she rushed to hug me.

"Stop that! In a letter! He proposed in a letter! Who does that?"

"Stevie D," Carlo said.

With an array of food on the table, Carlo and Alice pulled up chairs and joined us. It was warm and comfortable and fun and . . . family. In Texas, family here around me; I had never imagined anything like this in all the years I'd lived in Houston.

"Okay, I want to be serious for a moment," I said. That got their attention. "Now, as I said, I'm serious. I want to ask all of you, what's Stevie D like? In his everyday life, with you guys working for him, with his kids, all of it. You guys have been around him all your life, almost. Sal, you were a year behind him in high school, right?"

"Two; two years, he was in Rocco's class. You were a year behind him and Rocco."

"I know, but I was so wrapped up in Jimmy Toscano I never looked at another guy; that's why I'm asking. Carlo, what about you?"

"I only know him through work and family gatherings. Rocco was in the same class. And Cary was a freshman when Rocco and Stevie D were seniors. Cary might know something more about high school," Carlo answered.

"Okay. So, let's talk about what you know and what you've heard." I caught the look on Aunt Zorah's face. It was a suppressed smile as if she also knew what they might know and would wait to see who spoke up. I made a mental note of this; I'd play that card with her if I needed to do so.

"He's fair, at work, he's fair, but when he tells you what he wants done, you'd better do it and do it right," Carlo offered.

"What happens if you don't do it right?" I pressed.

Sal and Carlo looked at each other and laughed.

"I never wanted to find out," Carlo said, gestured by hunching his shoulders, saying, "Hey, it's Stevie D! You don't disappoint Stevie D!"

"When did he acquire this reputation? It sounds as if something -- what shall I call it -- undesirable would happen. Like what?" I pushed.

Again, the looks back and forth, this time Aunt Zorah was included and returned a "don't ask me" look.

"Maggie," Sal started putting his elbows on the table and lacing his fingers, "you don't understand about our kind of business. It's all about trust, absolute trust. And no one ever knowingly violates that trust."

Hmm. "And just what kind of business are we talking about? Criminal behavior? I ask because, see, I hold a license to practice as a Doctor of Psychology in the State of Texas, and if I move home, I will need the same license in New York State. Part of holding this license is the trust each state gives me that I will in no way be any part of criminal behavior. I'd be required to report it."

The table was silent. The guys looked at Aunt Zorah.

"Bedda, you-a think too hard! Things, they-a change over the years; it's-a no like the old days," Aunt Zorah said, then she pointed that finger at me again, "And-a only Carmine can a tell you about-a The Business!"

Well, at least that was consistent. "I respect that, Aunt Zorah. But do you understand why I ask?"

"Yes. And if-a you ever need to know, Carmine, he-a will tell you," she said.

"Okay," I had one last question, "What does the 'D' stand for in his name, Stevie D?"

Again, the three looked at each other.

Ethel pipped up, "Damien."

Ethel! Quiet all this time, and now she has an answer! We all burst out laughing!

"Damien? You're kidding! Are you sure? How do you know that?" I asked.

Carlo and Sal were saying about the same thing at the same time, through their laughter.

"I asked him," she shrugged one shoulder, "I just asked him."

All had their mouths open since their jaws had dropped.

"Damien?" I repeated.

"Yes. It's his middle name. It seems in grade school that Catholic school on the west side his parents sent him to, St. Something, well anyway, seems there were about five boys named Stephen in the class. The nuns took to separating them by using the first initial of their middle name, like Stevie A for Albert, and Stevie M for Michael, so on and so forth. He became Stevie D for Damien. There. Nothing notorious about it." Ethel seemed incredibly pleased with herself.

We laughed and shook our heads in disbelief.

"I gotta tease him about that," Sal said.

"I'd just keep it to myself if I were you," Carlo warned.

"Yeah, come to think about it, you're probably right," Sal reconsidered.

Ethel continued, "Maggie, he's a sweet man. He's wonderful with his children. He's like a taco --and I've come to love tacos since I've been here -- he's a taco: hard shell, but once you break through it, the meat is so good."

"I-a think you-a break the shell, Bedda," Aunt Zorah offered.

Sitting on the narrow ferry deck bench while crossing the strait between Bolivar and Galveston, the breeze felt so good in my face. It allowed me to relax, even meditate a little, and deep breathe in the sea air. This is it, I told myself. This is the weekend that defines the rest of my life. Am I ready for this? I asked myself. With marriage, I redefine me, or do I? I relocate, but then so might Alice. During this summer, my family was around me, and that had never happened since I left for college and divorced Jimmy. It was a significant change. But will Stevie D respect me for who I am? Would he adopt all the Sicilian husband behaviors we watched in our respective homes growing up? Or has time mellowed even that, and I just wasn't present to witness it?

When Stevie D met me in the lobby of The Galvez, he hurried to me. We embraced. He planted gently, a long loving kiss on my lips that surprised me, yet spontaneously I wrapped my arms around his neck and held him until we both had to come up for air. Once the embrace had space, we touched our foreheads together and smiled.

"How ya doin'?"

"Fine, now. Truly fine."

"Let's hit the buffet; the hotel is serving a buffet for breakfast and lunch each day during this weekend. I thought we could hit Guido's for supper."

"Oh, you don't want to go back to Patty's for supper? I think everyone is planning on a spread for tonight. Carlo and Sal are grilling chicken, ribs, and sausage," I informed.

Once our plates were loaded, we found a secluded table on the patio facing the Gulf and picked up our conversation.

Stevie said, "I was hoping that we might spend today together and talk about all the things that we've written about in our letters." He was careful not to say, "about the marriage proposal," I was sure.

"Ah," I truly felt his anxiety. "Okay. Today just us."

He smiled and relaxed, "Great! Mangia, I'm starving!"

"Didn't you eat breakfast? Oh, of course not, brunch buffet! I forgot," I corrected.

"And I was too nervous," he added with a mouth full of hash brown potatoes.

I tossed my head back, laughing! "Me neither! Couldn't eat a thing."

We chowed down with gusto.

Lingering over espresso and pastries on the patio, I especially loved the sheer panels that waved in front of all the apertures. It felt as if it were a scene in a movie: a romantic patio by the sea, gentle breezes flapping the sheer panels, and the loving couple engrossed only in each other, connecting with their eyes as they leaned into each other at a small bistro table.

Maggie! Snap out of it! "What next?"

"Well, how about a little shopping?" He more offered than asked.

"What did you have in mind? Souvenir shopping?"

"Hell no. The boys bought out the store back in July. I never saw so much junk! I was thinking more like a mall. Capra and Wilder start school next week, and I want to get them some new clothes for the first week. It's just kind of my thing. New outfits help them feel special. Stevens, I just give him money for the same. He likes to pick out his stuff now. So, what's a great mall for shopping?"

"Okay; it depends on what you want to spend. There's the mall at Kemah, sort of a neighborhood mall, or the Galleria in Houston, a bit into the city."

"The Galleria. Let's go!"

As we traveled north on I-45, the traffic headed for the Island was almost bumper to bumper.

"Oh, God, look at that! What a time we're going to have getting back!"

"Hey, I'm on a mini-vacation here; there's time!"

Once in the Galleria, Stevie D shopped in the best stores, and I couldn't help but notice that money was no problem. He picked out some great outfits for the boys, and as much as I knew about Capra and Wilder, I knew they were going to love the clothes. Stevie D certainly did know his kids. That was reassuring to me.

"Hey," he said as we strolled, breaking the silence.

"Yeah?"

"There's a Tiffany's here. Let's look."

I came to a dead stop. "What?"

"Tiffany's; let's go and look around."

"And what are we looking for?"

He took my left hand and, with his thumb, rubbed my ring finger. I caught myself gapping at the gesture. I pulled my hand away. "You're kidding?"

"Do you want me to drop to one knee right here, in front of Auntie Annie's Pretzels, because I will?"

It was a nervous laugh, "Don't you dare!"

"Tiffany's is this way," and he pulled me in that direction.

I was silent the entire route. When he opened the door to the jewelry store, and I stepped through, the sounds of the mall stopped, and the discrete aurora of the place impressed me.

He paused. I stopped abruptly. "What?"

He dropped to one knee, took my hand, and asked, "Margaret Ann Blake, my Innamorata, will you do me the honor and marry me?"

A very nicely dressed gentleman stepped up and asked, "How may . . . Oh!"

Stevie D, from his kneeling position, turned to the guy, and said, "Be right with you."

The salesman blushed.

"As I was saying, Innamorata, I love you, will you marry me?"

I had my hand over my mouth. I dropped my hand to grab his arm and bring him to his feet. "Yes, Stevie D Bataglia, I will marry you!" I said and we hugged.

The salesman clapped!

Without missing a beat, Stevie D turned facing the salesman, extended his hand to shake and said, "Steve Bataglia here, and my fiancée Dr. Blake. We've come for an engagement ring"

The gentleman shook hands with Stevie and offered, "My name is Geoff White, and it will be my pleasure to assist you both. I must say, this is a first, as far as I know, for Tiffany's! A proposal right in the store.

"Dr. Blake, do you have a cut in mind?"

"I'm sorry, a cut?"

"The shape of the stone, a cut, round, Marquise, pear," he offered as he headed for a showcase and stepped behind it. In a minute, he had a tray of fantastic selection of diamond engagement rings on top of the glass for me to consider.

I was stunned. They were all so beautiful! This is truly happening.

Geoff selected a pear-shaped stone, mounted with smaller diamonds on either side, and slipped it on my left-hand ring finger, and I let him as if it were someone else's hand.

"This shape is particularly pleasing and rather unusual," he said.

It looked huge, covering most of that knuckle. Oh, God! Oh, God! How expensive could it possibly be? But before all that had crossed my mind, Geoff had discreetly shown Stevie D a price tag. I caught the nod of Stevie D's head.

"Do you like it? Try on a few others, be sure," Stevie D said.

"Forgive me if I say it seems too big! I mean, what woman says a diamond is too big! Isn't that the dream, a huge diamond engagement ring?" I was aware I was babbling and felt my face flush.

Geoff had removed the ring and replaced it with another, just a bit smaller and round.

"You know, I did like that pear shape, but let me try that diamond shape . . ." I pointed to a ring.

"The marquis cut, try this one. It's the same weight as the pear," he told Stevie D as they passed the price tag between them.

"Well?" Stevie D asked.

"Excuse me if I'm a bit overwhelmed," I knew my face was still flushed.

Stevie D said to Geoff, "This trip here was a surprise I planned, so I guess it worked," he then turned to me, "Good surprise or bad?"

I looked at him, and all I could see in his eyes was love for me. I melted inside. This had never happened to me in my life, yet I heard many of my clients and other women friends describe this very moment. For my clients, it was the aftermath that brought them to me, disillusionment; but I must admit, there were also people I knew who still felt loved. I know my mom did, and I could see it between Zorah and Ethel. This is love, this look from him, this feeling in me, love. I hope he sees it in me for him.

I took a deep breath and exhaled slowly while relaxing. "This might sound crazy, but . . . just a bit smaller, and in the pear shape!"

The men laughed.

"When have you ever come across a woman who wanted a smaller diamond?" Stevie D directed to Geoff, who just smiled and reached into the inner case for a different tray of rings.

The next ring Geoff slipped on my finger was perfect. Pear-shaped baguettes on either side, gold band, and Geoff mentioned that the ring had a matching diamond wedding band.

"Stevie, if you don't mind, I've always wanted a plain gold wedding band. How about matching plain gold wedding bands?" He jumped forward and kissed me.

"I have just the set," Geoff said as he slipped the diamond off my finger and led us to another showcase. "Here, beautifully plain and 18 karats. Tiffany's handles only 18 karat gold. Dr. Blake, even the band on your engagement ring is 18 karat."

"Perfect," Stevie D said. "Are you okay with these?"

"Yes!"

Before I could say, "let me buy yours" or anything else I hadn't thought to say, Geoff was escorting me into a small, dainty private room and pardoned Stevie D and himself. I knew it was about the money, the purchasing of the rings.

Oh, God! Purchasing the rings! We're in Tiffany's! God! How much is the man spending? But then I recalled the look in his eyes, and I leaned back and told myself it was okay. It was all okay.

Fifteen minutes later, the door opened, and Stevie D carried a small Tiffany blue mini-shopping bag and said, "All set! How about a celebration drink?"

"Great! Exactly what I need!"

The hotel attached to the Galleria had an outstanding bar, quiet, dimly lit, and as cozy as I was feeling now. Stevie D ordered champagne. When the bottle came, the server opened it and filled our glasses. Once he left, Stevie D pulled the ring box out of the bag and got on one knee next to me at the table. He opened the box and asked, "Maggie, Innamorata, will you wear my ring?"

I was tearing up. "Yes."

Now he was on both knees as he placed the ring on my finger. He leaned in, and we kissed.

Applause caught us off guard! The people in the room were very aware of what was happening at our table and held up their glasses, shouting, "Congratulations!" and "Cheers!"

I was speechless. My gaze moved from the ring to Stevie D's eyes to the ring. I felt as if I were on a cloud. I hadn't ever felt so light before in my life.

"What's the matter?" Stevie D asked.

I laughed at myself, "Oh, I'm just trying to come back down to earth! This, this light feeling can't possibly be forever. I mean, life will go on as I know it, won't it?"

"Maybe not," he answered.

I twisted my glass by the stem. "I know. . . .I guess I'm moving. . . but don't press me right now for details because hearing myself say that means I've made a decision that I wasn't expecting to make right at this moment, okay?"

He was pleasantly amused, "Okay."

"And, please, no conversation about this at the Bay house."

"Then, how will you explain the ring?" he asked.

"Oh, the engagement is great, fine, but no moving talk. Leave that to Carlo and Alice; it seems they planned to shop for a ring this weekend, too."

"I want to invite you . . ." he started.

"I'd love to stay over at The Galvez. Get my head on straight before driving back to Bolivar."

"That's great, but not what I was going to ask," he had a grin on his face.

"Oh!" I was so embarrassed; I knew my face was flushed again.

"I'm scheduled to take a business trip to France at the end of September. Will you join me?"

"France? Paris?" as if I'd heard these names for the first time.

"We can drive into Paris, yes. But my work is in Le Havre, a port north on the English Channel."

"Why there?"

"That's where our products enter Europe," was all he said.

I hadn't expected an answer. At least a cryptic one was better than nothing.

"What? You look surprised?" he observed.

"You gave me a straight answer about The Family Business," I said before I thought.

He shrugged and smiled. "I trust you."

Another surprising admission from him; his trusting me was far more valuable than his loving me, and I knew it.

I just looked into his eye a moment. I still saw his love for me. "Yes, I'll join you," I said and added, "as long as we get to Paris," I replied. Gazing into his eyes, the crow's feet around them when he smiled, this trip would be our first get away, a first without family or kids.

"Pairs, absolutely. Thank you," he said, sincerely.

"Thank me?"

"Sincerely, Innamorata, I'm alive again, and it's all because of you."

This time tears rolled down my cheeks.

Back at the hotel, in Stevie's room, I excused myself for a bath. He said he would sort the boys' clothing, cut off the price tags, and separate the goods. He would also order room service for dinner instead of heading to

Guido's.

I lay back in the bubble bath and stared at the diamond ring on my left hand. I wondered just how many carats in my diamond. It was dazzling and felt so right. This day was the most fantastic day I'd ever had.

Our room service arrived. Wrapped in a luxurious Turkish cotton robe, compliments of the hotel, I joined Stevie in the living area. The spread was all finger foods, perfect for grazing while watching a movie. We cuddled, the sun was setting, and then something suddenly hit my awareness, and my insides panicked. I sat bolt upright.

"What's the matter?" Stevie D was confused.

"I just thought of something."

"Must be a big something the way you jumped."

"It is. Sex," I was dead serious.

He started to laugh. "Sex?" He couldn't stop laughing, "Why sex?"

"You might expect it now," I said, still dead serious.

Still very amused, and I wasn't, he said, "Well, at some point, yes."

"But not tonight."

He shrugged, "Okay. But why not?"

"See, you do expect sex tonight, don't you?"

"Maggie, slow down a minute. Breathe, breathe. Now tell me. What's got you spooked?"

I closed my eyes and breathed in and out a couple of times. "I think I've had enough for today. What I mean is Tiffany's, the engagement, blurting out I'll move back to Buffalo for you, all too much and enough for one day. I can't walk into that Bay house tomorrow and face my girlfriends with all the decisions I've made today plus having sex with you because it will be all over my face, and they'll read it, and I'm through.

"Way too much pressure! Let's just go with the engagement first; that's all for this weekend, the engagement. Carlo and Alice will have a ring, too, and they'll be all pumped about their engagement. That's enough for one family weekend.

"Oh, and no mention of France or Paris!" I was in full panic attack now. "No, no, no!"

"Let me make you a drink," and he was off the sofa and at the minibar. "How about bourbon?"

"On the rocks with water, please. In Texas, it's called bourbon and branch," I said nervously, then felt stupid.

Handing me the glass, he said, "Innamorata, what makes you comfortable, happy, is okay with me. I have the answers I came to hear, and now you can pace the remaining days."

I sipped the bourbon, "Really?"

"Yes, just let me know for scheduling with my job and the boys' schedules, okay?"

"Oh! I'm forgetting about the boys. Did they know you were going to propose?"

"In a word, yes," he was grinning again.

"Why am I not surprised?" I leaned into him.

"They all had their fingers crossed that you'd say yes. They like you a lot."

"I like them too. I'd be gaining children. Oh, God! I'm just realizing that."

"At least one, Capra; the older boys are pretty much on their own now, just drop-in visits for laundry and money."

"Where will we live? In your house?" It was, finally, a simple question.

"Anywhere you want to live, in Western New York. I want to sell that house."

"Donna?" I surprised myself how easy that was to say.

"Yes. Why would I bring my bride to a house with that history?"

I kissed his cheek. "Thank you."

"It will be a relief. I stayed for the boys. But with only Capra left at home, I think he'll be okay with a move."

"Oh, God, I've got to think about my license in New York State! I didn't take boards there; I wonder what the state expects?"

"Innamorata, how about you make a list of all the things that need checking into, send me a copy, and we'll tackle it together, later!"

I started to laugh. The bourbon had finally kicked in. I planted a big one on his lips, then said, "Deal!"

"Where do you want to get married?" he asked.

"So much for later! Where do you want to get married? In a church? Please say no," I told him.

"No. I do have a suggestion, but don't jump to an answer, and I'll be upfront about it, too. There's a business component to it, someplace where a scheduled meeting for all the families has been planned for almost a year; they'd be there already, and I think it might be a whole lot of fun for everyone."

I was sitting forward, looking at him spin this web of attraction, "Where? Vegas?"

"Yes! How did you know?"

"I guessed!"

"Well?"

"I don't have to answer right now, do I?"

"No. But I'm glad it's out there," he said as he raised his glass, and we toasted. Clink!

When we arrived on Bolivar, the women were on the beach, and the guys were on the deck. It was late morning. As we climbed the stairs, Carlo, Sal, and Cary got up, left Frank in a chair, and greeted Stevie D with a handshake and backslap. Frank finally joined them, reminding Stevie D they had met over the July Fourth weekend. I excused myself. I wanted to change into my swimsuit.

On the beach, Aunt Zorah and Ethel were under an umbrella sitting in chairs. I approached and stuck out my left hand.

"Ah!" She said something I didn't understand in Sicilian and pulled me down to hug my neck and kiss my cheeks.

"How wonderful, Maggie; let me see, let me see," Ethel joined the celebration. "Is it snug, dear? I don't want you to lose it in the Gulf."

"Yes, it is. Gotta run and get my dip in," I said, jogging towards the surf, wishing Ethel hadn't commented about losing my ring in the Gulf! She'd been hanging around Sicilians too long, the ever-present possibility of the worst thing that could happen.

Once I was wading into the sea, I recognized Dawn splashing Honey, then Patty on a raft, and Alice and one more woman. I squinted into the sun to see if I could figure out who, exactly, was talking with Alice. I headed in that direction.

"Hi! Cuz!" the woman called out.

I recognized the voice, "Ginger! What a pleasant surprise!" It was Cary's wife.

We hugged best we could, with the surf keeping us unsteady. Alice extended her left hand, and I eyed the massive diamond ring (larger than mine) with all kinds of diamonds surrounding the center round stone. "Oh God, Alice, that's beautiful!"

"Now, let's see yours," she directed.

"How did you know?"

"I was watching you with the aunts. Let's see!" Alice said.

I extended my left hand. I couldn't help but think that the simplicity of the center cut pear shape stone with a baguette on both sides and the 18K gold band was far more stunning, in my opinion.

"Wow! Girl! It's gorgeous!" Ginger gasped.

Alice was holding my hand, "Mag, it's the most beautiful ring I've ever seen, except for mine! And now I know what a boss man will spend on an engagement ring, the farm! How many carats?"

"To tell you the truth, I have no idea."

"What? Well, I'll be sure to ask the boss man," Alice said.

Patty, Honey, and Dawn joined us, and I had the opportunity to show off my 'gorgeous' ring again and again. I was feeling giddy on the inside. "So, this is the fun of it all," I thought. "This is what I missed when I married Jimmy at City Hall."

We could feel the sun getting hotter and hotter. The aunts had already abandoned the umbrella. I estimated about an hour had passed. Once the other women left the sea, I was finally alone. I paddled out just a little further and slipped my suit off, swimming parallel to the shore for several laps. I unexpectedly burst into tears! I started to tread water, I was sobbing, and occasionally gulping salty sea water. Oh! This can't be good! I quickly slipped my suit back on, and I started swimming back to shore. Once close enough to where I could stand, the sobs started, and I hung my head. What the . . .

"Maggie!" Stevie called out. That made my head pop up!

I ran the remaining way, and on shore, I almost leaped into his arms, sobbing.

He directed me under the umbrella. The aunts had left a towel behind. He covered my shoulders. It was hell-hot, but I was shivering. I couldn't stop sobbing. He pulled me close and encircled my body with both arms, holding me close, getting soaking wet, and just gently rocking. I couldn't stop, even thought I desperately wanted to stop. If I tried, the sobs came on stronger. He said nothing. When the sobs were stronger, he held me tighter.

When I was finally able to compose myself, he took the corner of the towel and gently mopped my face clean of snot and tears.

"You okay?" was all he asked.

"I guess so; who knows!" I answered.

"Let's get into the house before we melt."

I went straight to the shower under the house. I was the last one out of the Gulf, so I could stand under the cool water for as long as it took. I ended up lathering up my body with shampoo, and when I towel dried, I felt refreshed. Once I was inside, towel wrapped around me, I made a bee line for my room and fresh clothes.

When Stevie and I joined the group, he was in dry clothes that looked like Sal's.

During the buffet lunch the aunts spread out, my guy cousins, one by one, came up to me and ogled my ring. I watched Carlo's expression closest. He kissed my cheek and whispered in my ear, "I'd expect nothing less from Stevie D."

Hmm. Wow. My ring is the knock-out I believe it is.

"Hey, Stevie D!" Alice called out.

"Yeah," he called back.

"How many carats is Mag's ring?"

"Four."

"Nice!"

"Thank you!"

Now I knew.

My cousin Sal must have felt extremely comfortable with the company that day; he wore ladies' Bermuda shorts and a crop top, dangling pineapple earrings, and mules with faux feathers. After lunch, Dawn and Honey were huddled together on the backside of the deck; Frank and Cary found common ground; Stevie D and Carlo had a lot to say to each other. The remaining women gathered around the kitchen table. The aunts were excited about their upcoming road trip and grateful Ginger would be driving back with them. Cary and Carlo's, 'speedy' driving sometimes unnerved them. Alice whispered, asking me if Stevie D and I had set a date yet.

"No."

"Seems they were thinking about Las Vegas because there was a family business meeting scheduled there already," Alice commented rather casually.

"Really? Carlo and Stevie talked? When?" I was suspicious of the collaboration.

"I'm pretty sure Carlo checked in with Stevie D several times since he's been here. Most likely on one of those calls. What do you think, Vegas weddings? A double Vegas wedding?"

My head snapped to look directly at her. "You've got to be joking."

"Oh! I'm sorry, I thought that maybe you two had discussed it," Alice said.

"No. He did bring up the part about a family meeting in Las Vegas. But, now that I think about it, I don't remember exactly what he said about Vegas, what with him talking about Paris in September and all," I was rambling, racking my brain for more information.

"Paris in September! How romantic!" Alice perked up.

I became alarmed, "Alice, please do me a huge favor, say nothing about any of this to anyone, please! I have so much to think about, sort out," I pleaded.

Alice put her arm around me and gave me a side hug, "Okay, girl, I won't say a thing,"

As the sun's heat beat down, couples escaped to their rooms. Sal and

Patty, Honey and Dawn, Zorah and Ethel, I grabbed Stevie D's hand and led him to Patty's room. Carlo and Alice, Cary and Ginger, squeezed double air mattresses on the living room floor. Frank stretched out on a futon. This was the noon siesta arrangement.

Stevie and I flopped onto the bed, no conversation, and immediately fell asleep. I woke only because of the sound of scratching at the door. Moon wanted in.

Carlo and Alice and Cary and Ginger left each night with Stevie D, driving back to Galveston and their hotel rooms.

That night, I had just dozed off into sleep when there was a knock at my door, and Patty let herself in. "Why isn't Stevie D here in bed with you?"

"This is your first question?" I sat up as I adjusted the pillows.

Just then, Honey walked through the door, closed it gently behind her as not to wake anyone. "I'm wondering the same thing."

They joined me on the bed. "I asked that we hold off on sex for now. I've got to wrap my head around the decisions I've already made without the sex part."

"Decisions? You mean the engagement," Honey said.

I took a deep breath. "And moving back to Buffalo once we're married."

"I knew it!" Patty said, punching her fist into a pillow.

"Why are you surprised? Marriage to Stevie D comes with moving back home, and all y'all have been encouraging me to 'open to love,'" I mocked.

"Yes, yes, I know that, but hearing you say it brought it into reality for me," Patty said.

"You two were pushing me to marry Stevie; what's the problem?"

Honey said, "Maggie, there's no problem. I realize that we will lose you and Alice at the same time. Both of you, at the same time. How long have we been a foursome?"

"Wow, a long time; it started when we were in graduate school." It was a new point of view for me.

"Exactly," Patty said, "and I agree with Honey. It's the reality of both of you moving away. Like our kids are moving away all over again."

Honey sat straight up. "And I'm so happy for you! You found love! You never thought that you'd find love, and yet here it is! Immerse yourself in this love you have for each other. Move to the ends of the earth if you must. I'm telling you, it's visible! You can see it in him and you!

"More so than Alice and Carlo, but I think it's the age difference for the two of you. You're both older and have had marriages. That makes this different," Honey concluded.

"I agree. If you don't mind my saying, he seems puffed up! So proud of you and that ring! Girl, where did he get it?" Patty asked.

"Tiffany's, at the Galleria," I answered as I was admiring my ring.

"Our Galleria?" Honey asked.

"Yes, he surprised me. I was beyond comprehending what was happening! And you should have seen the rings I tried on, so heavy, and the stones from knuckle to knuckle!"

"Should have gotten one of those!" Patty teased.

"Wouldn't have been me."

"Well, darlin', we all have a lot of adjusting to do. When do you expect to have sex with that hunk of a man?" Patty didn't mind asking.

"Not this weekend! Getting engaged the way we did and my agreeing to move back home was enough surprises for this girl. But soon, maybe our next visit with each other," I mused.

Honey and Patty were moving off the bed and towards the door. They paused like cartoon characters, then turned, looking at me with frowns on their faces. Patty spoke, "Girl, you had better give him a going home gift. You need to leave him with the memory of some hot and heavy sex to keep him coming back."

"This is your advice?" I asked critically.

Honey chimed in, "I agree. You're engaged now, and no one is a virgin, by the way, so a good night or two in the sack is called for before he leaves," she pointed her finger at me, "doctor's orders!"

I started to laugh, but all along, I knew in my gut they made perfect sense.

As they opened the door to leave, Moon rushed in as if being chased. Once she jumped on the bed, she stood there looking and me and gave out the most unacceptable sound ever!

As Honey closed the door she said, "I guess she told you!"

Around eight Sunday morning, I decided I'd drive up to Kemah for shrimp. As I was pulling out the drive, Patty and Honey were under the house, showering after their dip in the Gulf, yelling at me, where was I going? Quicker than I can spell M.I.S.S.I.S.S.I.P.P.I. Honey, Patty, and Alice were in my car. We hit the road.

On the ferry, we climbed to that bench on the narrow deck. It was a calm morning. I took the back roads into Kemah, and with all the windows cranked open, we enjoyed the breeze. I thought about how this kind of spontaneous behavior would be difficult once back in western New York.

"Seems Frank is getting along well with the other guys," Alice noted.

"He's a mess," Patty offered.

"You think so?" Alice asked.

"You don't know the half of it," Honey added.

"Really? I work with the man every day, and I know he's depressed. Is it worse than the depressed state I can identify?" Alice asked.

"Yes, ma'am," Honey answered.

"Is there anything we can do?" I asked Honey. I knew that she saw Frank as his counselor.

"Nothing that a little love wouldn't cure; he took it hard when his wife left him. Their kids see more of her than him, and he's aware of that. He's just stuck," Honey said.

"So, what you're saying is he needs to get laid," Patty said.

"Exactly, but no one-night stand, he needs a . . . a whole experience. Something that will shake him up," Honey replied.

There was a reflective silence.

"You two thinking about getting married in Vegas, right?" Patty asked.

"It's come up," I answered, "but nothing has been set; there's a family meeting there, that's all," I was feeling nervous. Wow, news travels fast.

"Yes," Alice acknowledged.

My head snapped to look at Alice riding shotgun. "Yes? What do you mean 'yes'?"

Patty ignored me, "Well, make sure you do because once we're all in Vegas, we'll buy Frank a prostitute, maybe two," Patty said with a matter-of-fact tone.

There was a pregnant pause, then an eruption of laughter and cajoling broke out. I could hardly believe what Patty offered.

"What!? And who is paying for this?" Honey asked.

"We are. Think of it as a gift to a friend in need," Patty explained.

"Patty, we haven't talked at all about getting married in Las Vegas. All I know is that there's a family business meeting there, and Stevie D said so many family people would be there already, that's it," I repeated, trying to backpedal.

"Well, decide! Besides, I think it would be fun finding a couple of 'women of the night' for good ole Frank," Patty wasn't giving up.

"Honey, talk some sense into her!" I directed.

"Mag, I think it's a viable idea; it certainly would knock his socks off," Honey answered. She then said, "Get it? 'Knock his socks off? No pun intended!" She and Patty were enjoying themselves.

"I can't believe we are having this conversation," Alice said with nervous giggles.

"Where have you been the last fifteen years? I can. This is the type of role models we chose for ourselves, girl," I told Alice.

"No kidding!" Alice giggled.

Once back at the Bay house, I paid more attention, quietly, to Frank and his mannerisms and behaviors. I could see what Honey was talking about. In this social setting, it was apparent he was depressed, but to tell the truth, I couldn't assess to what degree. But if Honey said it was terrible, all I could wonder is if he was suicidal. On the job, back in the office, he always seemed so professional. He was kind of a father figure for me, though not quite old enough to be my father, but he had been in practice with Honey long before Alice and I joined them. I wanted to help but didn't know how or if there would ever be an opening from him for me to help. Best leave it all to Honey.

After Sunday supper, Aunt Zorah and Ethel began packing. They behaved like schoolgirls headed for summer camp. It seemed every time they passed Patty, they had to hug her for allowing them to live at the Bay house all summer. They invited Patty to Thanksgiving dinner at Ethel's home. Cary began loading the rental car. Two cars made it comfortable for all. They could rotate who rode with whom. One car could carry the bulk of the luggage. Plus, there had to be room for all the food.

Alice approached me and quietly asked if we could talk in my room. "What's up?"

"I want to ask you about our moving back to Buffalo . . . and convince you to get married in Las Vegas with Carlo and me," she started.

"Okay. But Stevie and I haven't exactly discussed wedding plans yet."

"Then let me get to my deepest concern," she sat on the bed.

Oh, God, she is deadly serious, I thought. "Alice, you just went pale."

"Really? Well, Mag, I want us to stay together in practice. Have you thought about us or our practice at all in all of this?"

"Somewhat. But my engagement was a surprise. Hey, Alice, what's the worry?"

"The worry is that there is no conversation between us about our practice," she said.

"In all fairness, this weekend is the first time we learned that the other is planning a move to Buffalo! So, relax, nothing is decided. And, of course, I'd love to open a practice with you in Buffalo. My thought is more around how difficult it is to become established and build a client base," I explained.

She sighed deeply, "No kidding. That scares me a little until I remember I'll be married, no longer on my own, my source of income. That's a relief; makes the idea of starting over in a new city tolerable."

"I agree. How about we keep the dialogue ongoing? As you and Carlo discuss what it will look like for your move to Buffalo, I'll keep you updated about the same with me. How's that?"

"Perfect. Mag, I needed some reassurance from you," she said.

"You got it, girl, we move forward together in practice, okay?"

"Yes! Whew! Maggie, I just . . . I . . ." she rushed me with a tight hug.

When we exited the bedroom, Alice started gathering up her belongings for the ride back to The Galvez. Stevie D was sitting on the patio. I approached him. "How about a stroll on the beach?"

"Sounds wonderful."

We headed down the stairs, walking towards the shoreline, saying nothing, holding hands.

I broke the silence, "When is your flight back again?"

He was silent, picking up seashells, then skipping them, badly, back into the Gulf.

"Well? When is your flight out?" I repeated.

He paused and looked at me, "Ah, I have no return flight scheduled."

I couldn't hold in the smile, "Oh?"

"Nope."

"And why not?" I was stepping closer to him.

"Well, didn't know how it would go, and I . . ."

I planted a big kiss on his face. As he began kissing me in return, it became a kiss that made me melt into his embrace, and I didn't want the kiss to end.

Finally, we came up for air while still holding tight. "What's your plan?" I asked.

"Got any ideas?" he replied.

"Let me drive you back to The Galvez tonight after Cary, Ginger, and Carlo leave here."

His face was coy, smiling, "Okay. That's a long round-trip drive for just a drop-off; it would be so much easier to ride with the guys."

I cocked my head, smiled, and said, "Yeah, maybe for a drop-off, but what about for an overnight?"

He planted a kiss so fierce and fast; we tumbled onto the sand and fell out laughing hysterically! We rolled onto our backs, then he rolled onto his side, propping up on one elbow. "You're serious?"

I rolled over as well and said, "Oh, yeah," and rolled onto him, kissing him again and again until he couldn't help but giggle.

I left Stevie D's room early Monday morning. I didn't want to miss saying good-bye to Aunt Zorah and Ethel. When I arrived at the Bay house, Aunt Zorah was frying peppers and eggs for sandwiches to take with them. That was the usual M.O. in our family: a long road trip equaled a stack of fried pepper and egg sandwiches. Fruit, cheese, bread, wine, paper cups, and olives completed the banquet for the backseat of the car. When I saw this, I had to laugh.

She eyed me. "Good-a morning," was all she said, and I knew that she knew that I stayed with Stevie overnight and had sex.

As Patty, Honey and Dawn joined me at the kitchen table for breakfast, their smug looks said it all.

Cary, Ginger, Carlo, Alice, and Stevie D arrived around ten a.m.. The cars were pretty much packed expect for the food. Aunt Zorah and Ethel had straw totes filled with "in case we need something," to keep at their sides in the back seat of the car. Kisses all around, as good-bye, and a huge hug to Patty for her hospitality.

Aunt Zorah was now in tears, "I-a want you to come to Buffalo for Thanksgiving, with me and Ethel, at our house," she said, wiping her eyes. "It's-a the least we can do for-a you."

They were off! The guys, I'm sure, annoyed the aunts by honking the car horns all the way to the main road.

Stevie D and I decided to stay Sunday night at The Galvez and avoid the post-holiday traffic back into Houston. But Monday morning, the traffic was terrible anyway. We went straight to my apartment because he was staying a few more days. I told him about Alice's concerns, about how she and I would love to have a practice together in Buffalo. He was listening intently.

"Why don't you and Alice visit Buffalo for Christmas? Come for the week between Christmas and New Year. Most offices close during that time anyway. I think it's a good time to get together with the people that might be able to help with some of our planning," he said.

"Really?" I began. Then, "Actually, that's not a bad idea. Alice has lived in the south all her life. A winter week in Buffalo might bring moving north into a new perspective!

"And I'm going to sit down with Frank and Honey about Alice and me leaving the practice here. I want everyone to feel good about what's happening, no fast moves that might hurt someone."

He reached over and placed his hand on my thigh. "Good plan."

"Who might these people be that can help Alice and me open a psychotherapy practice?" The real question was, who do you know and how legitimate are they?

He smiled. With a cagy tone, he answered, "I know a guy."

I laughed. "Stevie, opening up a psychotherapy practice needs state licensing for Alice and me, plus an office convenient for people, well-located. Marketing of some kind to draw clients; we'll need to become providers with the local health insurance companies. Maybe some of the health insurance companies we are listed with now might also be available in New York, so perhaps we can be listed there as well.

"Our practice isn't the same as The Family Business, Stevie. 'I know a guy' doesn't work." I was trying to be objective and, at the same time, separate my business from any Family Business connections.

"Okay. But how about you just keep an open mind? I've lived in Buffalo all my life, done business there, and, well, believe it or not, internationally. It might just surprise you that I know a guy!"

I was pulling into my parking space at my apartment. "Okay. But . . ." and before I could finish my sentence, he leaned in and kissed me.

"Don't you have to go to work?" he asked ending the discussion.

"Yes! Make sure when you let Moon out of her carry case that she heads directly for the litter pan in the bathroom. Patty spoils her, and that sometimes leads to 'accidents.' Here's the key, take my bag also, please; apartment 22, now get out! I'll be home by five!"

One last glorious send-off kiss, and off I went.

Three weeks later, I was on a plane for JFK. Stevie D asked me to meet him in New York City one day before our scheduled flight to Paris. I could have flown to Paris from Houston, but he insisted we fly together. I was happy he wanted it that way.

JKF and Houston Intercontinental were incredibly busy. But, arriving in New York, it didn't take long for us to find each other. After grabbing my luggage, he whipped me away in a limo into Manhattan, saying there was a surprise waiting for me there.

"What kind of surprise?"

"You'll see," he was coy. "Just enjoy the bridges. I love all the bridges. Have you ever walked across the Brooklyn Bridge?"

"No. The last time I was in New York City was on the high school senior trip."

Our hotel was on a small side street near Macy's and the Empire State Building.

"Quaint," was all I could think to say.

"It's a nice place. I know the guy," he said, smiling.

"Why am I not surprised!" And he did know the manager, who looked like he might have roots in India. As we rounded a corner heading for the elevators, I saw a couple seated near a huge fireplace. I took a quick look, smiled, and then did a double take.

"Rosalie?" I was stunned.

She popped out of her chair and approached me with open arms.

"What are you doing here?"

"That's the surprise," Stevie said, "Rosalie and Danny are joining us."

Danny spoke up, "It's a business and pleasure trip."

"Yes; Danny is part of my crew . . . team, and this is his first overseas assignment, and I'm introducing him around," Stevie D was explaining while we entered the elevator. He kept talking, "See, Danny and I will take the train out of Paris to Le Havre on Monday morning, take a break on Wednesday and wind up our work late Thursday; back to Paris for another weekend, and then home Sunday night.

"I thought you might welcome the company," he said, looking into my eyes.

I was taking it all in. Not the romantic trip to Paris I was expecting, but that might have mattered more if I were in my twenties, and he was my knight in shining armor. I mused to myself what Patty always said, "There is no Mr. Wonderful!" I decided it was very considerate of him, not leaving me alone in Paris while he worked. And my cousin Rosalie, my Woodstock buddy, oh yeah, we'd be just fine in Paris, just the two of us.

I loved walking the street of Manhattan. It was cool; the sun was setting earlier, the air, less humid. Dinner was at an intimate restaurant, dimly lit. The evening was romantic. I could see it in Rosalie and Danny also; there was no conversation about their children. I caught them once looking deeply into each other eyes.

I looked at Stevie D while he ate his steak. I felt warm and special and loved. The wine was helping, but all the concern and compassion and thoughtfulness Stevie had shown me since the moment I met him my first morning back in Buffalo facing my dad's funeral was no longer deniable.

We walked from the restaurant to Bryant Park, then found an igloo bubble, and had espresso and chocolate. Back at the hotel, we said our goodnights in the lobby.

Holding hands in silence, Stevie and I rode the elevator to the tenth floor. Our room overlooked the busy street below, now noisy with people and cabs. Once in the room, I quickly found my nightie in my suitcase and went directly to the bathroom. My heart was pounding. I caught myself giggling! There was a knock at the door.

"Hey! There's more than one person here who needs the bathroom!"

"Out in a minute!" I took one look at myself in the mirror then opened the door.

"Wow!" He wheeled me around out of the door frame. While closing the door, he said, "Hold that thought!"

I just laughed! Is this what romance looks like after thirty-five? I turned down the bed, climbed in, and grabbed the remote, checking for movies. Hearing the shower, I settled in with a late-night talk show.

Waking to gentle kissing on my neck, I stretched, embracing him, pulling him to me. He was naked. I was ready.

Rosalie and I were in frenzies the next day. Why we thought we'd miss our flight if we didn't leave for the airport eight hours early is beyond me. The guys finally relented; we headed for JKF six hours before our flight. Roaming airports is a favorite thing for me. Finally, we boarded. I hadn't seen my ticket for the JFK-to-Paris leg of our trip, so first class was another pleasant surprise. Flight attendants served us a light evening meal with wine; brandy and fruit and cheese; sleeping masks, pillows, and blankets. There was a movie, and headsets were complimentary.

Stevie D put his arm around me and pulled me close. The glow of lovemaking hadn't left me yet.

Our hotel in Paris had a view of the Eiffel Tower, which thrilled me. The staff called the place the Ram-a-DAN instead of Ra-MA-da.

Stevie D's plan worked very well. On Monday morning, he and Danny boarded a train for Le Havre. Rosalie and I walked with them to the train station. Twenty-four hours in Paris had affected them as they kissed us goodbye. I felt I was in a movie! Rosalie had the same reaction.

As the train rolled down the tracks, my cousin whipped a guidebook out of her purse, announcing she knew exactly what we needed to see, and she would try the French she learned in high school! And how long ago was that? We were off to an exciting start.

By the end of our first full day of sightseeing, I was so tired that I was afraid if I went back to the hotel, I wouldn't leave again for supper. Rosalie insisted we return to our rooms and freshen up. It was around four in the afternoon.

After a soothing bath, I'd fallen asleep when my intent was only a brief nap. There was a loud knocking at the door. I got up, adjusting the Turkish cotton robe snuggly around me, and called out, "I'm coming Rosalie! Sorry . . ." as I opened the door.

Standing before me was a man in a tuxedo, with a bottle of champagne in one hand and two glasses in the other. There were flowers in his lapel. He was clean shaven, looked like he had a fresh haircut, smelled wonderful; behind him a waiter stood next to a table-serving cart with domed covered plates on it.

"Hello," Stevie D said.

"Stevie?" I asked, squinting.

"Yes, may I come in; I've brought supper."

Dazed, I stepped back, and he walked into our room, followed by the waiter and the serving table.

The waiter went to work setting up the table, which included lighting a candelabra, and produced a bouquet of red roses. Stevie tipped him as he left. Stevie handed me a glass of champagne, then from the table, picked up a strawberry and plopped it into my glass. That made the gentle wine fizzle.

"What . . . you went to Le Havre!"

He clinked my glass with his, took me by the elbow, and guided me into the living area, and had me sit on the sofa; he sat next to me. "I was in Le Havre. I dropped off Danny, after introductions. I left him there. What better way to get into a new job?"

"But . . ."

"No buts . . ." He leaned in and gently, oh so romantically, kissed my lips.

I felt a flush coming on. I leaned back, away from him. "Stevie. . ."

He leaned with me, at the same time putting down his glass, taking my glass and setting it on the table as well. Then, he managed to open my robe, and began kissing my body, moving down my torso.

Oh. My. God. I'd forgotten what that felt like! Please, don't stop, was all I thought.

There was absolutely no keeping track of time.

The meals were quickly reheated in the microwave. We pushed the cart, minus the bouquet of roses, into the hallway.

Stevie took my hand, guided me into the bedroom, with a gesture he held my hand as I got onto the bed. He opened my robe again. Then he stepped back. Very slowly, and with no conversation, He untied the bow tie; then the jacket came off followed by the unbuttoning of the shirt. He unbuckled the cummerbund and flung it across the room. The shirt came off. Then he knelt on the bed next to me, took my hand, and gently placed it on his fly. I acknowledged by pulling his zipper down.

Oh. My. God.

Tuesday morning, I woke first. I quickly freshened up and returned to bed. Stevie was still sleeping.

If memory served me, yup, I thought as much. I gently woke Stevie. Stevie took a late morning train back to Le Havre. I called Rosalie.

"How did it go? Were you surprised?" she asked first.

"You knew!"

"Of course. My job was getting you back to the hotel on time. Now, what's up? You're free this afternoon, right?"

We decided on touring the Louvre.

When the guys were with us on Wednesday, they just wanted to rest, eat, and walk. No sightseeing, no shopping, only walk the streets and take in the atmosphere. Ending up at Shakespeare and Company was the highlight of the late afternoon. Thursday and Friday, Rosalie and I shopped for what we thought would be Paris-looking outfits to wear at home, and be so vogue. And souvenir shopping as well, was on the agenda. We spent the remaining weekend, the four of us, doing all the tourist things. It was great fun.

I couldn't help thinking that Paris really was magical. On the flight back to JFK, I wondered how I'd get back into my Houston routine after I'd seen 'Paree'?

"You call that a 'winter coat?' Burberry trench is not a winter coat," I told Alice. Our trip to Buffalo was in one week. Frank was kind enough to clear the schedule so we could fly out on December twenty-second and return to work on January 5th. The excitement was growing for me. Alice? A basket case; not only was this her very first Christmas east of the Mississippi, but it would include meeting Carlo's family and the Madonie's all at once. We were going over what she needed to pack for the weather. She didn't have one pair of what I call regular shoes. Her shoes were sandals, opened toes, sneakers, nothing that would stand up to snow, sleet, ice that's salted.

"In my defense, this Burberry is great in December in Houston when the temperature drops into the forties!" She was hugging her Burberry trench coat.

I started to laugh so hard I was rolling on her bed! "Alice, in Buffalo during the winter, the temperature falls as low as zero degrees, and sometimes lower. We need to shop!"

Foley's downtown had everything for winter, to my surprise. The sales lady said the skiing crowd shopped there first because it was less expensive buying in Houston instead of Maine or Colorado or Europe for that matter.

"How about a meal at Kim Son?" I asked. My assessment was all that Alice would need to keep her warm and comfortable from head to toe was in the bag (pun intended.)

"One more department, please," she replied.

"What could we have possibly missed?" I asked as I lofted half a dozen shopping bags at her.

"Nothing; let's go to the bridal shop and look at dresses," she teased. "Stop squinting at me! You may not want a wedding gown, but this is my very first wedding, and I do want a wedding gown! Please, we're already here. Let's just look?"

The department was enclosed with French doors at the entrance. Fortunately, there were wonderfully comfortable chairs. Checking my watch became my pastime.

"What about this one?" Alice asked as she hoisted up the skirt so she wouldn't trip on the hem of the very puffy dress.

"You look like a meringue."

She was swishing the dress back and forth, looking at herself in the floor-to-ceiling mirror.

"Say, what about your parents? Where are they now, still living in the ashram?" I interrupted her playfulness.

"Yes," she walked off the platform and plopped in a love seat with the meringue floating up as high as her head. The sight made me laugh. "Last phone call, I told them about my engagement. Also said the wedding would be in Las Vegas. Do you know what their reply was?"

"Can't imagine."

"They said great, getting to Las Vegas is much easier to book out of India than Houston. Then they asked what they could bring. Bring? I said, what about being the parents of the bride? Like Dad walking me down the aisle! And Dad said, well, wasn't I a little old for that, seeing I'm almost forty. Can you imagine?

"I ended up saying that their presence at the wedding would be wonderful, and I sincerely wanted them there to meet Carlo. Oh, get this, when I told them I'd be moving to Buffalo, they were more excited over that than me getting married. I pointed this out to Dad, and he said that Buffalo was a real city with real people, nothing like all the phony cowboys in Houston! And they encouraged me to have an agent rent the house out to anyone from either of the universities in the area. He's worried about renting the house!" She finally took a breath.

"Your dad is a character; I can hardly wait to meet him. Now, get out of the meringue, and let's go eat."

I called my mom that night. I asked her whether I should be thinking about a traditional wedding gown, or had I passed that milestone years ago?

"Oh, Maggie, Elizabeth Taylor has worn a white wedding gown several times! Besides, you never had a proper wedding to that Jimmy Calamari, now did you?"

"Jimmy Toscano, Mom, his band is Nickel Calamari. Do you think I'd look foolish? I mean, I have a vague memory of Stevie's marriage to Donna. She had a big wedding with all the bells and whistles."

"I've got an idea. Buy a few of those bridal magazines and look them over. If you see something you like, see if they have a shop in Las Vegas. Get to Vegas early and buy your dress!"

Wow. "Mom, that sounds like it could work! Thanks."

"So, what time does your flight land?" She had moved on.

"Afternoon. Stevie is picking us up and bringing us straight home. I'm sure Carlo will be with him. Alice is happy you asked her to stay with us. To tell you the truth, staying with Uncle Renato and Aunt Eve, she would be a basket case the entire visit. With us, she can relax, even ask us questions about family."

"Before you hand up!"

"What, Mom?"

"Are you bringing Moon? You'll be away more than a week, you know."

"No. I'm leaving Moon with Patty. But I'm bringing Moon to Vegas, and you'll take her back to Buffalo with you, okay?"

"Okay, doll. See you soon," and she hung up.

As predicted, Stevie D and Carlo stood waiting for us at the gate. Alice ran to Carlo. I knew I had a Cheshire cat smile on my face as I strolled up to Stevie D. Both hands holding luggage, I leaned into him, our foreheads touched.

"Hi."

"Hi yourself." He relieved me of my luggage. "Here, let me take those; anymore?"

"Yes, just one large piece."

"Follow me." We turned and headed down an escalator.

Again, a limo awaited, just like in New York. It was cold, blowing snow, but I paused at the curbside and asked, "What's with you and limos?"

"I know a guy," was all he said as he took my elbow and helped me into the limo.

"What happened to that hot Mustang you had last summer? The

convertible," I asked.

"Stevens, college, girls, in a word, usurped."

"Ah, I understand," I said, laughing.

Alice and Carlo wasted no time getting reacquainted, kissing, all the way to the front of the limo. Stevie and I were comfortable on the back seat, his arm around me, my leaning into him.

"How was the flight?"

"The usual; I got in a nap," I sat up, "Any plans for tonight? No, wait, tell me what this week's itinerary is," I said jokingly.

He had a smug look, "You are getting to know me! We're headed for your mom's. She's invited Carlo and me to stay for supper. After, the four of us are driving to Rosalie and Danny's house for a 'welcome to Buffalo' gathering for Alice. Carlo and I figured that meeting the cousins first might help Alice get comfortable. After all, the cousins are normal!"

"Speaking about normal, is Sal in town?" I asked.

"Well, that's a surprise."

"What are you talking about? Sal is no surprise anymore!" I joked.

"Let it be a surprise, okay?"

"Okay. Nice of Mom to invite you for supper; I'm guessing it's going to be something Sicilian."

"What else? The Madonie women are wonderful cooks, aren't they?" He nudged me.

"Ah, my name is Blake. So, you're saying that not being a good cook is a deal-breaker?" I was coy.

"I reserve the right to decide after all the evidence is presented!" He joked.

We elbowed each other back and forth a minute, laughing, then embraced in the best kiss ever.

As predicted, Mom's house smelled like sauce and homemade bread. She hurried Alice out of her snow gear and hugged. The confusion at the door caused me to miss, at first, that Aunt Zorah and Ethel were waiting in the kitchen to greet us as well. Quickly, the guys took our luggage upstairs, we followed. I showed Alice the guest room. But minutes later, she was in my room, sitting on my bed.

"This is really happening, isn't it?" She looked pale.

"What? The holiday, the family, the marriages? What could you possibly mean," I teased.

"Yes, all of it, it's here, it's real," she extended her left arm, hand flexed, gazing at her engagement ring, "Mag, I thought love, marriage, family had all passed me by. Secretly, I was so grateful for our friendship and that you were still single, too. And Honey, Patty, hell, even Frank, was family for me. When you came back to Houston after your father's funeral, and all your relatives followed you, I don't know if you're aware of this, but it was the most exciting time in my life. Then Carlo arrived!" She was welling up in tears.

I sat on the bed with her, "Alice, I had no idea."

"I know. Do you know how many years my parents have been globe-hopping? Fifteen! I know they earned it and all, but I do miss them." The tears flowed. "I do wish they were here for all of this."

"Well, they'll be in Vegas. Don't allow them to fly in and fly right out. Insist they hang around for a week or so," I offered.

The 'Sicilian voice' calling up the stairs for us to come to eat was Aunt Zorah's. We both jumped off the bed, one last stop in the bathroom, and down the stairs we flew as if we were teenagers again.

Oh, the spread Mom and Aunt Zorah and Ethel put out! Spaghetti with tomato and basil sauce, braciola, meatballs, homemade bread, and salad. No hesitation from the guys as they filled their plates.

"Innamorata . . ." Stevie called to me.

"Innamorata! Innamorata! You call Margaret Innamorata?" The people at the table froze a second.

Stevie D, surprised, looked at Mom, "Yes."

I didn't know what was going on.

"Zorah," Mom said as tears welled up in her eyes, "remember how Papa called mama Innamorata? Have you heard anyone use that term since they died? Oh, Stevie D," she placed her hand over her heart, "I just love that you call my Maggie Innamorata!"

Stevie picked up his wine glass, tipped it towards Mom, "Salute!"

Everyone followed. The atmosphere took a jolly turn after that.

"Hon," I turned to Stevie, "what was it you were going to say before we were so rudely interrupted?"

That made everyone laugh.

"I was going to tell you that braciola is one of my favorite dishes. Hon, can you make braciola?"

Again, a pregnant pause around the table.

"Ah, no, BUT I can learn!"

The laughter was warm. I knew I was home; Alice looked comfortable.

Carlo turned to her, "By the way, Babe, do you know how to cook?"

"Yes! Just bring me home that cow you slaughtered, and we'll throw it on the barbeque!"

"Ah yai yai!" Aunt Zorah cried, "Carlo, you come-a eat with Ethel and-a me!"

The limo again!

"You know a regular car like a Ford or Chevy would have been okay," I teased.

Stevie D laughed as the four of us climbed into the limo.

"Why? Don't you like riding around in a limo?" He was holding the door open like a good chauffeur,

I just shook my head.

There was a nativity scene on the front lawn of Rosalie and Danny's house, along with Santa and elves. Inside, a roaring fire, a tree as tall as the cathedral ceiling in the living area, garlands on the banister going up to the second floor; all families present, including their kids.

"Oh, wow! I'm not sure I'll remember all their names!" I told Rosalie.

"You did meet them at your dad's funeral; Dan and I thought having all the kids present would balance out the events, let them get to know you as you, especially since you'll be moving back and there will be more family gatherings," Rosalie replied.

Smiling, I said, "I like how you think."

"I'm going to seat you two," Dan was taking Alice's coat as Rosalie continued, "right by the fireplace and let the family come to you. What are you drinking?"

"Eggnog for me!" I ordered.

"Alice?"

One look at Alice: deer in the headlights!

"The same, thanks," she echoed.

Rosalie escorted us through the crowd; once we were seated, Rosalie called for attention.

"Hey! Everyone!" The room quieted. "We all want to welcome Alice McLeod to our family. As you know, Carlo and Alice were engaged to be married on Labor Day weekend. And, I think," she turned to Alice and me as she spoke, "it is going to be a double wedding because Maggie and Stevie D also got engaged that weekend!"

The family applauded.

Rosalie continued, "Now, I've seated the happy couples here so you can introduce your kids again. Let Alice learn who belongs to whom. I'm putting out the buffet, so drink up, and then we'll eat!"

Just then, Danny leaned in with a tray holding two eggnogs for Alice and me. Stevie D had a beer bottle in his hand, as did Carlo.

First up was Rosalie and Danny's kids, "Hi, Maggie, I'm John, he's Paul, and he's George," a happy Labrador retriever dog, I swear was smiling, with a tale moving a mile a minute was at the side of the boys. "And this is Ringo! Mom told us anything you want, we're to get it for you."

"Thanks, guys;" I turned to Alice, "Meet the famous, Fabulous Four!" John blushed, and the boys hurried away.

Alice turned to me, "The boys are named for the Beatles?"

"Yes, welcome to my family; you ain't heard nothing yet!"

Cary and Ginger had to practically drag their four for introductions; Maureen, O'Hara, Irene, and Dunn were typically disinterested teens. Their younger brother Dunn was doing a good impression of a teen even though he was only nine.

Angela and Jimmy, Uncle Carmine's only daughter and barer of progeny in that family, introduced Maria, Izzy (nickname for Isabella), and Car (shortened from Carmine, his grandfather.)

Rocco approached, introducing Drew. There were hugs all around.

Then Stevie D's kids followed to say hello. Stevens, Wilder, and Capra hugged me and said how excited they were that I was marrying their dad. From behind Stevie, I saw Lucy, his sister. I remembered her from the funeral. She and her husband Rich, Diana, and Elvis, all hugged me and welcomed me to their family. I introduced Alice.

I whispered into Stevie's ear, "Is Lucy the surprise?"

"No, she's family, and this is sort of our engagement party."

"There is still a surprise?" I was dying to know.

"Yes."

"Well, when do you spring it?"

"As soon as they get here," was all he would say.

Alice asked, "Is it over, the parade? I need the restroom." Off we went.

"Mag, may I laugh now? The kids' names! Maureen O'Hara?"

"Hey, in all fairness, Maureen is a girl, O'Hara is a boy . . ." I broke out laughing too. "Didn't I tell you? Why my cousins went so far off the beam for names is beyond me. I lived in Houston when they were having babies, so I know nothing of the stories around naming their kids. I mean, not one Luigi or Salvatore or Dominic like normal Sicilian families!"

"Maybe that was the motive," Alice said.

Heading for the buffet table, Paul handing me eggnog and people taking the opportunity to ogle our engagement rings, I heard a greeting go up at the front door, "Here they are! Finally! Always last to get even more attention!"

As I turned to see who it was, Sal walked towards me, arms outstretched. As I embraced him, . . ."Patty? Patty! What?"

"We wanted to surprise you. Sal wanted me to meet his parents. It seems the age difference didn't compute with his dad, so Sal said, next best thing, just bring me home," Patty quickly explained as we embraced.

Sal had everyone's attention, "Hey, you guys! This is Patty! Introduce yourself to her, okay, because I found the love of my life!" He held his hand over his heart.

All who had a drink in their hand held it high, and a communal "Salute!" rang out.

I quickly took Patty aside. "What about Moon? You were to pet-sit Moon for this week,"

"Honey has Moon, and Dawn, and the guy Dawn brought home to meet the mother!"

"Dawn brought a guy home?" I laughed a little. I was thinking how difficult it might be to meet the doctor/psychologist/mother of the girl you're dating, maybe even having sex with!

"I know," Patty said. "Would love to be a fly on the wall at that house this week. Maybe Moon will let us know what happened," Patty quipped.

"If only!" I replied.

While some were browsing the buffet table, Cary was telling the living area crowd the story about driving Aunt Zorah and Ethel back from Galveston with Ginger and Carlo. The crowd was laughing. I laughed so hard I thought I'd pee my pants. When that settled down, Carlo and Stevie begged Alice and me into the kitchen.

Rocco was waiting there, "Hey, my dad wants to have a meeting with the two of you tomorrow afternoon around three."

I knew immediately it was about business.

"Oh, how nice!" Alice said.

I gave her a look; looked at Stevie D, Carlo, Rocco, yup, this was all business. "Where?"

"Downtown where Dad keeps an office; Stevie D knows which building; he and Carlo will get you two there on time; okay, then?"

I looked at Alice again. Her affect was different, now serious as a heart attack.

"Okay; what time should we be ready?" I asked.

Stevie D answered, "Two-fifteen gives us plenty of time, especially in this weather. Carlo and I will be a part of this meeting, but I think you might have already figured that out," he looked at me with a smile.

I smiled back and took his hand, "Yes, I did."

"Ah, I'm a little lost here," Alice admitted.

Carlo put his arm around her, "I'm sure Maggie will catch you up tonight, okay? Now, let's get back to the party."

By ten p.m., I was exhausted. I wandered through the crowd; many of those with younger kids had already left, looking for my ride home. Found him, then looked for Alice. She and Patty were snug together on a love seat that faced the fireplace. I joined them.

"Ready to head back to Mom's?" I asked Alice.

"Yes, I'm beat," Alice replied, "and I'm on overload."

"Patty, where are you staying, and for how long?" I asked.

"Oh, at Sal's parents' house," she answered matter-of-factly.

Together Alice and I said, "What? Are you kidding?"

"No, not kidding. They invited me to stay with them for the holiday. Isn't that sweet?"

"And Sal," I asked, "where is he staying?"

"Maggie, he lives there, remember? With me. We have the guest room."

Alice reached over and gently put her hand under my jaw and closed my mouth.

"You're telling me that my Uncle Carmine and Aunt Lena invited you into their home, and you're sleeping with their son under their roof?" It was as if hell had frozen over.

"Mag, what's the surprise? We're all adults," Patty was missing the impact of the situation on me.

"This is not the Madonie family I grew up in, that's all I'll say," and I raised my hands in surrender.

"Stevie D walked up just then, "Say what? What won't you say?"

"Come on, Alice, our chariot awaits; tell you later," I said to Stevie after I hugged Patty bye.

Mom was deep into a TV movie when we arrived. We said good night headed for the stairs.

"Hey! Wait a minute. I have a question!" Mom called out.

I came back into the living room, "What, Mom?"

"And tomorrow? Anything doing tomorrow?"

"You know, don't you?" I challenged.

She leaned back in her overstuffed lounge chair, "If you mean the three o'clock appointment with Carmine downtown, then yes."

I turned back to the stairs, "Then you know as much as I do! Good night! I probably hadn't been asleep more than an hour when I woke while Alice was climbing into bed with me.

"Are you awake?" She asked.

"I am now. What's up?"

"About the meeting tomorrow, or rather later today; what's it about?"

"About our move back here, and I think about working in the family, but that part I'm just guessing at," I answered.

"Working in the family? You don't even know what exactly The Family Business is, let alone be recruited to work in the business! How weird is that?" She was settling in. I guess she was sleeping next to me the remaining night.

"May I make a suggestion about tomorrow?" I asked.

"Sure, shoot."

"Listen very closely, and, oh, I just thought of something, take notes! Not obviously with a legal pad, just in a pocket pad of paper from your purse, jot down key ideas and points as you hear and identify them. Will you do that? Then when we're back home, here, we can go over whatever is proposed, if anything is proposed. How's that?" I was facing her now, propped up on one elbow.

"I like going into a meeting with a plan. Night!" She rolled over.

Alice and I spent the late morning helping Mom made traditional cucidati (Sicilian fig bar cookies). It helped pass the time. Right after a lunch of last night's leftovers, Alice and I changed our clothes and waited for the limo.

Riding in silence was uncomfortable. Carlo, Stevie D, me, Alice, just looking out the window watching the scenery pass. As we climbed the stairs inside the Grand Foyer, I commented to Alice about how the building was a historical treasure. Uncle Carmine's office had windows facing the Grand Foyer. Stevie D graciously opened the door. As we stepped through, Uncles Carmine and Renato came from a back office and greeted us, as did Rocco.

"Bella Mia!" he said as he kissed me on each cheek. "Alice! It's been a long time since your graduation, in Houston!" " He kissed her as well. Uncle Renato and Rocco followed suit.

"Come in here, we'll talk." He led us into an excellent conference room. On the table was a carafe of coffee, cucidati cookies, and water.

"We were just helping my mom make her cucidati!" I told him.

"Your Aunt Lena had them done right after Thanksgiving. Girls, sit here, next to me, one on either side of me, yes, yes, that's better. You guys, I know you'll sit next to your girl, so, go ahead, get comfortable!"

I noticed that Uncle Renato sat opposite Uncle Carmine at the other end of the table. Rocco sat next to Stevie D.

"Have a coffee, relax; Maggie, do you remember way back when you brought Rocco home? I remember you telling me you were going to be a doctor of what goes on in the head, right?"

"Yes, Alice and I are psychologists."

"Remember I said I could use someone like that in my business?"

"Yes," I asked myself if this was going where I thought it might be going.

"Well today, all these years later, it's a lot different for The Business. Maggie, would you believe I pay for health insurance for all my employees? And most of my employees aren't even Italian, let alone Sicilian! Ah, times have changed. Employees come with families. And families need help.

"I've learned a lot in the last twenty years as our business changed. Now my employees pay taxes! Imagine taxes . . ."

"Do you?" I quipped, not even feeling the risk.

He laughed heartily, "Did you hear that, Renato? Do we pay taxes?" He was shaking his head, "No, no, doll," he shrugged, "we have a different arrangement. But my employees need something Rocco tells me is called 'employee assistance.' Do you know about this 'employee assistance'?"

"Yes, as a matter-of-fact, the practice we belong to in Houston is listed with about half a dozen health insurance companies for just that, employee assistance," I replied.

"Ah! See Renato! I knew this would work!"

"What? What are you talking about?" I was very anxious after his statement.

"Doll, remember, at your dad's funeral (God rest his soul), I told you that I would consider it a favor if you moved back to Buffalo for your poor widowed mother?"

I laughed a little, "Uncle Carmine," I looked at Stevie D, "in all honesty, I'm moving back because I'm marrying Stevie. I want to be clear about that."

"Same difference. Now, this here office, I think it's perfect for your practice," he wasn't skipping a beat.

I caught a glimpse of Alice's face. Her jaw was dropping.

"Our practice?" I needed to hear that again.

"As the employee assistance shrinks for my employees. This is how I repay my favor." He nodded to Uncle Renato.

"Maggie," Uncle Renato took up the discussion, "The Business's health insurance plan is written exclusively for us, Madonie Enterprises. We can bring on anyone we choose for this function. Right now, our employees must seek help elsewhere sometimes wait weeks to get an appointment. That is unacceptable. This is a huge deal, having our own employee assistance program if you and Alice accept."

I turned my chair to face Uncle Renato, trying my best to keep the sarcasm out of my tone, "Thank you, Uncle Renato, for the choice!

" With all due respect a psychology practice takes more than one employee assistance program to make the practice sustainable. Our Houston practice markets for clients with as many as six health insurance companies, and employee assistance programs is just a fraction of our business. We depend on clients coming in for counseling sessions, testing, and therapies.

"Once Alice and I have moved, we are hoping to open a practice that incorporates employee assistance programs, and in no way be employed by only one company, with all due respect."

"I don't see any problem with that," Uncle Renato answered, " as long as Madonie Enterprise employees and families have a first-serve basis with your practice."

I looked across the table to Alice. She was smiling from ear to ear.

"Okay, I think we understand each other," I said to Uncle Renato.

He looked at Uncle Carmine.

"Okay by me. "It's done!" And he stood.

I quickly stood as well, we hugged and kissed each other on the cheeks.

I sat and looked at them both, like watching a tennis match, "But, nothing can happen until Alice, and I secure our New York State licenses to practice as Doctors of Psychology in this state. I have no idea how long that will take. I'm researching it now, and we'll follow any protocol necessary for reciprocity."

Uncle Carmine asked Uncle Renato, "Renato, do we know a guy or what?"

"Yes, I believe we know a guy. I can get on that right away," Uncle Renato answered as he took a pocket-sized pad of paper out of his inside jacket pocket with a pen and started to make notes.

Oh, my God! It was my student loan thing all over again. I just sat in silence.

"Good plan?" Uncle Carmine was so pleased with himself as he stood, indicating the meeting had ended.

I got up as well and hugged him, "Good plan."

As we were delivering parting hugs and men shaking hands, Uncle Carmine has a grip on Stevie D. "Our Margaret, what a ball buster, huh? She knows about her business, and I'm telling you, watch your 'p's' & 'q's', she's something!"

Stevie looked relieved when Uncle Carmine released his hand, "Yes, sir", was all he said.

Leaving the office, pleasant conversation all around, as we stepped out onto the foyer balcony overlooking the grand foyer, Uncle Carmine called out, "See you Christmas Eve!"

Back in the limo, Stevie D gave instructions to the driver.

"Where are we going?" I asked.

"Someplace we can talk about the meeting, okay?" Stevie answered. He knew me well.

We ended up at the Anchor Bar. With an enormous plate of wings in and a pitcher of beer in front of us, the conversation flowed.

"First and foremost," I said as I licked my fingers, "these are magnificent! Now, that said, am I understanding correctly that the Madonie Family Business has a health insurance plan for their employees? And, we were just interviewed, for lack of a better word as the sole psychologist for this health insurance plan's employees' assistance program?"

"Yup, that's what I heard," Alice said.

"And what criminal element am I missing here?" I said to Stevie D after my second beer.

He laughed, "None. Not when it comes to the employees' assistance program. Satisfied?"

I licked my fingers, and then on a wild impulse, I licked the side of his face! "No, not satisfied."

"No, not satisfied with the offer, or no not satisfied just licking my face?" He asked as he wiped the sauce off his cheek. The beers were hitting me hard. The stress was far more than I imagined, and the alcohol was the release valve I needed.

The TV volume was turned up because a breaking news report began with the warning that lake effect snow was on the way. The reporter cautioned viewers to get home as soon as possible because Buffalo was about to be inundated with snow. We all cracked up laughing!

Alice sat with her mouth agape. "How much snow is that, exactly?"

"Enough for your first Buffalo blizzard!" Carlo answered as he helped her with her coat. We asked that the wings be boxed for take-out.

Back in the limo, Stevie leaned in and asked, "May I invite myself in for the night, you know how snowstorms are," with his coy smile.

"What about your kids?" I was coy in return.

"Mom has Capra this afternoon. She knew about the meeting with Carmine."

"Who didn't?" I said sarcastically.

He laughed, "And she'll keep him overnight, seeing we'll all be at her house anyway tomorrow for Christmas Eve. You're coming, right?"

"To your mom's? What about Uncle Carmine's? That is our tradition. Everyone and I do mean everyone packs themselves into my grandparents' house, which is now Uncle Carmine's house, on Christmas Eve."

He was silent a moment. "What was the best part of Christmas eve for you when you were a kid?"

Surprised, I had to think a minute. "Well, I think it was white pizza, then homemade Italian sausage on homemade rolls once the aunts got back from midnight Mass, you know, breaking the fast of not eating meat on Christmas Eve, for some reason," I answered.

"Old Catholic tradition; my parents don't do it that way. We have a gigantic meal around seven and then sit around drinking and snacking. The kids watch Christmas movies, you know, It's A Wonderful Life. Around midnight, we each open one gift, then home, so Santa knew where they were.

"How about you join us for our dinner at seven, then you and I can leave around eleven for Carmine's house and white pizza before midnight?"

"What about your boys?" I asked.

"You're forgetting Capra stays overnight with my folks. Now that I know what we're doing, I'll take his gifts there tomorrow. Stevens and Wilder will be in and out both days as they bounce between friends and family."

"Wow, you are a solution guy, aren't you?" He never paused as he arranged the events.

"I aim to please," he leaned in, touching forehead to forehead, "you," then kissed me. "By the way, I have friends in Las Vegas, Joy and Lonnie Earl King. He's a business associate; they have invited us to Vegas earlier than the business meeting date, hoping we'll stay with them. They want to get to know you.

"Joy asked me if she could call you and discuss the wedding, in case you needed any help, locally, you know stores, shopping, girl stuff, once you're in Vegas. You game?"

"How much earlier? And that is the question, isn't it? What are the dates of this Family Business meeting anyway?"

"You're kidding. I told you the dates," he was a little defensive.

"No, what are the dates of the business meeting?" I had turned in to face him directly.

"Monday, February ninth through that Friday, the weddings on Saturday, Valentines' Day. I thought I told you."

"Valentine's Day! Really? You're kidding, right?" It felt like a joke.

"Look, this meeting was scheduled a year ago. And, if anyone had told me then that I'd be getting married on Valentine's Day in Las Vegas after the meeting, I'd have chalked him up as crazy," he offered.

"Wow," I turned and leaned back on the seat. "Well, whatever you want to do. But it's going to be so difficult getting a wedding off the ground in a different city, at a hotel. Are you sure my meeting more people before the wedding won't be just another anxiety-packed encounter?" I wanted to back out of extra stuff.

"We're here," Stevie said as the limo pulled up in front of the house. The snow was whipping around, and the visibility was only an arm's length in front of us. We dashed into the house. Stevie and Carlo stayed over.

Around 2 a.m., we raided the fridge of the leftover wings, and sat around the kitchen table. We talked about everything. Christmas Eve; Las Vegas, the weddings. Stevie D handled all the details, reserving the wedding chapel at the Sands Hotel where the meeting was being held, the flowers, the reception, the invitations. Funny, I didn't mind. He asked me what I'd like with every step. I was grateful he was handling it because my head was spinning with moving from Houston, crashing in my mom's house, and Uncle Carmine's plan for our practice. Alice and I still needed New York State licenses to practice in New York and no way of knowing how long our request for reciprocity would take. It was so nice to see Mom happy. When I left in June, she was, at least, past crying every day. Once I left, Mom took sailing lessons on Lake Erie! Who knew she always wanted to do just that? It took Dad's death to free Mom, but that was life for a 1950s wife from a Sicilian background. So far, with Stevie D, I had no sense of my wings being clipped by the wedding ceremony.

Early Christmas Eve morning, the limo driver picked up Stevie and Carlo. After quick cups of coffee and biscotti, they were out the door. I had some last-minute shopping, and Mom was game. Alice couldn't believe we wanted to go out in all that snow! We told her that if we stayed home when there was 'all that snow,' we'd never leave the house between December and March! But to make it easier, we called a cab to take us downtown. We believed we could get everything we wanted between L. L. Berger's and A. M. & A's.

By the time we got home, getting ready for dinner with the Bataglia family was next. Alice was readying herself for the Eve with Carlo and his family, which then they would end up at Uncle Carmine's house and the Madonie Christmas Eve. When the doorbell rang, I only wanted a nap.

"Hey!" I looked past Stevie D. "What? No limo?"

"It's Christmas Eve! The guy has a family. I drove my dad's Caddy."

"It's almost a limo!"

"To be exact, it's a Cadillac Fleetwood Brougham Elegance; my dad always had the top of the line as long as I can remember."

I called out to Mom that I'd see her later at Uncle Carmine's. Alice already left for Carlo's house. She was a nervous wreck. Uncle Renato and Aunt Eve intimidated her because she had only seen Uncle Renato in his business attitude so far.

Jane and Leo Bataglia had a sprawling house in Orchard Park, a curved driveway and all. The pine tree in front of the house looked like one that could match Rockefeller Center's tree in New York City. Capra answered the door and immediately hugged me.

The meal was formal, delicious, and the house decorated in the best taste; expensive but warm and inviting. That's an art, having money but making a home that's a comfortable home, not just a showplace. By eleven p.m., Stevie D and I were thanking his parents when Capra ran out of the room and back just as fast.

He held out a gift at me, "This is for you!"

"Oh! I'm sorry I don't have anything for you . . . tonight," I said with a smile.

"But you do have something for me tomorrow?" He was in no way embarrassed asking.

"Right! Thank you," I accepted the box.

"It from all of us, I mean it's from Stevens, Wilder, and me. We picked it out together. Dad doesn't know!" he was pleased with that last bit of information.

"Do you want me to open it now? Or wait?"

"Yes, now!"

I quickly tore through the paper and opened the box; it was a Christmas charm bracelet in silver. The charms were a candy cane, a Christmas tree, a wrapped box present, holly, Santa's face, and a snowflake. I held it up to look closely at it sparkling in the light. Jane fussed over it, and Stevie D looked proud of his kids' choice. I kissed Capra and thanked him so much. Capra helped me put on the bracelet, making sure the clasp was tight. He was so pleased with himself.

"Thank you, sweetheart!" I said, hugging him, "Will your brothers be around tomorrow? I want to be sure to thank them, too," I asked.

"Yeah," he was blushing.

It took twice as long to drive back into Buffalo. The Skyway was closed to traffic because of wind and snow off the Lake. Parking was almost non-existent on the side street where my uncle lived. We got lucky when someone pulled out of a parking space and drove off.

I opened the back door into the kitchen and hit a wall of people. Following the aroma of pizza and homemade rolls, I started to weave my way around to Aunt Lena at the kitchen sink to kiss her hello. Wet hands and all, she grabbed Stevie and me by the neck and kissed us.

Uncle Carmine was at the dining room table, the head of the table, joined by the guys, my mom, Aunt Bertha, Drew, and Ginger for the traditional poker game. I made my way around the table to Uncle Carmine, who offered me his cheek, moving only the cigar in his mouth to the other side to receive the kiss. He never took his eyes off the cards. Stevie D hugged Aunt Bertha.

In the vast living area, the traditional tree stood, and the kids were involved with various board games around the tree. I looked up only to realize that a wire anchored the tree from the top of the tree to the wall on each side. I started to laugh. I pointed that out to Stevie D. The story is that grandpa had a huge tree just like this one when I was around eight. On Christmas Eve, the cousins were so rowdy that we knocked the tree over onto the floor. Our parents came flying into the living room, each grabbing their child, and the spanking began. Uncle Renato and Uncle Joe grabbed the tree, carefully standing it up again without disrupting the ornaments. But there, on the floor under the fallen tree, was baby Carlo, smiling and kicking! Aunt Eve screamed "My baby!" when she saw him. Quickly he was looked over to see if any tree needles spiked an eye or something. He was okay, but the rest of us got it good. After that, Grandpa secured the tree to the wall. The tradition continued!

"What are you two talking about?" Mom asked as she joined us.

"The time we knocked over the tree, and it fell on Carlo."

"On my God! That was horrible!" she said with hands on her face. "How was dinner?"

"Delightful!" I raised my arm and jingled the charm bracelet. "A gift from the boys."

"You mean your soon-to-be stepsons? It's gorgeous!" She was coy and giggling.

I looked at her and Stevie. "Wow, stepsons."

"It's true," Stevie added with a shoulder hug.

I made my way to the buffet table and looked for a corner piece of pizza. My family's pizza was always made in a rectangle cookie sheet, and I loved the corner pieces, more crust. Luckily there was a corner piece untouched. By one a.m., we were eating sausage on homemade rolls, dates, and fava beans and drinking wine. By two a.m., I had had enough! Stevie, Mom, and

I walked a couple of blocks back to Mom's house.

"Sleep in tomorrow?" I asked him.

"Sure. How about you and your mom come with me tomorrow to my parents' house and spend the day?" I called out over my shoulder to ask Mom. She yelled back, "Would love to! Not too early, though."

Stevie called back, "What? Noon is too early?"

"Yes!" Mom called back.

He looked at me, "Is she joking?"

"You heard her!" I said, laughing.

"Okay, how about two, twelve hours from now? Is that enough time?"

"Yes. Now go," I gave him a nudge.

"Not before . . ." he pulled me in close, kissing me sweetly. "Merry Christmas."

It was great that Christmas was on a Thursday. Friday morning, I packed an overnight bag, and Stevie picked me up in the Caddy that afternoon. We headed for Niagara Falls, Ontario. We both felt the need to be alone together. We checked into the Hotel Brock, Niagara Falls' hotel of the movie stars during the nineteen forties and fifties. I had always wanted to stay in the Hotel Brock and eat in their Rainbow Restaurant.

Once in the room, Stevie D presented me with a Tiffany blue box.

I recognized the box immediately. "What have you done?"

"Just open it."

I did. It was a set of diamond earrings, cut pear shape like my engagement ring, but dainty. "Stevie! You didn't have to!"

He backed me onto the bed; I knew exactly the thank you that would please him.

To my surprise, the cousins had managed a table at the Statler Hotel for their annual New Year's Eve bash. It was a gala event. Women wore evening gowns, men in tuxedos. I was thrilled. I had always fantasized about attending that ball when I was a kid. As soon as we learned about the event, Alice and I headed out to buy ball gowns. It was so much fun. That night, if I do say so myself, our group looking stunning: Stevie D and me, Alice and Carlo, Rocco and Drew, Sal and Patty, Angela and Jimmy, Cary and Ginger, and Rosalie and Danny. I teased the male cousins that this was the very first time, outside of weddings, that I'd seen them in a tux! But, of course, with Stevie, one look at him and I flushed as memories flooded my mind. His returned smile was to die for.

Around three a.m. I got in, and Stevie stayed with me, overnight. Alice went home with Carlo.

Alice slept the entire flight back to Houston. To our surprise, Sal and Patty were on the same flight. Sal changed seats with me so he could nap. Patty and I had a lot to catch up on. I hadn't talked with her at all while she was in Buffalo.

"Sal's parents are sweet. I've never met two people who love their kids more!"

"You enjoyed staying at Uncle Carmine's house?" I, for one, couldn't imagine this.

"It was more like staying at Lena's home. She has control of that home, trust me! Say, how did it go with you and Alice? Judging from how exhausted she is now, I'd say she might have been overwhelmed the entire time," Patty observed.

"That's putting it mildly. She was terrified meeting Carlo's parents but loved Uncle Carmine's idea for her and me going into practice as the employees' assistance program counselors for his business. He even has an office ready for us. I don't know if I think he's too pushy or extremely generous."

"Maybe some of each," Patty offered. "Any way you look at it, it solves the problem of establishing a practice in a new city."

"Then, in Uncle Carmine fashion, he turns to Uncle Renato and tells him to get us our New York State licenses!" I was as skeptical as I could be.

"NO! How? What about the exams you girls had to take? Certainly, another state may want an exam, too," Patty said.

"Exactly. I said we needed New York State licenses before we can work. It seems Uncle Renato 'knows a guy;' I need to start counting just how many times I hear that: 'I know a guy.'"

"All in all, it went well for you two, right?" Patty summarized.

I smiled. "Yes, it was wonderful. First thing when I'm back, Stevie asked me to get in touch with his friend's wife from Vegas, Joy King. It seems she wants to help me once I'm in Vegas. I thought that was very nice."

"You'll be packing up your home in Houston, won't you?"

"Yes. I'm sorry," I answered. This entire situation had equal parts of joy and sadness.

"No, no, don't be. Somehow, I never thought you two would ever move away. Yet, the excellent news is you both found love!"

"What about you, Patty? Have you and that tall, 'Italian stallion' in a tutu found love?"

She giggled, "Yes. As odd a couple as we appear, we're in love." Her face matched her declaration of love.

Watching her face and looking into her eyes, I could see just how truthful her statement was.

"By the way, when I go to Vegas early, will you bring Moon with you when you come for the wedding? We'll pass Moon off to mom, and she'll take Moon to Buffalo for me."

"Sure. She likes the beach and chasing seagulls. I'm always happy that she misses catching one."

I answered a call at work, "Hello, Dr. Blake here."

"Hi, I'm looking for Maggie Blake, Stevie D's fiancée; this is Joy King."

"Hi! That's me, Joy, I'm Maggie, how wonderful for you to call."

"I'm in Houston, Maggie, on business; I was hoping we might find some time to get together and discuss the wedding," she explained.

"I'd love that, Joy. Where are you staying?"

"I'm in the Galleria hotel. Are you available for dinner tonight, say around seven?"

"That works fine; meet you in the restaurant?"

"Great; I'll be wearing a red pashmina for the season," her voice smiled.

"Okay, red pashmina. See you then."

I stood in the doorway of the restaurant allowing my eyes to adjust to the dimly lit space. The most beautiful Asian woman I have ever seen approached me with a thousand-watt smile wearing a red silk pashmina, "Maggie? I'm Joy."

"Hello! You look stunning," just blurted out of my mouth, "and I'm in work clothes."

The maître d' showed us to our table, pulled out chairs for us, and draped napkins across our laps. While handing us the menus, the waiter asked if we'd like to see the wine list. Joy said, "Yes."

The meal was exceptional, and Joy was easy to be with.

I had no qualms about asking, "So, tell me, how do you and your husband know Stevie?"

"Through my husband's business, he works as an agent with INS."

Surprised, "INS, as in Immigration and Naturalization Service?" I was surprised.

"Yes, exactly; my father-in-law worked with the Madonie family long before Lonnie Earl got his assignment as an agent. Lonnie and Stevie knew each other years before they took over the reins from the older guys," she was so very nonchalant.

Here was my chance, a crack in the armor, "Do you know specifically what the Madonie business is?" I asked, trying to use humor.

Joy laughed hardily, even tossing her head back. Then she leaned in a little across the table from me, "Maggie, no one knows what that business is except the people Carmine Madonie tells himself. And, for the record, I'm not one of those people. No use spending time on that. Now, about your wedding; at the Sands, how incredibly special! Stevie D was lucky to get the wedding chapel, but he certainly booked early enough," she motioned for the waiter. "Dessert menu, please."

Early enough? Hmm. "Do you know exactly how early he booked the wedding chapel?" I asked suspiciously.

"July," she was smiling like a Cheshire cat.

"July!" I started to laugh. "Joy, we didn't get engaged until Labor Day weekend, and he already had the wedding chapel booked? What a sneaky guy."

"In his defense, he was booking, I think, three floors of room at the Sands for all the people expected for the business meeting and their families knowing there was going to be, at least, one wedding. I say he plans very well. I think booking everything well in advance is better than scrambling at the last minute. You can always cancel at the last minute but not necessarily get what you need at the last minute."

She made a lot of sense. "He sent you, right?"

She laughed that full-bodied laugh again, "No, Maggie, this is in no way a conspiracy to get you married to Stevie D. Although, he was nervous for a while, worried you might not come around. Boy! He has it bad for you, girl!" There was her full, beautiful smile again.

I quietly quipped, "So I've been told."

We got into details about flowers, the decorating of the chapel, some of the reception details. I told her about Mom's idea of looking through bridal magazines for a dress and then buying it once I'm in Vegas. She offered to look things up for me before getting there to give me an eyeballed assessment of any dress I might pick out. I liked the idea.

"Does Stevie D have a judge booked for the ceremony?" Joy asked.

"I think he does. I know the hotel can supply clergy for weddings if asked," I thought for a few seconds, "to tell you the truth, I don't know. I'm not a church-going person; I stopped attending Mass once I moved out of town for college. But, with my family present, and my first marriage was in a judge's chamber, I thought that I'd like someone more. . ."

"Spiritual? An officiant who represents a spiritual orientation yet not religious?" Joy offered."

"Yes. I think that's it. . . . But I haven't talked with Stevie at all about this."

"Next time you talk with him, bring it up. And, if you won't think I'm too forward or pushy, I'd like to offer my Teacher," Joy paused, purposely.

"Your teacher?" I asked.

"I'm Buddhist; the monk at the temple is certified to officiate at weddings in Nevada. I'd be willing to ask him if he's available for your wedding. Of course, only if you two are interested. Let Stevie know I offered when you talk with him about it, okay?"

The waiter was placing tres leches cake before us. "This is so rich! I love it," I said.

"Now, while I was walking this wonderful galleria, I saw Lord & Taylor. Let's look at wedding gowns. If you want to, I'm mean, I know you worked all day," she said.

"And you did too," I answered, "I guess we could take a few minutes if you're willing."

We were nodding yes in unison, our mouths full of that scrumptious cake.

I tripped over the cat carrier on the way to answering the door. My living area looked like a self-storage locker. Packers were in my house all week; much of my furniture was wrapped in plastic; the art from my walls was in crates; the only things not packed were my sofa, bed, kitchen table with one chair, and the TV. Limping the remaining few feet, tears rolled down my face.

"It took you long enough!" Patty said as I opened the door. "Oh, darlin'! What's the matter?"

"I stubbed my toe on the cat carrier," I sobbed, heaving the words out.

"Get her to the sofa, Patty. I'll get some ice," Honey directed.

By now, I was hysterically crying, allowing Patty to hold and rock me.

"Oh my God, Maggie! Talk to us; what's wrong?" Honey encouraged.

Hiccupping, running nose, eyes almost swollen shut, I managed, "I'm scared."

Patty pulled me close to her again, "Of course you are, darlin'! If you weren't, you wouldn't be normal."

Honey had her hand on my thigh. "She's right, and you know that, Maggie. Getting away a few days early to stay with Stevie's friends is the best idea. We've got to get you on that plane tomorrow. That's why we're here; we want last-minute instructions from you. That's why we came by."

"Darlin', go splash cold water on your face; I'll put on water for tea. Let's settle in and talk," Patty directed.

It took me a couple of hours to completely dump all my fears and what-ifs as the three of us sorted my clothing and packed several suitcases: one for Las Vegas, the others for Buffalo. As I talked and calmed down, I realized how overwhelmed I'd been since Christmas. If I'm this unhinged, what about Alice?

I plopped on the bed, "Have either of you checked on Alice? If I'm going crazy with all this, what about Alice? I haven't talked with her in a couple of days."

"Taken care of; we were at her house the other day, and Dawn moved in to give her a hand," Honey reported. "Dawn needed a distraction; she was driving me crazy, home on break."

"Isn't it weird that her parents . . ." I stopped myself. "I wish her parents would have come to Houston and been with her through the wedding and her move to Buffalo. But it isn't my relationship or responsibility.

"Alice has always appeared detached from her parents. Maybe because of all the traveling her dad did when he worked the oil fields. I hope she likes Buffalo; it's so different from Houston."

"I think Alice will be just fine," Patty said. "She's found the first true love of her life. As far as I can tell, that will carry her through all the changes coming up.

"You, on the other hand, darlin' have been burned once, aren't as flexible or trusting. But, from what I see with 'Mr. Wonderful,' it's going to be all right," Patty encouraged.

Honey paused like a robot, "Did I hear you right? You said, 'Mr. Wonderful' as a positive reference. I'm impressed."

"You did! You like Stevie, don't you? And I bet Sal helped you," I teased.

"Yes, I like Stevie D, and yes, Sal helped because he's always talking about home and his family. How could I not like Stevie D? Maggie, he opened your heart," Patty offered.

I thought about that a moment. Patty was right.

"Okay, kid, what next? How about we make a list of everything you can think of for the movers," Honey said.

"I'll take Moon home with me tonight. I'll be back in the morning for your airport run," Patty added.

Stevie and I must have called each other a dozen times in twelve hours before we got on planes to meet in Las Vegas and head for the King's home in the mountains surrounding the city.

"Welcome, welcome, welcome!" Joy bounced out of her home to greet us. Behind her was Lonnie Earl. One look at Lonnie Earl, and you would think of the WWE, too. He and Stevie D exchanged man-hugs. Their house seemed to be a ranch-style home from the driveway. But walk into the foyer, there was a direct line of sight to the balcony at the end of the living area. Once on that balcony, there was a level below and a level above tucked in Mount Charleston. Amazingly cool, fresh air, arid; a different kind of beauty from lush subtropical Houston; I could feel my muscles relax with one deep inhaled breath. I slowly exhaled.

Joy walked up next to me, "I love it."

"It's so peaceful; and a different kind of beauty. I've never lived in a dry place; Houston is subtropical, nothing arid about Houston. I do see why you like it."

"Follow me down the steps over there; I'll show you your rooms."

After dinner, Joy asked, "Stevie, did Maggie ask you about the officiant for your wedding?"

"I asked the hotel to line up a judge or minister. Why?" he answered.

"I asked my Teacher from my Temple if he'd officiate, and he's available," she offered.

He looked at me, "What do you think? We're talking about a Buddhist monk here, and neither of us are Buddhist, but then again, we're not Catholic either anymore; what are we?" He had a mischievous smile on his face.

He made me laugh. "What are we? That's a good question, Mr. Bataglia. What are we?"

"Now you're mocking me," he turned to Joy and Lonnie Earl, "She's mocking me. I think we're good people. That's what we are, good people." He nodded his head to punctuate his statement.

"What do you think our parents will say about a Buddhist monk?" I asked.

"Joy, are we talking about a shaved head, a long sari-type robe flung over one arm, flip-flops, and beads wrapped around the wrist, monk?" Stevie asked through that smile, holding back laughter.

"Yes, Stevie D, exactly! His name is Bhante Yeshi."

"Well then, okay!" He threw up his arms, Sicilian style.

"Are you kidding?" I asked.

He was serious a second, then "Why not? It feels different. We'll be breaking Sicilian tradition. Why not? We've both been married before; our families will definitely see this marriage as 'different.'

"I'm looking at it this way," he said, turning in his chair to look directly at me, "when I look at you and think of our wedding day at the Sands Hotel, surrounded by our Sicilian family, you in your traditional wedding garb, in front of a Buddhist monk in flip flops, it will make me laugh. I'll forget just how much you just irritated me!"

"Oh!" I snapped my napkin at him!

"How about we all go around to the Temple tomorrow and meet Bhante Yeshi?" Joy asked. "I want to be sure to tell him to wear leather sandals!"

"It'll be a great ride through the mountains," Lonnie Earl said.

"He speaks! Who knew?" Stevie teased.

Lonnie Earl lobbed a dinner roll at him.

Monday morning Stevie D was kicking himself for arranging all the family to arrive on Monday. He left early with Lonnie Earl for the city. The Texas Posse, as my friends became known, was scheduled to arrive Tuesday.

"That dress we talked about? Lord & Taylor is holding it for you. After that, I'll get you back to the Sands," Joy said during our breakfast on the balcony of her stunning home.

I was at the hotel by three. The family wasn't scheduled to arrive until after four. I had time alone in the suite, and I had my wedding dress with me. As if I had to sneak around, I undressed and put on my wedding dress, then stood in front of the full mirror in the bathroom.

I cried, careful not to drip on the dress. For me, it was perfect. It included a description from the store for the media. It said, "A tea-length, cap sleeve, boat-neck lace bodice, and a beaded lace applique skirt." I loved it.

Carefully I removed my dress and hung it in the closet. Mom most likely would be tired when she arrived, so I ordered room service.

Wrong. Mom was pumped to be in Las Vegas. She wanted to go out for supper and walk The Strip. I hadn't realized that this was her first time in Vegas. Was it maybe my third? Alice and I got out of town to Vegas a couple of times while in school. But, while we were walking, I noticed business cards all around. I picked one up; it was a card for a prostitute. Frank! Knowing my friends, they weren't going to forget about getting Frank laid. Mom and I stepped into a couple of casinos and played some slots. She just loved the 'outlandish,' as she called it, décor, or themes of each hotel/casino. I, on the other hand, was happily collecting ladies-of-the-night business cards.

Once back in the hotel, I tried on my wedding dress for Mom. She loved it.

"What shoes are you planning to wear? They've got to be special since they'll be so visible," she asked.

"Don't have them yet, but Lord & Taylor had a pair on display that caught my eye; I thought that might be our wedding shopping tomorrow if you want?"

"Oh, Maggie; I'd love it!" She approached to hug me, and I leaned in as not to crush my dress.

I was carefully getting out of my dress when Mom noticed the assortment of business cards. "And what, pray tell, are these for?"

I laughed, "Well . . ." once my dress was safely back in the closet, I sat on the bed, "it's about Frank. Will you keep a secret if I tell you?"

She sat, "Of course!"

"Mom, really; no Zorah, no Stevie D, no one need know because I'm not even sure if we're going through with it."

"Going through with what? Spill!" Her eyes were large and intense.

"Okay. Frank has been the steadfast pillar of our practice since the get-go. He was already divorced when Alice and I joined him and Honey, but Frank has emotionally pulled back over the years. This summer, when he came out to Patty's Bay house, it became clear that he was depressed.

"Then Honey confessed that she was seeing him as his counselor! Over Labor Day weekend, we were driving to Kemah for shrimp."

"I have no idea where that is . . ."

"Sorry, I'll skip that; long story short, we're planning on getting Frank a 'lady-of-the-night' for his first night in Vegas, hoping to improve his mood. It was Patty's idea, and Honey said it might help."

Mom just stared at me for a minute. Then I saw her squint. Ah hah! That's where I get that from!

"I love it! When do we start?"

"What? You love what?" I was confused.

"I want to be a part of it, getting the prostitute for Frank, have some fun, too, with all you gals. Stop squinting. What's wrong with that?"

"It's sex!" Where did my strict Catholic 'sex is a taboo until marriage' mother go?

"Hey, just because your father is dead doesn't mean I'm dead!" She got off the bed and wiggled a little, "It's ain't over until it's over."

Oh, please!

The Texas Posse arrived around two p.m.. The core families, Madonie's and Bataglia's, had the floor just under the penthouses; the next floor was all my cousins and their families, in-laws, and the Texas posse. The next floor below was for the Suits and their wives. After that, it was a crapshoot.

Alice and her parents were blown away by their rooms, next to Mom and me. The Texas Posse's rooms were great also, just not as large. Honey and Patty had their own rooms. Our receptionist Maureen and her husband had a room somewhere in the hotel, which didn't bother them. She was so surprised that we had invited them, all expenses paid.

Mom and I just arrived back from shopping. The light on the phone was blinking. It was Honey.

"Hey! We're here and ready to roll!" She announced.

"Where are you?" I asked.

"We were told the floor below you. Can we come up? We have business to attend to," she said with a sneaky tone.

"Do you mean . . ." I hedged.

"Yes, I do! His room is just down the hall," was the answer.

"Come on up!"

Mom heard me; she got the business cards and was reading through them. Every few, she threw one down onto the coffee table.

"What are those?" I asked as I picked up one by one.

"Prospects; your friends are on the way up here, right?" Mom said.

"Yes."

"Call room service and get wine! And a cheese and cracker tray, some fruit, there's work to be done!" Suddenly, Mom was large and in charge.

I called Alice, "There's a plan afoot. Get over here now!"

When I opened the door, Patty greeted me with Moon in her cat carrying case. I received Moon gratefully, and immediately let her out. She began a 'cat scan.' Honey unloaded two shopping bags of pet food, litter, her toys, and towels.

With wine in one hand, each of us began reading the business cards and setting aside those we thought looked promising? Then, one by one, we presented the girls we selected. The cards were all about looks and a phone number.

"This girl looks like a kid. She must be of age, don't you think? Anyway, she's in a Catholic schoolgirl skirt and shirt, bobby socks, and saddle shoes. What's not to like?" I pitched, shaking my head.

"Put that in this basket," Mom said. "I'll go next; this woman is named Leela. Her card advertises lingerie. I'm curious about the lingerie business. Think she doesn't make enough hooking?"

We all laughed.

"Okay, now me. Hear me out first," Patty said, "Her name is BeeBee, and she is plus size. Think about it, we really don't know what Frank likes . . . sexually."

"True," I said.

"Let's stop here and start making calls, okay? Get this going," Alice said.

"Me, first! What do I say?" Mom asked.

"Just tell her what we're up to," Patty said.

We looked at each other and then burst out laughing!

Mom had the phone in her hand, pressing buttons. "Hello, is this Leela? Hi! My name is Isabella Blake . . . no, I have the right number, you're a hooker, right?"

I was biting the side of my hand like a good Sicilian woman, holding back the laughter.

"Doll, just hear me out," Mom said. Then she proceeded to tell Leela about Frank and invited Leela to our room.

"Yes! Do you know a girl named BeeBee, or Lolli? You do! Great, bring them along! We're at the Sands. When you get in the lobby, use the lobby phone, and ask for Mrs. Isabella Blake's room. Remember my first name. There's more than one Blake here.

"Five. Perfect, thanks Leela, I look forward to meeting you!" And the call ended.

"Oh my god! They're coming here?" Honey squealed.

"Yes! My heart is pounding!" Mom started fanning herself with a napkin. "Do you believe it? I did it! The ladies will be here at five tonight!"

"How much?" Alice asked.

"How much? I never thought to ask!" We all bust out laughing again.

"We have a couple of hours; what do all y'all want to do?" Honey asked.

Silence.

"How about lunch? I'm hungry, and you can't make a meal from a cheese platter!" Patty said.

At five, we were sitting in the living area of my mom's and my suite, looking at each other as if we were in the waiting room of a dentist's office.

The phone rang, and Mom jumped to answer. She gave the room number.

"It's a go!" she said.

Finally, a knock on the door; Alice jumped up and answered it; the ladies introduced themselves to Alice, asking if they had the right place, and Alice welcomed into the living area.

I was taken aback because the three women dressed casually, expensively, and were genuinely nice-looking. Boy, I thought, that says something about me!

Mom was offering wine; we were getting comfortable. BeeBee took up an entire sofa cushion.

"My partners here told me I forgot to ask how much," Mom said.

BeeBee spoke up first, "Depends on what you have in mind . . . for Frank. It is Frank, right?"

"Yes," Honey answered. Then she went into a brief history about Frank, the divorce, the kids favoring their mother, how she'd watch the depression creep in along with social isolation. Since we were all in Vegas, she theorized, maybe we could help Frank enjoy, for lack of a better word, being in Vegas.

"Awe!" BeeBee said, "Y'all are so sweet and thoughtful! What a considerate gesture!"

We looked at each other and burst out laughing!

Honey asked, "Did I hear a 'y'all'?"

"Yes, ma'am," Beebee answered. "I'm from east Texas."

"Darlin'," Patty stated, "We're from Houston! Honey, me, and Alice. Maggie has lived in Houston over fifteen years. We're fellow country-women!"

"Is Frank from Houston, also," BeeBee asked.

Honey thought a moment, "I believe he is."

"Well, this is far more interesting now," she said.

"I guess that's one way of looking at it!" Patty said.

Leela said, "I get twenty-five hundred for all night."

"Oh, by the way, tell me about the lingerie business that's on your business card. Is it legitimate?" Mom asked, which shocked the hell out of the rest of us.

Leela didn't seem bothered at all. "It's a real business, the money I earn I put back in the lingerie business, pay taxes, and know I'm planning for a future."

"You're a real businesswoman. How wonderful!" Mom said.

I felt a little embarrassed by Mom's comment, but Leela sat up a little straighter and smiled broadly. Again, shame on me.

"BeeBee," Patty directed her attention, "What do you charge? How did you . . . start?"

"I'm less; Leela is elite," BeeBee said, and Leela smiled and nodded to BeeBee. "I started with an escort agency. I got the confidence that I could do well on my own, what with me being so big and beautiful (if I do say so myself). Anyway, I like sex. I think we can negotiate a price once I'm a little clearer on what you want for Frank," Beebee answered.

"And Lolli?" Alice said.

"We're all in the same range; it all depends on what you're looking for?"

Mom interrupted, "Is 'Lolli' your real name, dear?"

"Of course not! I don't think anyone uses their given names in this business."

Mom continued, "What is your given name, may I ask?"

There was a pause. I was nervous, thinking Mom had crossed a line or something like that.

"Maria Lopez-Schwartz. My dad was in the Air Force, and Mom is from Mexico. I grew up here in Nevada. I'm studying psychology at UNLV. I couldn't bear the idea of being debt-ridden once I got my degree with student loans. I make enough money that a PhD is my plan!"

I looked at Alice, who looked at Honey, who looked at Alice, and we looked at each other; PhD in psychology?

"Why, Lolli?" Mom continued.

Lolli hesitated a moment, "Ah, like Lollipop? You lick it."

Mom blushed. There's the Catholic mom I know!

"Okay then," Mom said.

Leela's beeper went off. She excused herself and headed for the bedroom. When she returned, she said, "Ladies, it's been fun meeting all of you. This is a first for me: a group of female friends hiring a hooker for a guy friend. I love it, though. I've got an engagement right now, so, best to all of you!" And she was out the door.

"Seems like we need to negotiate quickly!" Honey said.

"I've got it!" Mom announced. "Ménage à trois!"

I choked on the water I was drinking! "Mom!"

Mom explained, "Don't mind my daughter. She thinks she got here by the stork. It's every man's fantasy. BeeBee, Lolli, are you game? Oh, do you have costumes? Lolli, your business card had a picture of you as a Catholic schoolgirl. I like that. Can you do that tonight, say, around nine?"

"Wait, how much?" Alice questioned.

"Now y'all are cooking with gas!" BeeBee said. "Ma'am, you are so right about a threesome; all y'all are so cute! Will you give us a minute?"

"Sure," Honey said.

They went into the bedroom and closed the door. Then we could hear laughter! I guess if we were them, we would find it a real hoot too. After about five minutes, they came out smiling.

Lolli spoke, "We'll do it for fifteen hundred all night, and I'll dress as the catholic schoolgirl."

I choked, "Each?"

"No, Ma'am! For both of us! We're giving you a deal seeing how considerate all y'all are being for your friend. And I come as is!" BeeBee said, gesturing to her girth.

We quickly scanned our faces, "Sold!" Mom shouted. We all cracked up laughing.

"Sold?" I asked Mom.

"You know what I mean," she said.

"Nine tonight? Come here first; we want to deliver you in person!" Patty said.

"What?" Honey asked.

"Yeah," I joined, "Is that appropriate if there is such a thing as being appropriate here."

"You do want Frank to accept the gift, right? If we don't introduce them to him, how will he know it's all right?" Patty argued.

BeeBee spoke up, "I like that idea, more fun that way. We'll be here at eight forty-five." And the ladies left.

Once they were out the door, we all flopped back onto the sofas and burst out laughing!

"We did it! Oh my god!" Alice said.

"That's three hundred plus each. We can get that easily from the ATMs in the casino," Honey said.

"The ATM will only dispense in round numbers," I commented.

"Then four hundred each; they each get a tip," Mom said.

All nodded in agreement.

"How do we know if Frank will be in his room at nine?" Mom asked.

"We know because we just hired two hookers to make his life a life. That's how we know," Patty said.

"Right," Mom replied.

"I can't believe we're doing this," I said.

"Okay, let's regroup," Honey said as she got up and straightened up. "To the casino!"

Once on the casino floor, we headed in different directions seeking ATMs, and said we'd meet up in the café for a bite to eat.

Stevie walked up to me at the ATM, and I jumped when he touched me. "Oh! You startled me!"

"Sorry! You're pretty intense there. What's up?"

"Nothing, just getting some cash," I offered.

He tilted his head and asked, "Really? Why don't I believe it? You could just ask me."

"Please don't ask. I'll tell you about it later," I was hoping he'd buy that.

He shrugged and smiled. "Okay. By the way, I'm sorry we haven't had time for us."

I placed my index finger over his lips, "Stop. I already knew you had a full plate with The Family Business meeting. No expectations here while that's going on, okay? Mom and I went shopping this afternoon, Patty and Honey are here now, and Alice joined us. They are probably waiting for me at the café as we speak. So, you're good."

He hugged me as a couple of Suits passed us on the casino floor and teased, "Hey hey hey! Stevie D!"

In the café, I ordered a sandwich, quick and easy. I couldn't possibly have eaten anything else. I was so nervous.

Honey asked, "Any trouble at the ATMs?"

There was a collective, "No!'

Around eight-thirty p.m., we couldn't sit still. Finally, the knock on the door; BeeBee had changed into a lovely dress, but Lolli! She was so cute. Then I remembered it was a costume for sex with Frank.

"Okay, this is how I see it going down . . ." Patty started.

BeeBee had a broad smile, "Y'all are so funny!"

"What are we doing, robbing a bank?" Alice asked.

"Speaking of banks," BeeBee said.

Mom moved forward with the cash, "Of course! Here doll, knock him out!"

"Okay," Patty continued, "We knock on Frank's door, when he answers, we all walk in, introduce the girls by name, just by name, and say 'enjoy!' then just walk out! Simple, yet clear about what's going on."

We looked at each other.

"Then let's go," Lolli said.

One floor down and halfway up the hall, we stood at Frank's hotel room door.

Mom walked forward and knocked loudly.

"Just a minute!" Frank called out. He opened the door. His surprised look was an understatement.

Mom walked right past him, we followed, then Frank closing the door behind him. "Ladies?"

"Frank, I'm Isabella Blake, Maggie's mother. I want to thank you for all the encouragement you've given Maggie over the years. And the job! God! And the job!" She was shaking Frank's hand. He looked confused.

"Frank," Honey said as she stepped forward, "this is BeeBee, and this is Lolli. They're here for you."

"Night, Frank!" we individually said and left Frank with BeeBee and Lolli. I was the last one out of the room, closing the door behind me as I said, "Enjoy!"

When we made it back to mom's room, we burst into laughter.

"It's early. What next?" Patty asked.

"Let's just hit The Strip," Alice said.

"Let's," Mom said, heading for the door.

When I woke the following day, I was alone. I took advantage and soaked in a bubble bath. Today we planned on finding a maid-of-honor dress for Honey. (She refused to be called matron-of-honor.) I heard the door open.

"Hi! Where are you?" Mom called out.

"In the tub!"

"May I come in?"

"Of course."

"Well, you'll never guess who I met in the café," Mom began and perched herself on the toilet cover.

"Liberace."

"No! And he's dead, by the way. Oh, we could go to the museum dedicated to him," she answered.

I just looked at her, "Who, then?"

Frank!" she said.

"Really? What time was it?"

"Nine. Surprised me, too," she said. "He noticed me immediately and invited me to join him. And guess what?"

"What?" I decided to get out of the tub, and Mom handed me a super-soft towel sheet.

"He thanked me!" Mom continued.

"He thanked you. You mean he thanked you for . . ."

"Yes! He said he didn't know if I'd be comfortable talking about it, and I said, well, why not? Did he realize we interviewed the women before we rented them? He laughed."

"I bet he did."

"Seems he didn't get it immediately; he was confused, thinking it was a joke. It took the ladies a little convincing, and he was surprised when they said it was for his mental wellbeing; that's when he started to believe it wasn't a joke.

"He thanked me again, asked me if I'd convey his thanks to you, Patty, Honey, and Alice. He thought he'd be too embarrassed, but not in so many words."

"Then I guess the sex went well."

"Wonderfully well," she said with a whim of knowing.

My head snapped up, and I looked at my mother. "He told you?"

"Yes. He said it was his fantasy ever since college. Didn't I tell you it's every man's fantasy, a threesome?"

"Yes, you did."

"Want to know the best part?" Now she was acting like a schoolgirl after a date.

I stopped toweling myself, "There's more?"

"Yes. He took their numbers for while he's in Vegas! Isn't that great?"

I was speechless. This was my mother? I really didn't know this woman.

She got up to leave the bathroom, "Our work here is done!"

By Thursday, Alice and I were beginning to whip up into a wedding frenzy. Joy was the calming force. When she recognized that Alice and I were thinking in circles, she'd simply say, "Breathe, breathe, breathe."

Stevie D stopped by my room late that morning. "How's it going?"

"Okay," we hugged. "It's going to be beautiful. Say, I have a request," I broached.

"Shoot."

"How about an intimate dinner tonight with just us and the Texas posse; I would love that. I've been thinking that once they leave for Houston on Sunday, I don't know when I'll see them again."

"On one condition," he said with a suspicious smile. "What did you do to Frank?"

That surprised me. "Frank? Nothing."

"Something happened, and I think you know what. I remember this guy as one who continues to moan even after a six-pack, instead of talk and just never could be one of the guys! How hard is it to be one of the guys with us?" He added, puffed out chest and all.

"Even if one of the guys is wearing mules with faux fur?" I asked.

"Even in a bra and bikini pants, Sal still behaves like a guy! And Frank's a psychologist; he's probably encountered weirder people than Sal. Out with it! What did you do to Frank?" He flopped back onto my bed.

"We bought him a hooker. Oh, wait, I forgot," I was playing with Stevie now, "more accurately, we bought him two hookers."

It took Stevie D a minute, "What?"

"Ménage `trois!"

"You're kidding?" He was up leaning on one elbow.

"Don't you have a meeting to attend?"

He looked at his watch, "Yes, but this conversation isn't over!"

"About tonight, great idea, call catering and ask for Armaan. He's been my go-to guy in catering and does a great job. Tell him you're my bride."

I liked the sound of that; we kissed.

Armaan selected an intimate dining room on the penthouse floor with a view to die for of Las Vegas. It was just me and Stevie D, Alice and Carlo, Honey, Patty and Sal, and Frank. Stevie D was correct: Frank was animated and happy. Who knew sex could be so therapeutic? After dinner, Stevie and I were saying goodnight to our guests. Once the last person left the dining room, Stevie asked Armaan for coffee and another dessert. We sat down again at the table.

"Tomorrow, between the rehearsal and the rehearsal dinner, late afternoon, Carmine invites you to a brief business meeting with several of the business's partners." He was so matter of fact I almost missed the importance.

"Why?" I was more curious than impressed.

He shrugged, "If I were you, I'd just show up and see what happens."

"Okay. Do I send an RSVP?"

He leaned in and kissed me, "I'll let him know."

"Mmm, chocolate mousse! Let me have some of that!"

The rehearsal was complicated. Alice and Carlo would have a traditional approach. Alice's dad would walk her down the aisle to Carlo, and a rent-a-minister would officiate. Alice wanted me as her maid of honor, which I initially decline. That made Alice sad because we had been joined at the hip since graduate school. I thought about that long and hard. I had asked Honey to be my maid of honor and wondered if Alice felt slighted. She said no, she understood my choice. It hadn't bothered her. But on the other hand, being an only child, Alice felt as if she didn't have anyone else close enough to ask. I changed my mind and said yes.

"In your wedding gown? You're going to be my maid of honor in your wedding gown?" she had asked.

"Of course not! I'll wear one dress for your ceremony, and then quickly change into my wedding dress! How's that for flexible?"

And that's exactly how we played it at the rehearsal. It made the grooms and groomsmen laugh. Stevens was Stevie D's best man, with Wilder and Capra as groomsmen. Carlo asked his brother-in-law Danny as best man, with Cary, Rocco, and Sal as groomsmen. Carlo did insist that Sal wear a tux.

"And red socks," Sal stated.

"Red socks are okay; just the socks," Carlo warned.

Every time I turned and needed someone, Joy was there, realizing most of the women in my family were involved in the wedding party. Jokingly I dubbed her the wedding planner! Joy brought my dresses to the bride's room at the chapel, where I'd change between ceremonies.

At rehearsal, I didn't expose my groom to my wedding dress, we just clocked how long it took me to change from one dress into the other.

She also assisted Alice and her mother. It was interesting watching them. Alice's parents had been abroad for many years. The awkwardness between Alice and her parents was apparent.

Bhante Yeshi was right on time for the rehearsal. He stood out in his maroon sari and gold short sleeve shirt. He wore leather sandals instead of flip-flops. An amiable man, I was happy that we had previously met the week before at the Temple with Joy and Lonnie Earl. Bhante Yeshi gave us a copy of the official wedding ceremony he would use. It differed from what he would say for a wedding between two Buddhists but just as powerful. And he asked if we wanted to write our vows. I was surprised and relieved when Stevie D and I answered no at the same time.

Stevie D and I would enter the chapel and walk down the aisle together. For me, this was the most comfortable, meaningful way for two people who had previously been married and were no longer kids.

All in all, it took about an hour and a half for the rehearsal.

"Let's go," Stevie D said, taking my elbow while I was talking with Bhante Yeshi and Joy. "Please excuse us; we have an important meeting now."

On the penthouse floor, Stevie D opened the door to a cavernous conference room filled with suits. My immediate reaction was, "Oh boy! What the hell?"

Uncles Carmine and Renato approached me, kisses on each cheek, chit chat about how excited I must be feeling with the pending nuptials, all the while escorting me to a large conference table. In those few minutes, the men in the room quieted down, made their way to the table, and stood behind their chairs.

"Maggie, you sit here, next to me; Stevie D, next to her," Uncle Carmine directed.

Once I was seated, so did the men.

Uncle Carmine tapped the side of his wine glass with the ring on his finger, getting everyone's attention. "You all know my niece Doctor Margaret Ann Blake, my sister Isabella's daughter, and the daughter of our colleague and friend, George Blake, may he rest in peace."

There was a murmur of recognition.

He continued, "This is an auspicious occasion. Not only is Margaret Ann about to marry our esteemed colleague Stevie D Bataglia, but also, today, she becomes only the second woman to sit at this table, the first being, as you all know, my sister Zorah."

With the mention of Zorah's name, there was a louder murmur of general amusement surrounding Zorah, along with plenty of respect.

I was hanging on to every word my uncle was saying.

"Margaret, Maggie, has agreed to open her practice in Buffalo and be the shrink for our Business's employee assistance program under the Madonie Enterprises Health Insurance," Uncle Carmine announced.

Polite applause from the suits; I'm looking at faces now: Uncle Renato, Tony Ditalini, Ralph Zito; Russell Cellentani, Lonnie Earl King, Augustine Madonie, and Stevie D, of course.

"Being a doctor of psychology, it is crucial for Maggie that she understands The Family Business," Uncle Carmine continued. "I think about how important Zorah was way back when, and I think of Maggie that way now. I decided that makes it okay for Maggie to know about her Family's Business."

With that, the suits stood in place and applauded their approval. I felt a little confused. Stevie D was also standing. He leaned over to me and said to kiss Uncle Carmine. I stood, Uncle Carmine stood, we embraced and kissed each other on our cheeks, he hugged me again, whispering in my ear, "Your dad would be so proud."

All sat.

"Maggie, I'm no good at long stories, so Tony is going to tell you," Uncle Carmine said as he nodded at Tony Ditalini. Tony Ditalini stood at his place, but it didn't appear as if he was standing because he was so short.

All heads turned to see Tony.

"Maggie, it is my privilege to tell you about your family history. I won't go back to the beginning when your grandfather Carmine and his cousin Augustine came from Sicily and started The Business. I'll pick up the story in the sixties. That was a critical decade.

"The Families in the country were dying like flies on sticky paper, a slow and painful death. We knew we needed a change if we were to survive at all. At the same time, my oldest, Anthony, was accepted into pharmacy school. I was so proud. After a while, he was interning at a local hospital. We always talked around our dinner table, and one night, my Tony tells us how wasteful pharmacies were, pills returned to the pharmacy, once a patient was discharged or died, were destroyed. No one had the time or personnel to sort and restock the medications. No narcotics, mind you, just regular drugs, like antibiotics, other pain killers, vitamins, diuretics, stuff like that.

"I got to thinking about this. I was telling my goombah about the waste, wondering why the Feds don't stop the pharmaceutical companies from ripping off the country by destroying millions of dollars in medications and making new pills!

"Then, it was Debbie, right?" Tony looked at Ralph Zito.

Ralph nodded yes.

"Ralph's daughter Debbie was in school to become a surgery technician. You know, slap the knife into the doctor's hand? She was noticing how OR sterile supply techs threw away unused stuff. It was the same situation, with no one to sort and repackage.

"With the heat of the Feds on our necks, we started looking into this thing more closely. It was Zorah who knew a guy who worked for the Feds. She always ate downtown at the same greasy spoon near the Fed building, and he'd join her. She talked with the guy every day. One day she started asking questions about how companies' medical goods. He had a shine for Zorah and talked freely. She learned a lot, especially about having a Fed on our payroll.

"The next thing was getting the used goods out of the hospitals. My Tony's theory was that if you act as if you are going about your business with confidence, you can walk out of a hospital with anything. We tested this," he laughed to himself, and the men at the table all began to smile and murmur with the memory of what was about to be told.

"We turned to Zorah," Tony began, shaking his head and smiling big.

Now I'm transfixed. I think, please continue!

"One afternoon, Zorah walked into the hospital where my Tony was working, went to the pharmacy, and asked to speak with her 'nephew.' When Tony greeted her, he also filled a shopping bag she carried with returned drugs from a box labeled for destroying the drugs. Zorah walked out of the hospital without incident.

"That was all it took. Zorah was on a mission. She rounded up the old ladies in the neighborhood, and God only knows from where else, heaven forbid the Altar and Rosary Society!" He was interrupted by laughter.

"But we also needed quantity, so just visiting one hospital wasn't enough. My Tony got a few of his pharmacy classmates together. Well, long story short, the pharmacy guys were happy to help for the extra cash."

Tony sipped some water as the men murmured among themselves.

"We were shocked at how easy it was to walk out with shopping bags full of pills and surgical supplies. Okay, we could get the stuff. We started sorting in the kitchen of one of our Italian restaurants after hours. We figured the restaurant's kitchen had to be kept clean, just like the hospital. We hired pharmacists to sort the drugs, and we had to repackage the stuff. Some stuff needed to be sterilized. It all was a process, like any manufacturing.

"It was the end of Vietnam; we hired boys with any medical experience. But we needed customers. We knew it was too risky to sell in the states, and then it happened."

Ralph took over, "The hurricane . . ."

"Cyclone," Tony corrected.

"Okay, a cyclone in Pakistan," Ralph said from his seat. Tony sat. "We sent a few guys with medical supplies there and made a bundle. We were faster and cheaper than regular channels, and no paperwork. But we knew we needed an inside guy with the Feds. We went back to Zorah. As it turned out, her greasy spoon guy knew a guy, and he joined them for lunch one afternoon," Ralph looked to Uncle Carmine.

Uncle Carmine was smiling and shaking his head, remembering. "Zorah, what a surprise she was, you never knew who she knew, and this time she hit the jackpot. She hooked me up with a guy who was an assistant to the Secretary of State.

"The administration knew that countries around the world were in desperate need of medications, especially during natural disasters. They also knew that pharmaceutical companies looked to make money, and theirs was a closed market. But we could get in and out of a country quickly, efficiently. And bring the people immediate relief. Well then, wasn't that a good thing? And the administration knew in the overall scheme of things, no. Yet, if our family did nothing but what we proposed, in and out of a country quickly and quietly with medical surplus supplies and no narcotics, a man would be assigned from INS to protect us," he looked up smiling at Lonnie Earl King.

"That's when we met Earl Ray King." Shaking his head with a pleasant look, he turned to me and added, "Maggie, I can't count how many Secretaries of State I've talked with since then. And that's The Business. But understand, today our clients believe we are a medication disposal service."

There was a ripple in the room of men adjusting in their chairs, pouring more wine.

I sat stunned, still wrapping my brain around all that I heard.

"Maggie, let's be clear about one fundamental fact. We work with the permission of the administration in Washington, not the government. Only the people sitting at this table today know exactly what we do, including now you, Maggie. No one, capisce?"

"Yes, Uncle Carmine, capisce."

Again, with light applause as they all got out of our chairs, the men approached me. I quickly stood, shook hands, and was kissed on each cheek. Stevie looked proud. As the room emptied, Uncle Carmine beckoned me walking away from the crowd, "Maggie, I'm proud of you, and you do your mother proud, too." There were tears in his eyes. "Now go! Get married!"

Uncle Renato approached us just then and handed me two business envelopes. "Doll, don't lose these, one for you, one for Alice." He kissed me on each cheek, turned, and did the same to Stevie D.

Stevie D and I ambled down the hallway.

I started laughing! My family evolved from out and out criminal activity to illegal humanitarianism!

"Stevie, how big is this . . . project the family runs?"

"Worldwide, Innamorata, worldwide, with buildings everywhere for processing, packing and distributing. It's big."

"Wow."

"What's in the envelope?" he asked.

"I almost forgot," I paused and opened mine. "Oh no! It's my student loan all over again!"

Stevie D took the paper out of my hand. "It's your New York State license to practice as a Doctor of Psychology. What does that have to do with your student loans?"

"Remember, Rocco and the first favor?" I took the paper from him, rereading it, "My family is a little scary."

The rehearsal dinner was beautiful. Joy had created all the floral centerpieces. Armaan was filling wine glasses as the family entered the dining room. Frank Sinatra and Dean Martin were playing The Sands this week, and I learned they might drop in to wish us well. Really? The table sat twenty-eight. Mom, Alice's mom, and Joy selected the menu. As the unofficial wedding planner, I needed Joy to keep Mom corralled. As the wedding approached, simple rather than extravagant became my mantra.

Armaan and staff cleared the entree plates and served salad, cheese, fruit plates, and another wine. The doors to the room opened, and in walked Frank Sinatra and Dean Martin! Uncle Carmine was out of his seat in a shot, along with Stevie D and Uncle Renato. I only saw the men quickly get out of their chairs before I realized why. Stevie D brought the two stars over to me, Carlo, and Alice. The men congratulated us on our upcoming nuptials and handed us each a card. I thought, "How Sicilian of them."

Then the unthinkable happened. Uncle Carmine asked the men if they'd sing something. There was a huddle, and the two began singing Innamorata. There wasn't a dry eye at the table. Most of my family were out of their seats, hugging the stars, telling them how their father called their mother Innamorata; Mom said that Stevie D called me Innamorata.

What an incredible moment.

By eleven that night, the Texas Posse, including Maureen, our receptionist, was at my door, insisting we have a quick bachelorette party.

"Are you crazy?"

"No! Not at all. It's our rite of passage, now get some clothes on and grab your purse," Patty directed.

Mom was amused and pressed a one-hundred-dollar bill into my hand. That surprised me. I don't think she ever had done something like that before.

I woke with a headache, glad that the ceremony wasn't until four in the afternoon. Mom already had a room service table in the suite with various fruits, sweetbreads, and eggs.

"Did you have a good time?" she asked as I dragged myself out of my room and plopped onto the sofa.

I smiled, "Yes. I'm glad I went. After an hour or so going from one casino to another, we ended up at the Golden Nugget. I tried not to keep up with the girls and their drinking, but I guess I failed because I have a huge headache."

"That's dehydration. Make sure you finish this pitcher of water this morning and take two aspirin. That will do the trick," Mom directed.

"What I'd give now for Ethel's hangover cocktail! If I drink that much water, I'll be peeing all day. I don't want to be standing in front of Bhante Yeshi and have to pee."

"That won't happen, now drink up. Your body needs hydration!"

By early afternoon I was so much better. Joy arrived. While we were getting my wedding attire together, she paused, took my right hand, and slipped the most beautiful green jade ring onto my finger.

"What are you doing?" I studied the ring, a big oval jade stone sitting on a small woven gold basket with a gold band.

"It's our wedding gift to you and Stevie," she said.

"Joy! It's beautiful, but I couldn't. . ."

"Maggie, it's a Chinese custom to give jade on an auspicious occasion. Jade honors the Goddess Kuan Yin, Goddess of Compassion, and unconditional love. She protects and bestows blessings on those who honor her by wearing jade. From my heart to your heart, and from us to you and Stevie, may you love each other from here into future lives!"

I immediately hugged her, then held out my hand at arm's length and admired the ring. It was beautiful.

Joy said, "Now let's get you ready, you gather up your maid-of-honor dress, and I'll follow with your gown."

Alice and Carlo's wedding went smoothly. She was so excited. As I gazed into the wedding chapel, packed to the walls with family and friends, Carlo looked nervous. Everyone else was smiling.

As soon as they marched back up the aisle, I ducked into the bride's dressing room, where Joy and Mom assisted me into my wedding gown. Mom handed me a box.

"What's this?"

"It's a gift from the past, something borrowed, open it."

In the box was a diamond tiara. I recognized it immediately. Initially, a gift from my great-grandparents to my maternal grandmother on her wedding day. Each of my aunts and Mom wore this tiara on their wedding day. I had forgotten all about it. The last time I saw the tiara was on Rosalie; Angela had also worn it.

"Oh, Mom! I'd forgotten all about this!" I sighed as I reached for the precious heirloom.

Mom was fussing with it on my head, and Joy was handing her hairpins. I turned and looked into the full-length mirror. Wow.

"You'll keep it after the wedding, holding onto it until one of your cousins' daughters are ready to wear it," Mom directed.

"Okay. I'll guard it with my life. But you'll take it back home with you, right?"

"Yes. Moon in a carrier with one hand, the tiara in a box in the other hand! Just joking. I'll put it in our safe deposit box, where it lives between weddings," Mom said casually. "I'll give you the key when you're back home."

There was a knock at the door and the question "Ready?" from Stevie.

I took a deep breath, "Ready," I called back.

Joy opened the door, and I stepped through. Mom scurried past me so Wilder could escort her down the aisle, and Joy quickly joined Lonnie Earl.

His smile was electric. "Stunning!"

"Thanks."

We stood in the doorway to the chapel. Our family and friends all stood. The music hit its first notes, and Stevie and I proceeded down the aisle.

I felt my face in a wide smile. Please! No tears, I told myself.

Bhante Yeshi instructed the crowd to be seated; Honey took my bouquet of roses and Calais lilies as Stevie, and I joined hands.

Bhante Yeshi began.

Today Stephen and Margaret promise to dedicate themselves entirely to each other, with body, speech, and mind. For them, out of the routine of ordinary life, the extraordinary has happened. They met and now will transform their feelings into the path of love, compassion, joy, and equanimity. Today they attain enlightenment by perfecting their kindness and compassion to each other and the world around them.

Marriage is the vehicle to practice serving others. Love is wishing others happiness. Marriage is the equal commitment to the happiness of the other partner toward awakening. Our inner potential is developed through taking on challenges, not just through joy. We need people to practice compassion. Since their marriage is dedicated to the happiness of all living beings, those gathered here are the representatives of all living beings. Stephen and Margaret are happy today because they can share the joy of their love for each other with friends and family and because they can express their aspirations for the future.

Stephen, repeat after me: I, Stephen take you, Margaret, to be my wife, my partner in life, and my one true love.

. . .

I will cherish our friendship and love you today, tomorrow, and forever.

. . .

I will trust you and honor you.

. . .

I will laugh with you and cry with you.

. . .

Through the best and the worst,

. . .

Through the difficult and the easy,

. . .

Whatever may come, I will always be there.

. . .

As I have given you my hand to hold

. . .

So, I give you my life to keep.

. . .

Margaret, repeat after me: I, Margaret, take you, Stephen, to be my husband, my partner in life, and my one true love.

. . .

I will cherish our friendship and love you today, tomorrow, and forever.

. . .

I will trust you and honor you,

. . .

I will laugh with you and cry with you,

. . .

Through the best and the worst,

. . .

Through the difficult and the easy,

. . .

Whatever may come, I will always be there,

. . .

As I have given you my hand to hold

. . .

So, I give you my life to keep.

. . .

Bhante Yeshi asked for the rings from Honey and Stevens, one at a time. He handed Stevie my ring and directed him to place it on my left-hand ring finger.

Then he did the same with me to Stevie.

Bhante Yeshi continued:

It will take love to make your relationship work. This is the core of your marriage and why you are here today. It will take trust to know that in your hearts, you genuinely want what is best for each other. It will take dedication to stay open to one another and to learn and grow together. It will take faith to go forward together without knowing exactly what the future brings. And it will take commitment to hold true to the journey you both have pledged to today.

"By the power vested in me by the State of Nevada, I now pronounce you husband and wife! You may kiss your bride!"

Stevie pulled me to him, and we kissed the most perfect, gentle, loving kiss.

Once parted, I heard the applause; Bhante Yeshi was shaking our hands in congratulations, and we finally walked up the aisle for the reception line, standing next to Carlo and Alice for the good wishes of family and friends.

That took almost forty-five minutes. The four of us ducked into the bride's room to catch our breaths and wash our faces of all the lipstick smuggles before we had our wedding pictures taken back in the chapel.

As the photographer arranged my dress, I noticed that Stevie was amused about something.

"What?" I asked.

"Oh, I was just thinking," he said.

"Thinking about what? It's humorous to you; what is it?"

"The monk," was all he said.

"The monk what?" I didn't understand.

"Leather sandals," Stevie said with a huge smile.

I laughed. "I hadn't noticed," I said.

The four of us headed for the ballroom where the joint reception was beginning, I could hear the music waffling down the hallway. It was Innamorata!

"Oh! How sweet of you," I said to Stevie.

"You ain't seen nothin' yet," he replied.

Alice and Carlo entered first, and about fifteen minutes later, we did. It was then, when I looked at the band, did I recognize Jimmy Toscano and his most famous band Nickel Calamari.

"It's Jimmy! How did you manage that?" I asked Stevie.

He shrugged, "I know a guy."

I shoved him jokingly.

As we made our way to the main table, people were still coming up to us with hugs, well wishes, and cards. Then the surprise of all surprises, Frank approached with a lady on his arm. That lady was BeeBee!

"Maggie, Stevie, best of everything," Frank said, and BeeBee looked a little flushed.

"Ms. Maggie, I hope it's all right," she shyly asked me.

I pulled her in and hugged her, "Yes, BeeBee, it's all right!"

"I hope all y'all are happy forever," she gushed, shaking Stevie's hand.

While they were walking away, Stevie turned to me and asked, "Is that young woman who I think she is?"

"Yep."

After the bride and groom dance, Alice and I agreed that as couples, we would all waltz together; then, the aunts placed large satin shopping bags on our arms, an old Sicilian custom of paying to dance with the bride.

Spare me from one more old guy stepping on my feet! Now and then, Alice and I would catch sight of each other and roll our eyes.

I could see Jimmy approaching as some older gentleman was dancing with me. He tapped the guy's shoulder, who relinquished immediately, and then Jimmy put an envelope in my satin bag.

"Hi," he said.

"Hi! Thank you for playing at my wedding. I thought by now you'd be cost prohibited!" I joked.

"I'm doing it for you two, free, as part of my gift to you for your happiness. Something I failed to give you back when."

"Thank you, but no hard feelings here. We should never have married. We were on such different paths, in such different directions!" I said. "Forgive me?"

I stopped abruptly, "Forgive you? Jimmy, there is nothing to forgive you for."

"There is in my book. Forgive me, please." He was so serious.

We started dancing again, and I whispered, "I forgive you, Jimmy Toscano, I forgive you."

I had no idea the monstrosity of a cake that our family had ordered once we told them it was okay to have just one cake. It was massive and quite tall. We stood on each side of the cake, and the photographer assured us that we wouldn't be in each other's pictures cutting the cake. When it came to throwing the bouquets, Alice and I decided to do that together for more fun. What a frenzy that caused. Same with the guys and the garters. I laughed until my sides hurt.

By midnight I was exhausted. The band was taking a break, and Alice and Carlo approached Stevie and me.

"Hey, we want to get out of here," Carlo said, "but I think we should leave together, don't you?"

Stevie and I exchanged looks. Stevie replied, "Sounds good, let's go!"

I approached Mom first and told her. "Let me have your bag. I'll keep it for you, catalogue the names and gifts for the thank you notes, okay?"

"Sounds wonderful." I motioned to Alice.

"Isabelle, would you do mine also? I don't know half these people. They're all from Carlo's side," Alice was asking.

"Of course, doll, give it here."

Jimmy must have seen the four of us getting ready to depart the scene because the band started playing Strangers in the Night, and as soon as the band began, Old Blue Eyes took the stage and crooned. We were stunned.

I turned to Stevie and asked, "Did you know about this?"

"No," he was laughing, "my guess is your Uncle Renato!"

Accompanied by Frank Sinatra singing Strangers in the Night, we four departed our joint wedding reception.

The private elevator to the penthouse floor was lovely. Once inside our suite, we both collapsed onto the sofa.

Stevie spoke first, "Happy?"

"Yes. You?"

"Extremely."

"Want anything?" Stevie D asked.

"Ice water?"

"Coming up."

"What next?" I inquired as I accepted the water.

Jokingly, he said, "Do I have to spell that out?"

Laughing, I said, "No, silly, I meant for tomorrow?"

"Well, most of the family and the Texas posse have late afternoon flights. I thought if we just mingled around the Sunday brunch buffet, we'd get a chance to say goodbye to all of them."

"Great! Not too much effort. I already feel spent. By the way, when do we leave for our honeymoon that you are keeping a secret from me?"

"We leave Monday late morning."

"Okay. Where?"

"Toronto, we'll take in a few shows and then drive home via Niagara Falls," he casually said.

"Niagara Falls? You're taking me to Niagara Falls for our honeymoon?" I was laughing.

"No, I'm taking you to Toronto for your honeymoon," he corrected.

"Same difference!" I said, laughing. And why not? Niagara Falls is the honeymoon capital of the world.

You can't get more cliché than that after living in Buffalo most of your life.

Acknowledgments

One of the most influential people in my life is Carol Cowen Girgis. We met in an undergraduate creative writing class, both decades older than the other undergraduates. I joked that we were sisters-in-a-previous-life. Carol and her husband, Kamel Girgis, MD, and their home were a haven of unconditional love and acceptance during a challenging time in my life. I am forever grateful to them both.

Our writing professor was Honora Moore Lynch, Ph.D., (Lynch then, Honora Finkelstein at the time of her death.) She was the most unusual, generous English professor I ever met. She took the time to enter students' work, whether short stories, poems, or one-act plays (as assignments dictated), and surprised us with entries into small press publications or competitions, surprising us with publications and awards.

Carol, Honey, and I became fast friends. Before graduation in the spring of 1980, Honey invited me to her office and told me I was an excellent writer. She said my maturity, years as a registered nurse, and talent were the combination that would lead me to a professional writing career.

It did lead me to an application and acceptance into the Creative Writing Program at the University of Houston. Donald Barthelme was in residence each spring semester, splitting his time between City College New York and Houston. He became my advisor, mentor, and friend. I studied for three years with him. Rosellen Brown and Phillip Lopate filled out the fiction faculty. Before my final year of the master's work started, I began divorce proceedings. That sent me back to full-time nursing, and the revision of the novel I'd written as thesis lost priority.

There was a ten-year hiatus from writing when the divorce became final.

February 3, 1987, I met Bill W. Several years later, I met his surrogate, Patricia Ann Dwyer Futral, or Patsy. She and I have experienced an extraordinary friendship and sisterhood for over thirty years. And, in her, an undeniable champion of my writing career, my talent, and my heart's desire, without ever reading a word I've written! When I think I've produced something extraordinary, I read it to her! It is Patsy that I call when anything comes up.

July 23, 1989, Barthelme died. He had been a champion of writing talent that carried weight in my eyes. Now that was gone. I felt adrift.

During the 1990s, my desire for writing returned. It happened when a nursing colleague encouraged me to join the poetry workshop she organized, needing the credit for a poetry therapist certification. I attended, and, fortunately, getting back on the horse led to "off to the races!"

In 2000, I joined a women's online email support group. Women from around the world, sometimes numbering over thirty, weekly emailed each other on presented topics, support, or just for fun.

In the spring of 2017, one woman, Eva Glahan Atkinson, the counseling director at Brescia University in Kentucky, emailed me directly. Eva is a suicide prevention specialist and had made an appearance on the LA radio talk show, "Take My Advice," by Dr. Marissa Pei. Dr. Marissa was planning an interview with Karen Stuth of Satiama Writers' Resources, and Dr. Marissa wanted to gift ten people with a free hour of editing from her. Dr. Marissa asked Eva if she or anyone she might know be interested. Eva said yes, and submitted my name. One week later, Karen Stuth telephoned me. Karen Stuth was the second person in my life to tell me, out loud, that I was a gifted writer. She echoed Honey. Working with Karen has been a fantastic opportunity that feels like completing work Honey and I started all those years ago to build confidence in myself.

Eva's generosity in submitting my name to Dr. Marissa Pei's radio show is why I am here today, writing this Acknowledgment. The miracle of connection is not lost on me, and my gratitude to Eva and Dr. Marissa abound.

Along the way, lifelong friends have always checked in with me with "how's the writing going?" Not only Carol, but our other undergraduate buddy, Russell Luke, and a dear faculty friend, Daton Dodson, Ph.D.; my childhood girlfriend to this day Kathy Blatz Baumgarten; my dear friend Kathleen Joseph. We weathered Dr. Denton Cooley's recovery room/ICU and lived to tell tales about it. When I returned to my hometown, Buffalo, NY, I made new friends, and, now more than a decade later, Janice Rufino remains a friend, even after I retired from that very last hospital nursing position. Peter Adrian, MD, and Ann Tornabene, who gave me the gift of their time, and read a draft of this novel. Debbie Patton allowed me to send her 10 pages weekly, a self-imposed deadline that kept me writing.

I have been a student of Buddhism since my early days getting to know Bill W. It was a parallel path. Buddhism taught me that I am the only one who can create anything in my life.

During a retreat led by Ujotika Bhivamsa in 2016, a dharma name was bestowed upon me: Medha'vi' (A Wise One). One understands their dharma name because it is a carrot on the end of a stick, what one aspires in virtue. My dharma name is now informing my future goals as Medha'vi' Enterprise. Life became arduous once again, which sent me reeling. Yet, the Universe already had in place the next teacher I needed: Dawa Tarchin Phillips, leader/teacher of Mindful Leadership Tribe. When I became unraveled, Dawa's directions were clear: "Sit on your cushion and replace fear with courage and curiosity of the unknown." This I did. He has been a mentor to me all these years. I know in my heart that without his direction to live courage and curiosity, I wouldn't be writing this Acknowledgment. Deep bow, Dawa.

My goddaughter, Rachel Nocera Angrignon, has loved me unconditionally, non-judgmentally, and has had my back for over thirty years. Rachel, husband Tyler, their four exceptional children, Joe, Samantha, Juliana, and Sean, have always been there to help me when I ask and love me unconditionally. My gratitude to them shows up when I pop in on any day of the week at their house and cook an entire dinner for the gang.

My dad died in 1969. He was an Irish American man who never met a stranger. He read books to me, the newspaper and was a wonderful storyteller. Mom says I'm so like him, and he would be as proud of me now as she is.

I am also grateful to the Madonie fiction family in this book! The days I spent with them, immersed in their loves, food, trials, and kindness, were exercises for how I behaved in real life. Working it out through my characters made it easier to act well in reality.

There is a quote that has guided me over many, many years by German poet Johann Wolfgang von Goethe:

Whatever you can do or dream you can, begin it;
Boldness has genius, power, and magic in it.

When I recite this quote to myself, I become willing to take the next step, the next challenge, get into the next right action.

Deep Buddhist bow to all.

Morrigan Milligan

August 2021